PRAISE

ENSLAVED

"Another winning installment in the Eternal Guardians series will leave you eager for more as the action is unbelievably thrilling and the emotional conflicts are involving throughout.
—*RT Book Reviews*, 4 ½ stars

"Prepare yourself to be thrilled by incredibly hot warriors, strong heroines, a fabulous love story and diabolical villains that will leave you craving the next installment." —*Fresh Fiction*

ENRAPTURED

"Filled with sizzling romance, heartbreaking drama, and a cast of multifaceted characters, this powerful and unusual retelling of the Orpheus and Eurydice story is Naughton's best book yet."
—*Publisher's Weekly*, starred review

"Two characters whose love literally transcends time."
—*Smexybooks*

TEMPTED

"Endlessly twisting plots within plots, a cast of complex and eminently likeable characters, and a romance as hot as it is complicated." —*Publisher's Weekly,* starred review

"Ms. Naughton has taken the Greek Argonaut myth, turned it on its head, and OWNED it!"
—*Bitten By Paranormal Romance*

ENTWINED

"An action-packed creative wonder guaranteed to snag your attention from page one." —*Fresh Fiction*

"Do NOT miss this series!"
—*NY Times* bestselling author Larissa Ione

MARKED

"Naughton has tremendous skill with steamy passion, dynamic characterization and thrilling action." —*Publisher's Weekly*

"Elisabeth Naughton's MARKED gives an incredibly fresh spin on Greek Mythology that is full of humor, action, passion and a storyline that keeps you from putting down the book."
—*Fresh Fiction*

WAIT FOR ME

"Full of twists and turns, lies and deception, and the ultimate revenge, Wait For Me is a great romantic suspense read."
—*Night Owl Reviews*, Top Pick

"This book blew me out of the water. Wonderfully written with characters whose emotional turmoil seemed to jump off the page and grab you." —*Cocktails and Books*

STOLEN SEDUCTION

"This third book in the Stolen series is full of intrigue, secrets and undeniable love with characters you can't get enough of...an awesome read!" —*Fresh Fiction*

"An adventurous story of twists and turns, this story will keep you guessing until the very end. And the chemistry between Hailey and Shane is sizzling hot. Naughton combines passion and danger in one fast-paced story." —*News and Sentinel*

STOLEN HEAT

"This book has got it all: an adventure that keeps you turning the pages, an irresistible hero, and a smoking romance."
—*All About Romance*

"Stolen Heat is an awesome combination of deadly suspense, edgy action and a wonderful romance with characters that you'll laugh, cry and yell with." —*Night Owl Romance*

THE TEASING TOUCH OF DESIRE

"Are you okay?"

Titus leaned his back against the tree trunk. "Be fine…in a minute."

"Here. Sit." Gently, Natasa tugged on his arm, pulling him away from the tree and leading him toward the pallet of blankets and pillows against the tent wall. Warmth flowed from her hand into his; then softness enveloped his body, the cotton silky against the bare skin of his back.

She knelt next to him and rested her hands on her thighs. "What did they do to you?"

He leaned back in the pillows, closed his eyes, and relaxed as the last emotions seeped out of his body. "Nothing. Just—"

He drew in another breath then slowly let it out. He wasn't about to admit his biggest weakness to the girl he wanted to jump his bones.

"It hurt, didn't it? I saw the way you reacted when they were tying you to the tree, like you were in pain. Why don't you react that way when I touch you?"

His eyes popped open. She knew? For a smart guy, he was slow on the uptake when it came to her. Implications ricocheted through his mind. But the only thing he could focus on was the fantasy he'd been toying with before—the one of her in the black leather outfit, touching him, whipping him, ordering him to do any and every X-rated thing she wanted. "'Cause your touch feels good."

Her brow dropped low. "I don't understand. I mean, considering what I did to that guard back in Argolea, my touch should be worse, not better. Why am I different?"

"Don't know, just…"

Dammit, he didn't want to think anymore. He just wanted her to touch him again, to chase away the lingering pain, to make him feel alive. He needed it, more than he needed to know who she was or what she was really after.

"Put your hands on me again, Tasa. You're the only one who can."

Titles by Elisabeth Naughton

Eternal Guardians Series
(Paranormal Romance)

BOUND
ENSLAVED
ENRAPTURED
TEMPTED
ENTWINED
MARKED

Stolen Series
(Romantic Suspense)

STOLEN SEDUCTION
STOLEN HEAT
STOLEN FURY

Single Titles

WAIT FOR ME
(Romantic Suspense)

Firebrand Series
(Paranormal Romance)

POSSESSED BY DESIRE
SLAVE TO PASSION
BOUND TO SEDUCTION

Anthologies

BODYGUARDS IN BED
(with Lucy Monroe and Jamie Denton)

BOUND

ETERNAL GUARDIANS

ELISABETH NAUGHTON

EN

Cover art and design by Patricia Schmitt/Pickyme
Editing by Linda Ingmanson

For Dan,
Without whom none of this would be possible.
Thank you for making all my dreams come true, babe.

I must wrestle through time told by thousands of years
For the new king of gods hath contrived for me
Bondage thus shameful.
—Aeschylus, PROMETHEUS BOUND

CHAPTER ONE

Anxiety was a bitch he did not have the patience to deal with.

Nerves danced in Titus's stomach as he scanned the satellite image illuminated by the virtual screen in his suite of rooms at the castle in Argolea. The forest outside the Misos Colony in Montana was as quiet as ever. No movement. Nothing out of the ordinary. No sign of *her*. But just thinking about finding her, about *touching* her again, made his whole body vibrate as if on the edge of a precipice.

He curled his fingers into his palm, pulled his shaking arm back and covered his fist with his free hand before he could switch screens.

Think logically, dammit...

His heart raced. His adrenaline surged. If there was one skill he'd mastered over the years, it was control. Control over his body, his gift, even those around him. When he reacted impulsively, when he leapt without thinking, when he allowed his emotions to rule his actions...those were the times he got into trouble. Those were the moments that had led to his curse.

Common sense told him the Argonauts were growing suspicious as to why he'd been holed up in his room for days. His *I still feel like crap after getting my ass handed to me by Gryphon* excuse wasn't going to fly much longer. If he didn't pull his shit together soon, he was only going to create more worry. And yet...

He looked back at the image, reached out, and switched screens. To his disappointment, Maelea's beach house on Vancouver Island sat as empty as it had when he and the others had left it days ago.

"*Skata.*" He leaned back in his chair. Scowled. Called himself a hundred different kinds of stupid. He was starting to think she was a figment of his imagination. Except every time he remembered the heat that had rolled off her when she'd been close, and the feel of her skin against his when they'd touched, his entire body grew hard with an intensely deep craving he couldn't explain, even to himself.

She was real. And she was out there somewhere. The first person he'd been able to touch in over a hundred years.

A knock sounded at the door. Titus jerked forward, barely able to kill the virtual screen before the heavy wood door to his room pushed in.

"Hey, T-man." Phineus, his Argonaut brother, regarded him with speculation. "They're gathering downstairs already. What's taking you so long?"

"Theron's wondering what the fuck is up with you."

Phineus's unspoken words hit Titus hard. Even though the others knew he could read minds, they didn't always filter their thoughts around him or contain them in time.

Dammit...the trouble was already starting. Theron, the leader of their brotherhood, had made it crystal clear to Titus back at the half-breed colony that this "mystery woman" was of no use to their cause. If he found out Titus had spent the last three days searching for her, he'd be more than pissed. He'd be downright livid. And since Theron had the strength of Heracles on his side, a livid Theron was never a good thing.

Titus grasped his leather gloves from the desk where he'd been working and forcibly slowed his breathing. Just the thought of her—*Natasa*—burned a line of wicked heat straight to his groin. "Finishing up some work. They all set?"

Phineus leaned his broad shoulder against the doorframe and waited while Titus pushed out of his chair and reached for his leather breastplate, the one stamped with the seal of his forefather Odysseus, from the couch at his side. "Yeah, the Council's assembled and the rest of the Argonauts are there. All except Gryphon. He's waiting with Maelea. Tense as shit down there in that room, I gotta tell you. Especially with Nick hanging in the shadows."

Titus hated getting dressed up, but this was one of those rare occasions where he and the others just had to deal. Tonight was the official celebration marking the death of the goddess Atalanta, the female who'd made it her life mission to destroy Argolea and everything it stood for. They'd been hunting her for years. Only it hadn't been an Argonaut who'd finally killed her. It had been the female who'd brought his brother Gryphon back from the brink of insanity.

"Nick, Demetrius, and the Council all in the same place?" Titus snapped the straps in place and fixed the blue cloak so it draped over his left shoulder. "This oughta be fun."

Nick was the leader of the half-breeds, or Misos, and though he'd sided with the Argonauts in their quest to destroy Atalanta, he had a real attitude problem when it came to the Council of Elders, the body that advised the queen. One Titus knew stemmed from his childhood, when he'd been cast out of Argolea and his twin, Demetrius, had been spared and raised with the Argonauts.

"Fun?" Phineus tossed back with a frown. "Try borderline explosive. I'm just hoping we don't have to physically restrain anyone. I could do without fireworks for a few days."

Titus didn't want to have to restrain anyone either. Just the thought of touching someone else, even with the steps he took to keep himself protected, made him sick to his stomach.

He grabbed the leather tie from the desk, pulled his shoulder-length hair back from his face, and tied the mass at the nape of his neck. When he turned, Phineus was studying him with amused gray eyes. "Done primping?"

"Takes me ten seconds, pretty boy. I'm sure it took you at least thirty minutes to get gussied up."

A wide smile broke across Phineus's face. He ran a hand down his own leather breastplate—this one marked with the symbol of Bellerophon—then shrugged so the orange cloak over his shoulder swayed. "I make this look good. Admit it. You're jealous."

Titus snorted and moved forward, his boots clomping on the hardwood floor, the formal black trousers tighter than he preferred and cutting him off in places he didn't want to think about. "You give me a fucking headache. Let's go already."

He stepped past Phin in the doorway, careful not to touch the guardian. Even though the boundary of cloth would prevent any kind of transfer, he'd learned over the years it was just safer that way. The simple luxury of another's touch was something he'd come to detest.

Until Natasa.

Her fire-red hair, those plump lips, her high cheekbones, and gemlike eyes flashed in his mind all over again. And a sharp burst of heat rolled through his groin as he moved out into the hallway.

He needed to find her. He didn't care what Theron had to say about it or who she was. He just wanted to touch her one more time. To remember what it felt like to be touched himself. For just a few minutes, he wanted to be like everyone else and *feel* again.

Dammit, he deserved that after all this time.

"There is definitely something seriously up with you, man."

Phineus's thought plowed into him from behind, but Titus ignored it. He didn't care what his kin thought right now. He was too busy plotting how he was going to get through the next few hours without losing his frickin' mind then get back to figuring out where to look for her next.

They hit the grand staircase. Outside the castle walls, thousands of Argoleans had gathered in the streets of Tiyrns to hear the queen's speech from the royal veranda that looked out over the city and to be introduced to their savior. But below, the voices of Council members, Argonauts, and the "elite" who'd been invited into the castle for the post-announcement festivities echoed off marble columns and drifted up to Titus's ears. That and their thoughts. Too many to focus on, each unique and as irritating as fingernails scraping down a chalkboard, causing Titus's skull to throb.

Get through the next hour; then you can get back to what you really want to be doing.

Clenching his jaw, he moved down the stairs. When he reached the bottom step, a tingle rushed across his spine, and his feet halted their forward momentum. Awareness flowed like water over his skin, and a strange, familiar energy tickled the fine hairs all along his flesh. From the corner of his vision, something to his right moved.

Phin plowed into his back. *"Skata,* T, what the hell?"

Titus barely felt the blow. He was too focused on the dark-haired female who'd caught his attention. The one standing at the end of the corridor that led to the kitchen, wearing a server's uniform and holding an empty tray at her side. The one with pale features, a soft spray of freckles, and whose captivating, emerald eyes were locked solidly on his.

Eyes exactly like the ones he'd been dreaming—*fantasizing*—about for days.

His pulse picked up speed. He waited for her thoughts to pierce his mind, to prove it wasn't really her. But only one word got through. The same damn word that had lit him up like a Christmas tree back at the Misos Colony the first time he'd met her.

The same word that now held so many meanings, his entire body vibrated with an erotic blend of excitement and heat.

Fuck.

Sweat broke out along Natasa's nape as she stared down the corridor toward the one man…Argonaut…shit, *hero*…she'd hoped not to run into.

Just her luck…

She was already warm, and her body's irrational reaction to him wasn't helping matters. Pulling her gaze from his, she shoved the kitchen door open and stepped inside the crowded room.

Activity buzzed around her, preparations for the party in full swing. She wove through servers and cursed herself for taking a peek into the gathering room to see if Maelea had shown up yet. She hadn't missed the warning the leader of the Argonauts had issued when he'd ordered her to leave the colony days ago and never return. If he found out she was in Argolea, she'd be in a shitload of trouble. And if he found out what she really—

Her hand shook as she pushed strands of the dark wig back from her face. *Don't panic. Think, dammit!*

A server swept past her, jostling her on her feet. She reached out to steady herself, and her hand sank into something thick, soft, and cool. Natasa jerked back and stared at the creamy, white éclair filling coating her fingers. She'd smashed one of the confections sitting on the dessert table to her right.

Anxiety pushed up her throat. She swiped the goo against her pants, barely noticing the mess she was leaving behind. He'd *seen* her. Even with the wig, she couldn't go out there now. Any second he would plow through that door and come after her. And though the thought of him—*Titus*—being close again sent a thrill through her veins, *he* wasn't what she'd come here for. He wasn't the key to solving every one of her life's problems.

She turned before fate could change her mind and nearly knocked another server over. The male righted his tray filled with champagne flutes, but not before one toppled over the side and crashed to the floor. The shatter of crystal echoed through the entire kitchen.

Silence descended. Heads turned their way. The server's eyes widened; then he muttered a string of words Natasa didn't understand but suspected were filled with expletives. She held up her hands, tried to apologize, but his face grew redder with every second.

Natasa stepped back. "I… It's—"

The door across the room burst open. Natasa's head jerked that way. The Argonaut she'd tried unsuccessfully to banish from her mind filled her vision.

He wore tight black trousers that showcased his muscular legs, knee-high leather boots polished to a gleaming shine, a white tunic cinched in at the waist, and a leather breastplate stamped with the seal of Odysseus. Over his left shoulder, a brilliant blue cloak hung to his waist, anchored with a gold leaf, and his wavy brown hair was tied back with a leather strap. But it was his eyes—his knowing, hazel eyes—that she focused on. Eyes that bore into her own and told her she was in deep shit.

Dread pushed up her chest, latching on hard to her throat. They'd spent only mere moments together at the half-breed colony, but it had been enough. Enough for her to feel the relief in his touch and realize he was a distraction that could very well jeopardize the deal she'd made.

Perspiration gathered all along her spine. Her heart raced, and though her mind screamed *run!*, her body wasn't listening. Her attention shifted to his mouth. She'd wanted to feel that mouth against her own back at the colony. Wanted to sample it now. And she could. She could walk across the floor, slide her hand around his nape, ease up on her toes, find out if his lips were as stimulating as his fingers…

A bellow echoed to Natasa's left. She jerked that way, startled out of her trance. The red-faced server screamed words she still couldn't make out.

Maelea. Holy shit…Maelea. Natasa gasped and pressed a shaky hand against her throat. She'd almost forgotten what was important. She needed to focus on finding the female instead of fantasizing about hot, sweaty, world-class sex with the Greek god on the opposite side of the room. The kind of sex she'd gone too long without.

Like…forever.

She cursed her link to the gods for her weakness, and swiveled for the door at the far end of the kitchen.

"Natasa!" A voice—*Titus's* voice—rang out behind her, followed by footsteps—heavy ones.

Heat gathered in her stomach and sent fireballs of awareness all through her limbs.

No… Urgency overwhelmed her. She couldn't be distracted. Not now…

She pushed her legs forward and darted down a long hallway. Three archways opened before her. She didn't have time to wonder where each led. Rushing through the closest, she raced along a dark corridor until she hit a circular staircase that led both up and down.

Up or down…

"Natasa!"

Electricity sparked across the nape of her neck and rocketed down her spine, as if he were right behind her. As if he were about to grasp her. Stop her. *Catch* her.

She didn't have time to think. She could only react. And pray that she got away before desire tempted her to do something she'd forever regret.

CHAPTER TWO

"Titus!"

Phineus's voice rang out at Titus's back, followed by a thought that hit hard.

"Shit. What the hell is wrong with him now?"

Titus ignored his kin and darted down the corridor until he came to stairs that led to the upper and lower floors of the castle.

His adrenaline surged as he looked down at the spiraling metal steps. He couldn't see anything other than silver and darkness. Tipping his head back, he glanced up but saw no one ascending either.

Phin exhaled a heavy breath at his side. "What in Hades has gotten into you?"

Logic said she had to have gone up. Down would take her too close to street level. There were castle guards everywhere at the lower levels because of the festivities.

"He's seriously fucked…"

There was more to her than met the eye. She was—

"Dude." Phineus's hand closed over Titus's shoulder. He pulled hard, spun Titus around. His open palm cracked against Titus's cheek. "Snap out of it!"

Titus's head snapped to the side. Worry, confusion, and jolt of fear ricocheted through his cheek, shooting like a rocket into his chest. The air exploded from his lungs. His throat closed. Then pain spiraled through each cell in his body.

His strength rushed out on a wave before he could stop it. He collapsed to his knees, gasping. Fell forward on his hands. Tried like hell to catch his breath.

The emotional transfer didn't always dissipate quickly. He could control bits and pieces of it if he was ready, but he'd been so distracted by the thought of Natasa, this one had taken him completely by surprise. Luckily, if there was one thing he could count on, it was that the spearing, vicious pain still echoing through his limbs *would* eventually pass. But in the seconds it took to filter through and finally out, he was as weak as a baby, and fighting the urge to cry out like one.

"Fuck me," Phineus muttered, reaching for Titus's arm to haul him up. "What the hell is with you now? I barely touched you."

Titus weakly managed to knock Phineus's hand out of the way. "Don't...touch me."

"*Skata*. Something's wrong." "*I need to get Theron.*"

"Don't you fucking get anyone." Titus braced both palms on the floor, leaned forward and sucked back air. *Sonofafuckingbitch, that hurt.* "Especially Theron. I'll be okay...just...give me a minute."

He drew in a breath, then another. The emotions slowly receded, and synapse by synapse, his mind came back on line. But she was still there. Natasa. Circling his gray matter. Tempting him. Drawing him toward her with some uncontrollable power.

"*Skata*, man," Phin muttered, crouching down so he and Titus were at eye level, careful this time not to touch him. "What's going on? You went streaking out of that kitchen like you'd seen a freakin' Fate."

Not *a* Fate. *His* fate.

Or so something deep in his gut told him.

He wanted to find her, but good luck doing that right now in this state. Wherever Natasa had gone, he wasn't following. And even if he could, he had a pretty strong hunch if he tried, Phin would haul his ass to Theron and tell the leader of the Argonauts that Titus had finally gone completely wacked.

Which probably wasn't far off the mark.

His strength slowly returning, Titus eased back on his heels and braced his hands on his thighs.

Shit... Hearing voices was bad enough. He didn't want the others to discover the true extent of his weakness. The fact they knew he didn't like to be touched was more than he wanted to share. Argonauts couldn't be weak. They were strong. They were warriors. They were heroes. Not fucked-up mental cases that could be dropped with a simple touch.

Sweat broke out on his forehead, and he swiped it away. Anxiety pushed at his chest for the second time that day, but this time not from missing something he shouldn't be searching for, from fear of losing the only thing that truly mattered in his life. Serving with the Argonauts was the one thing keeping him sane. And it was high time he remembered that and stopped chasing a superhot wet dream that would only lead to more trouble he didn't need.

"I'm fine." Carefully, he rose to his feet, the lie coming easily to his lips—like always. But the disappointment lingered. And would, he knew, long after he'd gone back to his old, isolated life. "I picked up a thought from that servant who was causing a ruckus in the kitchen."

"What kind of thought?" Phin's brow wrinkled as he rose to his full height.

"A predatory one."

When Phin continued to stare at him like he was hovering on the edge of ape-shit crazy, Titus frowned. "Theron told us to be on the lookout for anything out of the ordinary, right? With the Misos delegation visiting for the ceremony and the Council in the castle for the day, we need to stay alert. Nick still thinks the Council has a spy planted at the colony."

Phin's gaze raked his features, and Titus's pulse picked up speed again. But whatever the guardian was thinking, this time he kept it carefully locked down. Which wasn't exactly a good sign.

"Why'd you hit the floor like that?"

"I've been under the weather, dickhead." Titus swiped at the sweat on his forehead again. "Why do you think I've been holed up in my room for days?"

"You should be better by now. Have you seen Callia lately?"

The last thing Titus needed was the queen's personal healer worrying over him again. She was the *only* person who knew his secret, and he didn't want to give her any reason not to keep her trap shut. "If I go running to Callia every time I have a little sniffle, Zander will get some crack idea we're having an affair. And I don't need Achilles's *I can't be killed* descendent on my ass, thank you very much."

He didn't give Phin time to answer, simply moved past the guardian. And this time made sure to intentionally brush his shoulder against Phin's to kill whatever lingering doubt remained.

Thank the Fates for clothing and armor that prevents the transfer. "We need to stop dicking around and get out there. Weren't you the one saying they were ready to start?"

Phin's boots echoed in the corridor at Titus's back. "You sure you're up for it?"

No, he wasn't up for hours of schmoozing with the Council and the colonists and celebrating Atalanta's death with his guardian brothers. He wanted to find the redhead. But that was a dream he was going to have to let die. For good.

"Let's just go get this over with." He pushed the door to the kitchen open once more. "And stop looking at me like I'm a two-headed dragon about to charbroil you, you putz."

Phineus didn't laugh at Titus's crappy joke. Instead, his unspoken thought reached Titus's ears. A thought that, at least, took Titus's mind off his own fucked-up issues.

"No, that would be the other way around, smartass."

Perspiration slicked Natasa's skin as she dropped with a soft thud onto the balcony of what she hoped was Maelea's room.

Straightening, she brushed the unruly curls away from her face. She'd ditched the wig and servant's uniform on an upper floor before climbing down the outside of the castle, thankful to be wearing the easy-moving black pants and fitted top again. The twenty-first century might overwhelm the senses with its abundance of technology, but she definitely liked the clothes.

She took a long, deep draw of late May air then let it out slowly. Yeah, okay, so it wasn't exactly great timing to be doing this, when the castle was abuzz with activity, but she didn't have much choice. She was running out of time, and Maelea was nearly her last hope. If the female couldn't help her...

She lifted a hand to knock on the french doors, and her thoughts strayed to the Argonaut who'd almost caught her in the kitchen. Her hand paused in the air. Sweat slid down her spine. Her pulse thrummed again.

What was it about him that called to her? It was more than his good looks, more than his warrior status and even the strength she sensed within. There was something there, something a place deep inside her wanted to explore. Something that drew her toward him like a parched traveler to an oasis.

A frown pulled at her mouth. A parched traveler? The analogy had never been more appropriate. And she didn't have time to waste thinking about it.

She tapped gently on the glass doors and squared her shoulders. Seconds ticked by in silence, seconds in which she held her breath and prayed this was it. Footsteps echoed across the floor. Then the doors pulled open wide, and an attractive female filled Natasa's line of sight.

The female's brow lowered. Natasa could all but see the wheels turning in her mind, trying to make the connection. Too bad she wouldn't find it.

Natasa stepped into the room and closed the doors quickly at her back.

"Who are you?" The female moved away, the pale yellow gown with the wide neckline and A-lined skirt rustling with her frantic steps. "How did you get here?"

Her hair was dark, falling like black silk down her back, her features pale. She was roughly the same height as Natasa, but where Natasa was curves and muscle, she was thin and frail. And the commanding tone she tried to take fell completely flat.

Natasa's gaze skipped past the female, and she scanned the room. She had the vague impression of plush furnishing, soaring ceilings, and a giant bed, but thankfully, they were alone.

Her focus homed in on the female she'd been searching for for the last month. "You are Maelea, correct? Daughter of Zeus and Persephone?"

Maelea took another step back, her dark eyes growing wider by the second. "Are you a Siren?" Her spine hit a chair in front of an elaborate stone fireplace. "Did my father send you?"

The Sirens were Zeus's female warriors who did his dirty work and covered up the evidence. While Natasa could see how Maelea would assume the worst, the correlation burned a place deep inside. "No. And I'm not here to harm you either. I just want information."

"Information," Maelea said hesitantly, her fingers gripping the edge of the chair at her back, as if it could protect her in some way. "I have none."

"I'm looking for Prometheus."

"The Titan? Why?"

"Personal reasons." And reasons Natasa wasn't about to share with this female. "You're Zeus's daughter. Even if he didn't tell you where he chained"—she pursed her lips, catching herself from giving too much away—"him, he might have told you something that will be of help to me."

Maelea considered a moment. "My father and I are not exactly on speaking terms. If you're otherworldly, and you know who I am, then you know that as well."

Natasa did know that, but she'd hoped. Panic forced a fresh layer of perspiration all across her skin. "Think, Maelea. Any minute detail may be of use to me."

"Why is it of such importance you find him now? Zeus imprisoned Prometheus millennia ago." Her eyes narrowed. "Why now?"

Because she was running out of time. And because if she failed…

No, she wouldn't think like that. Even if Prometheus didn't know the consequences to what he'd created, she did. She lived it every day.

"Who else might know? Can you think of anyone your father could have confided in?"

"This is important to you."

The words were a statement, not a question, and as Natasa's gaze focused on Maelea's dark-as-night eyes, she noticed that the female didn't seem scared anymore, rather…intrigued. "More important than you could ever imagine."

Maelea stepped away from the chair. Electricity crackled in the air. Legend said Zeus's bastard daughter had the power to sense energy shifts on earth. Could she in Argolea as well? Did she know who Natasa really was? And would she alert the Argonauts—alert *Titus*—to her presence?

"I wish I could help you," Maelea said, stopping a foot away, "but I can't. I don't know anything about Prometheus's imprisonment. I've not had contact with anyone from Olympus except my father, and that was only days ago. And our conversation was brief, if that. There was no mention of Prometheus or where he's bound."

The air leaked out of Natasa's lungs. She hadn't realized just how much she'd been banking on Maelea knowing something—anything—that would help her until this very moment. Months she'd wasted trying to find the female, when what she should have been doing was chasing a different lead.

Dammit, she was back to square one, with no idea where to look next and only this blasted heat to keep her company. She swiped at the sweat on her brow.

No, that wasn't true. She was back further than step one, because the end date was rushing up faster than even she'd anticipated.

"There are Titans in the human realm," Maelea said softly. "Those who didn't side with Krónos in the Titanomachy. Ones in hiding amongst humans. Have you tried them? Epimetheus, maybe? Prometheus's brother? It's possible he knows something."

Natasa huffed. "I already spoke with him. He's the one who suggested I find you. Epimetheus is a fool. Talking to him is as productive as talking to a wall."

Maelea's lips turned down. "Yes, I've heard that about him. But perhaps he knows more than he's letting on. Is there a reason he doesn't want you to find Prometheus?"

Oh yeah, there was. Because Epimetheus knew exactly *what* she was.

Her mind spun. And connections she hadn't made before clicked into place. Natasa lifted her gaze back to Maelea. "Has Epimetheus ever sided with Zeus?"

Maelea's brow wrinkled. "Not that I'm aware. But anything's possible, I suppose. Why? What are you thinking?"

What was she thinking? She was suddenly thinking Epimetheus had sent her after Maelea, knowing she'd fail. The question was…why?

There was only one place to find out.

She turned for the door. "Sorry to bother you."

"Wait—"

Maelea reached for her, but Natasa moved onto the veranda and closed the double doors before the female could stop her. She climbed over the railing and dropped down to the balcony below, landing with a soft thud on her boots. Then she waited, listening to see if anyone moved in the room beyond.

Nothing but silence met her ears. But from the balcony above, a male voice rang out. "*Sotiria*? They're ready for us."

"Gryphon," Maelea breathed.

Gryphon… He was an Argonaut. Natasa had heard that name back at the half-breed colony. She knew she should get inside before Maelea sent someone to look for her, but her curiosity got the best of her, and she waited, wanting to know if Maelea knew more than she'd let on too.

Fabric rustled, followed by soft murmurs and the distinct sound of kissing. And as she listened, a low ache built in Natasa's chest. When was the last time someone had hugged her? Kissed her? When was the last time she'd *wanted* someone's touch like that?

Warmth spread up her chest as she thought back to those few moments with Titus at the colony. Moments she'd foolishly relived in her mind a hundred times since.

"What's wrong?" Gryphon asked above.

"I'm fine," Maelea answered. "Nothing's wrong. I just…I had an interesting visitor."

"Who?" The concern in the Argonaut's voice jolted Natasa out of her melancholy and brought her focus back to the conversation above.

"I don't really know. She wasn't Argolean, but she was definitely otherworldy."

"She?" Concern gave way to suspicion. "What did she want?"

"To know if I had information about where my father is holding Prometheus."

Silence. Then, "Prometheus? Why?"

"She didn't say."

"Was she looking for the Orb?"

"It's a possibility, considering Prometheus crafted the Orb, but no, I don't think that was her goal. She didn't mention anything about it and I had the sense whatever she wanted from him was much more personal. I don't know why, but…"

"But what?"

Natasa held her breath.

"I sensed a very strong power within her. One not rooted completely in darkness but not bathed in light either. I can't put my finger on what it was, but my senses tell me whatever it is, it's on the verge of being released."

Shit.

"*Skata,*" the Argonaut muttered. "That kind of power anywhere near the Orb is not a good thing."

"I know," Maelea whispered.

So the Orb really was in Argolea. That explained why Natasa felt different here than she had in the human realm. And why she had such an uncontrollable urge to stay.

"We need to share this with Theron and the others before we head downstairs to the celebration," Gryphon said above. "Come on."

The others.

The Argonauts. Including Titus.

Natasa's pulse thumped faster. She pushed away from the wall and turned for the door she hoped was unlocked. Inside the room—another bedroom suite—she scanned the empty space, her mind already thinking ten steps ahead. To what she needed to do next. To the moment she was out of this castle and heading for the portal that would take her back to the human realm.

To where she would go after that.

Because, no matter what, she wasn't giving up.

"You're sure about this?" Theron asked.

Isadora stood beside Theron's desk in what used to be her father's office but was now the center for Argonaut business, arms crossed over her growing belly, listening to what Maelea and Gryphon had come to tell them.

The leader of the Argonauts looked less than thrilled with the news, and Isadora knew why. If this mysterious guest Maelea had encountered in the castle was the same female who'd shown up at the colony days ago, it meant things were heating up, not cooling down as they'd hoped.

Of course, the Fate had warned them after Atalanta's death that they'd won the battle, not the war, and Isadora didn't doubt for a minute that the gods were plotting a way into Argolea so they could get their hands on the Orb. She just hadn't expected it to happen so soon. Especially not now, when she should be out on the balcony overlooking the city of Tiyrns, presenting Maelea to the Argolean people.

"I'm not certain of anything," Maelea answered. "I can only tell you what I felt. There's more power in her than I've sensed in a very long time, from any one person who wasn't a god."

Theron glanced toward Isadora. "What do you think?"

Isadora chewed her lip. He'd told her of his suspicions and why he'd advised this Natasa to leave the colony and never return. "It sounds like the same girl. But how did she get here?"

"A delegation of Misos came across with Nick," Demetrius said from the couch behind Maelea. "Could she have come with them?"

The babe in Isadora's belly kicked out at the sound of Demetrius's voice, as if he too took comfort in the guardian's presence, and Isadora looked past Maelea and Gryphon toward her mate. Two more months until their son would be born. And hopefully then the permanent worry she saw in Demetrius's eyes would dim when he realized everything was going to be okay.

She smoothed a hand down her belly to ease both herself and the little one. "I guess she could have. She was at the Misos Colony long enough undetected. The question is, why risk coming all the way to Argolea? And why now? Nick's downstairs. I think we should include him in this discussion."

Demetrius pushed his big body off the couch. "I'll find him."

He reached for Isadora's hand and gave her a reassuring squeeze before heading to the door. And Isadora released a breath of relief as he left. Demetrius's public displays of affection came easier these days, but the fact he had willingly volunteered to seek out his twin, with whom he'd never had any relationship other than fierce animosity, was the best sign of all.

"Send Titus up here if you see him," Theron said to Demetrius.

Demetrius nodded and left. When he was gone, Isadora turned her attention back to Theron. "Tell them what you told me."

On a sigh, Theron rubbed his fingers against his forehead and leaned back in his chair. "When Titus found this female in your room at the colony, Maelea, she was holding a small book. More like a journal. Detailing the lineage of the gods."

With a confused expression, Maelea glanced toward Gryphon at her side, then back to Theron. "If she was looking for me, that makes sense, since Zeus and Persephone are my parents."

"Right," Theron answered, dropping his hand. "But the pages marked in her little book weren't yours. And they weren't Prometheus's."

"What pages were marked?" Gryphon asked.

"The ones related to Zagreus. Hades's son."

Gryphon reached for Maelea's hand, and Isadora's own stomach tightened at the fear and hatred she saw flash in his eyes. All the Argonauts knew what a loose cannon Zagreus was. Hades had unleashed his son on the human realm years ago, and though he had a reputation for being as vile and twisted as his father, since he didn't seem to focus on humans and he generally kept his little world of torture to himself, they left him alone. Going after Zagreus meant starting a war with Hades himself, but now it looked like that might be inevitable.

"You think she's working for Zagreus?" Gryphon asked.

"It's possible," Theron answered. "But more importantly, if she is, and she's here for Maelea, it means Hades hasn't given up his search for Persephone's daughter."

Maelea's face paled, and Gryphon wrapped his arm around her shoulders. He drew her close and pressed his lips against her temple. "He won't get to you, *sotiria*."

"And how do you plan to stop him?" she asked on a whisper. "You yourself told me since he's not an Olympian, he can cross into Argolea, like my mother."

Theron pushed out of his chair before Gryphon could answer. "No one will get to you. You're one of us now, and we protect our own."

The finality in his voice warmed Isadora's heart, and from the tinge of pink on Maelea's cheeks, it clearly warmed hers too.

Theron shifted his gaze to Gryphon. "I know you were planning to take her to your place on the coast for an extended holiday after the ceremony, and you both deserve that more than anyone, but for the time being, she's safer here in the castle where we can protect her."

"I agree." Gryphon looked down at Maelea. "*Sotiria?*"

"I'm okay with that." She squeezed Gryphon's hand. "As long as we're together."

Footsteps echoed near the open door, drawing attention.

"Demetrius told us to get up here," Phineus said, stepping into the room with Titus at his heels. "What's going on? I thought the party was about to start. Man, the council members do not look thrilled with all those Misos downstairs."

"Yeah, tell me something I don't already know," Theron mumbled. "Zander and Cerek can run crowd control for a few minutes."

He turned his attention toward Titus, whose hazel eyes were as focused as Isadora had ever seen them. As the guardian could read minds, he'd probably already picked up on what was going down. And though she couldn't be sure, something told Isadora he knew more than he was letting on.

"I need your super spying skills," Theron said.

Titus's gaze narrowed. "Why?"

"Because your mystery woman's back. And this time, she's not playing games."

CHAPTER THREE

The sands of time were sifting through the hourglass faster than he liked. And every second he had to sit here waiting for this melding of the minds to begin, the more he had to fight the urge to rip someone's fucking toenails out one by one.

Hades tapped his fingers on the armrest of the uncomfortable chair and stared across the gilded room toward his brother Zeus, whose head was currently tipped to the side as he shared hushed words with one of his bow and arrow-wielding, Barbie doll Sirens. At the moment, he'd like to rip Zeus's toenails out just to hear the fucker scream. What the bloody hell were they whispering about? And where in all hellfire was Poseidon?

Probably off fucking a sea nymph, knowing the son of a bitch. And most likely, *not* his wife. A frown turned Hades's lips as his thoughts strayed to his own wife. He couldn't help but wonder where *she* was right this minute. And with whom.

He hadn't seen Persephone in weeks. As per his agreement with her father, she spent half the year on Olympus and half with him in the Underworld. The few times she'd escaped to meet him in the human world during their latest separation weren't enough. He needed to see her again soon. Not simply because he wanted to string her up and ravage that sinful body, but because he needed to keep a close eye on her. His wife was as twisted and manipulative as he. And she wanted the Orb of Krónos just much as he did—maybe more.

The heavy door to the right pushed open, and Poseidon, the sea god, strolled into the massive room as if he owned the joint.

Day like all days...

The Siren straightened and stepped back, but a look passed between her and Zeus before she left the room. A look that said the King of Gods was up to something.

Zeus flashed his thousand-watt smile, the one Hades wanted to rip from his face. "*Adelfos*, I was about to send my Sirens to search for you."

Bullshit.

"No reason to worry about me," Poseidon answered, crossing the floor, his long legs eating up the space, his blond surfer hair blowing around his face as he moved. "Got tied up with business. Humans are always causing trouble, dumping crap and chemicals in my waters. Not to mention the creatures that need to be regulated, the storms that have to be redirected. Overseeing the world's oceans isn't as easy as, say"—he turned his blinding blue gaze Hades's way—"simply sorting souls."

Venom built in Hades's veins. The same raging fury he always felt when he was face-to-face with his pissant brothers. His condescending, kiss-my-ass brothers who'd taken the best parts of the earth and tossed him what was left: the fucking Underworld.

He tamped down the resentment, knowing he needed to stay focused so he could get this meet-and-greet over and move on to more important matters.

"Perhaps, brother," he said, glancing at his long fingers against the mahogany armrest, "humans wouldn't shit in your home if you took your dick out of those sea nymphs long enough to pay attention to what they're doing."

Poseidon's blue eyes turned icy, and a vein pulsed in his temple. "Why you little piece of—"

"Boys, boys, boys." Zeus sighed. "I didn't call you both here so you could get into a pissing match. We have a serious matter to discuss."

The King of the Gods waited until both Poseidon and Hades redirected their attention his way. "The queen of Argolea has the Orb of Krónos and two of the four elements she needs to release our father from Tartarus. I don't have to tell you what that kind of power, in the hands of someone so inexperienced and simple, would do to the balance of the world."

It'd fuck you over good.

Hades kept the thought to himself while Poseidon dropped into the chair to his right. Though Hades didn't want to see the

Orb controlled by an Argolean, the thought of the Little Queen pulling one over on his good-for-nothing brothers made him want to smile.

"We need to get to the other two elements before they do," Zeus went on. "It's time we put aside history and our petty differences and unite our powers."

What the fuck? Hades's gaze narrowed on Zeus. The King of the Gods never did anything unless it directly benefited him alone. Hades wasn't stupid. He'd seen the look that passed between that Siren and Zeus.

"Even if we find the last two elements," Poseidon said, "how do you plan to get the Orb? You just said the Argoleans already have it."

Zeus pushed out of his chair and crossed to the wide window that looked out over Olympus, a frown line forming between his brows. The Orb of Krónos was their father's get-out-of-jail-free card. During the Titanomachy, the war between the Olympians and the Titans, their father, Krónos, had ordered Prometheus to craft the Orb in the event he was captured. Prometheus, a Titan himself, had used the power of the four classic elements and created a disk-shaped object that held the strength to release Krónos from his prison. But Prometheus had never used it. Not after the Olympians had won and they'd locked their father in the pits of Tartarus. Not even after all these thousands of years.

No, Prometheus had always had a soft spot for humans and was afraid of what Krónos would do to the world in retaliation. So instead of handing the Orb over to the Olympians for safekeeping, the bastard had scattered the elements over the earth then hidden the Orb in Argolea—the one realm the Olympian gods couldn't cross into.

Hades had to admire the smart play. Though Zeus had created the realm of Argolea for his son Heracles and his descendants, he'd blocked the Olympians from entry, mostly to keep the Argonauts safe from Hera's vengeance. But he'd also done it as an act of good faith—so his son and all Argoleans could rule themselves. But now that detail had backfired big-time on the King of the Gods. Hades agreed that the power of the Orb couldn't be trusted in the hands of any Olympian, least of all his power-hungry brothers. But in another lucky turn of events—Hades wasn't considered an Olympian, and the realm of Argolea wasn't closed to him.

"There are ways," Zeus said, staring out at the view. "Ways we can discuss later." He turned from the window to face them, and whatever worry was previously etched into his features cleared. "What we need to focus on are the two remaining elements."

Double bullshit. "What would you have us do, oh great King of the Gods?"

Zeus turned his dark gaze Hades's way, and his cold stare clearly conveyed his displeasure over Hades's mockery. "I would have you focus your hellhounds and underlings on finding the water element before it's lost for good, *adelfos.*"

"And what of fire?"

"Leave that to Poseidon. He and I have already discussed…options."

A smug look crossed Poseidon's face. The two were in league together. That realization only infuriated Hades more. Though it shouldn't have surprised him. "Isn't fire more my expertise?"

"Not this time."

Yeah, they were definitely up to something. Hades looked from face to face. "Assuming we do find the last two elements, why then, dear brother, do we need you?"

"Because with our resources pooled, we'll be able find the elements faster together than we ever could alone."

There was something more, though. Hades felt it in the pit of his stomach. Some trump card Zeus was holding back.

A self-righteous smile spread across Zeus's face, almost as if the bastard had read his mind. "And because I hold Prometheus."

"That's not exactly a surprise," Hades countered. "Prometheus has been chained, what…? Over three thousand years? And after all that torture, the Titan has yet to tell you where he hid the elements. What makes you think he'll cooperate now?"

"I don't need him to cooperate," Zeus said. "I just need his daughter to cooperate."

His daughter…

A chill spread down Hades's spine. He'd heard rumors of a child, but after all this time with no sign or mention of her, he'd thought she was mere myth. Prophecy said Prometheus's child would lead to the downfall of the Olympian king—yet *another* reason Zeus had imprisoned Prometheus, so he could never procreate. But if what Zeus said was true, if Prometheus *did* have a daughter somewhere, and *if* Hades could find her first, it meant this whole game could be over much sooner than even Hades had planned. And it meant not only could Hades take control of the human realm like he wanted, but he could grind Zeus to dust in the process and claim Olympus for himself.

Excitement reverberated through his veins. Now, more than ever, it was imperative he get to Persephone and their son, Zagreus, before anyone else.

Careful not to show enthusiasm, Hades tipped his head and worked to keep the bite in his words when he said, "And where, oh great and glorious Grand Pooh-Bah, are you going to look for this mystery daughter?"

"That," Zeus said, leaning back against the windowsill, "is my worry, not yours. You just focus on finding the water element."

They were sending him on a wild-goose chase. Hades could feel it. He didn't know why, but he was certain they were plotting to use Prometheus's daughter for something cataclysmic.

Hades wasn't about to let them win.

"Are you in or out, *adelfos*?" Zeus's eyes sharpened. "Think carefully, because the choice you make now could change your life for good."

Hades didn't need to think twice. He already knew exactly what he wanted. And whose back he was going to stab to get it.

One side of his mouth curled into a vicious smile. "I'm already there, brother mine."

She was back. He hadn't imagined her after all.

Titus's nerves hummed as he moved past doors and scanned offices on the second floor of the castle. The guardians had been dispatched to do a thorough yet quiet search of the premises. With the Council milling around downstairs and all of Argolea in the streets outside, this was not the time to have a spy sent by the Prince of Darkness fucking around.

Shit, he had not seen that one coming. He pushed open a door, glanced around the empty meeting room, and moved on. She worked for Zagreus? How had he missed that? He passed through a sitting area and into a small kitchen, also empty. Perching his hands on his hips, he turned a slow circle and took in the room.

Zagreus... It explained a lot, though. Like why she was searching for Maelea, why she was asking questions about

Prometheus, why she was able to block his ability to read his mind, why, even, Maelea had sensed some great power within her. Dark power, obviously. A frown turned his lips as he eyed the table and chairs in the middle of the kitchen. But it didn't explain why he could touch her and not feel anything.

Movement outside the window over the sink caught his attention. He whipped that way just as something landed with a thud on the veranda.

A body pushed to full height, and his adrenaline surged. Fire-red hair blew in the breeze, and eyes—sparkling, emerald-green eyes—peered his way through the glass.

It was her. Natasa. Alive in front of him as if he'd conjured her.

Titus lurched into the sitting area and raced for the french doors that led to the balcony. Chants from the crowd growing impatient on the other side of the castle walls filled the air. The fresh scents of sea and salt wafted around him. His pulse raced while he scanned the empty balcony.

Where the hell…?

A thud echoed up to his ears. Followed by a voice, shouting, "Hey? Where did you come from?"

He rushed to the railing and looked down. A gardener holding pruning shears in his hand stood between rows of roses, staring after a redhead who was halfway across the courtyard. A redhead racing straight for the trellises covered in purple-flowered vines that climbed the castle wall.

Holy Hades, who was this female?

"Stop her!" he hollered, already tossing his legs over the railing and dropping to the ground. Normally, since they were in Argolea, he could flash wherever the hell he needed to go. But he still wasn't back to one-hundred percent after his recent injuries. And flashing was one of those things you needed to be in tip-top shape to perform.

She slowed and looked back. And then their gazes met. Fire flashed in the depths of her eyes. Fire and determination and a come-and-get-me challenge no man could resist.

"Signal the guards," he yelled at the gardener. "And alert the queen."

He didn't have time to contact Theron and the others. If he let this female out of his sight, he had a strong hunch he'd never see her again.

And aside from the fact she was working for the enemy, had infiltrated their realm, and had somehow gotten past the castle's security, something in his gut told him he had to see her again. Needed to…for reasons even he didn't totally understand.

She was already at the top of the trellis—at least thirty feet up in the air—by the time he reached the base, moving as smoothly as a seasoned cat burglar. She pulled herself up to the wall walk, turned and looked down. Grasping the trellis in his hands, Titus paused his hasty climb. The wind blew silky curls back from her face, and sunlight highlighted her creamy features. But it was the victory that flashed in her eyes that did him in. A victory that turned one side of her lips up in the sexiest smile and caused his heart to skip a beat with both awe and arousal.

"Wait—"

A dog barked. Voices echoed at his back. She jerked her head up to look toward the castle, and her smile faded. Those eyes grew hard and focused. Before he could reach her, she took off at a run across the castle wall.

"*Skata…*" Titus pushed his muscles into gear and climbed faster. He couldn't lose her now. He reached for the top of the wall. A loud, cracking sound echoed through the courtyard.

Every muscle in his body froze.

Another crack.

Oh…*fuck.*

He slapped the palm of his left hand against the wall walk and managed to hurl his right forearm over the edge. The trellis gave beneath his feet. Wood splintered and fractured. The entire section pulled from the wall and slammed to the ground.

Sweat slicked his skin. Muscles in his arms burned as he held his weight on the edge of the wall. He might be part hero, but he didn't have Theron's superhuman strength. And though he knew if he fell it likely wouldn't kill him, it would definitely shatter his legs, sidelining him for he didn't know how long. More time in a freaking hospital bed was not his idea of a good time.

A scream echoed. From his peripheral vision, he saw an eagle, diving straight for him.

Fucktastic. Where the hell had *that* come from? As if he weren't in enough shit already?

He ground his teeth, grunted, and pulled himself up. The eagle swooped low, screeched with a shrill that echoed off the inside of his skull, almost nailed him in the head then took off for the sky at the last second. Titus's fingers slipped. His legs swung out away from the wall. The weight of his body jerked on his arms.

Something soft brushed against his hand. He looked up to see the end of a rope resting near his fingers.

His gaze darted to the right. She—*Natasa*—was tying off the other end to the parapet. When she finished with the knot, she glanced his way, winked, then took off at a run.

Bloody hell...

He grasped the rope and pulled himself up. Chest heaving, he threw his leg over the ledge and climbed to his knees. He dragged air into his lungs then cursed the injury that had left him weak.

His gaze strayed down the walk in the direction Natasa had run. She stood at the corner where two walls intersected, another rope in her hand, looking back at him as if...checking to make sure he'd made it.

His breath caught. Slowly, one side of her kiss-me lips curled. And as his gaze zeroed in on only her, his blood flowed fast and hot. This time not from fear of falling to his death, but from excitement. Pure, unadulterated, sexual excitement.

No way was he done with her. Not by a long shot. No matter what Theron and the others said. Before this was over, she was going to be his.

Good gods...

Natasa swiped at her forehead, brushing aside the perspiration. She should have left well enough alone and let him fall to his death. Why hadn't she? And why in Hades did the man—no, nix that...*hero*—put the human term "Greek god" to shame?

Disgusted, she let her feet drop to the ground, released the rope and headed for the crowd in the streets outside the main gates. She didn't bother to see if he followed. Didn't trust herself. If it weren't for that stupid bird screaming like a banshee, she might not have looked back to begin with.

Keep telling yourself that, missy.

Her mind drifted to the sight of Titus pulling himself up on the wall walk. Muscular, sexy, panting to catch his breath. Her skin heated, and that internal temperature gauge she worked to control jumped another degree. She hoped he had the sense to check the rope before descending that wall after her. No way it would hold his weight. It had barely held hers.

Why do I freaking care?

More frustrated with herself than ever, she clenched her jaw and wove between Argoleans anxious for words from their queen. The crowd was thicker than she'd anticipated. They'd gathered in the mall in front of the main gates of the castle. She pushed and maneuvered her way through bodies. Her boot slipped on the cobblestone street and she nearly went down but caught herself at the last moment by grabbing on to a woman's arm.

"What…?"

"Excuse me," Natasa said, righting herself.

The woman jerked her arm back, frowned, and shook her head, then turned her attention back toward the castle.

Friendly. Another reason to get the hell out of here.

Natasa pushed through the crowd again. Finally, she reached the far edge. Drawing a deep breath of fresh air, she stepped up onto a sidewalk and scanned the marble buildings around her, then glanced back toward the crowd. A fountain rose up in the middle, one she hadn't noticed before. One made of shiny marble with jets of water shooting out into a circular pool. In the center, a giant of a man slayed a great minotaur, and around him, smaller but no less impressive, six other statues of men, each holding a different weapon, looked on in awe.

The Argonauts, Natasa realized. A memorial to the great heroes who had settled this realm. As she looked to the six below Heracles, she couldn't help but wonder which statue was Titus's forefather, Odysseus.

"Over there," a shrill voice echoed, cutting through Natasa's thoughts. "She went that way."

Natasa's attention jerked away from the statue, and she looked back at the crowd. Then froze when she saw the woman she'd bumped into pointing her direction. And beside her, the Argonaut who'd just been on Natasa's mind.

Shit. Shit!

She sprinted for the Gatehouse, the ancient building that housed the portal she'd used earlier to cross into Argolea. Caught wondering. Caught *daydreaming*. Dammit all to hell, the last thing she needed was to be caught by a man who was already a bigger distraction than she'd ever anticipated.

"Natasa, stop!"

Her pulse kicked up. The skin on her neck and spine prickled all over again. And heat flooded her veins. A heat she didn't have time for right now.

Brilliantly colored flags attached to light posts waved in the air above. More voices echoed at her back. More than just Titus's. Her boots hit the steps of the Gatehouse, and she skipped stairs to reach the top fast. Once inside, she paused to orient herself.

A guard moved out from behind a long counter, his armor flashing in the light of the setting sun. "Hey, you. Stop right there."

Her gaze landed on the door straight ahead. She pushed her muscles forward.

"I said stop!"

He stepped into her path. He was twice her size and probably well-trained in hand-to-hand combat. But she had determination on her side.

"You're not going anywhere, young lady."

Young? She wanted to laugh but didn't have time. "Move out of my way."

"Or what?" the guard asked, looking smug and arrogant.

She skidded to a stop, pulled one of the two silver daggers she kept sheathed at her lower back, and braced her feet. "Or I will cut you."

A low chuckle echoed from his chest. One that sent Natasa's temper boiling. She arced out with the blade, not to kill him, just to injure him enough so he'd get the hell out of her way. His arm swung out before she saw him move, and the dagger went sailing across the room to land with a clank against the black marble floor.

"I said stop," he muttered in a low voice.

Footsteps pounded at her back. Voices echoed from the steps out front. The guard edged forward.

Natasa's panic and anger peaked.

"And I said move!" She shoved both hands against his chest.

Power raced down her arms. Smoke rose up around her. The guard shrieked. His head hit the marble with a crack, then his body slid to the floor. Whimpering, he curled in on himself, but not before Natasa saw the holes in the front of his armor. Holes the size of her palms. Smoking. The skin beneath singed and black.

Wide-eyed, Natasa turned her hands over and looked at her palms, which were also smoking. How the hell…?

"Holy Hades," someone muttered.

She whipped around. Three men stood in the doorway. Three Argonauts. And at the front of the trio was Titus.

"Natasa," he said slowly, taking a step forward. "Stop."

She held her hands up in warning. Moved back. One step. Two. Stumbled through the doorway, unsure what she'd just done.

"You there!" Another voice rang out at her back. "Halt!"

She swiveled to find two more guards, each dressed in the same shiny armor as the first but holding spears, one standing on each side of the portal.

"Natasa," Titus said calmly at her back. Too calmly. And way too close. "No one's going to hurt you."

Her pulse roared. Her adrenaline surged. She didn't know what to believe. Nothing like that had ever happened before. Nothing…

Her gaze jumped from one guard to the other. They didn't look nonthreatening from where she was standing.

She wouldn't go back to being imprisoned. Not now. Not when she was so close to her goal. Her focus homed in on the portal, the stone arch shining like a beacon—her beacon to freedom. She stepped forward.

Both guards lowered their spears.

"Don't—" Titus yelled.

Natasa didn't wait for their response. She charged. The guard on the right thrust his spear out. She missed being skewered by a mere inch and grasped it with her palm. Heat radiated from her skin, and flames flared. The spear broke in two and turned to ash in her palm. Gasping, the guard yanked his arm back.

But the other thrust out his spear before she could deflect it. The tip grazed her side and tore her shirt. She sucked in a breath. Only, instead of shoving deep into her flesh as she expected, the guard sailed backward.

"Titus!"

She wasn't sure who yelled, but she whipped around to find Titus at her side. The guard and his spear lay sprawled across the floor.

"Stop running," Titus said, reaching out for her. "Let me help you."

Her chest heaved. She looked to the hand he offered. Then to the other two Argonauts behind him, moving slowly closer. And on both sides, the guards watching in shock.

He'd saved her life. Not knowing who and what she was. Even after she'd broken into his castle and burned that guard. And now he was offering help.

No one had ever offered to help her. Her pulse roared in her ears. No one could. At least not without demanding something in return.

"You can't help me." She lurched for the portal.

"Natasa! Son of a fucking bitch!"

Her body went flying. Air whooshed past her face, and the world swirled as she entered the portal. But something grasped her ankle just before she entered. Something warm and solid and tight.

CHAPTER FOUR

Titus hit the earth hard, his shoulder and hip taking the brunt of the impact. Pain radiated up his side and ricocheted through his limbs.

He rolled, and pine needles flew up around him. Natasa jerked her ankle from his grip and scrambled to her feet. Pushing up on his hands, he had the impression of towering trees that rose to the sky and blue-green mountains lingering in the distance. But the view was lost on him. And he didn't have time to wonder where they'd landed. The female already on her feet and racing away was his sole focus.

"Natasa!" His boots scuffed the dirt. He found his footing. She'd rounded a stump and was heading for the hillside that led to—he didn't know where. "Son of a bitch."

Phin and Orpheus should be right behind him. As long as no one else went through the portal and programmed in a new location, they would come through in the same spot. So long as she didn't get too far away, they'd find him.

He watched to see which direction she headed, then took off at an angle.

Her steps were near-silent, the push and pull of air in her lungs undetectable even though she had to be breathing hard. She was obviously trained how to disappear, but Titus knew a thing or two about hunting. And he wasn't going to be bested by some slim redhead who had somehow managed to give the Argonauts and every other fucking guard in Argolea the slip.

She appeared from behind a cluster of spruce. Just before she veered off again, he threw his weight forward.

Their bodies collided. A grunt echoed from her chest. He wrapped his arms around her and twisted so he took the brunt of the impact. More pine needles and dirt flew up in the air. He rolled, then wrestled her to the ground, pinning her hands above her head so she couldn't move. "Stop!"

"Let me go!"

"Not on your life."

She wriggled beneath him, but he held her tighter with his gloved hands. She stared hard into his eyes. Several second passed where the only sound was her labored breath, the only movement the rise and fall of her chest. And though her muscles remained tensed beneath him, and he didn't doubt for a minute she wasn't plotting a way to escape—or a way to crack his head open with a rock—relief spiraled through him. "That's better."

"Get," she said through gritted teeth. "Off. Me."

Not exactly calm. But better than before. If only slightly.

"When you tell me what you were doing in Argolea, I'll be happy to. Until then, I think we'll stay right where we are."

Her eyes flashed. "You saw what I did to that guard. If you want to live, I suggest you let go. Now."

Yeah, he'd seen the guard's burns, but he had a hard time believing she'd done that to the *ándras* on purpose. Granted, her skin was warm—warmer than he was used to—but it wasn't burning. And it definitely wasn't smoking, by any means. There had to be a logical explanation for what he'd witnessed back at the Gatehouse.

His bet was magic. She could be a witch, a sorceress, even someone just dabbling in spells. Gods knew he'd seen enough magical shit to know anything was possible. And she'd definitely looked as shocked as that guard, so he was pretty sure singeing someone wasn't a power she could just conjure at will.

"I told you back at the half-breed colony that our conversation wasn't over." He gripped her hands tighter and leaned down so their faces were only inches apart. "I suggest you start talking, *ligos Vesuvius.*"

Her eyes sparked at the nickname—little volcano—and he smiled at her reaction. Oh yeah, it definitely fit. He tried to read her mind. Couldn't. A fact that only intrigued him more.

"You want me to talk?"

"Start with what you were doing in Argolea. And why you've been hunting Maelea."

"How about I start with this?" She cracked her forehead against his. Pain spiraled across his scalp, throwing him off center. In a flash, she flipped him to his back, freed her hands and pulled a dagger he hadn't bothered to check her for from the small of her back. The blade pressed against his throat with deadly precision. "And this."

He froze beneath her. Shocked, awed and vibrating with excitement because when she'd slammed her forehead against his the only thing he'd felt was his own pain at the impact, not a single emotion seeping from her.

And, *fuck*, that was so freakin' hot. Not just the fact she could still touch him, but that she could kick his ass doing it.

"Not exactly what I had in mind," he managed. "Especially after I rescued you back at the half-breed colony."

"You—" Her eyes widened then narrowed to thin slits. "You didn't rescue me."

He fought back the amusement. And the desire roaring through his veins with the force of a freight train. She weighed less than half what he did, and even with the blade against his throat and not totally healed from his injuries, he could easily take her. But he didn't want to. He was enjoying her weight pressing down on his stomach and chest. Enjoying her bare hand pushing against his shoulder, her fingertips just barely brushing his collarbone at the edge of his shirt. Loving the absolute absence of any emotion transfer.

He worked to stay focused and not get lost in her. Worked to keep his brain online. "I all but carried you down to the infirmary after that panic attack."

Her eyes flashed again. She leaned closer but didn't move the blade. And holy Hera, this close he could smell her. Roses and…lemons. Underneath the floral scent he remembered from the colony, she smelled citrusy. And her eyes weren't just green. There were flecks of aqua floating in those mesmerizing irises. "I don't have panic attacks."

"My error. You must have been sleepy, then."

She drew back. A slow smile spread across his face—the first he could remember feeling in ages. Her eyes narrowed even more.

"You think this is funny? How funny will it be when I slit your throat?"

"You won't."

"Confident, aren't you?"

"Yeah, I am. If you wanted me dead, you would have let me fall off that castle wall. You didn't because you're not done with me."

Shock ran over her face. "I—"

"And that's fine by me, because I'm not done with you either. This, whatever it is between us, isn't even close to being over."

Her mouth closed. Her gaze held his. And in the silence...he couldn't tell what she was thinking. Which...only turned him on more. He always knew what those around him were thinking, feeling, plotting. He searched her expression for clues to her thoughts, but all he could see was surprise. And arousal. And the same damn heat searing his veins.

His stomach tightened. Beneath his pants, he grew hard. Oh yeah. He wanted this female. No matter who she was working for. Wanted her all to himself. At least for a little while.

She climbed off him and stepped back, the blade held out like a warning. "Go back where you came from, Titus. And forget you ever met me. I won't be returning to your realm—ever."

He rolled to his side, pushed to his feet, moving in slow motion so as not to spook her. A breeze rustled the trees at his back and blew a lock of hair that had come free across his cheek, the sensation normal. Familiar. Expected. The only touch against his skin he could count on these days.

Except for her. She could touch him. And he *had* to know why.

"I'm not going anywhere but where you're going," he said calmly. "Until I get what I want, you're stuck with me."

Her breath quickened. A flush rose up in her cheeks. She stepped back again, waving the dagger in front of her like a sword. "You're not going anywhere with me."

"Then start talking."

Voices echoed from the bottom of the hill. Several. Female. Natasa's gaze jerked that way. With her so easily distracted, Titus knew he could overpower her, but he didn't. He stood where he was and waited. Because even without her touching him, this was more fun than he'd had in months...no, years.

She faced him again, but instead of frustration and surprise, panic marked her features. "You have to go. Now. I'm not fooling around anymore."

His senses went on high alert. "Who's down there?"

She sheathed the blade at her back and bent to pick up a length of rope from the ground. The same kind of rope she'd thrown to him from the wall walk when he'd been struggling to make it to the top. Thin, strong, otherworldly rope that must have fallen out of her pocket when they'd been wrestling in the dirt. "No one you want to meet. Just go!"

The conversation with Theron flashed in his mind. Followed by the Argonaut leader's suspicions. He grasped her arm at the biceps. "I said I'm not leaving until we talk, and I meant it."

"Gods!" She swiveled, pushed both hands against his leather breastplate, and shoved hard. But she was only about five-seven and weighed *maybe* a hundred and thirty pounds, and her push didn't even budge him. And there was no heat in the movement. Not like when she'd attacked that guard. "I'm trying to help *you* now. Why won't you listen?"

"Natasa?"

Natasa froze against him. Titus looked over her head toward the tall brunette standing near an old-growth pine. The one decked out in full camo gear, her hair pulled back in a tight tail, her hand holding a blade the length of his leg. And behind her? Five more just like her.

"Shit," Natasa muttered, her eyes sliding closed.

Sirens? No, these female warriors weren't flashy enough. Zeus only recruited the sexiest, most alluring females into his private army. While these chicks weren't butt-ugly, they definitely weren't Siren material. And no way could he imagine a Siren being caught dead with a bandanna over her hair and camo face paint smeared across her cheeks and hands.

Natasa dropped her arms and turned to face their guests. "Ilithyia." She nodded at the others. "You're out earlier than I expected."

"And you're out later," the one in front, the one clearly in charge, said. "Who is this...*male*?"

The sneered word and the way her gaze raked Titus's body from head to toe put Titus on alert. He focused in on his gift, searching for answers to questions unasked. *"Argonaut, traitor, male"* were words that rose up from the group at his front.

"No one you need to concern yourself with," Natasa answered.

Ilithyia moved out of the trees and held her sword point out, her dark gaze zeroed in on Titus as if he were a fly she was about to grind to dust beneath her boot. "I must have missed the memo about Halloween coming early this year. But perhaps today we'll get a treat after all, ladies."

Titus didn't know who the hell these chicks were, but he'd had just about enough. He stepped forward, but before he could set their leader straight on a few very key points, Natasa moved fully in front of him. "He's my prisoner, Ilithyia, not yours."

Ilithyia slowed, and her brows narrowed, her gaze jumping from Natasa to Titus and back again. "Prisoner?"

Yeah…take that, camo girl.

Whoa—wait…prisoner? Titus's gaze snapped to Natasa, but from behind, he couldn't see her eyes. Only the defiant lift of her head that told him she was serious.

A shot of wicked heat rolled through his hips, along with mental images of all the different ways he could be her prisoner.

"Yes. Mine."

"He's not bound."

"I was just about to do that when you barged up on us."

Ilithyia's eyes narrowed even more. Tension crackled in the cool May forest. "Aella will not like this."

"This has nothing to do with Aella," Natasa answered in a hard tone. "She knows I have my own agenda. And she is not to interfere."

"Oh…the queen will definitely not approve of this."

"Natasa is so screwed."

"My gods, is he hot or what?"

"He's exactly what we've been waiting for."

Thoughts pinged around from the group, but Titus was too distracted to tell which was coming from whom. His focus had shifted entirely to Natasa. And, lucky him, her thoughts were the only ones he couldn't read.

"Fine," Ilithyia said after a long beat. "Bind him and we'll escort you back. We wouldn't want you to lose your prisoner along the way."

The smug way she said prisoner dragged Titus's attention away from Natasa and back to the Amazon glaring his direction

Amazon… shit. He looked out over the group. That was what these females were. Amazon warriors. He'd never run across one, but he knew they roamed the earth, just like the multitude of otherworldly beings that stayed hidden from humans. He quickly ran through what he knew of them: they didn't like the gods, they loathed men even more, and they marked themselves with the crescent moon.

He cut a glance at Natasa's arms, but her sleeves fell all the way to her wrists. He looked past her to the other females to confirm his suspicions, but they too all wore long sleeves.

Natasa turned his way and pulled the rope from her pocket. As she unwound it, he whispered, "What the hell is going on?"

"Shh," she muttered, grasping his wrists together, not meeting his gaze. "Do as I say. And for gods' sake, don't open your mouth. I can't protect you if you piss them off."

Protect *him*? Did that mean she wasn't one of them? Yeah, she was tough enough, but something in his gut said she didn't fit in with this group. He glanced back at the Amazons while Natasa wrapped the rope around his wrists. They'd spread out in a U-shape around him, their swords each drawn in aggression. But it was the glint of victory in the leader's eyes that told Titus he'd stumbled into something he should have left alone.

He didn't have a weapon with him. Nothing but his bare— well, gloved—hands. Sure, he could take a few down if it came to that, but he didn't like the idea of hurting a female if he didn't have to. He had no doubt he was faster than these chicks, which meant he could escape if he ran like hell. But what would happen to Natasa if he did that? Even if she was only *part* Amazon, he didn't have to read minds to know there was a power struggle going on here. A big one.

Where the hell was Phineus? Why hadn't he come through the damn portal yet? Titus lifted his bound hands and reached for the Argos medallion he wore on a chain around his neck, the one that was a beacon back to his order. He found nothing but skin.

Skata. He'd lost it. Probably when he'd been rolling around in the dirt with Natasa. Goofing off instead of doing his fucking job.

"Come," Ilithyia said after Natasa cinched down on the rope. "Queen Aella is waiting."

The twine cut into his skin, but Titus barely felt it. Because Natasa's eyes finally met his. And in their emerald depths he saw worry, and the unspoken plea *Do this. For me.*

His heart picked up speed, and that warmth he'd felt before came rushing back. Her prisoner. He could pretend to be her prisoner for a little while, couldn't he? Theron had told him to find out who the hell she was and what she was after. By staying with her, he'd only be doing his duty.

Images of being tied beneath her, of being forced to do whatever sinful thing she wanted rushed through his mind.

His blood pulsed, his heart raced, and any lingering doubt disappeared.

Yeah, he could do this. After all, they were just girls. What was the worst that could happen?

"Theron? We have a problem."

Isadora turned from her sister, Casey, and the prepared speech she was about to give and looked toward the leader of the Argonauts.

The sitting area in her royal office was full. In addition to Theron and her sister, several of the Argonauts were in attendance providing security. Zander and Demetrius stood across the room, quietly speaking, while Gryphon sat with Maelea on the blue velvet couch, his arm around her shoulder, her nerves as palpable as Isadora's since she had to face the crowd too. In seconds, Isadora was to step out onto the veranda that overlooked the city and address her people with the news that the evil goddess Atalanta was finally dead.

For most, that would be enough to set one's nerves on edge, but Isadora had bigger issues to deal with. Not only was the Council waiting in the ballroom downstairs with the Misos delegation—a race the Council deemed unworthy—but somewhere in the mix, Nick, the leader of the Misos—a man most hated by the Council—was wandering around, looking for the female that had been in Maelea's room earlier. Any number of fireworks could go off with the current mix of people in the castle, and the unease Isadora heard in Phineus's voice about some problem wasn't helping matters.

Theron pulled the communications gadget Titus had recently been experimenting with from his pocket and pushed a button. "What's going on, Phin?"

"We lost her."

"Dammit," Theron muttered. "Where?"

"Through the portal."

Isadora handed the papers to her sister and crossed the room to stand at Theron's side. Tension radiated from his powerful shoulders. Across the elaborate space, she felt Maelea's worry as if the female were right next to her.

"Well, go after her," Theron said. "Her coordinates should be easily accessible."

"Titus did go after her," Phin said through the com unit. "Grabbed on to her leg as she jumped through. But we can't follow."

Theron scrubbed a hand over his head in clear frustration. Casey—his mate—moved to stand on his other side. "Why not?"

"Because something's wrong with the portal. It's not working. Orpheus and I have tech guys here looking at it, but the panel's totally fried. We have no idea where they went or even if Titus can get back through this way."

Theron shot a look at Demetrius and Zander, then to Gryphon and finally Isadora. "And just how in Hades did that happen?"

"We're not sure. But, Theron? Man, you should see the guard down here. That female put her hands on him when he got in her way and tried to stop her. His armor damn near melted beneath her palms. Guy's got third degree burns all over his chest. Callia's looking at him now, but I've never seen anything like it. I mean, *skata*, even *I* can't do that."

Callia was Zander's mate and Isadora's other sister. She was also a trained healer. Gryphon stood from the couch and moved closer. Demetrius and Zander did the same.

Unease flitted through Isadora's veins. She could tell the guardians were all thinking the same thing as she. Phineus's gift was the breath of fire, bestowed upon those in his line from the Fates in honor of his forefather, Bellerophon, the great hero who'd slayed the Chimera, a gigantic fire-breathing beast. But Phineus rarely used his gift, for reasons Isadora didn't quite understand. And the fact he was telling Theron this female—this Natasa—had done something even he couldn't do, meant things were far worse than they'd all assumed.

"*Skata*," Theron muttered. He glanced toward Zander. "Phin, I'm sending Z to you. The queen's about to take the podium and Demetrius, Gryphon, and I can't leave just yet. Figure out a way to get that portal working again and find out where the fuck Titus is. Fire-and-brimstone shit goes along with our suspicions that she's working with Hades and Zagreus. As long as she's out of Argolea, that's all I care about. But I want Titus back ASAP. You got me?"

"Got it."

Theron clicked off the com unit and slid it back in his pocket. At his side, he squeezed Casey's hand and whispered, "Don't worry." Then he turned his attention to Zander. "Find him. The last thing I need is another lost Argonaut. *Skata*, you guys keep disappearing on me like fireflies."

Gryphon chuckled, and one side of Demetrius's lips curled—a smile Isadora loved to see. But her joy was short-lived.

As Zander headed for the door, she looked toward Theron. "Burnt armor? Who is this female?"

"I don't know," Theron muttered. "But we'll find out. Right now, let's just get this speech over and done with. This celebration is quickly turning into a friggin' nightmare."

Reluctantly, Isadora turned for the double doors that led to the veranda. She hadn't foreseen any of this coming, but then her gift of foresight wasn't exactly predictable, especially not now when she was pregnant. She waited while Gryphon and Demetrius opened the doors, then drew in a deep breath and prayed Theron was wrong.

They couldn't afford to lose any of the Argonauts, especially Titus. His gift of reading minds was too valuable to their cause.

CHAPTER FIVE

Titus didn't try to speak to Natasa as they walked through the forest. The looks she shot him and the way she tugged on the damn rope attached to his wrists whenever he slowed to glance around told him not to even try. If it were just the two of them, he'd have tugged back until she fell into him and her skin brushed his again, but the six Amazons with their blades drawn—three in front and three in back—nixed that little fantasy.

Still, his view wasn't all that bad. Natasa had one fine ass in those fitted black pants, and the way her hips swayed when she walked brought all kinds of other images to mind. Like what she'd look like dressed in a black leather bodysuit, wielding that rope like a whip and ordering him around in a sexy dominatrix voice.

He stepped over a downed log covered in moss and flanked by sword fern. Above, gigantic sequoias rustled in the wind. The weather was cool but not frigid, and the teasing warmth of early summer could be felt in the damp breeze. His gaze followed the thin layer of fog rolling through the maples and red alders. They had to be near a coast somewhere. In a place with gigantic evergreen trees. The redwoods, maybe?

He wasn't sure. All he knew was that they'd been walking for about three hours, and the rope was starting to seriously piss him off. As was the fact no one—not even the Amazons—seemed to like to talk. Their thoughts he could hear, but he'd stopped focusing on those about thirty minutes into their trek because they weren't telling him anything that would help his situation. It was mostly meanderings about hunting and skinning deer, concerns about their food supply and speculations about the size of his dick.

They might not be interested in men, but they obviously still thought about them.

His mind spiraled to what kind of 'agenda' Natasa had, and where the hell they were really heading.

Ahead, Ilithyia drew to a stop and held up her forearm. As a unit, the others halted and raised their weapons. Titus was so lost in his thoughts he didn't realize they'd stopped until he slammed into Natasa's back and nearly knocked them both down.

She grunted, pushed against him until he stumbled back a step, then glared over her shoulder.

A smile worked its way across Titus's mouth. She was gorgeous pissed. That flame red hair fanning out around her, the flare of heat in her eyes. He bet her skin was hot right now. Hot and soft and so damn alluring he wanted to feel it against him. Everywhere.

"A garrison," Ilithyia whispered in a harsh tone. "Spread out."

The Amazons moved with lightning speed, disappearing into the forest as if they'd never been there. Natasa tugged on the rope bound to Titus's wrists and quickly pulled him into a dense copse of trees.

Darkness surrounded him. He tripped over a downed limb, bumping into Natasa again, only this time she didn't seem to mind. She grasped him by the shoulders, whipped him around and shoved him up against the trunk of a tree the size of a house. Then she plastered her body to his and whispered, "Shh."

Titus's adrenaline surged. This close he could smell the lemon scent of her skin. Could feel the heat radiating from beneath her clothes. Blood rushed to his groin, messing with his thoughts. *Focus. Control.* To try to keep his brain on line so he wouldn't give away their location, he looked over her head at the trees around them.

The small area was more like a cave than a forest. The spruce so densely clustered, their limbs were devoid of needles. The packed groundcover told him some kind of animal had recently bedded down in here, and the foliage on the outside of the tree-lined circle was thick enough to block whatever lay beyond.

Footsteps pounded in the forest. Muffled voices reached their ears. Titus tried to focus on the words and thoughts of those around them, but Natasa's rapid breath drew his attention. And the way she gripped his sleeves tighter in her fingers, the way her heart raced next to his drowned out all other sound.

Instinct overcame reason. He lifted his bound wrists over her head, slid them down her back so his arms were tight around her. She didn't protest. If anything, she moved closer into the strength of his body. And yeah, she was warm—like he expected—but the tremble that rushed through her told him she wasn't quite as confident as she'd seemed earlier.

He lowered his mouth close to her ear, only just missed brushing her lobe with the tip of his nose. "Whatever's out there...I'll protect you."

She stilled against him, then slowly tilted her head back to look up. Heat radiated from her hands pressing into his sides, from her breasts resting against his leather chest plate. He wished he'd taken off the formal gear earlier in the forest. Wished right now they were naked, skin to skin, so he could see if she felt as good against him in other places. Wanted, more than anything, for her to rise up on her toes and press those plump, tender lips against his so he could know what it was like to be kissed again.

He couldn't remember the last time he'd been kissed. Couldn't remember what it felt like to press his mouth to someone else's, to taste their essence on his tongue. Couldn't remember how good it must feel to get lost in nothing but warm, blissful wetness.

She'd be all three, he bet. Not just in her mouth, but between her legs, where he ached to touch her, skin to skin.

"You can't protect me," she whispered. "No one can."

The finality to her words slowed his racing heart and brought his focus up to her eyes. They were so green, so fathomless, he wondered if he could see her soul. But they were also haunted. By a fear he sensed was the root of who she really was.

Her panic attack back at the colony whipped through his mind. Followed by the way she'd run from him in Argolea. He had no doubt whoever or *whatever* was out there was here because of her.

"Who's hunting you?"

Her gaze slid from his eyes to his lips, where it hovered, jacking his already overheated body temperature up another five degrees. For the first time in his life, he wanted to know the thoughts of another. Then she licked her lips, like she wanted to take her own sinful taste, and all that supreme control he'd mastered during his lifetime flew right through the trees. His cock swelled beneath his fly until need consumed him.

Kiss me. Gods, just kiss me.

"Natasa?" Ilithyia's voice rang out.

"Shit."

Natasa lurched back, her one panicked thought slicing through the sexual haze. But Titus's arms were still bound around her, and she didn't get far.

She struggled to break free, and amusement stole through him. He might not be able to read her thoughts clearly, he might wrestle with her expressions, but he recognized body language. She wanted him. Maybe not as much as he wanted her, but enough.

She jerked out from under his arms and smoothed her hair. Then held up a finger and shot him a look. "Not a word."

A broad smile spread across his face. Yeah, he'd discover who she was for the Argonauts. He'd uncover what she was running from and figure out a way to protect her for her. But he was going to have her for himself. Screw the consequences and whatever was keeping him from feeling her emotions. For the first time in over a hundred years, he wanted something just for *him*. And he wasn't going to walk away until he had his fill. No matter what happened next.

"They're gone," Ilithyia called. "We move on."

Natasa's chest rose and fell with her deep breaths. Color stained her cheeks. Heat all but rolled off her in waves. "Come on," she snapped. "And stay quiet. Don't make me hurt you."

"Hurt me, *ligos Vesuvius*. I want you to."

She narrowed her eyes. "You're playing with fire, Argonaut."

Warmth flooded every single vein in his body. This was about to get a whole lot more interesting. "I can't wait to get burned."

Natasa's adrenaline surged as they neared the compound. She was walking a fine line here. She didn't want to do anything to piss off Ilithyia any more than she already had. The Amazon already didn't like her. And being caught with an Argonaut wasn't improving her situation.

Stay focused. Remember why you're here. Remember what's at stake.

Behind her, Titus shuffled over a rock, and his shoulder bumped hers. Awareness trickled through, reminding her of that moment with him in the trees. When he'd looked at her as if he'd wanted to kiss her. When she'd considered—for one insanely stupid moment—rising on her toes and kissing him back.

Kissing him? *Kissing* him? She was seriously losing it if she was considering getting more involved with the hero.

Damn him for following her. Damn her for being so enticed by him. If she hadn't flirted with him on that stupid castle wall—if she hadn't *saved his life* then—they wouldn't be in this mess right now. Marching toward something that could end very badly for both of them if she didn't keep her wits about her.

Son of a bitch, she should be going after Epimetheus, not screwing around with an Argonaut.

"You're being cryptically quiet, *ligos Vesuvius.*"

Ligos Vesuvius… Did she *look* like a little volcano? Her irritation jumped another notch. "And you would be wise to take a cue from my silence."

That irritating, alluring smile spread across his lips again. "You want me. I know you do."

It was all she could do to keep from stopping, whipping around and telling him just what kind of trouble *wanting* him had gotten her into. What it was getting *him* into. But knowing eyes were watching, and if she had any chance of getting out of this mess, she couldn't draw any more attention. She settled for jerking hard on the rope and smiling at the sound of him grunting at her back.

A whistle echoed through the trees. Ahead, Ilithyia held up her forearm again, bringing the group to a halt. The Amazons lifted their weapons, their gazes scanning the forest. Titus's gaze darted up, and hers followed. Nothing but tree trunks and canopy as far as the eye could see.

She hated this damn forest. She always got turned around in here. If it weren't for the sentries who guarded the compound and sent scouts into the old-growth trees, she'd never find her way back.

Ilithyia whistled an answering tune. Silence descended; then an echoing song came from the branches ahead.

"Come," Ilithyia announced.

"Let me guess," Titus muttered. "'It's A Small World.'"

Natasa had no idea what he was rambling about, but her irritation kicked up again. She jerked on the rope and whispered, "Are you trying to get yourself killed?"

"That depends," he said close to her ear. Closer than she liked. His breath, like a whisper of fresh air, ran over her nape, under the collar of her shirt, sending a shiver down her spine. "On what you'll do to save me next time."

She swallowed hard. Fought back the arousal just being close to him fired off deep inside. "Don't be so confident I can. Knowing my luck, I'll probably be strung up with you."

The humor fled from his features. He shot a look at the Amazons ahead, then chanced a glance at those behind. "Where are they taking us?"

"Someplace hostile. Whatever you do, try to stay close to me. Go along with what I say. And for gods' sake, don't be funny. They don't do funny. Especially not from men."

"You think I'm funny?"

Good gods, he was…frustrating and arousing and sexy as hell, all at the same time.

She was in *big* trouble.

Two ropes dropped from the canopy with a thud that echoed through the forest. Their group came to a halt. Ilithyia grasped the ropes and turned, holding them out to Natasa with a smug expression. "Guests first."

The two-by-four tied to the end of each rope formed a plank wide enough for both her and Titus to stand side by side. But it wasn't the wood that concerned her. It was what waited above.

She tugged Titus up next to her. "Here. And hold on."

His gloved fingers closed around the rope to his left. Natasa did the same to the one on the right. The ropes tightened against her palm, and then the plank lifted, drawing them toward the canopy like birds in flight.

Her stomach lurched. She clenched her teeth and tried not to look at the ground disappearing below, the foliage rushing by way too fast. She hated heights. Hated that her life had been reduced to this. To relying on others. To making deals with people she should leave well enough alone. To siding with Amazons, of all people.

The foliage separated, and the hidden tree city of Antiope came into view. At her side, Titus muttered, "Holy Hades."

"Not quite," she said under her breath. "And don't mention him here either. His son is sort of a sore subject. In fact, don't mention anything. It'll be better for both of us if you just keep your mouth shut."

"What the hell are you doing with a bunch of Amazons?"

Natasa had asked herself that numerous times. But thankfully, she didn't have a chance to answer. Two sentries standing on the platform reached for the swing and pulled it forward.

Natasa jumped off the plank. Titus did the same. His hands were still bound in front of him, but there was no reason to lead him by the rope anymore. She let it fall to her feet. While he turned a slow circle and took in the city for the first time, she tried to see it from his point of view.

The Amazons were impressive with their hands. She had to give them that. Decks ran around tree trunks. Canvas tents formed houses. Rope ladders connected structure to structure, and everywhere you looked, the workings of a well-disciplined race could be seen as they went about their daily duties caring for both young and old, cooking food, sharpening weapons, living far above those who had no idea they were even there.

"Nymphs." Awe reverberated through Titus's voice. Several close by turned and stared his way. "Not just Amazons. Where are the men?"

"We don't need men," the guard to his left said, shoving him forward. He stumbled but caught his balance. She was Titus's height, dressed in the same camo gear as Ilithyia's squad, but Natasa knew from personal experience that Smyrna could be malicious. To the other guard, Smyrna barked, "Take him to the cage."

Oh, I don't think so. Natasa stepped in their way. "He's my prisoner. Not yours, and not Aella's."

Smyrna turned her venomous stare Natasa's way, but Natasa held her ground. She and Aella had worked out a deal. And she wasn't about to be intimidated by this brute. She lifted her chin and looked toward the other guard. "Take him to my tent."

The second guard glanced from Smyrna to Natasa and back again, as if unsure what to do. Long seconds passed in silence. Thankfully, this time, Titus kept his mouth shut.

Smyrna finally gave a curt nod to the other guard.

The guard grasped Titus at the arm and tugged. He looked back at Natasa with a *what the hell?* expression. Natasa's adrenaline peaked while he was led away. She just hoped to gods he didn't say anything that would make the situation worse.

When he was gone, Smyrna used her height advantage and leaned over Natasa, a move clearly designed to intimidate. "Aella will hear about this."

Natasa's back tightened. She had no doubt the queen of the Amazons would hear about it from Smyrna, from Ilithyia, from every single Amazon they'd come across. The question was, what the hell was Natasa going to tell her?

"I'm the only one who can grant you extra time."

The words—the deal she'd agreed to—echoed through Natasa's mind as she made her way toward her tent on the far side of the city. Perspiration formed on her forehead, and she swiped it away with her hand. Even with the Amazons' cooperation, she was running out of that extra time.

She pulled back her tent flap and stepped inside. A large redwood trunk took up the middle of the room. Decking ran all around it. Her pallet of blankets and pillows lay on the floor to the left. To her right were books and maps she'd acquired during her months of research. Two guards stood in the middle of the room tying Titus's wrists to D-rings bolted to the tree trunk above his head. Natasa tried not to watch—tried not to focus too much on why those rings were there…in every tent—and instead lit a lantern on a box by her bed.

Light illuminated the dark space. The guards stepped back. Natasa looked toward Titus. But unlike the cocky, almost teasing expression he'd sported all through their journey, now his features were tight, his lips compressed, and he seemed to be holding his breath, as if…as if he were in pain.

She glanced toward his arms, covered in the long shirt, but didn't see any marks or tearing of his clothes. The guards had removed his gloves but nothing else. Her brow lowered. "Leave us."

"That is not advised," the guard on the right answered.

Natasa had reached her patience limit about four hours ago. She couldn't remember the guard's name and seriously didn't care to. "Your advice has no bearing on me. And this does not concern the Amazons."

"Everything in our city concerns us."

"Not him, and not me. Now go."

The guard cast Titus a scathing look. One that screamed of malice and distrust—and—Natasa narrowed her eyes—heat?

Oh...shit. This was so not what she needed right now.

Reluctantly, the guard dragged her attention from Titus and glared Natasa's way. Then turned for the door. "We'll be right outside."

Yeah, Natasa knew they would. This was getting better by the minute. And would make getting Titus out of here *so* much easier.

The tent flap closed in the guards' wake. Natasa blew out a breath equal parts relief and frustration.

"Is this how all men are treated in your village?"

Titus's deep voice brought the fine hairs along Natasa's nape to attention. In addition to a chiseled body and gorgeous face, he had a great voice, deep with just a hint of rasp. And at the moment, it was even raspier than normal.

She turned away so she wouldn't be tempted by him. *Yeah right.* She was *always* tempted by him. "It's not my village. And yes, this is how all men are treated here. Amazons do not like men. Which is why your being here is a really bad idea. I told you not to get involved with me."

"You're not an Amazon."

It wasn't a question but a statement, and she didn't feel like being vague right now. She unhooked the small pack from her waist and dropped it on the floor. After sliding her remaining dagger from the sheath at her lower back, she set it them on the small table. "No."

From the corner of her eye, she watched him look up at his arms, bound to the tree above his head. Then back at her. But when she caught the gleam in his eyes, she no longer saw pain. She saw heat. A heat as hot as the one she'd seen blazing in his eyes when he'd looked at her in the safety of those trees.

"I could snap these ropes at any moment. I let you bring me here, *ligos Vesuvius.* Admit it, you wanted to get me alone so you could have your way with me."

Yes...

No!

Her frustration bubbled up, and she faced him. A frustration that grew to bursting with each miniscule curve of his lips. "I don't think you get what's happening here. These are Amazons, not children."

"They're still girls." He nodded toward the door. "Those two are no threat."

"Those two are the least of your worries. How many Amazons do you think live in this city? No idea? I'll tell you. At least eighty. And that's not counting the nymphs they protect who'd turn you over to the guards faster than you could cry foul should you so much as look at them wrong. Two Amazons wielding swords are nothing? Try the entire city bearing down on you because they not only hate men, they see you as a threat. You're only alive right now because I convinced them you were my prisoner. As soon as you challenge that, you'll be dead. I'm the only thing standing between you and the afterlife, buddy."

She turned for the door. She had to get away from him. There was something about him that riled her up. Distracted her. Made her *want*. And she didn't have the patience for that right now. Not when she was running out of time.

"Why are you?"

She stopped a foot from the door. Why was she? Good question.

A memory hit before she could answer. The gentle way he'd taken care of her at the half-breed colony after her panic attack. How he'd seemed as astonished by that fact as she was. How dangerous it had felt to be comforted by him. How *right*.

She might not have time to want. She might be dangerously close to an end she couldn't even think about. But she was cognizant of the difference between right and wrong. And though she knew she probably couldn't save the world, she wasn't about to turn her back on it either. Not the way her father had.

"Because you once helped me." She didn't face him. Couldn't. Because she was dangerously close to needing that comfort once more. And she, better than anyone, knew there was no such thing as comfort for her.

"Stay here and don't do anything to antagonize the guards," she said before he could answer. Reaching for the tent flap, she added, "I don't have to tell you the one asset Amazons see in men. Their last queen ordered all male prisoners be bound and crippled. I'll let you ponder why while I go meet with the Aella and try to save your life. Again."

CHAPTER SIX

Nick's skin itched to the point he could barely stand still.

He shifted his boots against the gleaming floor, scanned the ballroom of the Argolean castle from the shadows, and wished like hell he was anywhere but here. Fighting daemons was more enjoyable than this form of personal torture. Even being sliced and diced by the fuckers was a step up from pretending he was having a good time.

A shadow moved to his left, and the scars on his back tingled. Without even looking, he knew it was Demetrius moving up next to him.

"Thought you'd left already."

Nick's spine stiffened. They rarely talked. For years they hadn't even acknowledged each other's existence. While Demetrius had been chosen to serve with the Argonauts, Nick had been banished to the human realm. Those who'd exiled him as a child had expected him to perish, but he'd survived. In fact, he'd *thrived*. And now not only was he the leader of the Misos, he was also the Council's biggest fear because he was something not even the Argonauts could lay claim to. He was a true demigod.

"I was just about to." Nick pushed away from the wall, intent on getting away from this farce of a celebration and his long-lost brother with whom he had nothing in common, when a swish of pink to his right drew his attention.

His breath caught, his feet stilled, and for a heartbeat, it was as if time and place and fate had no bearing. Isadora moved down the ornate steps on the far side of the room with all the splendor and regality she'd been born into. Her pale gown was open at the shoulders, dipped into her cleavage and fell all the way to her feet.

Her short blonde hair had been pinned up, and the golden wreath of her crown sparkled under the chandelier lights and drew his gaze to the small gold drops at her ears.

But it was the smile on her face that increased the beat of his heart. The way she greeted each of her subjects, introduced them to Maelea and owned the room bursting with Argoleans and Misos and Council members dressed to the nines. And the way she looked his direction and that smile grew to a full-blown grin.

His soul mate.

"She doesn't show it," Demetrius said at Nick's side, "but she's nervous as shit about this celebration."

His brother's *wife.*

The air leaked out of Nick's lungs like a balloon pricked with a needle, leaving behind an emptiness that consumed him from the inside out. Reality settled in hard, and sound returned—the instrumental notes of the four-piece orchestra in the corner, the voices chatting around them, the clink of glasses and the scuff of shoes across the marble floor. As did the tightness in his skin that reminded him *this* was not his place. This was nowhere he'd ever wanted to be.

His gaze settled on the roundness of her belly. To what should be holding his child but wasn't. Awe turned to anger. And a bitter frustration he'd been living with for months, all because of the Argonaut at his side.

"She should be nervous. She's not a leader. She's a target."

Demetrius shot him a look. "What does that mean?"

Darkness bubbled up inside Nick. A darkness he fought every moment of every day. A darkness that preoccupied him with the reality that if his brother were dead, he could have the one thing he wanted most.

He ground his teeth, tried to hold back the words lingering on his tongue, but today the darkness was too strong. And part of him was sick and tired of holding back. "It means you're a bigger ass than I thought if you think she's safe now that our mother is dead."

Demetrius turned fully his way. "Do you have a problem with me?"

Nick met his brother's stare head-on. He didn't give a fuck who overheard them. He'd had it with this celebration and the in-your-face reminder of what should be his but never would be. "I've *always* had a problem with you. But today it's more than just the fact that your kind left me to die in the human realm. Look around you, *brother*. Look at the faces of your *Council*."

He waited while Demetrius scanned the crowd. Waited until Demetrius's gaze fixed and darkened on Lucian, the Council leader, who'd been staring at Isadora with malice and disgust all afternoon. And knew the exact second Demetrius finally cued in to a bitter truth Nick had figured out hours ago.

"Pat yourself on the back, *brother*. You and your Argonauts got your wish. You finally got rid of our mother. And in the process, you probably killed our soul mate too."

He waited for the darkness in Demetrius to roar to the surface—the same darkness that was in Nick, thanks to their twisted mother. Waited for the Argonaut to turn and pound his fist into Nick's jaw—a move that, for reasons he couldn't explain and didn't want to overanalyze, he *craved*. But Demetrius didn't move. He simply stared out at Isadora as if she were the antidote to his anger. And when she turned to look Demetrius's way and her smile turned to worry, Nick couldn't bear it anymore.

He left Demetrius standing on the edge of the room and headed for the door. The Misos delegates who'd crossed over with him would find their own way back. If he had to spend one minute more staring at something he was helpless to prevent, he'd go mad. Like his fucking mother.

He crossed the foyer, stepped into the early-summer sunshine and a courtyard full of flowering vines and swaying trees, closed his eyes and drew in a deep breath that did shit to ease the darkness inside.

"Nick."

Isadora's soft voice dragged his eyes open. He told himself not to turn, told himself to just walk away, but the soul mate draw was so strong, he couldn't stop himself.

She was a waif of a female. Too small, too soft, too…everything he'd never been attracted to but now couldn't stop thinking about.

"You're not leaving so soon, are you?" she asked. "I want you to stay."

"Do you? Do you really?"

Her eyes widened, and he knew his voice was too harsh, but he couldn't seem to keep the bite from his words. "Of course I do. You're as much a part of this celebration as anyone. Without you…" She lifted her slim shoulders, dropped them. "Without you, we never would have won."

Frustration, anger, yearning all coalesced inside him and overrode the only thing he could rely on: restraint. "You haven't won. You were safer *before* Atalanta's death."

"What do you mean?"

Don't say it. It wasn't his place. This wasn't his fight. He shouldn't even care what happened in Argolea. But dammit, she was *his*. "Your Council will overthrow you as soon as this celebration is forgotten. I see it on Lucian's face. I read it in his eyes every time he looks at you."

Shock at his bluntness ran across her features, but she didn't argue, and he knew from her reaction that she'd already considered that fact. "The Argonauts won't let that happen."

"You think the Argonauts are going to save you?" A smug huff slipped from his lips. "How long do you think they can last against the Council's army? Because trust me, *princess*, the Council's building that army as we speak. And when they have enough strength behind them, they'll convince your people to disband the Argonauts. Atalanta was the only thing keeping them alive, keeping *you* alive. There's no reason for the Eternal Guardians without her as a threat. Your Council doesn't give a shit about gods or elements or orbs or what will happen if Krónos is released from Tartarus. They only care about themselves. And self-preservation means eliminating anything that poses a threat to their control. The monarchy, the Argonauts, especially that child inside you."

Isadora's face paled, and she rested a protective hand against her swollen belly. "What would you suggest I do?"

Don't say it. Do not even think it. "Come with me."

A soft creased formed between her eyebrows. One he itched to kiss. "With you?"

He stepped close—too close. Her sweet scent rose all around him. Possessed him. "I can protect you. In the human realm, the Council can't touch you."

"But the gods—"

"They don't know where the colony's located. And I have ways to keep you safe. Ways the guardians and even my brother can't."

Her gaze searched his. And though he could see in her soft brown eyes that she was contemplating, something inside warned she was about to turn him down. "I can't leave Demetrius. He—"

That darkness surged before he could stop it. "You never had a choice. You didn't know you were my soul mate when you were stranded on that island. If you had—"

Pity filled her eyes. "Nick, I—"

A shadow shifted behind her, and the scars on Nick's back lurched to life. He didn't want her pity, dammit. He wanted *her*.

"You're mine too." He closed one hand around her nape. Used the other to tip her face up. Then he lowered his mouth to hers, kissing her in a way he never should. Kissing her in a way that made the darkness inside pulse with excitement.

She groaned against his lips. He kissed her harder, digging his fingers into her scalp. Her hands came up to rest against his chest; her fingers curled into his shirt.

She was drawing him in, pulling him closer. Victory flared hot in his veins.

She pushed hard, breaking the kiss, forcing him to stumble back a step.

Her chest rose and fell from her deep breaths. Her cheeks were flushed, her hair falling free from the decorative pins. She was gorgeous and pissed and *his*. The darkness pounded in his veins, begging to be set free, and a triumphant grin spread across his lips. He leaned down to kiss her again.

Her palm connected with his cheek, and a crack echoed through the courtyard. The sting of the blow rushed across his skin.

"That was a warning, Nick. Don't touch me like that again. Ever."

The darkness inside roared to life. Screamed for him to toss her over his shoulder, drag her into an empty room, and ravish her. Finally take what was his. Ruin her for everyone else, even her kingdom. And he wanted to. He *hungered* for it. But then he caught sight of the face in the shadows at her back.

Demetrius.

The darkness snapped and snarled inside him, gearing up for a fight he needed in ways he couldn't explain. Nick rubbed a hand over his jaw and didn't look away from his brother. "You want me, princess, admit it. You always have. I bet you're wet right now just from that kiss."

Isadora gasped. Demetrius stepped out of the shadows, the shock in his eyes replaced with fury and wrath and all the darkness Nick fought deep inside.

Finally...

"Step away from her, Niko."

Niko. Oh yeah, Demetrius was good and pissed now. He never used Nick's given name. No one did.

"Afraid she's finally come to her senses?" Nick asked. "That she's ready for a real hero? Trust me, *princess*, I won't need magic like my brother here to get it up for you."

"That's enough." Demetrius's hand curled into a fist.

It wasn't enough. It would never be enough, not for Nick. *Yes, you bastard, hit me. Haul off and beat the shit out of me. Let's finish this once and for all.*

Isadora pushed her way between them. "Both of you, stop it." She looked up at Nick with frustration and hurt alive in her familiar eyes. "What the hell's come over you? I don't need this right now. You're supposed to be my friend. Why are you doing this?"

Nick made the mistake of looking from his brother down to her. And though the darkness still whirred, one look was all it took for the soul mate bond to come screaming back.

It slammed into him. Stole his breath. A sharp pain sliced through his chest, one so intense it echoed through his entire body.

No... He was intentionally lashing out at her, wanting her to hurt because he hurt. Because he couldn't cope. Because he still wanted when it was more than clear she didn't want in return.

Regret and anger made his head buzz, and he stumbled back, turning away. His hands shook as he brought them together and opened the portal back to the colony.

"Nick, wait—"

He couldn't. Not even for her. And yet...

A tiny voice in the back of his head—a dark voice he wanted to ignore but couldn't—said he'd just planted a seed. Fear was the greatest motivator of all. And Isadora was smart. To save her child, she'd come to him.

He just had to be patient.

* * *

Natasa's pulse raced while she waited in the outer room of Aella's tent. She swiped at her brow and looked down at the perspiration on her fingers.

Just nerves. That was all. Nothing more.

She rubbed her hand against her thigh and tried to convince herself of that fact, but Aella's tent proved to be too much of a distraction. It was larger and grander than all the rest, made up of three trees decked together and strewn with canvas to create multiple, spacious rooms. The female didn't live as a peasant, like the rest of the Amazons and those they protected. Thick rugs ran across the decking beneath Natasa's feet. Colorful pillows in all shapes and sizes were scattered along the floor near the far wall to form a comfortable lounging area. A purple velvet couch and matching chairs were set up on the other side of the room. Intricately carved tables, golden candlesticks holding flickering candles, even gilded mirrors hanging on the tent walls rounded out the rest of the space.

For a moment, she was transported back to her mother's palace in Egypt. To the gold, the jewels, the richly colored fabrics and ostentatiousness when there had been so many outside the carefully constructed palace walls suffering in the blazing heat and dust.

That suffering—and the palace's careless attitude toward it—had been a point of contention between her and her mother. Between her and her mother's husband, the king. It had been the reason she'd run away at such a young age.

What a fool she'd been. So filled with ideals and the thought *she*, of all people, could make a difference. She hadn't made a difference. She hadn't even been able to take care of herself. Instead she'd been locked away. And now, the world as she'd once known it was no more.

The enormity of her situation bore down upon her, opening a hole the size of Mount Olympus in her chest. She should have been patient. Should have listened. Should have waited for her mother to tell her who and what she was. Maybe if she had, she'd know what to do now.

Canvas rustled on the far side of the room, jolting Natasa from her thoughts. Two guards stepped beneath the archway and moved forward, holding the flaps of the tent door open so the Queen of the Amazons could glide past.

"Thank you, Smyrna, Clymene." The queen nodded. "You may both wait outside."

The guards nodded and moved back the way they'd come, leaving Natasa to face Aella on her own.

Natasa bowed, wondering what the hell Smyrna had already told her. She wished she had her remaining dagger, but she'd known to leave it in her tent. No one armed was allowed anywhere near the queen. "Your Grace."

"Rise, Natasa. And tell me of your travels." Aella sat on the ornate couch. Though she was tall like all Amazons—literally towering over Natasa—she wasn't as hard. There was a softness to Aella's features, a beauty the others lacked. Her skin was pale, her hair dark and styled in curls that fell down her back. She wore khaki trousers, knee-high black boots, and a long blue tunic cinched at her waist with a stylish gold belt. And on her fingers and wrists, ancient jewels marked her as the queen of her race.

Natasa moved to one of the sitting chairs. She liked Aella. Had been relieved when the Amazon had agreed to protect her. But she was smart enough to know everyone in this world was out for only one thing: self-preservation. That didn't make Aella her ally in any sense of the word. "I know you've been told I brought a prisoner back with me."

"I was," Aella answered, clasping her hands around one knee. "A male, as I understand it. This surprises me, I must say."

"I didn't do so to upset you. It's just…" Gods, how did she rectify this? "He's important to my quest."

Aella's eyes narrowed. Natasa had told Aella she was searching for Prometheus, but not why. And she knew the queen had agreed to protect her in the hopes that when Natasa did find the Titan, he might be able to aid the Amazons with their little Zagreus problem. But that was a big maybe, and they both knew it. "How so?"

Shit. Perspiration slid down Natasa's spine. Lies ran through her mind, gathered on her tongue. "He knows things. About the gods. I'm prepared to leave here with him now. I only came back to"—*Come on, lie better than this. His life is on the line here!*—"to gather my things. And to thank you. For everything you've done for me."

Crap. Had she just said that? She was leaving Antiope with the Argonaut now? Great. Score one for not thinking faster. But now that it was out there, she couldn't take it back. Her future was going from bad to worse faster than she could blink. All thanks to her inability to leave well enough alone…or to leave one Argonaut she didn't need alone.

"I think," Aella said slowly," I would like to meet this male for myself. Before you go, that is."

Natasa's adrenaline jumped. *Oh, no no no.* That couldn't be good. Forget the fact Titus was an Argonaut—a fact Natasa was not about to share with anyone in this tree city—he was the exact specimen Amazons looked for when in need of a man. Strong, sexy, powerful, and handsome. Not to mention just a tad bit dangerous. Amazons loved danger. In fact, they thrived on it.

So do you.

Natasa shook off the thought and tried to figure out how to deter the queen. *Think, dammit.*

Aella pushed from her seat and gestured toward the tent's door. "Lead the way, my dear."

Panic cycled in. "But—"

A wicked smile spread across the queen's lips. "But nothing. I'm anxious to see for myself what has you so…flustered."

*B*ound and crippled…

The bound part, Titus didn't mind. Especially if Natasa was the one doing the binding. Hell, if she wanted, he'd let her do just about anything to him. Which totally went against everything he'd become thanks to his curse. But those few seconds they'd spent pressed up against each other in the trees hadn't been nearly long enough. And if the only way he could get more rubbing, more touching and a hell of a lot more skin-on-skin contact from her was to submit, he'd do it.

The crippling thing, however? Yeah, that wasn't happening.

The tent flap pulled open before he could get lost in the fantasy of her in that black leather dominatrix outfit, wielding a crop while he was tied to this tree, naked and ready. Excitement pulsed in his chest but quickly morphed to annoyance when the same two guards who'd strung him up stepped back into the room.

"Ladies…I was just thinking about you. How about some water? I'm parched."

"No one will know…"

"I want…"

The Amazon's thoughts and the way they inched forward put Titus on instant alert. His back tightened. He shifted against the ropes wrapped around his wrists. "Now hold up, girls."

Neither stopped. Both looked ready to devour him whole.

Shit. He twisted in his bonds. "The redhead said I was to be left alone." When neither backed down, he shot a look at the one on the left, the one eyeing him like fresh meat. "Hey. I know you. You're Medusa's sister, right? The resemblance is uncanny."

"Have you ever seen a chest plate like that?"

The blonde laid her hand over the seal of Odysseus. Titus flinched. Though they weren't touching his skin, they were way too damn close. "Ladies—"

"Take it off him," the brunette said. *"I don't care about the damn breast plate."* "I want to see his muscles beneath."

Oh, holy fuckballs, *no.*

Titus jerked hard on the rope. It scraped against the tree and loosened. But before he could pull free, the blonde wrapped her hand around his throat.

Emotions rushed from her hand into his skin and whipped through his body, condensing with the force of a bullet from a gun directly into his chest, stopping him from yanking free.

Excitement, arousal, *lust* bombarded him from every side, stripping away all thought, all ability to move. His muscles contracted and released. Pain rushed through his neck and ricocheted through his mind. His ability to read their thoughts fled. He tried to fight against the force, ground his teeth to stay in control, but the second Amazon tore off his breastplate, cape, and tunic and stripped him to the waist before he could find the strength to stop her.

"Like marble," the brunette said in awe, her eyes wide. "I've never seen anything like it."

"Touch him," the blonde answered, still holding him pinned against the tree with her hand. "Is he as good as he looks?"

They were talking about him as if he wasn't even there. As if he was a sculpture, not a man. He struggled beneath the blonde's hold, but the emotional transfer still radiated through him, like flickering electricity, zapping him of every ounce of strength. And it was getting stronger, the lust and excitement in her flowing faster with each passing second.

The brunette lifted her hand. A strangled *no!* echoed throughout the room, and belatedly, Titus realized it had come from him. But he couldn't do anything to stop her. Her hand landed against the bare skin of his chest, and another blast of emotions pummeled his body.

His arms sagged against the ropes. Pain ricocheted up his shoulders. Voices echoed through the tent, but his vision swam, and he couldn't make out the shapes around him anymore. From what seemed a great distance, canvas rustled and footsteps echoed. Followed by another voice. This one clearer. Softer. Oh so familiar. One he struggled to put with a name.

"Let go of him."

Pressure eased. Hands lifted from his skin. Titus's legs buckled, and he slid to the ground, landing with a thud against the floor. The ropes loosed from the tree and fell to the ground as his arms dropped.

"What the hell did you do to him?"

Someone knelt at his side. A female, but he couldn't see who. Couldn't read her thoughts. She lifted a fuzzy arm, and Titus tensed, mentally preparing himself for another zap that would knock him even further on his ass. But when her hand landed softly against his shoulder, there was no pain. Only warmth. A warmth that soothed the electrical charges flickering through him and eased the agony spiraling in his veins.

"We didn't—"

"Back up! Let him breathe."

Natasa. That was Natasa's voice arguing with the guard. And oh yeah, that was her silky hand sliding across his bare shoulder toward his neck, tipping his face up so she could look in his eyes, bringing not only heat but arousal to his flesh—his own arousal, no one else's.

Her gaze raked his features. Electricity arced between them— the good kind. And slowly her face came into view. Gemlike green eyes, flawless pale skin. Ruby red lips and the cutest spray of freckles, right over the bridge of her nose. "Tasa…"

Something dark—something *hot*—flashed in her eyes, but before he could decipher what it meant, her jaw hardened, and she let go.

She pushed to her feet. "He's not to be touched. Do you understand? He's my prisoner, not yours. Get the fuck out of my tent."

"But he's—"

"*Mine.* Now go."

A thrill shot through Titus at her words, but when he caught sight of the Amazon's tightening muscles, it quickly shifted to worry.

They both straightened as if they'd been slapped. Both reached for swords strapped to their hips. The one on the right mumbled, "We'll see about that. When the queen—"

"The queen already knows," Natasa said in a commanding voice. "Turn around and ask her yourself."

The guards whipped toward the tent opening. Titus struggled to see past them. Another female stood in the doorway. But instead of being hard and masculine like the others, she was tall, feminine, and gorgeous. And she was also staring at him as if he were a meal served up on a golden platter, just for her.

"*...Argonaut. The perfect specimen. Mine, not yours, foolish girl.*"

His head was still in a fog. He wasn't sure who'd thought the words, but he was pretty sure they'd come from the female in the doorway. The one whose eyes were practically glowing with excitement. The one, he realized belatedly, who had to be the Queen of the Amazons.

Skata. His situation had not exactly improved.

"Astiria, Lysa," the queen said, her eyes still locked on Titus, "step back."

Both guards did as they were instructed, moving toward the queen and the other guards behind her, but they didn't look thrilled. And even though Natasa drew in a deep breath as if tragedy had been averted, Titus could see that she wasn't convinced either.

The queen spoke in hushed words to her guards, her attention still fixed on Titus. The two who'd stripped him of his dignity filed out of the tent, followed by the two who'd remained stoic behind the queen. After several tense moments, the queen finally dragged her gaze away from Titus and focused on Natasa. "No one will bother you for the time being. Alert us if you need any...help."

Her gaze strayed back to Titus, and no, he did not like the flash of lust he caught in her blue eyes or the word that clearly came from her thoughts: *"Finally..."*

The tent flap swung closed behind them. Natasa knelt at his side, slid her strong arms under his, and helped him to his feet.

This time he didn't tense at her touch. His whole body relaxed, then came to life as if she had some magical ability to ease the aftershocks of the emotional transfer that had—only minutes ago—knocked him on his ass. "Don't think that one...likes me very much."

"I think she likes you too much." Natasa grunted, pushing him up. "Are you okay?"

He leaned his back against the tree trunk. "Be fine...in a minute."

"Here. Sit." Gently, she tugged on his arm, pulling him away from the tree and leading him toward the pallet of blankets and pillows against the tent wall. Warmth flowed from her hand into his; then softness enveloped his body, the cotton silky against the bare skin of his back.

She knelt next to him and rested her hands on her thighs. "What did they do to you?"

He leaned back in the pillows, closed his eyes, and slowly relaxed as the last emotions seeped out of his body. "Nothing. Just—"

He drew in another breath then slowly let it out. He wasn't about to admit his biggest weakness to the girl he wanted to jump his bones.

"It hurt, didn't it? I saw the way you reacted when they were tying you to the tree, like you were in pain. Why don't you react that way when I touch you?"

His eyes popped open. She knew? For a smart guy, he was slow on the uptake when it came to her. Implications ricocheted through his mind. But the only thing he could focus on was the fantasy he'd been toying with before—the one of her in the black leather outfit, touching him, whipping him, ordering him to do any and every X-rated thing she wanted. "'Cause your touch feels good."

Her brow dropped low. "I don't understand. I mean, considering what I did to that guard back in Argolea, my touch should be worse, not better. Why am I different?"

"Don't know, just..."

Dammit, he didn't want to think anymore. He just wanted her to touch him again, to chase away the lingering pain, to make him feel alive. He needed it, more than he needed to know who she was or what she was really after.

"Put your hands on me again, Tasa. You're the only one who can."

CHAPTER SEVEN

Natasa stared into Titus's mesmerizing hazel eyes and swallowed hard. She tried to resist, but there was something about him. Some pull she couldn't seem to fight. Some need growing inside her with every passing second.

She licked her lips. Shifted her knees forward even though she knew she shouldn't. Her gaze flicked to his bare chest. To his arms resting at his sides against the blankets, the shredded ropes still wrapped around his wrists. To his chiseled six-pack abs, rising and falling with his shallow breaths.

She wanted to touch him. Wanted to know if he was as hard and smooth as she imagined. As she'd felt pressed up against her in those trees. She lifted a hand, held it out, hesitated over his bare skin, her mind warring with common sense. "I—"

His hand captured hers, and a cool sensation slid from his fingers into hers. He tugged on her arm until her palm landed against the rock-solid surface of his chest.

A slow, gentle sigh escaped his lips.

The air churned around her. A fresh gust that filled her lungs, eased the fever she lived with every hour, and blew a calming breath all across her skin.

She drew it in. His spicy, masculine scent filled her nose. Tingles rushed over her flesh, soothing her irritable edges. And oh, he was hard beneath her hand. Silky skin over carved muscle and bone. Reflexively, she brushed her fingers against his muscles, loving the texture, the dips and angles of his rib cage, the way he groaned with every tiny movement.

As if she were the one who could soothe him. As if he needed only her.

Rough fingertips caressed the back of her hand and sent stimulating sensations all along her flesh. She glanced down, his tanned skin such a contrast with her much paler hand, then looked at his face. His eyes were once again closed, but unlike when those guards had touched him, this time pleasure toyed with his features. And a wicked, tantalizing smile curled his tempting lips.

That pull to him grew stronger. The irritability she was so used to eased. Normally, around others, she felt boxed in, trapped, and every breath was more stifling than the last. But next to him...*touching* him...all she could think about was what it would be like to brush her fingers over other parts of his body. What his naked skin would feel like sliding over hers. How thick and exhilarating he would be pushing deep inside her body.

"Gods," he whispered. "That feels so damn good."

It felt good to her too. She scooted closer and licked her lips again. "It doesn't hurt?"

"Are you kidding?" He chuckled, and vibrations zinged up her fingers, shooting straight to her center. "You feel like heaven."

Heat grew in her belly. An ache condensed between her legs, sending scorching threads of desire all through her core. The kind that overwhelmed the senses. The kind that begged to be sated.

His free hand closed over hers against her thigh. The frayed rope tickled her leg. He tugged again, not gently this time but quickly, until her weight shifted out from under her, and she fell against every hard, muscular inch of him.

She gasped, but the sensations rushing from his skin into hers were so invigorating, so restorative, she couldn't stop the sigh that slipped from her lips. And then she didn't want to because—oh gods—*he* felt good. The length of his body was flush against hers, easing the burn, calming her frazzled nerve endings, making her want in ways she never had before.

"You're so hot, *ligos Vesuvius.*"

His sensual voice cut through the haze. Pressure built beneath her ribs. "Too hot?" She tried to sit up. "I—"

His arms closed around her, and he held her tight as if he didn't ever want to let her go. "Not too hot. Never too hot."

Her lashes lifted. Slowly, she met his gaze, and her breath caught. Energy crackled between them. A sizzle and arc she felt everywhere. His eyes seemed to be looking deep inside a part of her no one else had ever seen. Little warning flags fired off in her mind. "You...you shouldn't be near me. I'm not what you think I am."

"What do I think you are?"

She had no idea. She just knew she didn't want to hurt him. Not like she had that guard. And the longer he stayed with her, the greater the chances she'd do just that. "I think...you're blind to the real me."

A chuckle rumbled through his chest, permeated her own, and brought another rush of refreshing tingles to her skin. His hand moved from the small of her back to her hair. His thick fingers sifted through her curly locks. "You know, the ancient Greeks thought having red hair was a sign of being a vampire."

She lifted her head to get a better look at his face. "You think I'm going to suck your blood?"

His whole body tightened beneath her, and a smile played with the edges of his mouth. "At the moment, I'm hoping you'll suck something else."

He was cracking jokes. She couldn't help it. She laughed. And oh, it felt good to laugh. To smile. She couldn't remember the last time the pressure in her chest was gone and a lightness like she was experiencing now floated through her limbs. "Titus, I—"

He lifted his head, and before she could get the rest of the words out, his lips pressed against hers.

Soft. Cool. Electric. Tingles rushed through her whole body. She knew she shouldn't let him kiss her, should be pushing away right this very second, but she couldn't. And when he nipped at her lower lip, when she felt the tip of his tongue slide across the seam of her mouth, she gave up the fight. She opened to him, drew his warm, slick tongue inside, and tasted him for the very first time.

Thought fled. Reason disappeared. All the protests she'd been about to voice drifted out of her reach.

He was like a waterfall. Like a cool flood of relief, pouring over her skin, easing the burn from the outside in. Rejuvenating her in ways she couldn't imagine.

She groaned. Or maybe he did. She wasn't sure. All she could focus on was the way he cupped her face in both hands. The way he tipped his head and kissed her deeper. The way his lush, tantalizing tongue tasted like sin and salvation against her own.

She'd been kissed before, but it had been so long ago, she barely remembered what it was like. And she knew it had never been as refreshing and consuming as this. Her muscles tightened against his. Her fingers dug into his chest. Her legs shifted open until his thighs pressed against the insides of hers.

Desire built, awakened inside her. His hand slid from her hair to her lower back to pull her body tighter against him. And oh, he was hard, and thick, and clearly as turned on her. That excitement grew. Overwhelmed. Possessed her from every angle.

His tongue probed deep into her mouth, tasted her everywhere, and she returned his kiss with the same enthusiasm, the same hunger. Time seemed to stand still as his mouth plundered hers. As he took what he wanted. As she let him.

Her head grew light. She needed air. Didn't want to break the kiss. Didn't want to let go. He nipped at her upper lip, soothed the spot with his tongue, then finally eased away so she could draw a breath.

"Gods, you taste better than I'd hoped."

She gulped in air and tried to tell him he tasted good too. But before her vocal chords could work, he kissed her again. Hard. Greedy. Deeply. Like a man starved. Like she was his very last meal.

Her brain turned to mush. Her body a pool of want. All she could focus on was *more*. But something inside warned she was losing control. That this wasn't a good idea. That as much as she craved his touch, this wasn't the right time or place. And if the Amazons outside heard what was happening inside her tent, they'd both soon regret it.

She pushed against his chest. She didn't want to let go but somehow found the strength to shift to her knees so there was space between them. "Titus. Wait. Just…give me a second."

"No more waiting. I want you."

His fingers dug into the cotton at her hips, and he tugged. She opened her mouth to tell him she wanted him too, that she wasn't trying to stop him, but that they both just needed to be careful. But then she registered the temperature around her. Not cool and refreshing like he'd been. But humid. Thick. Stifling.

Warnings fired off in her brain. The sexual haze cleared enough so she could listen. Something wasn't right. He couldn't be *just* an Argonaut. There was something else about him that drew her. Something she reacted to. Something that told her…she wasn't the only one keeping secrets.

"Tasa?"

She pushed away before his body could press up against hers again and somehow found her feet. The room spun, and she reached for the tree trunk behind her. He sat up, but she held out a hand to keep him from reaching for her once more. "No, don't. I…I need to think."

"Don't think. Come back. I know you want me. You have no *idea* how much I want you. Touch me again."

Minutes ago, he'd wanted answers as to why she was living amongst the Amazons, what she'd been doing in Argolea, why she'd been following Maelea. Now none of that mattered?

The air grew oppressive and claustrophobic. Her mind sputtered, trying to make sense of what had happened. She'd been tricked once before, and look where that had landed her. When he moved to his knees, she stepped back again, careful so he couldn't touch her.

"Natasa."

His voice changed. Tensed. Filled with a desperation that only kicked her nerves into high gear. "Wh-what are you doing to me?"

"I'm not doing anything," he said calmly. Too calmly. He held out a hand. "Natasa, come back to me."

She didn't know what to believe, didn't know whom to trust. He suddenly felt like some glowing, shimmering salvation, and she, more than anyone, knew things that seemed too good to be true usually were. "Who *are* you?"

Unease seeped into his eyes. "You know who I am."

"No, I don't." Panic flooded her voice, and she fought against it but couldn't keep it away. He was using magic or seduction or *something* unnatural to scramble her brain. "What the hell do you want with me?"

He moved to his feet, pushing to his full height. He was gorgeous in the dim light, half naked with his wavy dark hair loose around his face and those ropes hanging from his wrists. But he was also a threat. There were multiple people searching for her. Numerous beings that wanted her. And because he'd once been nice to her, she'd let down her guard. Assumed he could be trusted. Assumed—foolishly—he wasn't after the very same thing.

Panic turned to fear. She eyed her dagger on the box next to him. Knew she'd never reach it before he did. "Stay back."

"Natasa, I'm not going to hurt you. I'm here to help you."

There was that word again—help. The same word he'd used in Argolea just before she'd jumped through the portal. But he didn't really want to help her. He just wanted what she had.

"I don't want your help. I told you before I don't need your help. I—"

The tent flap jerked open, and they both looked toward the burst of light spilling into the room. Two guards stepped into the space and glanced between them—the same two who had tied Titus to the tree.

Relief immediately rushed through Natasa—relief that she and Titus had been interrupted—but then she caught the gleam in the guards' eyes.

"What's going on?" Natasa asked. "I told you—"

"Ladies." Titus turned toward the guards and held up both hands in a defensive move. "Let's not act hastily now—"

The guards moved up on both sides of him. Malice and heat and triumph swelled in their eyes. The taller of the two said, "The queen is ready for you."

Titus stiffened, tried to shift out of their grasp, but their hands landed on his arms before he could get a foot away. And the moment they made contact with his skin, his eyes rolled back, his features twisted and his knees gave out.

Natasa tensed. Yeah, she'd wanted him to back off so she could think, but not like this. They were hurting him. If anyone was going to hurt him, it was going to be her.

"Stop," she ordered. "What are you doing? He's *my* prisoner, not yours."

"Not anymore," the other guard said. A malevolent grin spread across her thin lips. "He's the queen's now. And the altar is prepared."

Oh shit.

They dragged Titus toward the door. Natasa closed her hand over the shoulder of the closest guard. "I said stop—"

The guard moved so fast, Natasa barely tracked her. One second she was holding Titus up by the arm; the next she had Natasa pinned to the base of the tree, a sword at her throat.

"Aella said you might be a problem," the guard sneered. "Therefore, you are to remain here, where you can't get in the way."

Natasa's breath caught at the contempt in the guard's eyes. The guard shoved Natasa's hands together, cinched a rope around her wrists, and jerked them high over her head. Natasa gasped. The guard looped the rope through the D-ring screwed into the wood and pulled hard.

Pain sliced into Natasa's skin. She winced. The guard laughed and stepped back.

Lysa—Natasa remembered her name now—tipped her head and grinned. "If you haven't figured it out yet, female, you are not invited to this ceremony." She leaned close, so close Natasa could smell the earthy scents of dirt and moss on her unclean skin. "The queen thanks you for your most generous...donation."

Natasa pulled on the ropes again. "Titus!"

Lysa chuckled, a menacing sound, and moved out of the room. The door flapped closed in her wake.

Alone, Natasa struggled against the ropes, but all her flailing did was cause the twines to dig deeper into her skin. Pain spiraled through her arms, slowing her fight.

Her chest rose and fell. Perspiration slid down her spine. She swallowed hard and tried to think clearly. She'd never witnessed one of Aella's so called "ceremonies" but she'd heard enough about them—and the males who were the sacrifices—to know what was about to happen.

Sickness rolled through her stomach and was followed by the memory of the way Titus had reacted when those guards had touched him. And how different it was from the way he reacted when she touched him.

She might still be rattled from that kiss, she might be afraid of her reaction to him and what he was really after, but regardless of anything he had or hadn't done, he didn't deserve what was about to happen. She'd brought him here. She'd led him to this. If she didn't do something to stop it, she was no better than the gods who'd cursed her.

She looked up at the rope and pulled hard. Fire ignited along her flesh. But the knots didn't give. She ground her teeth and pulled again. "Come on!"

Still nothing loosened.

Frustrated, she blew out a deep breath then remembered what she'd done to that guard back in Argolea. The way his armor had melted beneath her palms. She'd never been able to direct what was inside her before, but then the fever hadn't been as strong as it was now. Maybe there was a way…if she focused hard enough.

She closed her eyes, drew in a deep breath, and let it out. Then fought to center herself. And prayed this worked.

Did you hear what I said, son?"

Son. Zagreus ground his teeth and worked not to lose his temper. The word implied some sort of loving familial relationship, which this most definitely was not. But it wasn't every day the King of the Underworld paid you a visit. And Zagreus knew better than to piss his dear old dad off first thing. "I really don't see how this concerns me."

He also had better things to do than chase after his father's latest conquest. He moved through the rock archway and into his office, tossing the latest report he'd gotten about those damn nymphs on his desk. A fish swam past the floor-to-ceiling window that looked out over the underwater view.

Hades stepped up to his desk. "If Zeus and Poseidon find her before we do, it's going to concern you big-time."

Zagreus met his father's black-as-nights eyes. "Look around you, *Pops.* I don't give a flying fuck what the Olympians do. I'm perfectly happy right here where I've always been."

Hades's eyes flashed, and a muscle in his temple pulsed. From deep in the caves, a pathetic groan echoed along the rock walls. "How long do you think your little underwater torture tunnels are going to go unnoticed? If someone releases Krónos before we can stop them, the sick son of a bitch will confiscate everything you've built and probably set up residence in your humble abode. And if my brothers find the remaining elements before your mother and I do, they're going to lord it over all of us and likely still come after you. Do you think you're safe simply because you live in the human realm? You're not safe, *son.* You're living on borrowed time."

Zagreus straightened, and his jaw clenched. What his father said made a sick sort of sense, but he didn't want to get involved. He'd survived nice and long on his own ignoring the Olympian gods and their petty battles. "What about Atalanta's daemons? You did take control of her army after she died, didn't you? Why not just use them to find what you're after?"

"Because I need the greatest tracker on the planet. And that's you."

Smug victory spread through Zagreus. He *was* the greatest tracker. He could find anything. If he had enough time. The problem was, he couldn't just leave on a whim like he used to be able to do. He had certain…prisoners he didn't trust to the care of his guards. At least not for any extended length of time. "What is it you want from me?"

"I want you to find Prometheus's daughter."

"And what's in it for me?"

"Besides the ability to keep flying under the radar, doing whatever you damn well please?"

One corner of Zagreus's lips curled. "Yeah. Besides that."

Hades studied him, then said, "I'll tell you where your nymphs ran off to."

Excitement lurched in Zagreus's stomach. This could save him weeks of time. "You know exactly where they went?"

"Every single backstabbing one."

Zagreus's blood ran hot. And images of how he was going to string those nymphs up, how he was going to torture them and make them pay rushed through his mind. No one left him. No one dared and got away with it.

"How?" he asked skeptically.

"My daemons intercepted a few of the creatures protecting them from you."

Zagreus tipped his head and considered what his father was offering. This was Hades's specialty. Making deals, manipulating the outcome. But Zagreus knew his father never offered a deal unless it included something he desperately wanted. The only reason he was here now was because he needed someone who resided in the human realm full-time to do his bidding. The Olympians—and Zagreus's parents because they ruled the Underworld—operated under restrictions in the human realm, only able to stay roughly twelve hours at any one time. "What about Mommy Dearest?"

"Your mother and I have…an understanding. She wants to find Prometheus's daughter as much as I do."

Zagreus huffed. Persephone never did anything unless it was exactly what *she* wanted to do too. "And she'll stand against the Olympians? Even her father?"

"For me she will."

Zagreus wasn't so sure. But then, his parents' sick and twisted relationship was beyond his comprehension, so what did he know? "And all I have to do is find this female, and my part of the bargain is done."

"Yes," Hades answered.

Zagreus pursed his lips. It was asking a lot, considering he'd have to leave his tunnels. But the payoff...

He grew hard just thinking about those nymphs.

"Fine. I'll do it. But I want the location of my nymphs first. As soon as they're back in my lair where they belong, I'll find the female you can't seem to live without."

Hades's eyes flashed. He didn't like the addendum. But Zagreus wasn't about to back down. Because if his father had come to him, that meant he was Hades's last chance at finding the chick. The God-King of the Underworld wouldn't bother to look sideways at his only son if he didn't have to.

"Agreed," Hades said. "But if you double cross me, this" —he gestured to the cenote that made up Zagreus's lair— "will be the least of what comes crashing down around you. Your nymphs are in the Amazon tree city of Antiope, in the redwoods on the northern coast of California."

A wicked grin rushed across Zagreus's face. "Amazons, you say? I haven't had an Amazon in quite some time."

"Try not to go hog wild." Hades turned for the door. "And don't forget to bring me Prometheus's daughter, or you will regret it."

Titus's head swam.

He was aware of someone dragging him, of hands closed tight over his arms tugging hard. But he couldn't think straight. Couldn't focus on even one watery object rushing by. The emotions bombarding him from every side were too strong—greed, anger, lust. A helluva lot of lust that wasn't turning him on in the least.

He was dragged up some kind of stairs; then the guards swung him around and pressed him back against a cold, rock surface.

Before he could make sense of his surroundings, his arms were jerked away from his body. Shackles closed over his wrists. His legs were pushed apart and strapped to something solid.

The guards stepped back. The emotional transfer slowly faded, and, weak from the impact, Titus drew a shaky breath, then stiffened when his vision cleared and he caught sight of the faces around him.

Dozens of Amazons and nymphs, all looking on with excitement and curiosity. He was on some kind of stage. In the darkness, torches alive with flickering flames illuminated the space. And somewhere close, drums beat a steady rhythm while voices echoed a chant he couldn't make out.

Okay, this was not looking good. He tugged against the restrains, but was too weak to make them budge. *Shit*. This was not the fantasy he'd been daydreaming about. Had he made a crack about these warriors being girls? He was suddenly wishing he hadn't been so cocky when Natasa had tried to warn him.

Natasa…

Skata, where was she? He couldn't remember what had happened after those guards had come into her tent. Worry gathered beneath his ribs. His gaze raked the crowd, searching for her in the sea of faces.

The chanting grew louder. The crowd parted, and then he saw her. Not Natasa, but a tall, slender female dressed in a flowing green robe with an ornate golden headdress decorated in multicolored feathers. Jewels dripped from her ears and throat and wrists and fingers, and desire burned in her eyes as she drew close.

Titus swallowed hard. He recognized those eyes.

The Queen of the Amazons.

He tugged against his bindings—harder. But her heated gaze didn't waver. It was fixed solely on him.

Fuck…*me*. This was not good. Not by a long shot.

The queen moved up the stairs. The drums beat faster. The air grew thick and constrictive. She stopped in front of him, closed her hands over the lapels of her robe, and tugged. The garment fell in a pool at her feet, leaving her dressed in nothing but jewels.

Holy Hades. Titus couldn't help but stare. She was butt-ass naked. And yeah, unlike her warriors, she was gorgeous and totally built, with the mark of the Amazons, a crescent moon, tattooed over her right breast. But she wasn't the female he wanted. And he was seriously *not* interested.

"Um, look." He tugged on the restraints. "I'm flattered, really, but I think you've got the wrong idea here."

The queen turned away as if he hadn't even spoken; then she held up her hands. A hush fell over the crowd. "The gods have seen fit to send us a prize. Tonight we thank them for their generosity."

The gods? Not even. The gods didn't give a rip about anyone but themselves. Before Titus could point that out, the rock at his back moved, and a loud scraping sound echoed through the night. The entire slab shifted. His feet left the ground. His eyes widened. The motion stopped abruptly, leaving him lying flat on his back, staring up at the starry sky.

Skata. His situation had not improved. This wasn't just a stage. It was an altar. And, holy *fuck*, he was the sacrifice.

He pulled hard on the restrains. "Hold on—"

The queen climbed up on the stone slab and stood with her bare feet on each side of his thighs. He tensed, but thankfully, the fabric of his pants prevented any kind of emotional transfer. Then she looked down, and her eyes locked on his. Hard amber eyes. Eyes that glowed as if she were possessed.

Titus's adrenaline lurched. He struggled harder against the cuffs, twisted his wrists, then caught sight of the jeweled dagger she held in both hands high over her head.

Every muscle inside him froze.

"For all those who came before," the queen announced in a loud and confident voice, "and for all those who will come after because of this sacrifice, we give thanks."

She lowered to her knees, sat back on his lap, and grinned. But her eyes were clouded, distant, possessed. And Titus had the ominous feeling she wasn't looking at him, but through him. To something…he didn't want to see.

"And when his seed is finally spent," she finished, her glowing eyes growing wider, "then, my sisters, we shall feast."

CHAPTER EIGHT

Natasa's fingers were still smoking when she sneaked out of her tent. She could barely believe that had worked, but the singed ropes proved it hadn't been a fluke. Power rushed through her, infusing her with confidence. If she could direct it, maybe—just maybe— she could beat this thing before it killed her.

Chants rose up in the air, followed by a voice, singing some kind of garbled song to the beat of multiple drums. The sounds were coming from the amphitheater.

She stayed in the shadows, darting around tents and tree trunks as she crossed the city. When she reached the crowd, she couldn't see anything besides the golden glow of torches and the backs of spectators gathered for a show.

She spotted a tree with limbs low enough to climb, wrapped her hand around the first branch, and pulled herself up. In seconds, she was above the crowd, with a clear view of the stage.

Her breath caught, and sickness rolled through her belly. Titus was shackled to the altar. He was still wearing his pants, but Aella straddled his lap, a dagger held high above, and her naked body was swaying and grinding against him, moving to the beat of the drums like she was gearing up to fuck his brains out. But the wide-eyed *holy shit* look on his face wasn't one of arousal. And the way he was yanking on those ropes told Natasa he wasn't enjoying a single second of this.

Mine. Some deep-seated possessiveness bubbled up from inside, rolled through every part of her, and spurred her into action.

Frantic, she glanced around the crowd. She was seriously outnumbered and the measly dagger she had left wasn't going to save Titus. Aella's guards blocked the stage, armed to the hilt, preventing anyone from interfering with the ceremony. She looked down and around, but didn't see anything that would help. Then she noticed a child's bow and arrow set leaning against the side of a tent. The kind the Amazons used to train their women.

An idea hit. She looked at her fingers. She didn't know if it would work. But if she didn't try, he was going to die.

For reasons she didn't understand, she wasn't ready to lose him. At least not like this.

Never had Titus been thankful for his curse until this moment.

Not only were the Amazon queen's eyes freakin' glowing, she was shaking and rubbing against him like something was trying to claw its way free from her body.

He was never going to look at jiggling breasts the same way. This was not a turn-on. It was a major-ass turn-*off*. And shit, he did not want those things touching him.

He swallowed hard and jerked against the bindings. He couldn't move them even a centimeter. The only consolation was that as soon as she did touch him, he'd be in too much pain to pay attention to what she was doing to his body.

And skata, *do not even think about what she's going to do to your body.*

Closing his eyes, he imagined Natasa's fire-red hair and those mesmerizing green eyes to distract him from that first touch of skin against skin. Wondered—again—why she'd pulled away from him back in her tent. She'd wanted him. He'd known it even if he couldn't feel the emotions from her.

A whir echoed through the air. The queen jerked against his legs. A scream rose in the night.

His eyes shot open. The queen lurched to her feet on the stone slab, standing over him and batting at her head. The feathers in her headdress were smoking and burning. She knocked the heavy metal adornment from her scalp. It cracked against the slab, then dropped to the wood decking with a thud.

Gasps rose up from the audience. Furious, the queen whipped toward the crowd to see where the arrow had come from.

Another whir cut through the silence. The queen flinched. This time the banner just to the right of her head ignited in flames.

"Guards!"

Screams echoed.

Titus lifted his head to see what the hell was going on. Nymphs and Amazons rushed in every direction. The guards scrambled, armor clinking. Another whir echoed through the air, then the queen's robe, lying where she'd dropped it on the stage, bust into flames.

"Natasa," the queen growled. She pointed toward the trees on the far side of the crowd. "Find her!"

Excitement flooded Titus. She'd come for him, even after she'd been so freaked out in her tent. He pulled against the bonds and searched for her in the sea of faces.

The queen leapt off the altar and lurched into the crowd.

Another whir. Another banner caught fire. Titus pulled and wrestled with the bindings. If he could just break free… If he could get to her…

"There!" A voice rang out clear.

Before Titus could track where the guard was pointing, an entire tree exploded.

A thud echoed to his right. He strained to look behind him. Natasa pushed to her feet yards away, her eyes as intense as he'd ever seen them, her face illuminated by the flames around her, making her look like a fire-goddess.

Relief and hope and excitement shot through his entire body. Then quickly shifted to bone-chilling fear. At her back, closing in fast, an Amazon raced toward her with sword held high.

"Behind you!"

Natasa dropped the bow in her hand and reached back for her dagger. Panic overwhelming him, Titus strained against the cuffs with every ounce of strength left. She didn't have time to react. She—

The chain anchoring one wrist gave with a snap. The other burst free. He bolted upright, kicked out at the shackles around his ankles. Couldn't take his eyes off Natasa.

She whipped around. The Amazon knocked the dagger from her hand, and it went flying. Natasa stumbled and hit the end of the stone slab with a grunt. Titus's heart lurched into his throat, and he reached for her but she was too far away.

"Natasa!"

The Amazon pulled her blade back, but before it could slice deep into Natasa's flesh, the warrior jerked. Her blade cracked against the stone slab, hit the wood decking, and slid down the steps of the stage. Then her body slumped to the ground with a thud. A black arrow stuck out of her side. Blood pooled all around her body.

Natasa's eyes grew side. She scrambled back. More shouts echoed from deeper in the city, and her head whipped that direction just as Titus's did. Blood-curdling screams reached his ears, followed by hooves pounding the earth and male voices rising in the night sky.

Natasa lurched to the railing and looked down. Shock raced over her features. She stumbled back, turned, grabbed her dagger from the ground, and raced toward Titus.

"What the hell's happening?" He fumbled with the bindings on his right ankle. That arrow hadn't come from her. And he was pretty sure it wasn't an Amazon weapon. Which meant it had to have come from someone or some*thing* else.

Natasa sheathed her blade, then unstrapped his other leg. "Zagreus's army found us."

"Zagreus...*as in Hades's fucking son?*"

Her hand closed over his upper arm, and she pulled him from the altar. "I don't know how, but be thankful. I wasn't going to be able to distract Aella's guards for long with my flaming arrows."

Heat built in his veins and shot straight to his belly.

She tugged him out of the torchlight and into the shadows of a tent. As soon as they were covered by darkness, he closed his hand over her wrist, yanked her close, and captured her mouth with his own.

She gasped in surprise, but he didn't let it slow him. He dipped into her mouth, slid his tongue along hers, and reveled in the warm, wet taste of her. That and the fact he couldn't feel anything other than the heat of her body, the silkiness of her skin, and the pulse in her veins that indicated she was alive.

He pulled back and brushed his finger over her soft cheek. "You did it again. You saved me. You do care."

"I..." A frown turned her lips. But he saw the desire in her eyes. And the heat. "I haven't saved you yet. Save your thanks for someone who deserves it."

He kissed her again. Quick. Safe. Chaste. Not at all like he wanted to kiss her. "I will. When we get out of here and are finally alone, I'll thank you properly. That's a promise."

Something in her eyes warned that wasn't a good idea, but he ignored it. She'd come back for him. That meant something.

He grasped her hand and led her around the other side of the tent. A sound that was oddly similar to a horse whinnying or a goat baying rose up from below. The clank of steel against steel echoed through the trees. He peeked over the railing and watched an Amazon lunge at a man dressed all in black with a thick beard, his head shaved and painted white with a black stripe down the middle.

"Zagreus, you said?" Titus asked in a whisper.

"His satyrs," Natasa answered, her voice thick. "Evil satyrs who thrive in his pain palace. That's why the nymphs are here. The Amazons protect any otherworldly females being hunted."

Titus looked closer and realized the man—no, satyr—wasn't wearing shoes. Where feet should be, hooves peeked out beneath his pants.

He turned to look at Natasa. Her gaze was fixed on the battle below, but when she lifted stormy eyes to his, he saw fear.

He squeezed her warm hand. "Zagreus isn't going to catch you."

"He's not the one I'm afraid of."

Emotions brewed in her eyes. Emotions he couldn't feel in her skin or read with his mind. He wanted to ask what had spooked her. Wanted to know who and what she was hiding from. But this wasn't the time or place. And when she glanced away and blinked several times like she was holding back tears, he told himself whatever happened, he had to keep her safe.

"Come on."

He tugged her with him. Crouched low so they wouldn't be spotted and moved behind another tent. The battle echoed from decking to their right. Zagreus's army had reached the city.

Skata, he needed a weapon. He scanned the area as they ducked from one shadow to another. Any kind of sword would suit him just fine right about now.

"We need to get to the ground," he told her.

Natasa pulled back on his arm when he would have rounded another tree. "This way."

He followed, thankful she hadn't let go. She tugged him around another tent, then drew up short and gasped.

Titus hit her from the back, looked up, and realized why she'd stopped.

A satyr sniffed the air once, muttered, "Not a nymph," then lifted the sword in his arm and swung.

"Get back!" Titus knocked Natasa out of the way and lunged for the beast.

Natasa screamed. Titus hit the goat man in the waist, and the two toppled to the decking.

Titus's head swam. The satyr's emotions pummeled him, but he fought against the emotional transfer. Pain ricocheted through his body, and in a rush he realized most of what the beast was conjuring was hate. He could funnel that. Like Atalanta's daemons. He let the hate feed him.

His arm felt like dead weight, but Titus hauled back then plowed his fist into the satyr's jaw. The beast's head cracked against the decking. Titus did it again and again, until blood pooled from the creature's mouth and his hairy arms went limp against the wood.

"Titus!

Natasa's hand tugged at his shoulder. Warmth flowed into his bare skin, slid beneath his ribs, and condensed. He stumbled off the beast and swayed. Natasa turned him, wrapped both arms around his waist, and pulled his weight against her, keeping him from landing on his ass.

"Breathe. Gods, just breathe."

The emotions receded, and slowly the haze cleared. Probably not any faster than they would have if he'd been alone, but man, he liked that worry in her eyes. Liked the panic in her voice. Liked the way she was holding him tight.

"Are you okay?" she asked.

"Yeah, I—" He gave his head a shake. He needed to let go of her. They didn't have time to screw around.

He didn't want to let go, though. Man, when she got close, he swore he lost brain cells.

He looked down at the satyr at his feet and noticed the blade. Reluctantly, he eased out of her arms and knelt to pick it up. "Let's just get the hell out of here."

"I was thinking the same thing." She turned, took a step, winced, and reached out for the trunk of a tree.

His gaze shot to her leg and the ripped black fabric against her thigh. "*Skata*, you're hurt."

"I'm okay." She pursed her lips, steadying herself against the tree. "It's…not deep."

Blood stained her pants. Titus pressed a hand against the cut, realizing the satyr's blade must have gotten her before he took the beast down. She hissed in a painful breath. He pulled his hand back. Fresh blood stained his palm.

The wound was shallow but long. She'd be okay, but the sight of her blood tossed his stomach on a sea of nausea and helplessness. "Hold still."

The battle echoed below while she leaned back against the tree hidden in the shadows and rested her weight on her good leg. Titus recoiled at the stench but yanked open the satyr's coat and tore the shirt from the beast's hairy chest. When he came back, he knelt in front of Natasa and tied the garment tight around her thigh. "This is going to stink. I'd give you my shirt if I had one." He looked up. Tried to smile. "Kinda lost mine."

"I'm glad you didn't lose your pants too."

His fingers stilled against her warm thigh. "You are?"

She nodded. Torchlight from somewhere close reflected off her face. Made her skin look darker, her hair redder, her eyes flicker with dancing flames. And even though there was a war raging around them, he felt frozen in time. Like she was the only person for miles.

"About what happened before," she said, "in my tent. I'm…not exactly stable. In a lot of ways. You should know that before anything else happens."

His heart beat faster. "Neither am I. In a lot of ways."

Her gaze locked on his. Slowly, he pushed to his feet. Watched her watching him with the same intensity. The same need.

"You should go without me," she whispered. "I'll just slow you down. I don't want anything else to happen to you…because of me."

She was trying to save him again. Being the hero when that was his job. Her heat surrounded him. Warmed him. Gave him a strength he'd been lacking, not just today but every day. Gave him purpose… Something he'd lost during the long course of his life. "I'm not leaving you, *ligos Vesuvius*. I told you back in the woods you were stuck with me. I meant it."

The tiniest smile pulled at the corner of her mouth, but it didn't reach her eyes. Those darkened with secrets and...pain. A pain he was desperate to ease. "You can't save me, Titus."

She'd said something similar before. At the portal, when he'd offered her help. No matter what Theron and the others said about her, they were wrong. He knew deep in his soul that she wasn't evil.

Now, more than ever, he was determined to prove them, and her, wrong. "But I will. That's a promise."

Any news?"

Cerek turned from the virtual computer in Titus's suite and frowned as Demetrius stepped in the room. "Nothing. His Argos medallion hasn't gone off, and for whatever reason, I can't find it. He of all people knows to keep that damn thing on."

More good news. Just what Demetrius needed.

Evening pressed in from the arched windows that looked out over the sparkling city lights. The party was winding down, and Isadora and the others were downstairs saying their good-byes. Demetrius knew he should be by Isadora's side, but he couldn't go to her. Not yet.

He looked to Orpheus. "What do you think?"

Orpheus crossed his arms over his broad chest and scowled. "I think the Argonauts' little gizmos are crap if one measly female can so easily screw with not only the portal but your silly tracking devices."

"Hey," Skyla said, shooting her mate a look from the seat next to Cerek where she'd been helping the guardian try to crack Titus's computer. "They're your silly tracking devices now too."

"Don't remind me."

"And she wasn't just a measly female," Skyla added. "She's something more."

Orpheus scowled but stepped forward and squeezed Skyla's shoulder. "If she was a Siren, maybe then I could buy her super-warrior skills. But we know she wasn't."

Skyla faced the computer, her long blonde hair falling over her shoulder as she moved, and flipped screens. "From what happened at the portal, no, she definitely isn't a Siren. She's stronger. Any ideas?"

"She's not a nymph," Cerek said. "Too tough."

"A fury?" Orpheus asked.

Cerek cut him a look. "No way. Too hot."

Orpheus exhaled a sound that was part shock, part amusement. "Since when do you notice hot or not?"

Cerek turned back to the computer, feigning disgust. "I might not act on my base desires like you, daemon. Doesn't mean I don't notice."

Orpheus looked to Skyla and raised his brow. Skyla shook her head in a *Well, what do you know?* way and grinned, then refocused on the computer screen. She bit her lip. "Great power... She could have been a muse, I suppose."

"Nah. Not submissive enough."

Skyla's green eyes sparked when she glanced at her mate.

"What?" he asked.

"Get to know a few muses in your day, did you, big guy?"

Orpheus's grin widened. He leaned close and kissed her temple. "Not as well as I know you, Siren. And they never wanted to play. Not like you."

Demetrius fought from rolling his eyes at the direction of the conversation. Honestly, he really didn't give a rip who or what the female was. He was too busy stressing. And wishing like hell he hadn't seen what he'd just seen.

Pain tightened his chest, making it hard to breathe. The memory of Nick kissing Isadora sent every inch of his skin throbbing with a mixture of rage and helplessness. He should have plowed his fist into Nick's jaw. He should have stayed and talked to Isadora instead of turning and walking away. But he hadn't been able to do either. Because seeing them together like that... It was like looking at a scene from the future. Of what *could be* if he did the right thing. If he just stepped aside and finally let her go.

His brother was right. He couldn't protect her here. Not her and the baby. The Council would move on her soon. If not before she delivered, then right after, when she was at her weakest.

He couldn't keep her here, not if it meant her life. But the thought of handing her over to Nick...

"Demetrius? Are you listening or what?"

He cut his gaze toward Orpheus. The guardian's gray eyes were fixed on him as if he'd grown a third eyeball. Which he felt like he had. Words echoed in his head, but he couldn't make sense of them. Isadora... She was the only thing that made sense. She was the only thing that ever had. "What?"

"I said," Orpheus went on, exasperation in his features, "do you think she's a witch?"

Thought slowly came back. Demetrius's brow lowered. He and Orpheus—though they were no blood relation—were both part witch, and if this female had fried the portal the way Phin and O said she had, it was a possibility she was part witch too. But something about that simple explanation didn't add up.

Wondering, though, gave Demetrius something to obsess over besides his mate. And what the hell he was going to say to her when the last of the partygoers downstairs were finally gone.

He crossed his arms over his chest. "I think it's time we spoke with Delia."

"The coven leader?" Cerek turned back to the screen, but there was a look in his wide brown eyes. A look Demetrius couldn't quite read. "If it's all the same, I'll let you two handle that one without me."

Interesting. Cerek, afraid of a witch? He'd never shown any fear around Demetrius or Orpheus. And, come to think of it, the last time the Argonauts had visited the coven—when they'd been looking for information about the sorcerer who'd kidnapped Isadora—Cerek hadn't seemed afraid then. Of course, *then* Demetrius certainly wouldn't have noticed what the hell Cerek was up to. *Then* he hadn't been paying attention to anything but what was happening to Isadora and what he was going to do.

A lot like now.

"Groovy." Orpheus kissed Skyla's temple once more and pushed away from the desk. "Let's do this. The sooner we figure out where the hell Titus went, the sooner we can get back to more important things. Like playing."

Skyla grinned as they headed for the door and called out, "In that case I'll dig out my whip."

"Oh, Siren." A wide smile spread across Orpheus's face. And danger and heat brewed in his eyes. "I can't wait."

In the hall, he winked Demetrius's way. "Admit it. You're so freakin' jealous you can barely see straight."

Demetrius's jaw tightened, but he kept his focus directed ahead. Yeah, he was jealous. But not of Skyla. He was jealous of the relaxed relationship the Siren had with the Argonaut. The type of relationship he wished he had with Isadora.

Pain sliced deep again. Because he feared, relaxed or not, soon they wouldn't have any kind of relationship at all.

They found coats in an empty tent. A flashlight and a fresh canteen, the strap of which Titus hooked over his shoulder. When he tried to grab a blanket, Natasa tugged it from his hands and threw it on the floor. They didn't have time to pack, for gods' sake.

"Which way?" Titus asked as they crouched in the shadows, scanning the trees and decking. Blades striking blades echoed from below. Screams from nymphs who had to be scared out of their minds. Grunts and gasps as Aella's warriors battled Zagreus's hired thugs.

"Natasa?" Titus asked, squeezing her hand. "Which way?"

Her head snapped his direction. She blinked twice. Hadn't realized she'd been zoning out. The sounds of battle were growing closer, as if they were overrunning the city. And—*shit*—were those flames rising from the canopy behind him? She hadn't started that, had she?

She swallowed hard and rose to her feet, wincing at the pain spiraling up her leg. "Toward the west end of the city. There's an exit. And I'm thinking we need to hustle and get out of here before *that* reaches us."

He twisted to look over his shoulder, muttered, "Fuck me," then pushed to his feet. "Come on."

They wove around tents and tree trunks, staying as far from the battle as they could. Warmth spread down Natasa's leg. She knew without even looking that the cut was bleeding more than she'd thought.

They reached the far end of the city, deserted and quiet. Natasa rested her weight on her good leg and grasped the railing while Titus searched for the rope ladders she'd told him were rolled up and stored against the trees. This was the exit she used to come and go from the city, and it was usually guarded by at least one Amazon. But not tonight. And that didn't settle Natasa's nerves any.

Anxiety spread beneath her ribs. In her attempt to do the right thing, she'd caused more damage than if she'd left well enough alone. The cyclical pattern of her life kept repeating itself, and she seemed helpless to stop it.

"Found it," he called. He latched the end of the ladder on the hooks drilled into the decking and flung the ladder over the side. Then he stopped to look at her. Concern tightened his features. "Are you okay?"

"I'm fine." She shook his hand off her arm—the one that felt way too damn good—and climbed over the side. Darkness beckoned from below. "Let's just get out of here."

Pain radiated up her leg, making her weak. She grasped the rungs of the rope ladder and moved slower than normal, trying to compensate for her injury.

She reached the bottom, breath heavy, legs tired. Grasping the trunk of a nearby tree, she stepped off and swiped at the sweat running down her forehead.

Titus moved off the ladder at her side and looked through the trees back toward the battle. They were at least a hundred and fifty yards from the action, but the screams still echoed through the night and the red glow of flames high above was growing stronger.

"Man, either Zagreus has a serious axe to grind with your queen, or he's got a hard-on for those nymphs."

"It's the nymphs." Her stomach rolled. She couldn't think about what was happening back there. "And she's not my queen."

He looked at her. Seemed on the verge of asking something. She held her breath and waited. She knew he had a thousand questions, and he deserved answers to them all, but they didn't have time to get into any now. And she didn't know what she was going to tell him when he finally asked.

"Which way gets us out of here the fastest?"

Relief pulsed through her veins. Relief that he hadn't posed the tough questions. Relief that he wasn't blaming her for what had happened back there. She was carrying enough guilt over that already. "That way."

"Come on."

He grasped her hand and pulled her into the darkness of the forest. Shadows and mist surrounded them. The air was cool, slapping at her face, but it didn't stop the sweat from slicking her skin or the heat that seemed to consume her from the inside out.

Don't let it be happening now. She breathed deep and ground her teeth in the silence. She needed more time. Needed to figure out how to get info out of Epimetheus.

Tingles radiated from Titus's palm into hers, then up her arm, cooling at least part of her as she limped along next to him. That moment in the shadows, when he'd been tending her wound, slammed back into her. The worry in his eyes. The heady need in his voice. The draw to him that seemed to overpower even her common sense.

A lump formed in her throat. She didn't want him dead. Didn't want him hurt because of her. But the longer they were together, the more volatile she'd become. As soon as they got to safety, she had to figure out a way to lose him once and for all.

Her thoughts were so messed up, she didn't hear the roar until Titus tugged on her arm, pulling her to a stop. Her bad leg gave, and pain stabbed through her all over again. He wrapped an arm about her waist and pulled her close, keeping her from going down.

Gods, he felt good. So cool where she was hot. Even through the thick fabric of the military-style coat they'd picked up, he was like a breath of fresh air, easing the fever growing inside her.

"That doesn't sound like a stream," he muttered.

She strained to listen. And caught the faint roar reverberating through the misty trees.

"It's not." Panic closed in. They'd been heading toward the coast, not into the hills away from danger, like she'd thought. She always got turned around in these damn trees. "I—"

Hooves pounded the earth. Shouts echoed at their backs. Natasa whipped around. Six, seven…no, more like ten satyrs were bearing down on them.

"*Skata.*" Titus stepped in front of her and lifted the blade in his hand. "Go!"

She reached back for her dagger. "I can fight."

"You're pale as shit, and you can barely stand. Get the hell out of here before it's too late!"

He was protecting her again. Even after everything she'd gotten him into. Something in her chest cinched down tight. Something she didn't understand and wasn't prepared for. Something that told her losing him was no longer an option.

"Go!"

Her temper flared. The heat inside her grew stronger. "Not without you." She grasped the sleeve of his open coat and pulled hard. "I didn't just betray the people who were protecting me so you could get yourself killed by some freakin' satyrs."

"Natasa—"

A crash echoed through the underbrush. Natasa twisted that direction. Instinct ruled before thought. She lifted her hand toward the satyr now only yards away. Heat and energy erupted in her palm. A fireball shot through the air, hit the beast in the chest, and ignited his coat in flames.

A scream tore through the trees. Hooves skidded against the earth. Shouts reverberated. Natasa's eyes widened at what she'd just done.

"Holy Hades," Titus gasped. "How did you do that?"

"I don't..." She looked at her palm, then glanced back at the flaming beast rolling across the ground. Shock and sickness pooled in her stomach. "I don't know."

"Do it again."

Openmouthed, she glanced past the satyr she'd hit, toward what Titus was staring at. More beasts. Dozens of them, racing their way. And through the mist and trees and red glow of flames, a man astride a giant black horse. Only he wasn't just a man. Even from this distance, Natasa could feel the power and darkness radiating from his body.

"Do it again, right now," Titus said more urgently. "That's Zagreus."

Fear shot through every inch of Natasa. Hades was hunting her—all the gods were. If he'd had any suspicion she'd been hiding out with the Amazons, of course he'd send his son, the greatest tracker on the planet, to chase her down. She'd been stupid to think she was safe here. Especially after those nymphs arrived.

She wasn't going to be caught. Not by any god, and not by the Prince of Darkness. Her body took over. Thought fled. She turned and ran.

"Natasa!"

She didn't stop. Didn't think about her wound. She tore through the trees. Then skidded to a halt when she reached the edge of a cliff overlooking the churning Pacific.

Titus drew up short at her side, breath heavy. Waves crashed against rocks fifty feet below, and the sound of hooves closing in at their backs grew louder.

"Shit," Titus muttered. "If you have any idea how you hurled that fireball, you better do it again. Fast."

Natasa jerked around, realizing too late that instead of sprinting away, she'd run right into a trap. In her panic, she'd lead them out onto some kind of point. There were no more trees, only rocks beneath their feet and a drop-off to darkness and swirling danger in every direction.

She lifted her hand and tried to conjure the same energy she'd created before. Nothing happened.

"It's not working." Fear tightened her throat and caused her voice to rise. "It's not working! What do we do?"

"*Skata.*" Titus grasped her arm tight at the biceps and jerked her back toward the ledge. "We jump."

CHAPTER NINE

The frigid water tore the air from Titus's lungs. His body rolled through churning waves and slammed into stone. Pain, like a thousand tiny knives, stabbed at every inch of his skin, but he braced his feet on the rocks, pushed away, and kicked hard, swimming toward what he hoped was the surface.

Somewhere on the way down, Natasa had let go of his hand. Panic spread beneath his ribs as he gasped in the cool night air. The waves lifted and lowered his body, crashing in churning white foam against the cliff. Darkness surrounded him while water ran in rivulets down his face, blurring his vision.

He treaded water, turned a circle, and searched for her in the darkness, not wanting to call out and alert the beasts above to where he—*they*—had landed. But he couldn't find her. Panic turned to bone-melting fear. If she'd been swept out to sea or thrown against those rocks...

Water splashed, followed by her head breaking the surface not ten feet from him.

Thank you, Dimiourgos.

She was gasping for air when he reached her. He pulled her tight against him and whispered, "Don't make any sound."

Her hands landed against his bare chest. Her body pressed up tight to his. His open coat floated around them. "Where are they?"

He looked up toward the cliff. It was so dark—no moon—that he couldn't see more than a few feet. The sound of pounding surf twenty yards away was his only source of information on the distant to the cliffs.

"I don't know." He wrapped his arms around her slim body, holding her close. He didn't want to make a move for land until he knew they were safe. "If we're lucky, they'll either think we're dead or that we're too much trouble to come after."

"If we're lucky," she whispered. "We haven't been lucky yet."

He couldn't see much more than the whites of her eyes. He shivered again, but damn, her heat felt so good against him, he didn't care.

He wasn't sure about the luck part. Yeah, he was isolated from the Argonauts, still wasn't any closer to figuring out who she was, and because of her, he'd almost been sacrificed in a pretty twisted Amazon sex ceremony, but this wasn't the worst date he'd ever had. In fact, he wasn't all that upset over the events of the night. Because no matter what, they were still together.

You are so fucking screwed. One touch and you're obsessed.

Obsessed was pretty accurate. He'd been obsessed with her since the moment he'd touched her back at the colony. Obviously, he hadn't been using his legendary brain much. He wasn't sure why Phin and Orpheus hadn't followed him through the portal, but he knew the Argonauts had to be looking for him. And twisted as it was, even if he could alert Theron and the others as to his location, he wasn't ready. Not yet. He wanted more time alone with the gorgeous creature clinging to him like he was her last lifeline.

"You're shivering," she said softly. "You have to get out of this water. We can't wait much longer. Stay close to me while we try to get to shore. I'll keep you warm."

He hadn't even noticed he was shivering until she pointed it out. That was how gone he was around her. But he knew she was right. Even with her abnormally strong heat plastered to his front, it wasn't going to take long for his body temperature to drop and for hypothermia to set in. "Wh-why aren't you shaking from the cold? And wh-why are you always so warm?"

Damn, he sounded really tough right now, didn't he?

She tore her gaze away from his and grabbed on to his hand. "We'll skirt the edge of the cliff. Try to see if there's a ledge of some kind."

"O-okay." A rush of frigid water washed over his abdomen, sending another series of shivers all through his body. He was too cold to argue right now.

Water splashed in his face. He swam with one arm, trying to keep his head above the surface, trying to stay focused in the ice-cold liquid. Wave energy grabbed on and pulled them in. He hit the rocks with a grunt, turned, and reached for Natasa. Another wave dragged them under, and he kicked hard, pushing them back up to the surface.

Son of a bitch... He shook the wet hair from his eyes... Couldn't see shit. Just a little light so they could figure out where the hell they were... Was that too much to ask?

And then, as if a Fate had actually been listening—which he knew wasn't the case because the Fate's had abandoned his ass a long time ago—the dark clouds parted. Moonlight shone down, illuminating the cliff, the white-capped waves, and near the point, a rocky ledge and what looked to be a cave beyond.

"Tasa," he managed, his teeth knocking together. "There. Swim hard."

He couldn't feel his fingers or toes. The water grew thicker. More like syrup than surf.

"Just a little farther, Titus. Come on."

His vision blurred again. The rocks came and went. A hand tugged at his arm. A warm hand. One that felt so damn good. Tremors racked his body. The hand pulled hard, and then he broke the surface and cold stone pressed against his torso.

Natasa's other hand wrapped around his shoulder, yanking him out of the water. He rolled to his back on the rocky ledge, drawing frigid air into his lungs. He closed his eyes and focused on breathing. Gods, he was tired. That had taken a lot more energy than he'd thought.

"Don't pass out. Come on."

More tugging. She forced him to sit up. Wind chilled his cheeks and lips, but he didn't care. He liked that voice. *Really* liked it. He couldn't remember why but he only wanted to hear more of it.

"Stand up. It's not far."

The room swayed—was he in a room?—he didn't know. Water—yeah, that was water—squished between his toes. The scents of salt and seaweed filled his nose. Something warm brushed his chest.

Hands grasped his jacket, yanking it from his shoulders. The garment fell to the ground at his feet. "Sit."

He moved as if on autopilot. This uncontrollable shaking was really irritating. Wrapping his arms around his bare waist, he lowered himself to the ground. Rocks pressed against his ass and spine.

Thoughts came and went. Water. Cold. Night. "We…need…to make…a…fire."

"No time for that. You're already hypothermic."

Hypothermic? Okay, yeah. That wasn't good. Fabric rasped. A thud echoed. Hands tugged him forward, away from the rocks at his back, and then warmth closed in from every side.

He trembled again, then sighed as heat seeped into his skin, surrounded him, consumed him. His eyes slid closed. His breaths slowed and evened. In a daze, he realized Natasa was at his back, leaning against the rocks, pulling him in to the radiating heat of her body. Her mostly *naked* body.

Her arms wrapped around his torso, her legs around his waist. And wow, her bare skin felt good. So hot. So right.

She ran her hands up and down his chilled arms, across his chest, stimulating blood flow. Her warm breath spread down his neck, sending another quake through every inch of him. She tightened her arms and squeezed her legs to hold him tighter. And though he still shivered from the cold, he leaned his head back into the hollow between her shoulder and neck and smiled. All he had to do was shake a little and she'd plaster that hot little body against his? He could work with that.

"You're smiling," she whispered. "I'll take that as a good sign."

"You feel good. Been a long time."

She was silent for a moment, then said, "How long?"

His smile grew wider. A wicked shot of heat rolled through his groin. "Nine inches. At least. Maybe more. Definitely more."

She chuckled, and though he knew it couldn't be, even more warmth seeped into him with the movement. "That's not what I meant. Though I'm now suddenly glad Aella didn't get to see that for herself. What I meant was, how long has it been since someone's been able to touch you?"

His smile faded, and his mind spun out across the years. Reminding him of things he'd done, things he shouldn't have done, things he wished he could change. "A hundred years."

"I know Argonauts have long life spans, but…really? Have you always not been able to touch?"

"No. I'm a hundred and sixty-seven. The no-touching thing was a curse."

"From whom?"

He sighed, snuggling back deeper against her body. She answered by holding him even tighter—which he liked. "A witch."

"Why?"

"Because I used her."

"Her powers?"

He shook his head. "When I was younger, right after I joined the Argonauts and learned how to use my gift, I didn't often think about who I was using it on."

"What kind of gifts? Do you mean your fighting abilities?"

He wasn't sure why he was telling her this. He'd never told anyone. But he couldn't seem to stop his lips from moving. And part of him didn't want to. Maybe it was the hypothermia making his brain soft. "No. I can read others' thoughts."

"*What?*"

Her torso grew warmer against his spine and shoulders but not across the middle of his back. Was she wearing a bra? Damn, he really wished she'd taken that off too. Wanted to feel her nipples pressing into his skin.

"Can you read mine?"

Her voice pulled him from remembering her tongue sliding against his, the way she'd straddled his hips, what he'd wanted to do to her before they'd been interrupted. "Not yours. Not always. Every now and then a word gets through, but it's not enough to know what you're thinking. You seem to affect me in many different, unusual ways, *ligos Vesuvius*."

She was silent for a minute. Then relaxed against him. "So what happened? With the witch?"

Maybe she *did* like it. She didn't seem upset or on edge as he'd expected. He let her warmth cradle and soothe his tired body. "We had a fling. It wasn't serious on my part. But when she figured out I'd read her mind and used that to get her in bed, she wasn't happy."

"I bet not."

Her hands were still gently rubbing up and down his arms, and he took that as a good sign. If he'd shocked her with that revelation, she wasn't showing it. "I felt bad, but, honestly, I was young. I didn't care about anyone but myself."

"So she cursed you?"

Regret burned like a hot, sharp knife. "To touch others and feel everything they do. Every emotion I'd ignored. And then she killed herself."

"Oh."

The regret built and condensed beneath his breastbone, just as it did every time he let himself think of the past. He'd been young and stupid, and he'd deserved what that witch had done to him, but he was tired of dwelling on the past. He'd learned his lesson. Now he only wanted to go on enjoying the relief Natasa could give him—for however long it lasted. "By dying, she pretty much guaranteed that curse would never be broken. Until you."

Her chest rose and fell with her slow breaths. And in the silence, he wondered what she was thinking. He liked that he couldn't read her. Liked that she was a mystery, because unraveling that mystery was becoming a challenge he couldn't seem to stop thinking about. But right now, he wanted to know if what he'd told her had changed things between them.

Exhaustion tugged at him. He fought it, waiting for her to say something—*anything*—but she remained quiet. Water crashed against the rocks, a rhythmic whoosh and slap that lulled him, relaxed him, and made him sink deeper into her heat. Vaguely, he remembered there was something they were running from. Something he should be worried about but couldn't totally remember. And honestly, right now he didn't care. All he wanted was to go on enjoying this moment, in case it didn't last.

He drew in another breath. Felt the sticky fingers of sleep and finally gave over to the darkness. But as he drifted off, he heard her voice. Soft. Sexy. So damn alluring, it conjured fantasies that swirled behind his eyelids and warmed places she wasn't even touching. Places he wanted her to touch. At least once.

"I know all about being cursed. But I'm not your savior, Titus. And when you realize what it is about me that affects you, I have a feeling you won't be so anxious to help me anymore."

"Let me do the talking," Orpheus said.

Demetrius eyed the tent city in the hills outside Tiyrns where he and Orpheus had flashed after leaving the castle. Lights illuminated the canvas walls and multicolored flags flying high atop tent poles. Leaves lay scattered across the forest floor, crunching under their boots with each step in the moonlight, and the air was cool—an early-summer chill that spread through his skin like a virus.

Which was a lovely thought. As was the realization that a virus—even a really nasty one that left him quaking on his deathbed—was preferable to the misery currently sweeping through his heart every time he thought about Isadora.

Demetrius's witch senses prickled and tingled as they drew close to the coven. For hundreds of years, he'd denied his lineage, but in the last few months, as he trained himself with Orpheus's help, the spells were coming easier. And he was growing more accustomed to reading his body's reactions to the natural world around him.

Another thing he had Isadora to thank for. Without her, he never would have experimented with his abilities. He wouldn't have found a part of himself he didn't know was missing. He wouldn't be alive.

Sharp pain condensed beneath his breastbone, and he rubbed a gloved hand across his chest, hoping to alleviate the ache.

It didn't help.

"You okay?" Orpheus asked.

"Fine." Demetrius dropped his hand. "Which tent's hers?"

Orpheus gestured for him to follow, and Demetrius fell into step at his back.

At this time of night, most of the inhabitants of the city were asleep. But a few faces peered out as they passed. Delia—the coven leader—operated several illegal portals, and Argoleans often ventured into the city to cross to the human realm without the Council's knowledge. But it was all on the down-low, and usually it was prearranged. Demetrius knew it was only a matter of time before they were greeted by Delia's lookouts.

They reached the far end of the city. Ahead, a giant, pavilion-sized tent rose against the night sky, blocking out the moonlight and mountains beyond. A female witch with purple-striped hair pulled the tent flap open and faced them. "Delia's been waiting for you."

Of course she was. If Demetrius had sensed the magic gathered in this place before even reaching the city, Delia had sensed they were on their way.

Orpheus ducked under the flap. Demetrius followed, his gaze skipping from the circle of witches kneeling on pillows on the floor to his right with their hands joined and their eyes closed, swaying in what seemed to be some kind of spell-conjuring ceremony, to the group at his left, speaking in hushed voices.

Quiet descended, and gazes peered their direction. The tent was smaller than he'd thought, this space like a small gathering area more than a pavilion. That or walls blocked off rooms he couldn't see and wasn't sure he wanted to know about. A sliver of unease shimmied through him. Even though he was learning about his abilities, he wasn't sure he was totally ready to embrace his heritage. Especially not the woo-woo, *we-are-one* nature shit the witches in that circle were conjuring.

The grouping parted, and Delia stepped forward, her eyes glinting, her long, white hair illuminated by the candles spaced around the perimeter of the tent. "It's been a while, Orpheus."

"Delia." Orpheus lowered his head, a movement that took Demetrius totally off guard, because Orpheus never bowed to anyone. "We need your help."

Delia's eyes sharpened, shifting Demetrius's way. And under her scrutinizing gaze, Demetrius tensed, knowing she was examining, assessing, and judging.

She stepped back and gestured for them to follow. "Come. Away from the circle."

Relief flitted through Demetrius but turned to unease as he moved under an archway and into another room, this one smaller and cozier than the last. Instead of open and barren, it was decorated with plush couches, soft throw pillows and blankets, and reflective surfaces that shone off every wall.

Witches used mirrors as seeing objects. Demetrius hadn't mastered that ability yet, and at the moment didn't really want to know what Delia could see.

She turned to face them. "You're here to discuss the girl."

Orpheus cast a look at Demetrius. Even without asking, Demetrius knew what he was thinking. *Bingo, we were right.* "So Natasa is from this coven?"

Delia looked his way. "No. And she's not a witch."

"Then what is she?"

"Something of great value."

"To whom?" Demetrius asked.

"To everyone."

Okay, this was already getting irritating.

"She fried the portal at the Gatehouse," Orpheus told the witch. "That's why we're here. One of our Argonauts went through with her, and we can't find him. If she's not a witch, we would appreciate anything you can tell us about her."

Delia pursed her lips, then said, "I sensed when she crossed into this realm."

"So she can conjure magic," Demetrius said, "but she's not a witch. That tells us a lot."

The coven leader didn't answer. Simply looked at him with a blank expression. And Demetrius's frustration with her jumped another notch.

This was a waste of time. He should be trying to figure out what he was going to do about Isadora and the Council, not wasting his time here chasing dead ends.

He was just about to leave when Delia turned to look into the mirrors around her. "What was she after in this realm? Did you find out before she crossed?"

Sandy brown hair fell over Orpheus brow when he cocked his head. "She told Maelea she was looking for information about Prometheus."

"And which Argonaut went through with her?"

"Titus," Orpheus answered.

"Not ideal," Delia muttered. "And Titus's forefather? From whom does he hail?"

"Odysseus."

Delia turned and stared hard into Orpheus's eyes. "Are you sure?"

Orpheus glanced uneasily at Demetrius then back again. "Pretty damn. Why does it matter?"

Delia shifted her weight. "It matters because if she is what we think she is, he is likely the only one who can stop her. And yet because of his curse, he is the one from your order who will be most distracted by her."

"And what in Hades does *that* mean?" Demetrius asked. O sent him a *calm the hell down* look, but Demetrius had reached his limit. "Curse? Stop her? Look, whatever you're dancing around, just spell it out for us. If Titus is in some kind of danger, we need to know."

Delia held his gaze. Seemed to debate something. Finally said, "Titus was cursed by one from my coven years ago. That female you mentioned...because of the power inside her...has the ability to distract him from that curse. And that distraction will blind him to who and what she really is."

Orpheus's eyes narrowed. "And what is she?"

"Our best guess?"

Gods, Fates spoke more plainly than this chick. Demetrius frowned. "Yeah, if that's all you've got."

Delia pursed her lips. "Unquenchable fire."

Silence settled over the room like a thousand ton weight had just been dropped. And in the aftermath, Demetrius's stomach tightened with both fear and apprehension. His gaze shifted to Orpheus, who was staring back at him with a *holy fucking shit* expression.

If what Delia suspected was true, then it meant Isadora wasn't going to be safe anywhere. And if Natasa really was unquenchable fire...

Frantic, he turned toward the witch. "Why does it matter that Titus's forefather is Odysseus?"

"There are those who believe," Delia said, "that through his line, Odysseus passed along the gift of hidden knowledge."

"About Natasa?"

She shook her head. "During his travels, Odysseus was imprisoned by a nymph named Calypso. Calypso was the daughter of the Titan Atlas. Atlas is Prometheus's brother. Which means Calypso is Prometheus's niece."

When they only stared at her, she heaved out a sigh as if they should already know this. "Some think that before Calypso let Odysseus return home to Ithaca, she gave him the gift of hidden knowledge. Zeus threatened Atlas and any other Titan who wasn't already imprisoned with Krónos in the underworld with death should they share what they knew about Prometheus's imprisonment. But he didn't forbid the passing of a gift."

Understanding finally dawned. Along with shock. "Are you saying Odysseus passed this knowledge to his descendants," Demetrius asked, "and Titus knows where Prometheus is chained but just doesn't realize it?"

"No," Delia answered. "I'm saying...it's a possibility. However, it's also a possibility this hidden knowledge only relates to the location of Calypso's island. Her name in direct translation means 'concealer.'"

True, but either way, if they could find Calypso, Titus could read the goddess's mind. They might be able to find Prometheus before Zeus and the other gods. They could stop Natasa from what she was about to do.

"Who would know for sure?" Demetrius asked.

Delia shrugged in a noncommittal way.

"Epimetheus." Orpheus's eyes narrowed on the witch. "He lives in the human realm. Keeps to himself. I've met him a few times. A complete moron, but"—he glanced at Demetrius—"our best shot to find out if this theory is true or not."

Prometheus's brother. Also a Titan, and the father of afterthought. Demetrius had heard stories about the elder god; he'd just never had any desire to seek him out. But now…

He refocused on Delia. "What did the witch curse Titus with? You said it was one from this coven."

Delia sighed again. "I shouldn't—"

"Screw shouldn't," Demetrius said. "We passed shouldn't a long time ago. You said Titus's curse interferes with his ability to read Natasa. How?"

Delia frowned. Debated. Then finally said, "She cursed him to feel the emotions of any he touches."

"Which is why he wears the gloves," Orpheus muttered.

A lot about Titus suddenly made sense. "Assuming Calypso passed this hidden knowledge to Odysseus, how does Titus unlock it?"

"In that," Delia said, "I am no help "

Orpheus looked toward Demetrius. "What do you think?"

What did he think? Demetrius couldn't stop thinking about Isadora. And their baby. And what could be his last chance to save them both. "I think it's the only lead we've got."

Orpheus turned to Delia. "Thank you." Then to Demetrius, "Let's go."

They moved for the door, but the witch's hand on Demetrius's forearm stopped him. "Be careful, Guardian. Some decisions have irrevocable consequences."

She knew. He didn't know how, but she was talking about Isadora and Nick and what Demetrius was considering doing. That heart his mate had awakened swelled beneath his ribs. "And some people are worth it. I don't care what happens to me. As long as she's safe, that's all that matters."

He pulled away, heading for the door Orpheus had already exited. But at his back, he was sure Delia muttered, "And what about her people?"

He was in an oven. Being roasted like a turkey dinner.

Images of flickering flames and a slamming door dragged Titus from deep sleep. He opened his eyes and blinked several times. Darkness and a faint moon hung above. Waves crashing against rock echoed to his right and the scent of salt hung heavy in the air.

Sweat slicked his back. He pushed up on his hands. Chill air spread across his overheated skin, instantly cooling him. Surveying his surroundings, he realized he was in some kind of rock overhang. It wasn't a cave, really, but enough shelter from the wind and prying eyes to keep them dry and safe.

A moan echoed at his back. He glanced over his shoulder, peering through the dim light. Natasa sat leaning against the wall directly behind him, her head tipped to the side, her curly red hair matted and damp over one slender shoulder. Her eyes were closed in sleep, and her arms hung at her sides, but without even touching her, he knew she was the reason for his fiery dreams.

Gods, she was beautiful. Beautiful and mysterious and all he could think about. Heat rushed to his belly, slid into his groin. Memories of the way she'd wrapped her body around his to keep him warm flickered in his mind. His cock swelled and hardened, and other, more enjoyable ways she could warm him flooded his thoughts.

He brushed a hand over her arm, hoping to rouse her, to tempt her, to kiss her. Alarm registered at the first touch. Her skin was hotter than he'd ever felt it.

"Tasa?" He placed his palm on her forehead. She moaned, moving her head toward his hand, but didn't wake.

He hadn't been dreaming. Her flesh was on fire. He shook her. "Natasa."

She groaned, but still didn't wake. His gaze spread down her torso, over her breasts covered only by the thin white bra, to the black pants plastered to her hips and legs. Finally landed on the makeshift bandage tied around her thigh.

He tugged at the bandage, pulled it free, then grasped the tear in her pants and ripped it open wider so he could get a better look.

The wound was red and inflamed, no longer bleeding but swollen, the edges oozing. Infection had already set in. Faster than it should have for one shallow cut. He shifted his hand back to her forehead. She moaned once more and leaned into his hand.

Skata, she was burning up. He needed to do something to cool her fever or she could seize. At this point, risking a secondary infection to her wound was less of a concern than watching her die.

He pushed to his feet, leaned down and wrapped his arms around her. She grunted, resting her hands on his biceps. Her burning head fell against his chest. Fear and panic mingled inside him. "Come on, Tasa. I need you to wake up."

She was like deadweight in his arms. He carried her toward the water and scanned the area. When he found a place where the waves weren't crashing too strongly against the rocks, he headed that direction. Lowering her to her feet, he wrapped his arm around her waist and slowly eased them both into the water.

He gasped at the frigid bite, but she was so hot next to his skin, her heat quickly eased the chill. Bracing one hand on the rock ledge to keep the waves from knocking them into the cliff, he held her tight. "Wake up for me, baby," he whispered, running his fingers up and down her lower spine. "Open those pretty eyes."

She moaned, leaned her head against his chest as if still sleeping, but her legs grazed his, and her arms tightened around his waist.

Man, he could get used to this. Her wrapped around him, leaning on him, needing him. And as he slowly felt her body temperature lower, he couldn't help but see how the situation had reversed. Hours ago, she'd been the one saving him. They seemed to have this back-and-forth thing going. Where she couldn't walk away from him and he couldn't walk away from her. Now more than ever, he was determined to figure out who she was, and how he could help her.

His fingers brushed her hair to one side, and he noticed the triangular tattoo on the back of her neck.

He shifted her in his arms to get a better look. The triangle wasn't fancy, just straight lines and identical angles. Nothing someone would purposely have tattooed on their skin unless it meant something personal. But this didn't look like ink to him. It looked—he shifted his forearm covered in the ancient Greek text closer to compare the lines and markings—like something she'd been born with.

Everything inside him stilled.

Her erratic body temperature, the fact Maelea had said she was searching for Prometheus, Natasa's admission that people were after her, her inconsistent, almost volatile reactions, his strange ability to touch her...

A tingling grew in his chest, slowly drifted up until his thoughts were a whir in his mind. He looked down at her face, resting gently against his shoulder, her eyes closed, her long, dark lashes forming crescents against her pale skin. And realized what he would have figured out with his superstrength brain had he not been so obsessed by her touch.

She was fire. He didn't know why or how it was possible, but he was certain she was the element the Argonauts and gods were all desperately seeking.

His heart pounded hard. Options, scenarios whirred through his mind. Theron and the others already thought she had some dark agenda. If they found out she was fire, they'd use her as a weapon. The same way they'd used him all these years to get an upper hand in their battles.

"Don't stay...in water...too long," she mumbled against his chest. "He'll come... Will think I...failed."

His brow lowered. He tried to read her expression. Couldn't. "Who, baby?"

Zeus? Hades? Both were desperate to find the remaining elements. The waves rocked them in the water, but she didn't answer. Her breathing slowed, and as she drifted to sleep, her temperature seemed to normalize. But his heart was racing. And he was starting to shiver again.

Realizing he was going to be no help to either of them if hypothermia set in, he climbed out and dragged her with him. Water ran in rivulets down their skin. She was still groggy and out of it, but this time when he lifted her, she curled into his arms, and the urge to protect her, to take care of her, overwhelmed him.

He carried her back to the shelter of the overhang and reached for her now-dry coat. He dabbed at the wound on her leg. Her face tightened, as if in pain, but when he placed his bare palm over the cut, she tipped her head and sighed. Her breaths slowed once more and evened out. He felt her forehead again, counting minutes as they ticked by in silence.

Her temperature was already slowly creeping back up.

"*Skata*."

She needed medicine. A healer. Something to take care of the fever before it burned her alive. He could open a portal back to Argolea, but there was no way he was letting Theron get close to her now.

He glanced up and around. Zagreus and his goons had to be long gone. Judging from the position of the moon and the reduced cloud cover, hours had passed since their run-in. He didn't have time to wait to make sure. By morning, Natasa's fever would be worse, and though the water had cooled her slightly, something about her mumbled warning set his nerves on edge.

"Here, baby, drink this." He grasped the canteen they'd lifted before running from the Amazon city and brought it to her lips. She grunted, tried to push it away, but he forced her to drink. Licking her lips, she leaned back against the rocks and sighed again, never once opening her eyes.

"I'm gonna get help, *ligos Vesuvius*. Don't worry."

She didn't answer. He didn't expect her to. He set the canteen next to her hand, then gently brushed the hair away from her face, grimacing at how hot she was already. Grabbing her jacket from the ground, he went back to the water, then dunked it in the ice-cold ocean. The frigid garment would make him cringe, but he knew it'd feel like sweet relief to her.

She sighed when he draped it over her, seeming to melt into the rocks.

He leaned close and pressed a kiss to her forehead. And felt his heart take a nosedive into an ocean he was starting to think he might never be able to swim free from. "I'll be back. Dream of me."

CHAPTER TEN

"**D**aemon attacks are down in the area since Atalanta's death," Helene said as she sat in front of Nick's desk in his office at the colony and made marks on her trusty clipboard. "But Kellen reported this morning that a new pack was sighted outside Whitefish. And we're hearing word of attacks at small outposts deeper in the Rockies."

Nick had never expected his mother's beasts to stop their hunt for blood simply because she was now dead. But he'd hoped for it, even if he'd never said so aloud. He studied the report Kellen, one of his best scouts, had generated. "Send a unit to the Whitefish area to check for signs. And another to scour the acres south of the lake."

Helene nodded, her shoulder-length, light brown hair falling over her face as she looked down at her notes and made another mark. The movement dragged his attention away from his own papers, and he watched with detached interest as she brushed the lock back and tucked it behind her ear.

Her jaw was strong, her skin creamy, her features feminine and attractive. She'd been his go-to person for the last two years, had been instrumental when they'd relocated the colony here from Oregon, and was probably the closest thing he had to a friend. And yet he knew virtually nothing personal about her. Not about what she did after she left him for the day or who she hung out with or even how she'd lost her leg as a child.

"There's one more thing," she said.

She lifted her head, and her eyes widened when she realized he was watching her. A blush spread across her cheeks. A blush that told him she was aware of him on a level he *should* be aware of her.

And yet, even with that knowledge, he felt nothing inside. Nothing but anger over the fact the gods had cursed him more than any other. Ever since he'd learned Isadora had fallen for his brother, he hadn't been able to get it up for any female. Even one as sexy, available, and interested as the one sitting right in front of him.

She quickly glanced back down again and made a mark on her paper. Her cheeks turned pinker. "Um...the therillium supply will need to be replenished soon. You've been so busy with the scouts and the celebration in Argolea, I was thinking it might be time to pass that job on to someone else."

Nick's jaw clenched at the memory of that celebration, and his back tingled at the thought of what lived beneath the colony. "No one else goes into the mines. End of subject. And I don't want it brought up again."

Helene's gaze snapped to his. Questions brewed in her dark eyes, but she didn't ask them.

After a long pause, she sighed, then looked back down at her notes. "I guess that's about it."

She pushed to her feet, and guilt slithered through Nick at the disappointment showing on her face. Guilt that he wasn't what she wanted him to be. That he couldn't be more. Followed by another shot of anger that whipped and burned through every inch of his veins.

He was tired of doing and being and having others depend on him. Exhausted from the duties and responsibilities of running the colony and being the person everyone turned to in a crisis. He was on a circular path that seemed to have no end. And now, thanks to his inability to restrain his temper, he'd done something he shouldn't have. Which meant the one tiny piece of joy he had in his life—seeing his soul mate now and then even if she'd never truly be his—was gone.

His mood darkened. As if on autopilot, he rose from his seat and followed Helene toward the door. Her limp was less visible these days, the new prosthetic obviously working better than the last. He wanted to ask about it. Knew he should say something to clear the air but couldn't find the words. Didn't even know if he wanted to.

She pulled the door open, then drew up short.

Kellen's tanned face filled the doorway. "Helene." He looked past her and focused on Nick. "We've got a problem."

Always a problem. Always another fucking problem.

Nick tamped down the resentment. "What's happened?"

"We got a call on the satellite line. One of the Argonauts is stranded and requesting help."

Nick's jaw clenched. *Let it be Demetrius.* He was in the mood for a good bloodletting. At the moment, it was the only thing he could think of that might improve his mood. "Which one?"

"Titus. And he's not alone. The redhead? The one that was here a week or so ago, looking for Maelea? She's with him."

She was running. Her feet were bare. The ground dry and covered in a thin layer of dust. Her muscles ached, but she pushed on, the fabric of her dress flapping in the wind around her ankles.

Breathe. Focus. Draw on the strength inside you.

Her mother had spoken those words to her. Years ago. So many, Natasa could barely remember when exactly. But her mother's voice rang in her head. Louder now. So very clear. As if she were right behind her, urging her on.

The dirt road blurred. And a blast of heat rolled over Natasa, dragging the air from her lungs, flinging her forward with a force that swept her off her feet. She hit the ground with a grunt, landing on her hands and knees. Dirt flew up around her, making her cough. Blinking to rid her eyes of the grit, she looked over her shoulder to see what had hit her. Then gasped as the landscape began to change.

Her homeland swirled as if made of a magical fog. No more mud huts or pyramids; even the palace on the hill where she lived with her mother had disappeared.

Rolling over the mountains, a smokeless fire as big as a sandstorm came straight toward her. So hot she could feel its heat burning her skin, even miles away.

Breathe, Natasa. Focus. Draw on the strength that is inside you. Good or evil, the choice is yours.

Fear consumed her. She didn't want to focus. Didn't care about good or evil. She needed to run.

She dragged herself to her feet. Pushed her muscles forward with every ounce of strength she had inside her. The fire roared closer. Panic swelled in her chest. Fiery heat licked at her back, igniting the skirt of her dress in flames that crawled up her legs.

"No!" She swatted at the flames, trying to put them out. She couldn't stop running. "Help me! Someone!"

She batted furiously, couldn't smother them. Panic morphed to bone-melting fear. She tried to rip off her dress. Her fingers got stuck in the folds of fabric. She sobbed and pulled harder. The fire across the hills thundered close. She looked up just as it devoured the tree she'd been reading under. And her eyes grew wide when she realized it wasn't just a fire. There was a face within the flames. A face that was blowing the blaze all across the land, igniting everything in an unquenchable fire. A face she'd seen in her mother's drawings.

The face of her father.

Her eyes grew wider. Horror whipped like a wind blown straight from the fires of the Underworld.

She looked up at the sky, and screamed into the burning wind, "Why are you doing this?"

An eagle screeched high above, swooping overhead. Her gaze followed. The eagle sailed over a man, standing not a hundred feet away. Flames licked at his feet, but he wasn't burning. At least not yet. Her breath caught. Recognition flared.

Titus…

Her heartbeat picked up speed. She pushed her feet toward him, grasping her burning skirt. She had to save him. Had to help him…

Just as she reached him, his face shifted, the nose growing longer, the chin sharper, the hair not dark and shoulder length but short, blond, and sun kissed. And all around him, a cool, blue aura erupted.

"I can help you. Come to me and live."

She heard the voice in her head, but the lips didn't move. Confusion swamped her. This wasn't her Titus. This wasn't what she wanted to be running toward. She knew she needed to go, to flee, but her legs wouldn't move. A hand extended. A hand bathed in the same blue aura. Not scorching and hot but cool and refreshing, offering her…relief.

Her heart screamed no, but her mind told her it was the only way. She reached out. Energy flowed from his fingers to hers. A crackle of power across the empty space that told her the face in the blue glow—whoever he was—was more than relief. He was a god. And stronger than any she'd known before.

"Yes, child. I'm the only one who can stop the flames. I will cool you so you have more time. You have but to promise to give me one tiny thing…"

Titus paced the outer room of the medical clinic in the colony, his jaw twitching as he waited for news.

The muscles in his chest tightened, and he ran a hand over his sternum to ease the ache. Thankfully, Nick had sent a helicopter to pick them up, but when he'd reached Natasa again, she'd been lying so still against the rocks, for a moment he'd thought she was dead.

The memory of that—the gut-wrenching fear he'd felt and the way she'd mumbled "No, no, no…don't take me back to the water," over and over—was still enough to make him draw in a breath, then let it out slowly in an attempt to regulate his pulse.

She wasn't dead. She'd been hotter than hell, but alive. He'd held her close all through the flight back to the colony, and for whatever reason, she'd cooled slightly under his touch, but not enough. Now, as he paced the waiting room, all he could think about was whether or not they'd been too late. Whether or not the infection had spread. Whether or not he was going to lose her so soon after finding her.

A lump formed in his throat. One he couldn't swallow. The door behind him opened, but he didn't turn to look. Couldn't. He closed his eyes.

Don't let her be dead. Please don't let her be dead.

"I brought you clothes."

Nick. It was Nick.

Fixing an impassive look on his face, Titus turned. Fresh clothing sat on the chair, and Nick stood in the doorway, his massive arms crossed over his chest, the long sleeves and fingerless gloves covering the ancient Greek text on his forearms and the backs of his hands, just like Titus's.

His gaze skipped to the Misos leader's face. Hard jaw, amber eyes narrowed in speculation, the UV clinic lights above reflecting off his shaved head and highlighting the long, jagged scar on the left side of his face.

He didn't seem thrilled to see Titus, but then Nick never seemed thrilled to see anyone. "Thanks."

"My men said you ran into some trouble with a tribe of Amazons. And Zagreus."

Titus tugged off the seawater-scented coat he was still wearing and reached for the long-sleeved Henley, thankful for something clean. He really wanted to take a shower but couldn't leave Natasa. "You could say that."

"Zagreus is not someone we want to fuck with."

Zagreus wasn't someone the Argonauts wanted to fuck with either. Titus tugged the clean shirt over his head. "He didn't follow us."

"How can you be sure?"

"I scouted the area before I called you. Zagreus and his goons were long gone."

"What the hell were you doing with a tribe of Amazons?"

That was a story Titus wasn't ready to get into yet. He glanced toward the door. "What's taking so long? I need to see her."

Nick turned to look through the empty doorway. "Lena will tell us when there's news."

Titus flexed his fingers and resumed pacing. Worst-case scenarios flashed through his mind, and that fear he'd been fighting came raging back.

"You look like shit, you know," Nick said.

Titus huffed and ran a hand over his head. His hair smelled like the ocean and hung to his shoulders in knotted waves. A rubber band to tie the mess back from his face would be good, but he didn't even have the urge to go look for one. "I'm fine."

"You don't look fine; you look fucked."

Titus hesitated midstep, and realized the thought had come from Nick. He'd been alone with Natasa so long, he hadn't heard another thought in hours. And the shock of it was enough to remind him just how much he needed to be near her again.

"Look," Nick said, "As much as it doesn't overjoy me to do so, I need to alert Theron that you're both here."

Titus jerked around. "Don't do that."

"Why not?"

"Because"—what the hell was he going to say?—"Theron's distracted with everything happening in Argolea."

"Yeah, right."

Shit, even Titus knew that was a stupid excuse. He scrubbed a hand down his face. Nick was a smart guy, and if Titus lied to him, he'd only run to Theron anyway to double check his story. His best shot was honesty at this point. Or partial honesty.

"Theron thinks Natasa's working for Zagreus. That she was in Argolea to find Maelea for that reason. That's why I called you for help instead of taking her there."

Nick's eyes narrowed. "Is she?"

"No. Most definitely not."

"How can you be sure?"

Because he felt it. Deep inside. In a place he'd never felt anything before. But he knew that wouldn't be enough to convince Nick, so instead, he said, "Because Zagreus came after her too. He wouldn't have done that if she were working for him."

"Unless she changed her mind and was running from him."

He'll come for me. Will think...I failed.

No, he didn't believe that. He shook off the thought. She'd been feverish and mumbling those words. They didn't mean anything. Plus, her working for Zagreus wasn't a logical explanation, not with everything he knew about her.

"She wasn't," he said firmly.

Nick tipped his head and studied Titus speculatively. "What is it about her that's got you in such a knot? It's more than the fact she's attractive. I've seen you barely glance twice at an attractive female. Why is this one so special?"

Because she's mine.

Another burst of understanding ricocheted through Titus. Holy shit... She was his soul mate. It wasn't the element drawing him to her; it was a deeper connection, one he'd never expected—never *wanted*—to find. Until now.

"I...I don't know," he lied. His head felt suddenly light. His skin cold and clammy. He swallowed hard and tried to mask his reaction, but knew he failed...miserably.

Nick stared at him so long, sweat broke out all over Titus's skin.

"You look like you haven't slept in three days," Nick finally said.

"I'll be fine."

"Fine or not, you look like you're in over your head."

A truer statement had never been uttered. Titus shook it off. "I'll sleep on a chair in her room. I won't let her out of my sight. Just do me this one favor—don't tell Theron and the others we're here. I promise nothing bad will happen to the colony. As soon as she's better, we'll leave."

"And go where?"

Titus didn't know. He just knew he wasn't losing her. Not to the gods, not to the Argonauts, and not to some fluke infection. Not when he'd finally found her.

After several long, tense seconds, Nick turned for the door. "You can stay. For now. Mostly because I don't feel like dealing with anyone from Argolea. But if any strange shit happens, you and your chick are out of here. Got it?"

"Got it." Grateful, Titus nodded. "Thanks."

Nick paused in the doorway. "Don't thank me yet. I have a knack for fucking things up myself. An hour from now you may be wishing you'd found refuge anywhere but here."

His boots echoed down the long corridor, and Titus drew in a breath, then let it out slowly.

His soul mate… *Skata*, he should have figured that out sooner.

He dropped into a chair and rubbed his throbbing temples. The click of shoes from the hallway brought his head up.

Lena, the colony's healer, came into the room, her brown ponytail swinging at her back. "Titus?"

Fear stabbed through his heart. He pushed to his feet. "Yeah."

Don't say she's dead… Please don't say she's dead…

Lena crossed her arms over the clipboard in her hands and pulled it against her chest. "We were able to close the wound and treat the infection. Her temperature has come down."

Relief as sweet as wine whipped through Titus and dragged the strength from his legs. He dropped back into his chair and closed his eyes. *Thank you, Dimiourgos.*

"There's more."

Apprehension tightened his chest. He glanced up. "What more?"

"How did you…?"

He rose to his feet. "Just answer the question."

Lena pursed her lips. "She's still running a fever above 102. It's not as bad as it was, but we can't seem to bring it down. And we can't find any reason for it either. No other infection, no underlying health problem. It's like…"

"Like it's part of her," he finished, reading her confused mind.

She nodded. "Right now she's stable, but there's no telling if it will creep back up again. The infection wasn't nearly as bad as the fever."

Which meant her increasing temperature wasn't from infection after all. It was from the fire element.

I'm unstable. In a lot of ways…

He swallowed hard. "Can I see her?"

"We were hoping you would. Marc and the others who brought you here told me her temperature seemed to lower when you were touching her. Maybe you'll be able to have an effect on her my healing skills can't."

That didn't make any logical sense to Titus, but he nodded and followed Lena into the hall.

Sconces lit the corridor. The medical clinic was located in the lower levels of the Misos Colony, which was really just an old castle built on an island in the middle of a glacial lake.

Lena stopped outside a heavy wood door. "We'll check on her in a bit. If you need anything, let us know."

He muttered his thanks. On a deep breath, he pushed the door open, then stepped into the dimly lit room and looked toward the bed.

The scent of institutional cleaners met his nose. Medical equipment filled the perimeter of the white room, and a small window high on the far wall looked out over the lake. But it was Natasa, lying with her head on the pillow and her body covered by a thin blue blanket, who drew Titus's attention.

His heart bumped. Someone had brushed her hair. Shimmering coppery-red curls surrounded her face, looking like swirling fingers of flames against the white pillow, which seemed so fitting now. He let the door close behind him and moved quietly toward the bed. An IV was hooked to her hand, but there were no other machines attached to her body. Her skin was still pale but thankfully had more color than when he'd been holding her in that helicopter.

Something in his chest contracted hard as he stared at her. A feeling he wasn't prepared for. Yeah, she was his soul mate—he knew that now—but there was another connection between them. Something more. Something he sensed on the edge of his mind that he couldn't access.

Slowly, he stepped around the bed and touched her forehead with the back of his hand. Warmth immediately flowed from her into him, but she sighed, leaned into him, seeming to need his touch as much as he needed hers.

His chest vibrated with a thousand emotions. He grasped the shirt he'd just put on, tugged it over his head, and dropped it on a chair. The bed was standard hospital fare—single and barely wide enough for one, let alone two—but her temperature had cooled when he'd held her before. He hoped now that the infection was gone, whatever connection they had would somehow cool her even more.

He climbed into the bed, rolled to his side, and tugged the blanket over them both. She didn't open her eyes, but she shifted his direction and curled into him. And when he wrapped his arms around her, the sigh that escaped her lips was like the sweetest, softest, most beautiful music he'd ever heard.

In that moment, everything made sense. She wasn't just the second half of his soul. She was so much more. Their fates were tangled together, and he knew somewhere deep inside that she was destined for more than just being used as a pawn by the gods. She was destined for greatness.

An odd tingle started in his chest. His whole life centered around duty, around his service to the Argonauts, but she was changing his priorities. And he had an ominous feeling if she asked him, he'd go to the ends of the earth for her.

Even if it meant forsaking his Argonaut brothers to do so.

CHAPTER ELEVEN

Zagreus paced the living room of Epimetheus's home in the wilds of Arizona and looked out at the early morning orange-and-pink sky swirling behind angry red mountains.

This place was in the middle of freakin' nowhere. He had no idea how the elder god lived way out here in the sticks with no one around for miles and didn't lose his fucking mind.

"Here, here." Epimetheus rushed into the room, holding a silver tray set with a delicate china teapot, two cups, and saucers. He set it on the coffee table. "I brewed it fresh."

Stringy silver hair pulled free from the tie at Epimetheus's nape, falling forward over his wrinkled face. He wore a tan garment that looked like a muumuu over black pants. Bare feet with brittle, too-long, yellowish toenails peeked out from the cuffs. He pushed the wire-rimmed glasses back up his nose, poured steaming liquid into one dainty cup, and handed it to Zagreus. Zagreus lifted one brow as he gazed down at the pale green concoction.

Epimetheus poured his own cup, smiled, then took a sip. When Zagreus only stared at him, he gestured with his hand. "Drink, drink. Sweet nectar from the gods." Then, under his breath, "and the local goat."

Forget what he'd *thought*. Epimetheus had already *lost* his fucking mind.

Zagreus set the cup down untouched and waited until the god situated his frail body on the plastic-covered couch. "I want to know about a redhead. Otherworldly. Great power. A mark in the shape of a triangle on the back of her neck."

Epimetheus swirled the liquid in his cup. "A female, did you say? Don't you have enough females?"

"How many I have and what I do with them are my business, not yours."

"It is, it is." Epimetheus eased back his seat. "I meant no disrespect."

Zagreus ground his teeth. Epimetheus might be an elder god, but he was as docile as a flower, and as dumb. He was, however, one of the oldest beings on the planet, which was the only reason Zagreus was here now.

"A triangle, you say? Did you see it up close?"

"No. From a distance. When she turned, her hair flew over her shoulder. Do any of the gods bear that symbol?"

Epimetheus chewed on his lip. Abruptly, he set his tea on the coffee table and jumped to his feet. Then he rushed out of the room without a word.

Just like a cat.

Zagreus brushed his duster back and perched his hands on his hips. The sounds of papers crinkling and books clapping echoed from the next room.

He didn't have time for this. He should be back at his compound, showing those nymphs just what happened to those who tried to leave him. As it was, he'd left Lykon in charge. And though he'd told the satyr the nymphs were not to be touched in his absence, he knew Lykon's control would snap before long.

However, that girl—the marking—had been too alluring to ignore. And the power he'd felt from her…

He'd made a deal with his father, but this might turn out to be way more lucrative.

He tapped his hand against his thigh. Ran his fingers down the soul patch under his lip. From the direction of the hall, Epimetheus called, "Was the triangle skewed? Upside down? Did it have any other markings through or around it?"

Where the hell was the old fart? "No," he called. "Point up. No other markings, lines or shapes."

Several minutes went by in silence. Zagreus stepped toward the door, wondering if the elder god had gotten a hair up his ass and split.

Epimetheus appeared as if from nowhere and thrust a book into Zagreus's face. "I found it!"

"Holy Hera, old man." Zagreus lurched back. "Don't *do* that."

"Sorry. Sorry." Epimetheus brushed past and set the open book on the coffee table, then pointed at the page. "Like this?"

Zagreus crossed the floor and looked down. The simple triangle was in the center of a page filled with other ordinary geometric shapes. "Yes."

"The triangle has many connotations. In Western society, it represents the Trinity. The Father, Son, and Holy Ghost. It's often drawn to show the number three. It can be linked to time—past, present, and future. To the metaphysical world—spirit, mind and body. Occultists use the triangle as a summoning symbol. It's often contained in a circle in these cases. Point up can also indicate strength and stability. Or the presence of male energy. Point down—"

Zagreus clenched his jaw. "What about in *our* world?"

"Oh, well. In our world, there are many indications for the triangle. But point up"—He flipped the page. Four triangles filled the empty space. Two up, two down. One point-up triangle was empty. The other had a line drawn through it perpendicular to the base—"indicates either water or fire."

Zagreus stepped closer to the book. All four triangles were marked. One for each symbol of the four main elements—earth, air, water, and fire.

A tickle started in his belly, grew with strength and infused him with excitement. "Are you saying what I think you're saying?"

Epimetheus stared over his glasses with a blank expression. "Saying what? Am I saying something?"

Holy shit. The elder god didn't even realize what they'd found. The female was—

A knock sounded. Epimetheus jerked that direction, his beady eyes growing wide. A grin split his face. "More visitors! I don't know what to do with myself!"

Zagreus could think of a thing or two, but he held his tongue. Picking up the book, he studied the symbols and ancient Greek text in the sidebar. "Get rid of them."

Epimetheus waved his arms and shuffled toward the hall. "I'll have to make more tea. Oh, but this is turning out the be quite the morning!"

Zagreus moved through the archway and into the dining room where he wouldn't be seen. Voices echoed from the front of the rustic house. Several. Male. Epimetheus's excitement echoed off the walls.

Dumb shit. Couldn't follow a simple order. Luckily, though, he was harmless. Which was the only reason Zeus let him wander out here in the sticks and didn't bother much with him.

Grinding his teeth, Zagreus looked down at the book. *"Fire is the strongest and most powerful element, but it is also the one with the least endurance. One of the four classic elements, it can be separated into two types— Aidélon (destructive fire), and Aidês (benevolent fire). The most fundamental of all the elements, fire can give rise to the other elements if manipulated correctly."*

The last words echoed in Zagreus's head, followed by the memory of his father's recent visit and the revelation that the balance of power within the world would likely soon change. Was it possible this girl was both Prometheus's daughter *and* fire?

An ambition he'd never had ignited deep inside him. Fuck his parents and what they wanted. Things could change *his* way if he played his cards right.

Footsteps echoed from the other room. Zagreus slid back into the shadows, closed the book, and listened.

"Yes, yes," Epimetheus said, shuffling through the hall. "Come this way. I've made tea."

Voices muttered words Zagreus couldn't make out. He shifted closer to the open door.

"No thanks," a deep voice said. "We're not staying long. We just have a few questions."

"Argonauts." Epimetheus's voice rose with excitement. "This is a treat. It's been quite a morning so far. Quite a morning."

Zagreus shifted so he could see around the corner. Two males stood in the room, towering over Epimetheus, one bigger and taller than the other, with a tree-trunk legs and a menacing look. The second…light brown hair, muscular body… There was something vaguely familiar about the way he held himself.

"What do you know about Odysseus?" the familiar Argonaut asked. "Specifically his time with Calypso."

"The nymph?"

"Yeah."

"Hm." Epimetheus chewed on his lip and lowered himself to the kitchen chair. "Calypso is a Nereid. The daughter of Atlas. She captured Odysseus during his voyage and imprisoned him on her island for seven years. Wanted to make him her eternal husband.

She enchanted him with her singing. Oh, she has a lovely voice. They became lovers." His hand landed on the table, and he looked up. "Penelope threw a tizzy-fit when she found out. It was all the rage in the heavens. Odysseus, he was quite the scoundrel, you know, even before he'd been a soldier in Ithaca."

The Argonauts exchanged frustrated glances. And Zagreus rolled his eyes. *You don't know how much I feel your fucking pain.*

"What do you know about their relationship?" the big Argonaut asked. "Did Calypso *give* Odysseus anything?"

The way he said the word "give" perked Zagreus's ears.

Epimetheus gnawed on the inside of his cheek and furrowed his brow. "A boat. Wine. Bread." He looked up again. "Some say a loom."

"Nothing   else?"   the   familiar   Argonaut   asked. "Nothing…hidden?"

Epimetheus bit his thumb, then looked back down at the surface of the table. "Well, I once heard someone say she gave him knowledge. But it wasn't more than a myth, so I didn't listen very closely."

The Argonauts exchanged looks again, only this time, hope sprang to life in their eyes. Zagreus's gaze narrowed. What the hell were they up to?

The big Argonaut rested his hand on his hip. "Did this person—whomever he was—say how to unlock that knowledge?"

Epimetheus blinked at them. "With a key."

The Argonauts shifted their feet. One raked a hand through his hair. The other blew out a breath. Frustration floated like thick smoke in the air around them.

"Any idea what kind of key?" the familiar Argonaut asked.

"Of course I know what kind of key," Epimetheus responded, his brow wrinkled with irritation. "What do you think I am, a moron?"

No, we know you're a shitacular moron. Zagreus was ready to toss the elder god out the window. Getting anything useful out of him was more painful than pulling pubic hairs.

"The key is the Orb of Krónos."

The Argonauts both looked up sharply. "How?" the big one asked.

"Calypso is my niece," Epimetheus said matter-of-factly. "And Prometheus is my brother. Links, Argonauts. Everything in our world is linked to everything else. In order for Calypso's knowledge to be unlocked from Odysseus's mind, he has to be near the Orb, which in turn must contain or be near all four elements. Unless, of course, one believes in the turnings of fire."

"The turnings of..." The familiar Argonaut shook his head. "Run that by me again?"

"The turnings of fire," Epimetheus repeated. "First into sea, half of the sea into earth, half of the earth into rarified air. The turnings or transmutation of the four elements into one another."

"Wait." The big Argonaut held up his hand. "You're saying one element can be mutated into another?"

"For the sake of the hidden knowledge? Yes. So long as you have fire. Fire is everything, Guardian. Of course, you also need Odysseus, and I'm afraid the hero is long dead."

The Argonauts looked at each other. They didn't seem fazed by that last revelation.

"Thank you," the familiar Argonaut said, turning Epimetheus's way again. "We appreciate your time."

"Wait." Epimetheus rose from his seat. "There's no reason to rush right off. Don't you want some tea? I made it from scratch."

The familiar Argonaut patted Epimetheus on the shoulder as if he were a child, which wasn't far off the mark, since the ass-hat gave up information like one. "No. But thanks. We gotta run. Next time."

Epimetheus walked them both to the door. When Zagreus moved out of the shadows and looked around the corner, he clenched his jaw. The fucker was waving at them as if they were long-lost friends.

"Come back soon," the elder god called. He shut the door, sighed, and walked back toward the kitchen with a shit-eating grin on his wrinkled, old face.

The Argonauts had acted like they knew where Prometheus's daughter might be. Otherwise they wouldn't have been so excited and eager to leave. She'd been with an Argonaut on that cliff beyond the Amazon city. Who, in the human realm, had the Argonauts aligned themselves with?

And then he knew.

"Where's the Misos colony?"

Epimetheus gasped and jumped back a foot as if he didn't realize Zagreus was still there.

Zagreus's jaw tightened. He was done playing games. "Don't give me shit about not knowing. I know you know."

"H-how?"

The darkness inside him—his link to the Underworld—swirled like a hurricane. "You're not as isolated as you think, old man. I know a lot of things." He glanced toward the mantel in the living room and the small wooden box sitting innocently on its surface, then back to the elder god. "Even about your box."

Epimetheus's jaw dropped open, and fear paled his face. Skirting the table, he sidestepped into the living room and grasped the box, then pulled it against his chest in a protective move. "You can't take it. Please don't take it. It's all I have left of her. All that matters in the world. Please, *please.*"

Tears dampened the pathetic god's eyes, and victory welled inside Zagreus. That wasn't all of Epimetheus's wife Pandora that was left, but he'd save that nugget of information for a better time.

He leaned forward, enjoying the panic in Epimetheus's features. "Then tell me exactly where the half-breed colony is located. And don't even think about trying to lie. We both know you're too dumb to pull it off."

Natasa was floating. Her body felt light, cool, refreshed.

She groaned, stretched her arms over her head, and sighed. Something cool pressed against her spine. Something muscular and smooth at the same time. Something that felt so incredibly good, she instinctively wiggled back against it.

She opened her eyes, blinking into the dim light, then looked slowly around.

This wasn't her tent in the Amazon tree city. She was in some kind of fancy room. Intricate moldings framed a darkened window across from her. Heavy velvet curtains hung on each side. She was in a bed, a soft mattress beneath her body, a thin sheet covering her skin. And across her hip, lay a cool, solid weight that sent tingles up and down her torso.

An arm. She looked down. An arm marked in ancient Greek text.

She shifted slowly to her back and looked into Titus's sleeping face. His eyes were closed, his wavy, dark hair falling over his bare, muscular shoulder. His head resting on the same plump, heavenly pillow she'd been sleeping on.

She didn't know where they were, didn't know how they'd gotten here after running from Zagreus's army and jumping into that ocean. But suddenly, she didn't care. She was alive. He was alive. The fever was no longer baking her brain, and the reasons she'd convinced herself she couldn't have him seemed to fade into the background.

Her pulse pounded as she rolled to face him. His arm slid from her belly to her hip. A thrill of tingles rushed through her pelvis.

Heat gathered in her belly and slid between her legs. But this wasn't the same kind of heat that burned and threatened. This was the kind that made her want. Made her crave. Made her think of nothing but him.

She leaned forward, pressing her lips to his. Drew in a breath of his musky scent and shivered. Gods, he felt good. Soft. Warm with life yet cool and invigorating at the same time.

He made a small sound, not a grunt or a moan, but it was enough to encourage her. She kissed him again, shifting closer so her body came into full contact with his. Her lips brushed his mouth again, and gently she slid her tongue along the plump curve of his bottom lip.

The arm across her hip flexed, and his hand flattened at her lower back. A low growl built in his throat, and then he opened to her, drew her tongue into his mouth, and kissed her like he couldn't get enough.

Heat pulsed through her pelvis. He rolled to his back, dragging her on top of him. One hand combed through her hair, gripped the back of her skull, and tipped her head so he could kiss her deeper. The other pressed against the top of her ass, pulling her tighter to him, forcing her legs to open, to straddle his hips. She rubbed against his growing erection.

A tremble rushed through her. She moaned at the taste of him, at the warm wetness of his mouth. Flexed her hips and smiled when he lifted his own and pressed right where she wanted him most.

She was breathless when he pulled back, when he opened his gorgeous hazel eyes, when he looked up with heat and lust and every ounce of need she felt rushing through her. "You're awake."

Her smile returned. She rubbed against him again. Loved the way it caused him to suck in a breath. "You noticed."

His gaze sharpened, searching hers. "How do you feel?"

"Horny."

A slow smile spread across his luscious lips, and he laughed, a sound that was sweeter than anything she'd ever heard. Deep. Rich. Sexy. One that felt even better rumbling from his chest. "I can see that."

She lowered her head and nipped at his square, chiseled jaw. Then brushed her lips across the dark stubble covering his skin as she worked her way toward his ear.

"I meant," he managed, swallowing hard, "how are feeling? Light-headed? Nauseous? Hot?"

She licked his earlobe, drew it into her mouth and suckled. He trembled and tipped his head to the side, offering her more access. "Very hot. But this time just for you."

She kissed the soft skin beneath his ear, kissed her way down his neck, loved how silky soft his hair was against her cheek. Before she could reach the hollow at the base of his throat though, he threaded his other hand into her hair and carefully pulled her away. "Wait."

She shifted her weight back and looked down. Concern darkened his eyes. A concern that caused her heart to bump.

"You've been a little out of it, Tasa. I need to make sure you're okay before we…"

The room was dark, only a sliver of light shone in around the edge of the curtains, but even in dimness she could see the pink tinge to his cheeks. And she loved that he was nervous. That he was worried. That he was thinking of her when he could so easily take everything she was offering without even asking.

Gently, she tugged his arms down to her waist, shifting so she was sitting on his lap. His erection pressed against her sex, and it was all she could do not to grind against it. "I'm fine, Titus. Much better than before. And I'm thinking clearly. Very clearly."

Disbelief swirled in his eyes. He moved his hand from her leg—which she now realized was bare except for a bandage wrapped around her left thigh—to her forehead. Feeling, she knew, for her fever.

"You were so hot."

"Don't you think I'm still hot?"

He smiled again. "Scorching. But I like this heat a whole lot better than the last."

She did too. She leaned forward and touched her lips to his again. "You cool me."

"I know. I just haven't figured out why."

Oh, he had the softest lips. "Mm…"

"I don't want to do anything to hurt you, Tasa," he mumbled against her mouth.

"You can't." Then she realized he might not be worried *just* about her.

She eased back, resting her hands against his muscular chest. A scattering of fine, dark hairs covered his pecs. "What I have isn't contagious—like a virus or anything. It's just…part of me."

"I know."

She stilled. Remembered how he'd told her—on that rock ledge—that he could read minds. "You…know?"

He nodded. "I know about the fire element. And I don't care. I'm not going to let anyone get to you."

Her skin grew hot. Her pulse picked up speed. If he knew about the element, did he also know about the side effects and what would happen if she didn't find Prometheus before it was too late?

He sat up, wrapped his arms around her, and kissed her again. And she realized she needed to push him away, to talk to him about this, but his lips were so soft, his mouth so wet and inviting, she couldn't stop herself from taking another decadent taste.

Her hands landed against his shoulders. She opened to his kiss, her tongue slicking over his, again and again. Between her legs, he grew thick and hard. Her need for him rose to exponential levels.

"Gods." He nipped at her lips. "I was so worried. You scared the shit out of me, baby. Don't do that again."

She swallowed hard. Knew that was inevitable. The dream— seeing him standing in those flames—rushed through her mind, bringing urgency back to the forefront. This conversation was getting too deep. If she told him about the side effects, she'd have to tell him the rest. And she didn't want to do deep… Not right now. Not unless it involved him deep inside her.

She kissed him again. Loved the way he trembled whenever she touched him. Easing away, she grasped the hem of the nightgown, dragged it over her head, then dropped it on the floor beside the bed. "I don't want to talk, Titus. I just want to feel. Make me feel."

His eyes darkened. Lust and need swirled in their hazel depths. His fingers tangled in her hair, and he dragged her mouth back to his. And then he kissed her like no one had ever kissed her before.

Yes, yes. Just this…

Energy coiled beneath her skin. Excitement tightened her stomach. She gasped when his tongue thrust into her mouth, then sighed at the exquisite taste of only him. His other arm tightened around her waist and he lifted her, then moved out from under her body and pushed her back on the mattress.

Tingles rushed all over her skin as his weight settled against hers. She wrapped her arms around his shoulders, opened her legs to the push and pull of his hips, opened her heart to a man she had no business wanting but suddenly couldn't let go.

Tomorrow she'd tell him the rest. Tomorrow she'd figure out what to do next.

CHAPTER TWELVE

Titus pulled back from Natasa's mouth and looked down at her.

His pulse was a roar in his ears, his cock so hard, he was afraid if he moved this would be over long before it started. He thought he'd been dreaming, but now, as his gaze ran over her face, as he took in every freckle, every inch of creamy skin, every tiny imperfection that made her real, he realized he wasn't fantasizing. This was happening. She had started it. And he was the luckiest son of a bitch on the planet.

"You are so beautiful."

A blush rose in her cheeks. Her warm, silky fingers tiptoed down his back until they rested on the waistband at his hips. She fisted the fabric. "Don't talk. Kiss me."

She lifted her mouth to his. He let her draw him into the kiss, let her take the lead and slide her tongue along his. He wanted her to enjoy, wanted her to feel everything. Told himself to be gentle with her. Even if she thought she was fine, he didn't want to rush things.

The memory of how hot she'd been, how close he'd come to losing her, tightened the space around his heart.

She lifted her hips and rubbed against him. Mumbled, "More."

He moved his hand across her bare shoulder, then down her chest until he finally found her breast. Soft skin filled his hand. He rolled her nipple between his thumb and index finger, swallowing the groan from her mouth. Relished the way it echoed deep inside his chest.

Her hand moved to his hair, tangling in the long strands. The fingers of the other worked their way under his waistband and brushed against the dimples on his lower back while he kissed her ear, the pulse point at her throat, while he nibbled his way to her shoulder.

"Titus…that feels so good."

She had no idea. Not a single emotion flowed from her into him. No pain. No memories. Nothing but sweet, blessed warmth that jacked him even higher.

He kissed his way down to her breast and finally brought it to his mouth. His tongue flicked the sensitive nipple. She groaned, arched, pulled his hair until a lick of pain shot across his skull.

Gods, she was so sexy. On fire—in a good way—and *his.*

He'd never wanted anyone to be his, had never wanted the burden or responsibility of a soul mate but now couldn't imagine being without her. He kissed her other breast, laved his tongue over the nipple, and suckled. She scraped her fingernails against his scalp. He worked his way down her stomach, circling his tongue around the soft indent of her belly button and pressing soft kisses to her pale, perfect skin.

Her scent excited him. Aroused him. His cock throbbed as he pushed her legs wide, as he slid lower. He eased back to look down at her in the dim light.

"Oh, *ligos Vesuvius.*"

She was wet and swollen and hot. He parted her with his fingers and breathed against her mound. She planted her feet against the mattress, grasped the sheet with both hands at her hips, threw her head back, and groaned.

Mine, mine, mine… The words roared in his head. He was a man possessed, and he didn't even care. Lowering his head, he licked her center. Then swallowed the sweet, tart, sexy taste of her on his tongue.

"Oh, gods, Titus…" She lifted her hips, fisted the sheet, and pressed against him. "More."

He licked her again, loving every groan and mewling sound she made. He glanced up her body, watched her closed eyes tighten, watched pleasure slide over her features.

All mine…

He wanted her panting. Wanted her as desperate for him as he was for her. He flicked his tongue against her clit again and again, ran his finger down her sex, found her opening, and pressed inside. Every muscle in her body tightened. He stroked deeper. Flicked faster. Suckled.

Fire filled in his mouth, his heart, his soul. She screamed out her release and quaked beneath him. Finally collapsing against the mattress in a sweaty, sexy lump.

Victory pulsed in his veins. He brought her down gently, kissing her inner thigh, her hip, brushing his lips against her lower belly. She was drenched from his mouth, from her climax. His cock ached to be inside her, but he didn't want to hurt her. He pressed his mouth against the curve of her breast and rested his forehead against her chest. Bracing his hands on the mattress, he breathed deep to calm his raging urge.

Her fingers slid into his hair. Stilled. "What's wrong?"

What's wrong? He laughed, then groaned because the friction made his dick that much harder. "Nothing. Everything's finally *right.*"

"Not right," she whispered. "Not yet anyway."

She flipped him to his back. His eyes flew wide, not just at her strength but at her determination. She stripped his pants, climbed over his hips, grasped his cock in the tight grip of her hand, then lined herself up and lowered, taking him deep with the very first touch.

Holy…*gods*…

Sensations bombarded him from every side. Her slick, tight channel clenching around him. Her soft, silky skin cradling his hips and thighs. The press of her palms against his chest and the weight of her body lifting, lowering, taking him deep again and again.

He grasped her hips, rising to meet her downward stroke. Searched her eyes for any sign of discomfort. But he only saw power and need and fire. A blazing inferno that consumed him and filled that place inside that had been empty for so long.

He sat up, wrapped his arms around her, pulled her tight, and captured her mouth as she rode. She groaned. Opened. Kissed him so deeply.

This was better than anything he'd ever felt. Better than all those years alone. Better than worrying about a world he couldn't change and always doing what someone else wanted him to do.

"Come with me, Tasa."

"Yes." She rode faster. Her fingers slid into his hair; her palms radiated heat against his scalp. Her body claimed his. "*Yes…*"

His climax burst through him like a volcano erupting in a plume of heat and light and combustible energy. He felt her tighten around him, heard her cry out her own release. Knew in those moments something inside him had just blown wide open too.

And somehow also knew, in the connection he shared with her, that turning away from the Argonauts, choosing her over everything else, might very well lead him to a place he couldn't return from.

Isadora sipped the cup of tea that wasn't doing much to calm her frayed edges and looked out the window at the sparkling view of Tiyrns.

The hour was early—dawn shone over the buildings and spires of the city—and though she was tired, she hadn't slept more than an hour or so the night before. She leaned back against the wall in the window seat, pulled her knees up as far as she could, and winced when the babe inside her kicked hard, telling her he didn't appreciate being squished.

"Okay, okay," she muttered, stretching out her legs again on the soft seat cushion. "I get it. You're already like your father. Demanding and irritatingly stubborn."

A door clicked open somewhere close. She looked up, then smiled when her sister, Casey, peeked around the corner of Isadora's bedroom suite. "You're up earlier than I expected. No luck sleeping?"

Isadora frowned and smoothed a hand down the t-shirt stretched tight over her belly. "None. This kid already doesn't like me. I thought that wasn't supposed to happen for several years."

One corner of Casey's lips curled. Silky purple pajamas with wide cuffs at the wrists and ankles covered her slim body. "I wouldn't know. But if memory serves, my grandmother said I was a handful from the time I was in diapers. Maybe it runs in the family."

"There's a comforting thought. Where's Theron? Isn't he going to miss you at this hour?"

"He was tossing and turning last night. I kicked him out of bed because he was keeping me up." Casey tucked a lock of dark brown hair behind her ear. "I think he's still in his office with Zander, discussing 'strategy.'"

That so-called "strategy" would be finding Titus. Isadora knew Theron wouldn't sleep until each of his guardians was accounted for. He worried over them like children, which was an ironic thought coming from her. At one time she'd been more afraid of Theron than she had been of her father.

She nearly laughed at that realization. Her life had been so easy back then. Now she had an entire kingdom to worry about. And a husband she hadn't heard from since the scene in the courtyard with Nick.

Casey sat at the end of the window seat, tucked her legs up under her, and held out her hands. "Let me feel."

Sighing, Isadora moved her hand back, and Casey rested both palms on her stomach. The baby kicked out again, right under her fingers, then managed what felt like a double backflip.

Isadora winced and shifted. The kid was going to crack one of her ribs if he wasn't careful. Oh, he definitely had Argonaut genes.

A wide smile broke across Casey's lips. "That is so cool." She moved her hands out slightly and down an inch, feeling for the little bugger. But before Isadora could tell her it didn't *feel* cool, her eyes widened, and her gaze shot to Isadora's. "Oh my God."

The shock on Casey's face put Isadora on instant defense. She placed a protective hand over her belly. "What? What's wrong?"

Casey pulled her hands back, but the wonder and joy were both gone. Worry lingered in her violet eyes. "Why didn't you say anything? It's been hours."

Casey had the gift of hindsight. Which meant by touching Isadora, she'd just seen what had happened in the courtyard.

Isadora's mood slid right back into the depressing depths it had been in earlier. "What is there to tell? It happened. It wasn't my fault. It's not going to happen again."

"But Demetrius…"

"Demetrius is an idiot if he thinks there's anything going on between me and Nick." But even as she said the words, worry rippled beneath her ribs. "And before you ask, no, I don't know where he is. Between the celebration and dealing with the Council, I didn't get a chance to talk to him after. And when I went looking for him, Phineus told me he'd left with Orpheus to track down a lead about Titus."

"Men," Casey muttered.

Isadora pushed off the bench seat because she couldn't sit still any longer, struggling only slightly at the shift in her center of gravity. Casey reached for her, but she moved out of her sister's grasp and fixed her pajama bottoms. Two more months...

"Do you want Theron to call him back? Demetrius is wearing his Argos medallion."

Anger pushed aside the worry. Isadora paced the small living area of her suite, her bare toes—which she couldn't even see any more beneath the swell of her belly—sinking into the plush white carpet. "No, I don't want that. If Demetrius can't get it in his thick skull that I'm with him because I want to be, then he can just stew in his stupidity."

Pity crept over Casey's features. "Maybe it's a good thing he's not here right now."

Isadora scowled her sister's way, then immediately regretted her aggravation. She was getting worked up over something that wasn't even real, but she knew how Demetrius thought. Knew, even after their binding ceremony and everything they'd been through, that he still didn't believe he deserved her. Didn't believe he was worthy. Didn't believe she could love *him*. When was he going to get it?

"*Ilithios*," she muttered.

The babe in her belly kicked out several times, as if he agreed, and Isadora rubbed a hand over the growing bulge to soothe the kid. Even their baby got it, dammit.

A knock sounded at the outer door. Isadora said, "Come in," without bothering to ask who was there.

Her other sister, Callia, moved into the room. Disheveled auburn hair hung to Callia's shoulders, and her light blue cotton pajamas were rolled up on one leg as if they'd been twisted in sleep. But it was the look of distress that showed clearly in her eyes that forced Isadora to take a breath and calm her temper. "I felt something. Is everyone okay?"

As they were all three connected through their link to the ancient goddesses, the Horae, they could each feel when one was in trouble. Or frustrated, as was the case now. Casey crossed one leg over the other, looked toward Isadora, and shrugged. "Okay is a relative term at the moment."

Callia's worried gaze darted to Isadora. "What does that mean?"

Isadora sighed again. "It means some men in this family have no brain. Or refuse to use the tiny one they were born with."

Relief spread over Callia's pretty face. "Oh, just that? Their brains tend to run due south more often than not."

Casey laughed.

Isadora rolled her eyes. She wished that was what this was about. The fact Demetrius hadn't touched her like that in weeks was another reason she was nearing the edge of her sanity. Every time she made a move, he wiggled out of her grasp, muttering something about not wanting to hurt the baby.

At least he was calling it a baby now and not a thing. That was an improvement, right?

Callia rested her hands on Isadora's belly the same way Casey had, but because Callia's gift was a healing one, not vision centered, she only smiled. "Baby seems good. Pulse is a little high, but nothing to worry about." Her gaze lifted to Isadora's. "What did Demetrius do this time?"

"The question is what didn't he do?" Casey said.

When Callia glanced her way in question, Casey relayed what she'd seen in the vision. And when she was done, Callia's gaze snapped back to Isadora. "What are you going to do?"

"What can I do?" That anger and frustration she'd worked hard to tamp down came steamrolling back. "If he wants to brood, I can't stop him. And I've got other things to worry about right now, like where the hell Titus is and what this Natasa person was doing in our realm."

"Cerek and Phineus were able to get the portal working again." Casey swung her foot and pursed her lips. "But there was no location logged in the data stream. And Theron told me earlier that Skyla wasn't having much luck with Titus's computer. Though this is of interest… She was able to figure out that he's been searching satellite images of Maelea's house on Vancouver Island and the forests outside the colony since they brought Gryphon home."

"Searching for what?" Callia asked.

"Not what," Casey answered. "Who. Skyla thinks he's been looking for Natasa. They met at the colony."

"I know." Callia lowered herself to the window seat next to Casey. "I was there."

Her sister was lost in thought. About what, Isadora didn't know. She'd been in the room too when Titus had brought Natasa to see Nick, but she didn't remember anything weird happening then. Or Titus's reaction to the redhead, for that matter. Then again, she'd been distracted at the time.

She sighed and resumed pacing. "So we're no closer to learning anything."

"Maybe not, but…" Casey bit into her bottom lip.

"But what?"

Casey looked up. "I wasn't going to bring this up, but I overheard a conversation Theron was having with one of the guys via com unit."

"About what?" Callia asked, tuning back into the conversation.

"I guess when Orpheus and Demetrius left here, they went to see Delia."

"The witch?" Isadora asked in shock. "Demetrius went to the coven?"

He'd gone without her. That hurt almost as much as the fact he hadn't tried to talk to her after the party. She'd supported him through so much, was the one who'd encouraged him to embrace his heritage. The fact he could so easily push her aside sent her temper through the roof.

Casey nodded. "I couldn't make out much, just Theron's side of things, but he mentioned something about an unquenchable fire."

Everything inside Isadora stilled. Even the baby slowed its frantic ballroom-dancing jig. An icy chill spread down her spine. "Say that again. Are you sure he said unquenchable fire? Those exact words?"

"Yes." Casey's brow furrowed. "Why?"

Isadora reached for the arm of a nearby chair and lowered herself into the seat. "Oh my gods."

Callia pushed to her feet. "Isadora? Are you okay?"

Isadora held out a hand to keep her back. "I'm fine. It's not me or the baby. It's…" She dropped her hand and looked at her sisters. "Unquenchable fire. Some call it Armageddon, others the Apocalypse. Whatever the term, it's a reference to the end of days. A fiery inferno that's supposed to spread all across the entire human realm and destroy every living thing in its path."

Casey and Callia exchanged *holy skata* glances. Quietly, Callia said, "How do you know about this?"

"When I was in school, studying to rule just in case our father was never able to produce a male heir, it was covered in the ancient texts. Prometheus, as you know, is the one who gave fire to humans. But he was worried Zeus and the other gods would one day lay claim to what shouldn't belong to them. It is written that should that day ever come, he would rather see the end of all things than the human realm in the hands of the gods."

"What are you saying?" Callia asked. "That Prometheus is planning to destroy the earth? How could he even do that? He's still imprisoned by Zeus."

"He could if he planned this long ago," Casey said quietly. "He's the father of forethought. Who's to say he didn't put a time limit on things. If the Orb wasn't found by a certain date, if its pieces weren't uncovered by a specific time... He could have even put conditions on power shifts within the heavens. These are gods we're talking about, not humans or Misos or Argoleans who live in a finite universe."

Shit. That made a lot of sense. Isadora's pulse picked up speed.

Silence settled over the room. Then Callia said, "If that's what this is... If the guys have found evidence it's coming..."

"Then Titus isn't the only one in danger." Isadora's thoughts skipped to the hundreds of colonists at the Misos Colony. And to Nick. Though she was still pissed at him for what he'd done, she didn't want him harmed. And she'd never forgive herself if she didn't do something—anything—to save the people her father had forsaken.

She pushed to her feet.

"Where are you going?" Casey rose too.

"To get dressed. Someone has to find Titus before it's too late. Our heroes aren't getting the job done."

"No." Callia's eyes widened with understanding. "It's too risky this late in your pregnancy."

Through their link with the Horae, and with the help of the Orb, the sisters were able to see into the present. They'd used that gift once, and it had worked, but there had been repercussions.

"What other choice do we have?" Isadora asked. "Maelea said she sensed great power within Natasa. Stronger than any god. I'm not going to sit back and do nothing when we can harness our gifts together and find Titus. The Argonauts aren't making any progress. They're only wasting time. And contrary to what you both think, I'm not a piece of glass. I'm stronger than I look."

Casey pursed her lips, then looked to Callia. "She does have a point."

Callia frowned. "Don't do that. You're supposed to back me up." Then to Isadora, "Look, even if I wasn't worried about the effects on the baby—which I am—I'm more worried about you. I know you're strong and tough, but you've been through so much. And you're the only heir to the throne we have. Casey and I can't rule. The Council will never recognize Max. If we lose you, the Council wins. And Zander, Theron—all of the guys, especially Demetrius—will be pissed if we take the chance."

"Leave the Argonauts to me." Confidence swelled inside Isadora. A confidence she was growing more accustomed to with every passing day. If nothing else, her father had taught her how *not* to rule. "This is a matter of life and death. Some things are bigger than one person."

When Callia frowned, Isadora softened her expression and added, "If I feel a twinge of *anything*, I'll pull away. I promise."

Casey pushed to her feet. "Promising and doing are two very different things."

Isadora knew that better than anyone. She lived with it every day.

She pushed aside thoughts of her mate, squared her shoulders, and glanced between her sisters. "As queen, I promised to protect my people. And those people include the Misos. No matter what, I'm not about to fail them. Now hold out your hands. It's time we stop letting the men screw everything up and find that Argonaut once and for all."

Natasa's pulse raced as she rested her head against Titus's shoulder and fought to slow her breaths.

Sweat slicked her skin, and his arms held her tight, but for once she didn't feel claustrophobic. There was no heat. Just cool, tingling sensations that reverberated all through her veins, into her limbs, even down her fingers.

"I…" His voice echoed against her ear. "Wow."

A smile spread across her lips. Wow for her too. She could still feel him inside her, softening slightly but still *there*. Still long and thick and gloriously naked. "I'll take that as a compliment."

He chuckled, and the sound resonated from his chest into hers. Felt so damn good. "Next time I promise to do all the work."

"How soon can there be a next time?"

He stilled beneath her, and she felt something—a shift in him somehow. Confused, she pushed up on one hand and looked down.

His hair was mussed, his features relaxed, but there was something in his eyes. A doubt. A worry. A fear that hadn't lingered there before.

She rolled off him, tugging the sheet up over her body. Nerves ignited in her stomach, reminding her they might have this incredible chemistry, but there was an ocean of things between them they needed to discuss.

"How did I get here?" she asked, figuring starting with easy was the best bet all around. "And where is here? I have a vague recollection of a hospital room, but this doesn't look like the same place."

"We're at the Misos Colony. I called Nick, their leader, and asked him to pick us up."

"The colony?" She tensed. "Does anyone else…?"

"No." He smoothed his hand down her arm. "No one else knows we're here and Nick promised to keep his mouth shut."

"Oh." She relaxed back into him and stared up at the ceiling's intricately carved wood beams. "And this room?"

"We moved you here after your temperature cooled. Thought you'd be more comfortable. Well—" a smile curled through his words "—I think Lena and the other clinic staff though we'd both be more comfortable. We didn't fit well in that single bed together."

She was comfortable with him. Very. The memory of him pressing deep inside made her hot all over again. She bit her lip.

He rolled to his side, facing her, and chuckled. "I might not be able to feel your emotions but I can definitely feel your body temperature heating up. Give me a minute to recover, okay? I may be a hero, but you have a tendency to overwhelm me."

She smiled, the tension inside her easing. She closed her hands over his forearm lying against her belly. "I suppose since you haven't had sex in a hundred years, I could cut you some slack."

"Oh, I have sex."

Her fingers stilled against the Argonaut markings on his arms. "You do?"

"Yeah. Why? Does that surprise you?"

"No. I just thought… Well, you said you couldn't touch anyone." *Except for me.* "That it had been a hundred years."

"I haven't. But I'm not celibate. A guy has needs."

She froze beneath him. Didn't know what to say.

"Ask me, *ligos Vesuvius.*"

She looked his way and narrowed her eyes. "Are you reading my mind?"

"No." He smiled. "But you're getting hot again, and I can tell this time it's not from arousal."

He was right. She was heating up. She hated that her emotions were so closely tied to that damn element inside her.

"I just…I saw the way you reacted when the Amazons touched you. You were in pain. How do you…you know…deal with that and keep it…hard…enough….to have sex with other"—*shit*—"people?"

His cheeks turned the slightest shade of pink. "It's a complicated process of clothing and condoms and making sure they don't physically touch me."

"They who?"

He glanced away, and his cheeks grew pinker. He was embarrassed. The knowledge sent an odd thrill through her. "There are a couple regular females back in Argolea who know what I like."

That thrill turned to a quick shot of dislike. Had *she* done what he liked? She didn't know. Suddenly, she wanted to know a whole lot more. And who these females were who were throwing themselves at him. "And what is it you like?"

His arm tightened around her waist, and he nuzzled her ear. "I like being inside you. Naked. Feeling every part of you. Gods, your whole body melts like liquid fire when you come."

He was being cute. And sexy. And he was damn good at both. But she suddenly couldn't stop thinking of him with those "regular" females.

She literally felt her temperature rising. It was stupid to get so worked up. She hadn't known him before a few days ago, and back when he was fucking these other females, she'd been frozen anyway.

"Tasa." He lifted his hand from her belly, used his index finger to tip her face his way, and forced her to look at him. "They can't touch. That's the rule. And usually they're restrained because I don't trust them. They agree to it not because of me, but because of the bragging rights for sleeping with an Argonaut. I hate it. It's clinical at best. But it's the only thing I've found that works. I wasn't built to be celibate."

She could feel that. He was still semi-hard against her thigh, even in the middle of this fucked-up conversation. He was obviously built for pleasure and release. And though her anger had subsided, the thought of him giving that pleasure to someone else burned a path of fire straight to her gut.

"I'm sorry." She looked down at his lips. Couldn't meet his eyes. "I told you before I'm..." *Emotionally volatile. A raving lunatic. Pathetically jealous.* "...unstable."

His luscious lips curled. "And I told you I am too." He kissed the corner of her mouth. "Being with you... It's not even a comparison. Just thinking about the sounds you made, the way you climaxed... The way you felt coming around me... *Skata*, it's making me even harder, right now. Can't you feel that?"

She smiled because she *could* feel it. And because this conversation was off-the-charts *insane*. Burning with embarrassment, she wrapped her arms around his neck and pulled him close.

He kissed her throat and breathed cool against her skin. "You've ruined me for anyone else, you know. There's no way I'll be able to go back to that after this."

The thought eased the sting. Made her sex clench. But then she realized what it meant. And guilt slithered in. Guilt for making such a big deal over something that—in a few weeks—wouldn't even matter anymore.

If she were normal, if she had any kind of future, he'd be the sort of guy she'd want to spend it with.

She couldn't tell him what his words meant to her. But she could give him something he'd been waiting for.

"Titus, the element inside me... It's getting hotter. I went to Argolea in the hopes maybe Maelea could tell me where Zeus chained Prometheus. He's the only one who knows how to stop it. He gave it to me. He's...my father."

He pushed up on his arm and stared down at her. "Your father? But how…?" His gaze raked her features. "That makes you like…four thousand years old."

"Technically, yes." She rested her hands against his shoulders, loving the way his muscles flexed beneath her fingers. "But chronologically I'm only twenty-nine. I was trapped in a frozen state for over three thousand years."

His brow wrinkled. She could see he was working through the probability of that. "Run that by me again."

She pushed against his shoulders and leaned back in the pillows. Explaining all this when his touch was a teasing chill she liked too much made it hard to focus. "My mother was a nymph who was seduced by Zeus. They had a love affair, but when Hera found out, she flipped. To protect my mother, Zeus turned her into a…well, a cow. People say a beautiful white heifer, but really, she was a cow. I think he did it because he's an ass. I mean, he could have picked anything, but a cow?" She shook her head, pulled her knees up, and wrapped her arms around them. "Hera was so pissed he'd tried to protect her, she banished my mother from Greece and cursed her to wander the wilds as a beast."

He didn't say anything, just leaned on his elbow and stared up at her, dumfounded. Okay, springing the Prometheus card on him probably hadn't been the smartest thing for her to do, but now that it was out there, she couldn't take it back. And part of her didn't want to.

"Zeus did nothing to stop Hera, and my mother had no choice but to leave the only home she'd ever known. She wandered for years. What Zeus didn't plan for though was that during that wandering, she'd accidentally come across Prometheus, whom he'd already imprisoned. I guess she felt bad for the elder god—they were basically in the same kind of prison but with different walls, both exiled and alone. Whatever she said must have resonated with Prometheus, because though he was still chained, he retained the power to ease at least part of her suffering. He changed her back into a woman."

Titus slowly sat up. "I know this story. Io. The nymph who was turned into a cow was Io. You're Io's daughter?"

Natasa swallowed hard. The sheet fell against his waist. Light from the edge of the curtains glinted off his strong, solid chest. Faintly she wondered what time it was—what day—but the shock and awe alive in his features kept her from asking. "Being the father of foresight, Prometheus has the gift to see into the future. He also told my mother that one day she'd reach Egypt, and there, far from Hera's sight, Zeus would eventually break the wandering curse. To thank him for the hope she'd given him, my mother, uh, eased his...um, suffering."

"Hold on." Titus held up a hand. "While Prometheus was chained to a rock, your mother..."

Fucked him blind?

Natasa's cheeks burned. "Ah...yeah. She, um, relieved him...as much as she could while he was bound. I was the result."

Titus chuckled. "Gives new meaning to the title of that ancient Greek play, *Prometheus Bound.*"

He was cracking jokes. A little of her embarrassment ebbed. "I guess you could say that."

She swallowed. "My mother eventually reached Egypt, and Zeus did rid her of Hera's curse. And there she married an Egyptian king—Telegonus—my stepfather. But when Zeus found out what had transpired between Prometheus and my mother, he came looking for me."

"Wait. I know this one too. Prometheus foresaw that a descendent of Io's would lead to the downfall of Zeus."

She nodded again. He didn't look shocked anymore. Just...interested. And that calmed her anxiety. "I was in my late twenties by then. I had only recently been told about Prometheus. When Zeus appeared in the form of a dove, I wasn't afraid. I mean, doves aren't scary, right? It was only after—after he took me away from my home—that I realized why."

"So he froze you in some kind of perfect state for more than three thousand years? Why didn't he just kill you?"

"Because by killing me, he'd also kill the fire element. And he knew he'd one day need it."

"How did you get away?"

"I have no memories of that time. It was like being in a coma. One day you fall asleep, the next you wake up and years have gone by. Only in my case, it was thousands of years. I don't know what changed, but for some reason, I came awake. I was in a cave high in the mountains of Greece. I didn't wait around to see who—if anyone—had saved me. I got as far from there as I could. Then, after I'd adjusted to the changes in the world—which I'm still not totally accustomed to yet—I went looking for my father."

"To fulfill your destiny," he said quietly.

His eyes were so intense, his gaze so focused on her face, her heart bumped again. "No," she whispered. "I'm no hero, Titus. I'm not looking for Prometheus for any reason other than to find out how to stop the fire inside from consuming me."

"Destiny's a fickle thing to play with."

"I wouldn't know. At the moment, I'm just trying to make it from one day to the next."

"That's why you were with the Amazons, isn't it? Because you were hiding from Zeus."

She drew in a breath, then slowly blew it out again. "Yes. The Amazons don't have any particular love for the gods. Though Aella and her warriors have their own issues, they were more than happy to help me so long as I helped them."

"What were you going to do for them?"

"Find a way to stop Zagreus from bugging their tribe."

"That didn't work out so well."

No, it hadn't. And a sliver of guilt whipped through her when she thought of what had happened at the Amazon city. Though she was pretty sure Zagreus being there was not her fault. "I wasn't trying to hurt anyone. That guard in your realm...I didn't even know I could do that."

"I know."

His utter faith in her shook her to her core. No one else had ever believed in her. Why him? And why now? She stared into his hazel eyes. And saw that flash of worry again.

He was holding something back. Her pulse picked up speed. Her skin grew hot all over. She searched his eyes for answers.

He was a smart guy, the descendent of Odysseus. Even if he wasn't willing to admit it, he already knew what would happen if the fire consumed her first.

Her heart clenched. "You should get as far from me as possible," she whispered. "I don't want to hurt you."

He reached across her body, hooked a hand over her hip, and tugged her beneath him, until her body was flush against his. "You said that before and I didn't listen. I'm not listening now."

She pressed her hands against his chest and tried to push him away. "Titus—"

"Stop."

She stilled beneath him.

His eyes were intense as ever. His stare, unwavering. And gazing up at him, her heart took a hard, painful tumble. "I told you you're not getting rid of me, and I meant it." He brushed a curl away from her temple. His voice gentled. "We'll figure this out. We've still got time. I'm not letting you go, Natasa. Understand? You're mine now."

His...

He bent his head, brushed his mouth over hers, and kissed her gently. Deeply. And her entire body responded. Not just to the kiss, but to him. To what he was willing to do for her. To his steadfast vow to protect her.

She knew it was wrong. She knew it was selfish. But she didn't want to give him up either. Wrapping her arms around his neck, she pulled him close and arched against his strong, muscular body.

No one had ever wanted to help her before. She hadn't even considered that someone like Titus could be out there. She hadn't thought to wait for him. But maybe there really was a chance they could do this. Maybe he could help her find her father and get rid of this blasted element.

And maybe...just maybe...she wouldn't have to go through with the deal she'd made with Poseidon after all.

CHAPTER THIRTEEN

Demetrius flashed into the courtyard of the Argolean castle. Memories of seeing Nick and Isadora here the day before bombarded him, but he pushed them aside. Right now he needed to get to Theron.

"Hold up, D," Orpheus muttered at his back.

He ignored Orpheus and headed into to the castle. At this hour—nearly six a.m.—the castle was quiet. Guards glanced their way in the main foyer but barely paid them any attention. He headed for Theron's office.

Light spilled through the doorway into the darkened corridor. Voices echoed from inside. Theron's and Zander's.

He stepped into the room. Z and Theron were studying what looked like a map on a virtual screen near Theron's desk. Both looked his way when his boot steps quieted.

"Well?" Theron asked. His gaze flicked from Demetrius to Orpheus at his back. "Anything?"

"More than you may want to know," Orpheus muttered, stepping around Demetrius. "We just had ourselves a nice little chat with Epimetheus."

"The Titan?" Zander asked. "How in Hades did you end up there? I thought you went to see about a witch."

Demetrius moved into the room and told them about their visit with Delia and how that had led them to the elder god. When he was done, Zander's shocked expression said it all.

"*Skata*," he muttered. "And I thought Krónos was the one we had to look out for."

"So did we. 'Things are going well for you?'" Orpheus mocked in his best Zeus impersonation. "'Here, bend over and I'll fuck you in the ass a few times to liven things up.'"

Theron ignored his sarcasm. "We need to get to Titus and stop Natasa before its too late." Urgency formed deep lines in his forehead. He looked back at the map. "Based on what little we were able to get from the portal's records, we've narrowed it down to the western half of the US. Cerek and Phin are searching this area here—"

"Dad?"

The voice of Zander's eleven-year-old drew their attention. Zander's brow wrinkled with concern. "What are you doing up this early, son?"

Max rubbed his left eye. Blond hair stuck out all over his head, and his pajamas hung off his slim frame, looking two sizes too big. But the Argonaut markings visible on his hands proved he'd soon grow into his lineage. And since he was Zander's son, and a descendent of Achilles, he'd grow into it well. "I couldn't sleep. I went to see Mom, but she's not in bed. I thought maybe she was with Aunt Isadora, you know, because of the baby and stuff, but she isn't in her room either."

A shot of unease echoed through Demetrius. Theron turned toward Zander. "Go find out if everything's okay. D?"

Demetrius looked over. "Yeah?"

"Go with him."

His heart pounded hard in his chest. He should. But so much else hung on finding Titus. He knew Isadora wasn't in danger—because of the soul mate connection, he'd feel it if she was. Right now, he'd be far more help to her by finding Titus than on dealing with what had happened between them earlier. "No. I'm sure everything's fine."

Liar.

He pushed down the thought before it could run away from him and stepped toward the desk. Zander and Max left, and Orpheus moved up to the table. Demetrius tried to stay focused while Theron ran through what he and Zander had figured out while they'd been gone. Contacts on the west coast had reported a fire burning in the redwoods and an Amazon tribe completely decimated. Though there was no official confirmation, Theron obviously thought Titus and Natasa were somehow involved.

Footsteps echoed from the hall. Demetrius turned when Zander poked his head back under the doorway. And the anger that flashed in his blazing silver eyes put Demetrius on instant alert.

"What's wrong?" Theron asked.

"Ask her." Zander tugged Casey into the room behind him. Max shuffled in after them, eyes wide and, this time, very alert.

"All right, all right," Casey said, jerking her arm from Zander's grasp. "You don't have to get so bent out of shape."

"Acacia?" Theron's eyes hardened. He stepped away from the desk and pinned Zander with a look. "What the hell's wrong with you?"

Casey moved between her mate and Zander and placed a hand on Theron's chest. "It's okay. I'm fine. Don't get mad at Zander. I expected you'd all find out sooner rather than later."

Theron's confused gaze snapped to her face. "Find out what? What's going on?"

She pursed her lips and looked down at the floor.

"*Meli?*" Theron prodded.

"Okay. Promise not to get mad."

Everything inside Demetrius went cold.

"Tell us what's happened," Theron said, trying for patience with his soul mate but not quite getting there.

"Well…" Casey wrung her hands together. "I couldn't sleep. And I had this feeling that Isadora couldn't either. So…I went to see her."

Panic spread through Demetrius. "Where is Isadora?"

Casey's worried gaze skipped from one face to another, then finally settled on Demetrius. "At the colony. With Callia. We pooled our gifts to find Titus. He's there. With Natasa. Isadora went to talk to them and find out what's going on. And…"

His heart nearly stopped. She'd gone to the human realm. Without him. Without any kind of security. To face someone who could quite possibly be working with Hades. The god who still held a contract on her soul.

The darkness inside that Demetrius fought to keep down bubbled to the surface. His voice turned to ice in his throat. "And what?"

Casey sighed. "And to see Nick. "

* * *

Nick scrubbed a hand over the prickly hair on the top of his head. He needed to shave his damn scalp again. Thing grew like a weed. "Okay, let's seal off that tunnel. I don't want anyone else getting hurt in there."

Kellen rolled up the map detailing the tunnels beneath the colony. "Will do."

He turned away from Nick, signaled to the other men he'd brought with him, and headed for the far end of the cavern. Lantern light shimmered off rock walls and stalactites hanging from the ceiling. Water dripped somewhere close, and a chill spread straight down Nick's spine as he watched them go. From the castle entrance, numerous tunnels fanned out under the high mountain lake. They were meant to disorient any who ventured too close to the colony. But they weren't all stable, and this was the second tunnel collapse they'd had in the last month. Thankfully, this time, only a sentry running patrol had been caught in the falling debris, and his injuries were minor. Next time, they might not be so lucky.

"I expected you to hide from me. I didn't expect it to be way down here."

Nick's stomach lurched into his throat when he recognized the voice. Slowly, he turned and looked toward the silhouette behind him. And the female he'd been dreaming about and cursing this whole last day.

Isadora perched her fisted hands on her hips. She wore loose gray pants and a tight–fitting black shirt that accentuated her breasts and the swell of her belly. But even in the dim light he could see the glow of her blonde hair, the tilt of her jaw, and the fire in her eyes that he both hated and admired. "What are you doing here?"

"You have one of my Argonauts. I want to see him."

She'd come because of Titus. Not because of him. He should have expected as much and yet…disappointment dropped like a stone weight into his belly. He shifted his feet on the uneven rock floor and hooked a thumb through his belt loop. "Can't keep track of your heroes, huh? As I recall, you lost the last one as well. Effective leadership there, princess."

"And I see being an asshole runs in the family. Where's Titus?"

She must have had an argument with his brother. Demetrius never would have let her come here alone. A small thrill rushed through him. "Ask me nice and maybe I'll tell you."

Her eyes flared, and she stepped forward. "I'm done playing nice with you, Nick. Some things are more important than your petty problems."

He leaned close. So close he could smell her sweet scent. "You're my problem, princess. You always have been."

Her eyes softened, just a touch. Just enough to tell him she pitied him. "I know. And I'm sorry. But you're going to have to suck it up and deal with it, just like I am. Your people are in trouble, Nick. Big trouble."

His people. He was sick and tired of *his* people. Of serving them. Of leading them. Of making all the tough decisions like what the hell to do with the damn tunnel that had caved in. What he wanted was to let someone else deal with the shit. And to take what was standing right in front of him.

"Regardless of how pissed I am over what you did," she went on, "I don't want anything to happen to you. I care about you. You're family."

Family. As in, the blacklisted, good-for-nothing brother-in-law. Not the man she loved.

And yet...she was here. Of her own free will. On his turf. Maybe he could still convince her this was where she was supposed to be.

He reached for her elbow, closed his fingers over the delicate bones, and tugged. Anger and arousal swirled in his stomach and fired through each of his veins. A tiny voice in his head screamed *don't do this again*, but he ignored it. Just as he had the last time. "Why don't you show me just how much you care, princess?"

A tiny gasp escaped her lips. Her body brushed against his, the swell of her belly preventing him from feeling all of her like he wanted. He tipped his head and leaned down to kiss her.

Her fist met his stomach. And the force of the blow doubled him over with a grunt.

"I told you not to touch me like that again." Isadora's angry voice met his ears. "I wasn't kidding."

Nick wrapped a hand around his middle, rubbing at the sore spot. He was more shocked than hurt. But for a girl—for a pregnant girl—she hit pretty hard. Demetrius had obviously taught her something. "You came to me, princess. Don't forget that."

"Trust me. I won't. And I won't be so quick to do so again."

"You will. You and drama seem to go hand in hand. I think you like stirring the shit. In fact, I'm pretty sure that's the whole reason you're here now. Not to warn me about any so-called trouble, but because you just can't stand not being the center of attention."

Her face paled. "That's a terrible thing to say."

He huffed and pushed aside the guilt that tried to creep in. "No, terrible is you throwing yourself at me, then playing hard to get. Tell me, does your shitty husband know you're such a cock tease?"

Footsteps pounded the rock floor, and before Nick could look past Isadora to see where they were coming from, a fist slammed into his jaw, knocking him off his feet.

Isadora shrieked. Nick stumbled backward and knocked into a stalagmite. Rock and debris broke loose from the tip, crumbling to the cave floor at his feet. Hands grasped the front of his shirt and hauled him around, slamming him against the cave wall.

"Demetrius! Stop!"

"You son of a bitch," Demetrius growled, ignoring Isadora. "I was going to give her to you, you bastard. But not now."

A gasp echoed through the cave, but all Nick could focus on was his brother's enraged eyes. They were roughly the same weight, but Demetrius had him by at least an inch, though at the moment, Nick didn't give a fuck. The coppery tang of blood slid across his tongue. And with that darkness roaring in his veins, urging him on, one corner of his mouth twisted in a sneer.

This was better than kissing Isadora. Or tormenting her. This was the bloodletting he'd been hoping for for months.

"Even you don't want her?" Nick grunted. "Yeah, she's turned out to be a real catch, hasn't she?"

Demetrius's grip tightened on Nick's shirt. And he leaned so close, Nick could feel the darkness radiating from him too. "Give me one reason not to beat the fucking life out of you."

Footsteps pounded close, and voices echoed through the tunnels. Kellen and the others who'd been checking out the cave-in tore into the room. Nick waved them off. "Don't touch him. He's mine." Then to Demetrius, "You think you can take me? Try it."

"Oh for gods' sake." Isadora's voice bounced off rock and echoed in the air. "You're both complete morons if you think this is helping. Kill each other for all I care. I've had it. You"—she tipped her chin toward Nick—"with your *I don't give a shit* attitude, and you"—she turned her fiery gaze upon Demetrius—"thinking you *own* me? No one *gives* me away." She threw up her hands. "I'm done. I'm done with both of you."

She turned for the tunnel that led back to the lowest level of the castle. For the first time, Nick realized Isadora's sister, Callia, was standing near the door to the entrance of the colony. "Come on. Let's go find Titus before it's too late."

"He's upstairs, in one of the suites."

"Thank the Fates we don't have to go searching for him," Isadora muttered. "The sooner we get this done, the sooner we can get the hell out of here. I'm suddenly sick of the view."

Footsteps echoed and slowly faded. Silence descended, settling in the tense air. The only sound was the thump of Nick's heartbeat roaring in his ears. He waited, expecting Demetrius to haul off and plow his fist into his jaw again, but the blow never came. Instead, Demetrius let go and stepped back. Then his face paled, and worry crept into his dark, usually guarded eyes.

"*Skata.*" Demetrius scrubbed a hand through his hair.

And standing there, watching, Nick had a memory flash. Of the way his brother had looked strung up in the Council's chamber after Demetrius and Isadora had come back from that island. How lost he'd looked then. How Isadora had been the only one to believe in him. How she'd convinced her father to abdicate the throne to her, stepped in, told the Council to go to hell and stopped his execution.

What they had was stronger than the soul mate bond. It was the kind of connection that defined you, that made you who you were. The one thing in the world you'd sacrifice, knowing you'd never be whole again, all to keep the other safe.

"You love her."

Demetrius sucked in a breath.

"No," Nick clarified. "I mean, you *really* love her."

"Don't fucking mock me."

Nick wasn't. At least, he wasn't trying to. Sweat broke out on his forehead. He didn't care that his men could still be listening. That the private life he worked so hard to keep private from those he protected was slowly drifting away. He'd known Isadora felt something for his brother, but all this time he'd assumed it was the soul mate bond keeping them together. He'd thought that his own bond to her was just as strong. Now...

Now he knew it wasn't even close. He may want Isadora. He may never be able to stop the soul mate draw to her. But she didn't love him. And she never would.

"Go to her."

Demetrius closed his eyes. "She doesn't want me, you idiot. Didn't you hear her?"

"Yeah, she does." Nick swallowed the lump in his throat. "She's just pissed, and with good reason. You were a dick."

"Now you're telling me to stay with her? *Skata*, you're the one who said she'd be safer here with you."

"I'm an asshole. What the hell do I know?" When Demetrius rubbed a hand over his eyes, Nick found himself with a choice. To go after what he wanted, or to do what was right. And shit, though he wanted nothing more than to be a selfish prick, something inside wouldn't let him.

"She loves you, you moron. Even I can see that. Are you really dumb enough to let her get away?"

Demetrius stared at the cave wall. Defeat rippled across his features. "You're right about the Council. They'll move on her as soon as they think they can."

"So don't let them. You've got the Argonauts on your side. Use them. If you and those girly men you hang around with can protect a whole realm, you can figure out a way to protect her."

Demetrius turned to look at him. "Why the change of heart? We both know you want her too."

Nick's skin prickled. He could lie, or...he could be honest with...himself. "I thought there was a chance she might one day...want...to be with me. But I can see now that's never going to happen, thanks to you."

Darkness filled Demetrius's eyes. "She deserves better."

"Than both of us?" Nick huffed. "I'm not arguing with you there. But for whatever reason, she wants you. And no matter what I do, I'm never going to be you. No one is ever going to be you."

Their eyes held. And in the silence between them, Nick's chest pinched. He was losing her again. Which was an absurd thought, considering she'd never really been his. But that didn't make the hurt any less. In fact, if possible, he was pretty sure that made it a thousand times harder to take. To see your future standing in front of you and not be able to reach for it... That was the definition of true misery.

"Go to her," Nick said before he could change his mind.

Indecision brewed in Demetrius's eyes, then was slowly replace with hope. He stepped toward the tunnel that ran back to the colony, but stopped and turned back. "What about you?"

Nick tucked a hand in his pocket. Tried for his I-don't-fucking-care attitude. Knew it came off weak and pathetic. "I'm not soul mate material."

Demetrius stared at him. Opened his mouth to say something. Closed it.

With one last nod, he headed down the dark tunnel.

Alone, Nick turned to survey the barren room. Kellen and the others had left somewhere in the middle of the conversation, which was the only plus Nick could see. Everything else—his future, his purpose, his reason for getting up in the freaking morning—was bleak. What the hell did he have to look forward to now that he knew for sure he'd never have his soul mate?

He didn't know. He only knew that he couldn't stay here. He needed out.

Titus rolled toward Natasa in the morning light. She lay softly sleeping on her stomach, her back rising and falling with her gentle breaths, her red hair fanned out around her on the pillow.

His heart contracted. He slid his leg over hers and tugged her into the curve of his body, not wanting to let go of her. She made the softest mewling sound but didn't wake.

Arousal speared through his groin. Though he wanted nothing more than to push her legs apart, lift her hips, and slide inside her from behind, he decided letting her sleep was the more heroic thing to do, especially since only a few hours ago, he'd been worried that fever was going to burn her alive.

He ran his hand down her smooth back, loving the texture of her flesh beneath his hand. The sheet fell loosely at her hips. In the pale light, her skin was luminescent and no longer hot to the touch, only slightly warmer than his.

Their conversation from earlier ran through his mind. He brushed her hair aside and studied the triangle on her neck. Prometheus's daughter. What kind of sick son of a bitch gifted this kind of curse to his child? The ramifications of what he'd discovered trickled through him. It was going to consume her if they didn't find the god before it was too late. And what it would unleash...

He squeezed his eyes tight. Duty and desire warred inside him. He couldn't abandon her, but every instinct he had as an Argonaut fought against his own personal wants.

A knock sounded at the door. He lifted his head and looked that way. Quietly, a voice—Callia's voice—called, "Titus? Are you in there? I need to talk to you."

Shit. What the hell was Callia doing here? And how did she know *he* was here?

Fucking Nick...

He looked back down at Natasa. She hadn't even stirred at the knock. She was obviously more exhausted from the last few days than she'd let on.

Worry rippled through him, but he tugged up the sheet and pulled her hair back over her neck, covering the mark. Quietly, he climbed out of bed, pulled on his pants, then crossed the floor and gently cracked the door open.

Relief washed over Callia's features. "There you are. Everyone's been looking for you."

He shifted, making sure she couldn't see into the room. One glance into the hall told him she was alone. "What are you doing here?"

"Helping you." "I came with Isadora. She needs to speak with you."

Titus went on instant alert.

"Don't worry. The Argonauts aren't with us."

He searched her mind and discovered she wasn't lying. She couldn't hide her thoughts from him the way Zander could.

Nodding, Titus slipped out the door and closed it tightly behind him. His instincts screamed keeping Natasa out of whatever the queen was up to was his only move. "Lead the way."

Halfway down the hall, he realized his feet were bare, his hair wasn't tied back, that he hadn't shaved and that he wasn't even wearing a shirt. Not exactly an acceptable way to meet the queen, but he didn't give a rip. His mind was ten steps ahead, planning how they'd get out of the colony and where they'd go next.

The hallway opened to a great living room, flanked by an enormous fireplace and arched windows that looked out at the blue-green lake. Morning sunlight glistened off its surface like a thousand sparkling diamonds, but it wasn't the view that stopped Titus dead in his tracks. It was the queen.

And Theron, and Zander, and Phin, and Cerek. All staring his way as if he'd sprouted horns.

"Shit," Callia thought. *"When did they get here?"*

"Sorry." The queen cringed. *"They just arrived."*

"Skata," Phineus muttered, moving forward. "Where the hell have you been, you mad fuck? We've been looking everywhere for you. Ever hear of your Argos medallion? That's why we wear them, numbnuts."

Titus held up his hands to block Phin from touching him and stepped to the side. Phineus pulled up short, staring at him in question.

Sweat broke out on Titus's forehead. He was getting way too used to Natasa's touch. It was messing with his reaction time. "What are you all doing here? I was going to contact you later."

Yeah, right. It sounded good, at least.

Theron's brow dropped low. "Where's the girl?"

There was no friendliness in that tone. It was straight up, leader of the Argonauts business-cold. Titus's back tightened. "Sleeping."

"Where?"

"In a bed." Theron and Zander exchanged glances, but whatever they were thinking, they kept closely guarded. Titus's anxiety jumped to a higher frequency. "She's not working for Zagreus and Hades like you thought. She's not a threat."

"Oh, yeah, she is."

The one thought got through, but Titus couldn't figure out from whom it had come.

Theron pushed off the arm of the sofa he'd been leaning against and unfolded his arms. "T, she's not what you think."

Fuck that. They didn't know a thing about her. "She's—"

"She's Prometheus's out." The queen stepped forward, her arms crossed over her bulging belly, her expression hard and serious.

Footsteps echoed from the hall. Demetrius moved into the room, his gaze locking on Isadora.

Isadora glanced his way, but her expression hardened, then refocused on Titus. "We're pretty sure she's the unquenchable fire ancient texts wrote about eons ago. The end of all things, should Prometheus never be set free. Lena told Callia about Natasa's erratic temperature. We know about the fire in the redwoods and the charred Amazon city. If she is this unquenchable fire, then she has to be stopped before whatever is inside her burns free."

Titus's jaw flexed. "She's not evil."

He wasn't turning her over to them so they could lock her in another freaking cage. They didn't understand what she...

He looked from face to face. They were all blocking his ability to read their minds. Which meant only one thing.

They weren't just talking about locking her away. They were talking about killing her.

"No." He shook his head. "Not happening. Don't even fucking think about it."

"Titus," Isadora said carefully. "No decisions have been made, yet. But we have to consider all possibilities. This is bigger than all of us. This is the fate of the world. You can't turn your back on that."

Yeah, he could. He considered telling them the rest—that she was the fire element—but knew that wouldn't save her life, at least not a life she wanted to live. Being caged was no sort of life, and he wasn't condemning her to that again.

Tension surged in the room.

"Be sensible, man," Phineus muttered. "She's just a girl."

A girl who meant more to Titus than anything else ever had, save his order. He sent a scathing look Phin's way, then glanced from face to face again. Pleading with his eyes, he finally said the only thing he could. "She's *not* evil."

Theron's stare darkened. "You're about to make a choice that can't be changed, Guardian. Be sure it's the right one."

CHAPTER FOURTEEN

Silence echoed through the room. Titus's pulse pounded hard. He stared Theron down. "There is no choice."

Theron's jaw clenched. He looked toward the queen. Unspoken words passed between them. To Zander, he said, "Go get her."

Zander pushed away from the wall. Titus scrambled to block his path. "Don't, Z."

Zander's expression softened. "Come on, T. You know I won't hurt her."

Titus believed that, but it was Theron he didn't trust. The leader of the Argonauts was all business unless it came to his soul mate. If the roles were reversed, if it were Casey they were talking about, this wouldn't even be a question. "You're not touching her."

Isadora turned to her sister. "Give me the Orb."

Callia pulled the Orb of Krónos from a bag slung over her shoulder and resting against her hip. The circular-shaped disk caught the light shining down from the ornate chandelier. It was divided into four chambers, two of which were filled with the elements they'd already found: air and earth. The other two—directly opposite each other—were empty. The stamp of Krónos, the king of the elder gods and the bitch of a god the Argonauts were trying to keep locked in the Underworld, shone brightly in the very center.

They'd risked bringing the Orb to the human realm? Something else was going on here. Titus's gaze flicked past Zander toward the queen, then to Theron. "What the hell is this about?"

Isadora held the Orb out to him. "Just hold it. See if anything comes to you."

Comes to him? What the hell were they smoking?

"Take it, Titus," Theron said. "We know about the witch's curse. You can either cooperate or we can knock you on your ass and make you hold it."

Sweat spread down Titus's spine, and his pulse roared. They knew about the curse. He looked warily at the Orb. They were playing some kind of game. Trying to distract him so they could go after Natasa. So they could—

"Stupid son of a bitch." Zander grasped Titus's wrist in one hand, grabbed the Orb from the queen with the other, and slapped it into Titus's palm.

Emotions flowed from Zander into Titus—anticipation, fear, anxiety—followed by a shot of gut-wrenching pain that stole Titus's breath and sent him doubling over. But there was something else. A low buzz echoed in his ears—the same one he always heard when he was near the Orb—and it was growing stronger. Muffled words, ancient voices, sounds he couldn't place bombarded him.

One voice cut through all the rest.

"Titus. Oh gods…what did you do to him?"

Natasa's voice.

Heat spread through Titus's body. He needed to see her face and tried to turn and look, but the pain intensified, followed by a tingling in his fingers that grew stronger, then rocketed into his arm and shoulder and finally shot straight to his brain.

He gasped. Synapses fired. Images flashed behind his eyes. An electrical current arced through every cell and exploded in a burst of white-hot fire.

"He's seizing!"

"Titus!"

Sound dissipated. His brain felt like it was on overload, like it might explode. The flood of information didn't stop.

Then everything came to a screeching halt. Sound slowly returned. The draw and push of air in his lungs. His rapid-fire pulse. He blinked several times. And stared up into Natasa's worried face. Her lips were moving, but he couldn't hear her voice. Heat seeped into his skin—her heat—warming him from the outside in. And those were her fingers against his arms, his face, turning him to look at her.

He was lying on the hardwood floor. Behind her head, the fuzzy outline of a chandelier hanging high above came into view. When had he lain down? He didn't remember hitting the ground. Didn't remember anything but holding the Orb and—

Holy skata.

His eyes grew wide. Muffled words echoed to his ears, grew clearer. Familiar voices, not of ancient heroes but of his kin.

"Titus?" Natasa cradled his face in her hands. "Talk to me."

"No, don't touch him," Callia said somewhere close. "Just let her."

"Fuck the gods." Demetrius. That was Demetrius's voice, but Titus couldn't see the guardian. All he could see was Natasa. Her emerald-green eyes, her red hair like a halo of fire around her face, her sweet, tempting lips he knew were so wickedly soft.

"Do you think it worked?" someone said.

"We'll see," someone else answered.

"He can't read her, right?" Theron. That was Theron talking about him like he wasn't in the damn room. Talking about Titus's soul mate like she was a thing, not a living, breathing person.

Anger raged through his blood. He struggled to sit up. He wasn't going to lose her. Not to the gods and not to the Argonauts. He knew now how to find her father. Clarity and knowledge had spread from the Orb into him like they'd hoped, but he wasn't sharing an ounce of it with them.

"Gently," Natasa said, grasping his shoulders and easing him upright. "Take deep breaths."

Gods, he loved that she cared. Loved that she was here. Her fingers were warm, her scent swirling in the air to make him light-headed. Loved…her.

He gripped her hand for stability and to keep her close. Lena had left her fresh clothes, which she'd changed into before coming out to find him. Instead of the nightgown she'd been wearing when they'd moved her from the infirmary, she was now dressed in slim jeans and a fitted white T-shirt. And he was thankful. Thankful the Argonauts couldn't see all of her because that was only for him.

He leaned back against a couch and kicked his legs out in front of him. Then turned his glare toward the others in the room. "What the hell was that?"

"You tell us," Theron answered expectantly.

Titus glanced from Theron to the queen and back again. He was going to have to play this good if he had any hope of getting them to back down. "I don't know. But it wasn't all that different from what I get when someone touches me. Thanks, Z, by the way."

Zander shoved his hands in his pocket. Shifted his feet.

Silence settled over the room.

"Epimetheus might have been wrong," Demetrius said quietly from the far side of the room.

Natasa shot a worried look down at Titus.

He squeezed her hand to try to reassure her. And to warn her not to say a word. He glared toward Theron. "You're basing your info on the father of afterthought? Since when is the fool of the gods considered reliable?"

Theron's jaw clenched. He stared hard at Natasa. Beneath Titus's hand, her temperature jumped. "I think it's time the redhead and I had a nice long chat about Prometheus. Alone."

"No fucking way." Panic resurged. Titus found his feet and used the wall to push himself up.

Natasa moved quickly in front of him and pressed a warm hand against his chest. "It's okay. I'll be fine."

His gaze raked hers. She didn't know what she was doing. "No, *ligos Vesuvius.*"

She let go, stepping away before he could stop her. He reached for her but his limbs were still too weak to follow, and he slumped against the wall.

Squaring her strong shoulders, she turned and faced the leader of the Argonauts. "You want to talk. Fine. We'll talk. Prometheus is my father. And at the moment, I'm all that's standing between your life and death."

Hades sat in the leather chair and tapped his long fingers against the stone slab that made up his desk. Wide windows looked out at the swirling red sky and black, jagged mountains far off in the distance. Cries of agony and despair floated on the hot wind, their owners paying for whatever misdeeds they'd done in life.

There'd been a time when he'd enjoyed the suffering. When he'd drawn strength from the misery. But now only disdain rippled through him as every sound met his ears. He was sick of the dead.

Sick of being the one responsible for judgment, sentencing, and punishment. He was ready for a major life change, and he was counting on his son to make that happen.

The door to his personal study pushed open, and fury raged through him at the lack of a knock. But when his wife, Persephone, swept into the room in her deep purple gown with her black-as-sin hair falling like a waterfall down her back, that fury twisted to uncontrolled lust.

"Kore…" He pushed from his chair, lurched down the three steps and caught her in a fierce embrace. She'd been with her mother on Olympus, and he was starving for her.

"My king."

He yanked her close and took her mouth in hard, vicious kiss. One that was both punishing and erotic at the same time. Lust swirled in the air, overpowering every sense. She answered by scoring her nails across his back and biting his lip hard enough to draw blood. The coppery taste slid over his tongue, mixed with her essence and the wine she must have drunk earlier in the day. He growled low in his throat, kissed her harder and had her pinned against the wall before he realized it wasn't time for her to return to the Underworld. Not yet, at least.

He pulled back from her mouth, looked down into her dark and sinful eyes, and tamped down the lust, for a moment. "Your father let you go?"

A wicked smile curled one side of her lips. "I convinced him I was too miserable to stay on Olympus without seeing you for at least a fortnight."

He knew that mischievous look. And he knew his brother. "You mean you whined so much he was more than happy to get rid of you for a few days."

"Something like that." Her eyes darkened. "Your females can't satisfy you the way I can. Tell me, husband. Did you miss me?"

"More than life itself." He dipped back down to kiss her again. Stroked his tongue against hers until she moaned. He had his pick of females when she was gone, but he preferred her to anyone else. And it wasn't all that fun toying with his slaves when she wasn't around to watch…or interact.

She tightened her fingers against his shoulder and lifted one leg, wrapping it around his hip, kissing him back with every ounce of passion he was showering on her. The heat of her mound pressed against his swollen cock, and she pushed her hips forward and back, rubbing herself against him. Her dress fell down her leg. He ran his hand up the sweet, sensitive flesh until he found her ass, then squeezed.

"Little minx. You're going to make me spend in my pants."

"Not yet, husband." She tipped her head so he could bite her neck, then sighed even though he knew it had to hurt. "I've something to tell you. I didn't come back just for this, though *this* is more than enough to draw me home time and again."

"No?" He closed his lips over her earlobe and tugged.

"No. I came to tell you our son works against us. He moves to take Prometheus's daughter and the fire element for himself. They are one in the same."

Hades's lips stilled against her throat. He pulled back to look into her dark eyes. "How do you know this?"

"I overheard Zeus and Athena discussing strategy. Zagreus recently visited Epimetheus. Suspicions rise that the elder god told our son where the fire-girl is hiding."

Hades slowly lowered his wife's leg to the floor. "How would the ass-hat know that?"

"Because she travels with an Argonaut. And Argonauts also recently visited Epimetheus as well."

The Argonauts. Fury flared in Hades's veins. He let go of Persephone and stepped back. The meddling heroes were always fucking with his plans. And because they were now hiding Maelea—*the Stain*—from him, he had no more use for them. He should have ground them all to dust when he had the chance.

"Where?" he said between clenched teeth. "Where is she hiding?"

"I don't know exactly. But Zeus's Sirens tracked Zagreus and his satyrs moving north. We know the Argonauts have joined forces with the half-breeds. Athena suspects they move toward the half-breed colony."

Of course that was where the Argonauts would be hiding the girl. He wasn't sure why they weren't protecting her in Argolea where the Olympian gods couldn't cross, but he was thankful for the fact she was still in the human realm. It was easier to take her there than to have to slink around Argolea. Even though he and Persephone—not technically Olympians—could cross into the blessed realm of the heroes, there were places there inaccessible to them. Like the queen's bloody castle.

No one knew where the half-breed colony was located, but if Athena was tracking Zagreus north...

Another shot of boiling fury whipped through Hades's veins when he realized who else had betrayed him. His brothers—Poseidon and Zeus—were moving on their own, without contacting him. Against the pact they'd agreed to.

Fucking shagging pile of shit. Not that it surprised him, but it did royally piss him off.

He turned his rage toward his queen. "Our son will be punished for this."

"Of course. And the element? What will you do with her when you have her?"

She was Prometheus's daughter. As far as Hades was concerned, the elder god had gotten off easy being punished by Zeus in the human realm rather than locked in Tartarus with Krónos and the other Titans like he deserved. His daughter wouldn't be so lucky.

"She's mine."

Persephone's eyes flashed. "Only if I get to watch."

Lust reignited in his groin—a lust he'd have to delay, at least for now. "I wouldn't have it any other way. Come, Kore. We have a battle to begin."

CHAPTER FIFTEEN

Natasa turned a slow circle and took in the large room with the curved floor-to-ceiling windows that looked out at the black lake and the sun moving higher in the sky. A long table surrounded by chairs filled the space. Against the far wall sat a sidebar. It was some kind of formal dining room built to seat at least thirty. Or an interrogation room designed to intimidate.

The door closed with a snap, and she turned to face the leader of the Argonauts. The same man—*hero*—who'd kicked her out of the colony weeks ago when she'd come looking for Maelea. Her body temperature rose with every second that passed, but unlike the last time they'd faced off, now the fire inside was stronger, and a sense of purpose pulsed through her.

His face was hard, his jaw tight. He was as big and muscular as Titus, but his hair wasn't as long, and there was no humor or kindness swirling in his eyes.

He didn't step farther into the room, just crossed his arms over his broad chest and widened his stance while he stared at her.

"You're the unquenchable fire all the ancient texts talk about, aren't you?"

She lifted her chin. Refused to back down. She'd been imprisoned, tortured, burned. She wasn't afraid of one measly hero. "My father's lasting gift."

"Why were you in Argolea?"

No sympathy from the hero. Well, that would make this easier, she supposed. "For the same reason I came here originally. To find Maelea."

"To destroy her with your fire?"

"Why would I want to do that?"

He shrugged. "The gods don't care for her."

"I hold no ill will against Maelea. I went looking for her to see if she knew anything about where my father is being held."

Doubt darkened his eyes. "Why?"

"So I could find him. Contrary to what you might believe, being the destined destruction of the world isn't a hell of a lot of fun."

"Are you saying you're not working for Hades and Zagreus?"

"I'd have to be mental to work for the God-King of the Underworld, or his son."

"That remains to be seen. Answer the question."

No humor either. This guy had to be a real joy at parties. "No, I'm not working for Hades or Zagreus."

"Who are you working for?"

"Myself."

Silence spread across the room like a vast ocean. He was debating whether or not she was telling the truth. She didn't care. She only cared about keeping Titus safe.

His eyes finally narrowed. "How can the fire inside you be stopped?"

It can't. But Titus can slow it.

The thought registered immediately, followed by a shot of fear that speared straight to her heart. She didn't want this Argonaut knowing anything about her relationship with Titus. For reasons she couldn't explain, she had the feeling he'd use it against her. Or Titus.

She fixed an impassive look on her face and crossed her arms over her chest, mimicking his stance. If he wanted to play the part of a bully, so could she. She was, after all, flame and destruction. "I suppose you could *wish* to stop it. Though that hasn't worked well for me. Maybe you'll have better luck."

His tensing jaw told her he didn't appreciate sarcasm. Tough shit. She didn't appreciate being treated like an object.

His palms landed against the sleek table's surface with a slap, and he leaned forward, his eyes full of distrust. "I don't know what kind of game you're playing, but you'll not do it with one of my Argonauts."

The heat inside her intensified. "I'm not playing any game. And your Argonaut is a thousand times the hero you are. Let's stop dancing around. We both know what you plan to do with me. I'm not about to let that happen."

Theron drew back. He continued to stare, but this time with surprise in his eyes. "Titus is Odysseus's descendent. He's the most logical of any of the guardians. He never leaps without thinking through every possible scenario, and he's the last one of us to be ruled by his emotions. But that fire inside you is fucking with his mind. And every hour he spends with you not only turns him into something he's not, it jeopardizes his future."

For the first time since their conversation began, Natasa didn't have a smart comment to toss back.

The thought that the fire element somehow affected Titus's thought process hit hard. His inability to walk away from her, his need to help her slowly lit off a whole new set of worries.

"You can threaten all you want," Theron went on, "but know this. If Titus tries to help you escape, then he's the one who will suffer. There are consequences to betraying our order. If you care about him at all, you'll think long and hard about what happens next."

Natasa's skin grew hot. Her heart picked up speed. Perspiration formed along her forehead.

Theron moved for the door and pushed it open. The blond guardian who'd touched Titus earlier stepped toward him from the hall.

"I want her placed in a holding cell," Theron said to him. "Until we can move her to a secure location away from the colony, I don't want anyone near her. Especially Titus."

Footsteps sounded from the hall, cutting through Natasa's frantic thoughts.

A dozen men in armor rushed by. Theron drew one soldier to a halt. "What's happened?"

The man's face was taut, his features grim. He was a half-breed. Not nearly as big as the Argonauts, but strong. Natasa remembered his light green eyes, and realized he must have been one of the men who'd brought her and Titus to the colony. "We're under attack. Satyrs have been seen moving up from the south. And word is there's a horde of daemons not far behind them."

Oh, shit...

"*Skata,*" Theron muttered. "Where's Nick?"

The half-breed's features twisted into a scowl "No one knows. We can't find him."

"Perfect." Theron looked toward the blond. "Zander, get her secured, then find Demetrius and start the evacuation process. We need to get the colonists moved over to Argolea in case this goes bad. Then find your mate and the queen and make sure they get the hell out of here. Gods know those females do what the hell they want, when they want." To the half-breed, he said, "I'll gather the Argonauts."

The half-breed nodded. Footsteps pounded in the hall again as he and Theron left, and then Natasa was alone, staring into the face of the blond, strikingly handsome Argonaut who'd brought her man to his knees only minutes ago.

Her man?

Her skin grew even warmer. Yes, Titus was her man, and her heart and head were suddenly in a fierce battle over what to do. Something that only kicked up her fear and agitation more.

She narrowed her eyes. "I don't like being manhandled."

"So I hear." The blond's silver eyes sparked. "Right now, though, girlie, you're not the one I'm worried about. Let's go."

Satyrs? *And* Daemons? *Fuck...*

Titus tugged on his shirt and shoved his feet into the boots he'd kicked off only hours ago. His strength had returned, and now he had only one thought: to get to Natasa before his worst fears came true.

The bed in the room they'd shared was a mess of blankets and sheets, and he could still smell that unique lemony scent he now associated with her. As if she were still here.

He dropped onto the side of the bed, leaned over, and laced his boots, ignoring Callia standing in the doorway, her arms crossed, a pitying look in her violet eyes.

He didn't need pity right now; he needed action.

Footsteps echoed from the hall. He lifted his head.

Zander stepped into the room, tugging—*oh, shit*—Natasa in after him. "Close the door, *thea*."

Callia quickly shut the door and locked it. Confused, Titus pushed to his feet and looked from face to face. "What's going on?"

Natasa turned toward Zander. "I thought you were supposed to lock me up."

"I probably should. But something tells me he'll"—he nodded toward Titus—"figure a way to break you out no matter where I put you. You can both thank me for saving you a step."

Shock rippled through Titus, followed by bone-melting relief. He reached for Natasa's waist, threaded one hand into her hair, and pulled her into his arms. A muttered "Thank you," slid from his mouth just before he kissed her sweet, tempting lips.

"I was right."

The thought came from Callia, followed by a whispered, "See?" But Titus barely cared. All he could focus on was the silky soft skin beneath his hands and the warm lips pressing against his own.

Relief slid to concern. Her skin was hot. Too hot. But he could cool her. He was confident now he was the only one who could.

"Titus, wait." He drew back at Natasa's worried voice. "I don't want to be the reason—"

He looked over her head toward Zander. "Why?"

The Argonaut flashed a lopsided grin and tossed his arm over Callia's shoulder. He angled his head toward his mate.

"A hunch," Callia said. "One doesn't have to read minds to see the obvious."

"Titus," Natasa said again. "I'm not going to get between you and your or—"

Titus leaned down and kissed her once more, cutting off her words. In the few seconds he'd held the Orb, everything had become clear, including what they needed to do next. "Theron's an ass. Forget about him."

She huffed. "No argument there, but—"

"I know how to get to your father."

She froze. "You do?"

He nodded. Gods, he loved when she looked at him like that, like he was the only thing she needed. "Call it ancient intervention. I'll explain it all later. We need to make tracks before Hades and Zagreus catch wind you were here."

Fear washed over her features. A fear that heated her skin another degree and amped his urgency. He let go of her waist, grasped her hand, and looked toward Zander. "What will you tell the others?"

Zander shrugged. "I'll think of something."

He tightened his fingers around Natasa's. "Theron will be pissed."

Zander's eyes sharpened. "Theron's wrong on this one. A guardian's soul mate"—he looked toward Callia—"isn't something you mess with."

Kinship reverberated in Titus.

"Soul mate?" Natasa asked, her brow drawn low.

"Theron's distracted right now," Callia said. "If you're leaving, you need to go soon."

"Hold on." Natasa pulled her hand from Titus's and pressed her fingers against her temple. "Everything's happening so fast. I need to th—"

From her pocket, Callia pulled out the Orb. The circular disk sat in the palm of her hand, the chain hanging between her fingers. Natasa jerked that direction. Froze.

The same buzz Titus had felt before in the presence of the Orb lit off in his head, but now he knew why. "You're giving this to us?"

"No." Callia grinned. "Isadora would kill me if I lost the Orb. But there's no reason you can't use it while you're here, right?"

It took only a split second for her thought—and meaning—to reach Titus. And he was suddenly thankful not only for Zander, but for Callia too. He owed them both, big-time. Expectantly, he looked toward Natasa.

"Between your power and the Orb's," Callia said to her, "you should be able to open a portal. It'll save travel time."

Natasa glanced warily from Callia to Titus, then back to the Orb. Cautiously, she stepped forward, then carefully ran her finger down the edge of the circular metal. "I…I wouldn't know how."

"The same way you fried that guard's armor and threw that fireball at Zagreus's army," Titus told her. "Center yourself."

"You charbroiled Zagreus's satyrs?" A wide smile cut across Zander's face. "Sweet."

Callia nudged the guardian in the ribs. Zander twisted out of her reach and muttered, "What? That's more than any of us can do, *thea*. Even Phin."

"You…" Slowly, Natasa turned to face Titus. "…trust me."

Surprise echoed in her voice, but there was something in her eyes… A feeling, an emotion he couldn't quite read. Something that made him wonder what the hell Theron had said to her. "You already know the answer to that question."

"I know you did, I just…"

Tears filled her eyes. She wrapped her hand around his neck and pulled him down for a hard, swift kiss.

A happiness Titus had never known washed through him. And his knees nearly buckled from the strength of the emotion.

Across the room, Zander laughed. *"Payback is a total bitch. And this is gonna be fucking fun to watch."*

His head felt light as a feather by the time Natasa let him go. She blinked several times and hugged him tight. Dazed, Titus couldn't stop the smile creeping over his face.

Natasa let go. "Okay." She faced the Orb in Callia's hands again. "Let's do this. Where are we going?"

"Ogygia."

She glanced over her shoulder with wide eyes. "Calypso's island?"

He nodded.

"Wow. Okay. You know where that is? Because that's not exactly on my map of frequently traveled destinations."

He tapped his temple with his index finger. "Thanks to the Orb, baby, I know a lot of shit I didn't before. You open the portal, and I'll take us there."

Natasa drew in a breath and placed her hand over the metal disk in Callia's hand. "Here goes nothing."

"Stay together. Single file. Don't push. Everyone will make it through."

Isadora pressed a hand against her lower back and drew in a breath as colonists filed past her toward the portal Zander had opened. They'd rounded up most of the people they could find and corralled them in the ballroom, the biggest room in the castle. Chandeliers sparkled above. Light pouring from the open portal bounced off intricately carved dark wood beams high overhead, the arched windows looking out at the lake below and the fancy long tables and chairs. But all Isadora could focus on was what was happening outside the castle, beyond the safety of the lake, where Hades and his son Zagreus were either lying in wait or already battling the colony's soldiers and her Argonauts.

She looked around the busy room, searching for Demetrius. He and Callia had gone to check the other floors for lingering colonists. And dammit, where was Nick? That low ache she'd been dealing with the last few hours flared again, and she pressed harder against the spot, wishing she'd held her tongue and hadn't said those things to Nick in the tunnels below.

Of all the times for her to get pissy with him. But it wasn't like she'd known Hades and Zagreus were about to attack, right? She drew in another breath that didn't completely fill her lungs because the kid was taking up so much space, blew it out, twisted to the right and left, hoping to ease the pain. Demetrius she would deal with later. But Nick had a responsibility to his people. He should be here right now. Where the hell was he?

"My lady."

The small voice drew Isadora's attention. She looked down at the cherub face. A girl, about five, with curly dark hair cut short, smiled up at her. The right side of her face—from cheekbone to forehead—was puckered and scarred from what looked like some kind of recent burn.

These colonists had already been through so much. Isadora's frustration with Nick and Demetrius slid to the wayside. She knelt in front of the girl as best she could with her large belly, bringing them to eye level. "Hi there."

The girl lifted a doll. Her right arm and hand were also puckered and scarred. "Minnie said to tell you it's coming soon."

A woman placed a hand on the girl's shoulder. "Marissa, now isn't the time." Then to Isadora with pink-tinged cheeks, "I'm sorry, Your Highness. I tried to tell her no. She doesn't understand royal etiquette yet."

"It's okay." Isadora glanced toward the girl's mother. "This isn't exactly a time for etiquette, either." She looked back at the girl. And the name and description—and especially the doll—finally clicked. "Marissa... I think you might know my sister, Casey."

Marissa's eyes lit up. "Is she here? I haven't seen her in so long."

Casey had saved the child from a daemon attack months ago, when the colony had been housed in Oregon. "No, she's across the portal, in Argolea, where you're going with your mother. You'll see her soon."

The girl clutched her doll and jumped up and down in excitement. "Minnie will be so happy."

Isadora smiled, then remembered what else Casey had said about the child. She was a soothsayer, like Isadora, and she used her doll as her medium. But whereas Isadora couldn't see into her own future, this child might be able to.

Suddenly, the girl's words took on new meaning.

"Marissa," Isadora said calmly, trying to get the child's attention once more as people passed. "You said Minnie wanted to tell me it's coming. What's coming, honey?"

"It" could be anything. War, death, Hades himself. Isadora's nerves hummed as a hundred different options raced through her mind.

"It," Marissa said as if *it* were common knowledge. "That which will change your life forever." She pointed to Isadora's belly. "The future."

The baby? Oh, good Lord. Of course it was coming soon. Anyone with eyes could see Isadora was as big as a house and would deliver sooner rather than later.

Feeling foolish for getting so worked up, Isadora pushed to her feet with a grunt. So as not to make the child feel unappreciated, she placed a hand on her belly and smiled down at the girl. "You're right. Soon. But thankfully, not today."

Marissa smiled. "Soon. Do not be afraid. Everything happens for a reason. Even pain and death."

Isadora's heart stuttered. Horrified, the mother hushed the girl and whisked her away.

Pain and death? What did *that* mean? Those nerves that had settled just moments before came raging back.

Loud footfalls echoed from the hall, but Isadora was too wrapped up in her neurosis to turn and look.

A hand on her shoulder dragged her around. "Isa? Are you okay?"

Isadora forced down the foreboding threatening to overwhelm her. "Fine. I'm fine. Did you find anyone else?"

Callia shifted to the side so the crowd could move past. "No one. It looks like we've got everyone." Her brows drew together. "Are you sure you're okay? You're pale."

No, she wasn't okay. She was freaking the hell out. Pain and death were not things she wanted to contemplate right now, especially with regard to her baby. She looked past her sister and spotted Demetrius heading her way.

Her heart took a hard, slow tumble. His hair was messed, his features set and tense, but his eyes warmed just a touch when they met hers from across the room. And though she wanted nothing more than to remain mad at him, she couldn't. She needed him. Now more than ever. And, dammit, she understood what he'd been trying to do even if she didn't agree with it.

That didn't mean she was going to let him totally off the hook, though.

He stopped in front of her, searching her features, she knew, for a clue as to her mood. And this close, she could feel his heat and smell that musky scent she always associated with him. The babe in her belly kicked out, and she winced.

Concern tightened his features. "*Kardia?*"

Isadora rubbed at the tender spot where she'd been round-housed then moved her hand to the pressure intensifying against her lower back. "Dumbass?"

Callia chuckled and covered her mouth with her hand.

Demetrius scowled. "I see you're still pissed."

"Your powers of deduction are stunning."

He perched his hands on his hips and glared down at her. He was twice her size, but she knew he'd never hurt her. At least not intentionally. "You should go back to Argolea."

"Telling me what to do again? It didn't work last time."

"It never works with you, *kardia.*"

"And yet you keep pushing."

"I keep *hoping* you'll wise up and listen."

She narrowed her eyes and stared hard into his. At her side, Callia muttered, "Um, I'm gonna go see if Zander needs any help."

Callia's footsteps faded in the distance. The crowd was thinning, only a few dozen colonists waiting to cross into Argolea, but all she could focus on was her mate, the *ándras* she loved above all else and whom she wanted most in the world to be happy.

"Are you ready to admit I won't be safer here?" she asked.

"On a good day, you would be. This just doesn't happen to be a good day."

Gods, he was stubborn. And though she hated that about him, she also loved it. "I'm not afraid of the Council."

"You should be. They don't want you to rule."

"You didn't either for quite some time."

He sighed. "Isadora—"

"Look. The Council is just going to have to get used to the fact I'm not backing down, and I'm sure as hell not going anywhere. Just like you're going to have to get used to the fact I don't want Nick. I don't want anyone but you. And if you keep trying to push me away like you've been doing, all it's going to do is make me dig my heels in deeper. You are mine, and that's the end of the story. I love you, and I'm not giving you up, no matter how much you piss me off. Got it?"

Ever so slowly, his eyes softened, enough to push aside what was left of her anger. "I don't know what the hell you see in me."

"Sometimes I wonder the same thing, and then all I have to do is look at you, and I know. You're *my* hero, Demetrius. All mine. I have no reason to live without you."

"*Kardia…*" He wrapped one arm around her waist and drew her against him, then leaned down and tipped her face up to kiss her. The tug was gentle because of the baby, but his kiss was filled with need and desperation.

Home.

It was the only thought she had. The only one that mattered. His lips were soft, his body warm and so very muscular. And held tight in his embrace, she didn't even care that people were looking or that danger lurked outside. When they were together like this, anything…*everything* was possible.

He eased back, gazed down into her eyes, and brushed a hand against her lower spine, as if she were the most precious thing in the world to him. Which, she knew, she was. "Will you *please* go back to Argolea now?"

"Not until the battle's over and I know you're safe."

He breathed out a sigh of frustration. "Isadora—"

"Speaking of which." She grinned because she knew she'd won, then eased out of his arms. "Theron and the others could probably use your help."

The intense light from the portal dimmed, and Isadora turned toward Zander and Callia, both of whom were heading her way.

"Everyone's across?" she asked.

"Safe and sound," Zander answered, rubbing his hands together.

"*Kardia,* don't fight with me on this one."

She didn't plan to. No way she was leaving him here with Hades right outside. "Callia and I will stay unless it becomes necessary for us to go. In which case, we'll contact Casey and have her open the portal for us. That decision is nonnegotiable."

At her back, Demetrius blew out a hard breath.

Callia's features morphed from amused to concerned. "Isa?"

"What?"

Her gaze shot to the floor where Callia was looking, and the puddle of blood forming between her feet.

CHAPTER SIXTEEN

Ogygia was not what Natasa had expected.

Sweat slicked her skin as she stopped in the shade of a palm and lifted the shirt away from her breasts, fanning her overheated flesh. Sunlight beat down from above. Warm earth radiated heat from below.

Of all her luck, to land somewhere sweltering when she was already battling this bloody fever.

"You okay?"

Natasa dropped her shirt, working for indifference when she faced Titus. She didn't want him worrying about her, not when he'd just risked everything for her. And she was still stressing over that fact. *Was* he not thinking clearly around her? How would he be reacting to her if she didn't have this damn element inside? "Fine. You?"

Sweat slicked his skin too, but unlike her, the heat made him look sexy and desirable. Not weak and pathetic. He'd taken off his shirt and tucked it in the back pocket of his pants. A thin sheen coated his rock-solid chest. His wavy hair was tied back, two day's worth of dark stubble shadowing his strong jaw. Warmth reignited in her belly when she remembered tracing the line of that jaw with her lips...with her tongue...

He stepped in front of her and placed his palm against her forehead. Deep lines formed around his eyes and mouth. Before she could push his hand away and reassure him she was okay, he reached for the hem of her shirt and dragged it up. "You're too warm. You need to take this off."

She swatted at his hand. "Titus. No. Someone could see me."

He chuckled and easily pulled the garment over her head. "Who's gonna see you other than me? Besides, I like looking at your breasts, *ligos Vesuvius*."

She frowned, feeling totally vulnerable in nothing but her bra and jeans, but he was right. The air rushing over her bare skin felt a thousand times better than under that shirt.

He knelt in front of her and pulled a dagger from a sheath at his hip. "Don't move. I don't want to cut you."

"Whoa. Wait. What—?"

He grasped a handful of denim at her thigh and pulled the fabric away from her leg. Using the tip of the dagger, he pierced the fabric to create a hole, then set the weapon on the ground, grabbed her pant leg, and ripped it free of her leg.

Okay, that was like the sexiest thing he'd ever done. Wait, no...what he'd done to her in that room at the colony with his mouth...with his body...*that* was the sexiest, but this was damn close. She didn't want to admit danger turned her on, but him kneeling in front of her, shredding her pants with a dagger...? Total turn-on.

The fever was seriously baking her brain.

She rested her hands on his shoulders and tried to stay still while he repeated the process with her other pant leg. When he was done, she was left in nothing but boots, cut-off shorts, and her bra, and all but panting.

"This looks better." He pressed a gentle kiss against the scab on her leg, then rose to his feet. "Cooler?"

Hell, yes. But she frowned for effect. "They're a little short, don't you think?"

He glanced down her body and smiled with what she could only define as appreciation. Then he leaned around her side, slid his hand up the back of her bare thigh until he gripped one cheek, and squeezed. "Not too short for me."

Cool tingles spread along her ass, up her spine. Desire pooled in her belly, tightening her sex. She couldn't stop herself. She rose up on her toes and pressed her hands against his hard, slick chest to keep from falling over. One touch and she was putty in his hands.

Just fuck me. Right here. That'd cool her down for sure. She still didn't understand how, but simply touching him was more relief than stripping naked could ever be.

He grinned that devilish, sexy-as-sin smile and grasped her hand, pulling her along behind him. "Come on. Lots more land to check before sundown."

Disappointment rippled through her body, but she tamped it down and told herself no matter how much she wanted him right now, she wasn't going to use him like that. The Argonauts used him to read minds, to tell them what others were thinking or feeling. She didn't want him to ever think she wanted him only for what he could do for her. Because it wasn't true.

"What happens at sundown?" She stepped over a downed log, wishing they were back on the beach so she could dunk herself in the ocean one more time. Or ten.

"We find a quiet, sheltered place for the night where I can ravish you."

Her whole body tightened. She hadn't realized her feet had stopped until he chuckled and stepped in front of her again. "Like that idea?"

"Yes," she breathed.

He cupped one hand around her jaw, leaned down, and brushed his lips over hers. And those tingling, cool, refreshing sensations shot through her whole body from that one spot, easing the fever just enough, bringing her focus back to what was important.

Him. Keeping him safe. Finding this nymph so they could locate her father. And getting rid of this fire inside her.

When he eased back, his eyes were so fathomless she was sure she could see eternity if she looked hard enough. This had to be the real him. Not the reserved, carefully calculating guardian Theron had described. "Titus…"

He brushed his thumb along her jaw. "Yeah?"

"I should have told you."

"About the element?"

She shook her head. "About the fire."

"It's okay," he said softly. "It's not your fault."

"No, but—"

He cupped her face in both hands. "Do you know why you need me, Tasa?"

Because you're sexy as hell. Because you protect me. Because you're the only one who cares. "I—"

"Because I can cool that fire inside you."

He smiled and brushed a lock of hair away from her forehead. "I love when you're confused. You get this gorgeous little line, right here."

He ran his finger between her brows, and she frowned. "I don't—"

"Understand? I didn't either. Not until I held the Orb. You know how you said you didn't know why you'd been freed from Zeus's prison? It's because Zeus trapped you in the air element. He figured you'd be safe there since he had possession of it. What he didn't know was that Orpheus was going to steal it and hide it for thousands of years."

"Orpheus?"

"One of the Argonauts. He's really Perseus's son reincarnated, but that's a whole other story. What's important is that when O remembered where he'd hidden the air element in his former life, found it again, and placed it in the Orb, that freed you from your prison. He found the air element about three months ago."

Three months ago... That was about the time she'd awoken. Natasa focused on a branch behind him. Stunned and...well, enlightened. "That's why so much time passed."

"And why you don't remember any of it. Thanks to Orpheus, you lucked out. Zeus would have used you long ago if you hadn't been hidden."

And she never would have met Titus.

Her gaze found his again. "That's some knowledge you've come into."

He grinned. "There's more."

"More?" She wasn't sure she wanted to know more.

He slid his arms around her waist and pulled her close. Her temperature ticked down pressed up against him like this, and she felt herself growing weak in the knees, just like every other time he touched her. "I cool you not because you're my soul mate, but because of Calypso."

She rested her hands on his forearms, loving the feel of him against her but overwhelmed at the same time. "You're throwing things out at me really fast. Soul mate?"

He chuckled, leaned close, and kissed her ear. His sweet, refreshing breath ran down her neck, and felt so damn good. "We'll get to that later. When my forefather, Odysseus, was stranded on this island by Calypso, he bathed in a special pool. One drawn from the water element. Traces of that passed to his descendants. To me. I'm the water to your fire, *ligos Vesuvius*."

Her brow furrowed deeper. He looked so smug and proud of himself. What he was saying was crazy, and yet, in some insane way, it made sense. "You're saying the water element's here on this island?"

He shrugged. "Yeah, I guess."

"Then why aren't you looking for it? Your Argonauts—"

"Because I don't care about the elements. I only care about you."

Her mouth dried up, and love—a love she'd never expected to find—filled the space inside her chest. This *had* to be the real him. "Oh, Titus."

He kissed her again. His lips were cool and soft, his tongue wet and so damn tempting sliding along hers. Coaxing a groan from her chest. Making her ache. Making her need.

He smiled that wicked grin. "I am going to have my way with you later. But first I want you sweating. And panting. And so damn hot you're begging for me to cool you from the inside out."

She already was.

A shiver raced down her spine. One born of anticipation and excitement. Fantasies about what he'd do to her ricocheted through her mind as he let go of her, as he tugged on her hand and pulled her after him. But they quickly shifted to doubt and worry when she realized she needed to tell him the rest. Needed to tell him about the deal she'd made so she could search for her father these last few months. But she was afraid. Afraid of what he'd say and do when he learned the whole truth. Afraid of losing him because of a stupid mistake she now couldn't change.

Her heart raced. She stepped around a tree and tried to steady her quaking voice. "So what is this soul mate thing you and Zander both mentioned?"

"It's a curse. From Hera. She had a major grudge against Heracles, and when Zeus created the Argonauts and the realm of the heroes, she was doubly pissed. So she cursed him, and all the Argonauts' descendants, with having only one soul mate. The one person he wants most in the world, but who is the worst possible match for him."

He smiled again, a dazzling grin that supercharged her blood. "But in our case she screwed up, because I'm water to your fire, baby."

His perfect other half... Her entire body lit up with understanding. No wonder he was so drawn to her. Not just because of the elements, but because of a deeper, more sinister reason.

Yeah, water could extinguish a flame, but if the fire was too strong, if there wasn't enough water to douse it, it would turn that water to steam and continue pillaging the land.

She knew too much about destiny. It wasn't something you could change. She was destined to free her father...and with Titus's help, now she had a chance. But this curse of Hera's...this horrible destiny the goddess had bestowed on each of the Argonauts...guaranteed they wouldn't wind up together.

The hope and excitement she'd held on to moments before withered and died. All she could do now was pray that she found her father before it was too late.

And that the fire inside her didn't destroy Titus before that happened.

Nick rolled his shoulder and stepped over a downed log.

The terrain was steep, his breaths heavy. Sweat slicked his skin, but he didn't care. Every step away from the colony was one step closer to freedom. He was done doing for others. Done being the one everyone turned to. Done—

Pain ripped through his chest. He gasped in a breath, reached out for the trunk of a nearby tree, and came to a stop, trying to figure out what the hell had just happened to him.

Nausea rolled through his stomach, and another burst of searing pain shot beneath his ribs.

Isadora.

His heartbeat picked up speed and adrenaline surged through his system. Something was wrong with her. The soul mate bond was screaming that she was in trouble.

His body moved before his mind clicked into gear. He whipped around and pushed his feet forward, picking his way down the hill, jumping over downed logs and around saplings and brush. He had to get to her. He had to help her. He had to—

The scars on his back tingled. And the air around him went from early-summer cool to bone-chilling frigid. His boots skidded to a stop.

Daemons. Leftovers from his mother's ragged army.

His adrenaline surged. The guns strapped to his hips were no use against their tough skin. He reached for the blade he kept strapped to his back just as the first beast emerged from the trees.

At least seven feet tall, with the face of a cat, the ears of a dog, and horns like something straight out of hell, the beast was a gruesome mix of ugly. The only sign he'd once been human was his body. Tall, lean, muscular, dressed in fighting gear and wearing a long trench coat that hid a multitude of weapons. But this monster was not human. Not anymore. And it was here for blood.

The daemon sniffed the air. Bloodred eyes settled on Nick and flared to life. "Half breed."

Three more daemons emerged from the trees at the monster's back. The first motioned them forward with a snarled twist of his gruesome lips. "We've found lunch, boys."

Two stepped forward. The third remained motionless, narrowed eyes blazing. "We're under orders from Hades."

Nick gripped his blade in both hands. They were working for the King of the Underworld now? Fucking fantastic.

"Screw Hades," the one in front said. "I'm hungry."

"He was clear," the other answered. "Only the colony."

Everything inside Nick went still. Hades knew the location of the colony. Their cover was blown. His people…

Isadora…

The darkness he kept locked inside surged and exploded. A red rage colored his vision. He roared and charged, swinging his blade. Metal sliced into flesh, cracking against bone. Howls echoed through the trees. Nick ducked, whipped around, avoided claws and jagged teeth. The first daemon hit the ground with a grunt. In a fury of movement, Nick stabbed his sword through the heart of the daemon on his right, yanked it free, spun and decapitated the other in one clean move.

One look and he realized the fourth—the one who'd hesitated at the back—was gone. All that remained was a bloody mess of cloth and bone.

Daemons weren't truly dead until their heads were separated from their bodies. Chest heaving, Nick lifted his blade and decapitated the other two, then pushed his legs into a sprint and headed for the ridgeline.

He reached the top and looked down into the valley below. His heart dropped like dead weight into his stomach.

A battle raged on the banks of the glacial lake. Daemons and satyrs, Argonauts and half-breed soldiers in a duel to the death. In his peoples' greatest hour of need, he'd abandoned them.

His gaze shot across the shimmering water, to the island that held the castle, invisible to the naked eye. The therillium ore was still masking its location. Hades hadn't discovered it yet. There was still time.

He grasped a boulder, took a step around it, intent on heading down to join the battle. Another shot of blistering pain ripped through his chest, bringing every cell in his body to a halt.

His gaze shot back to the rocky island in the middle of the lake.

The battle would have to wait.

"**B**reathe, Isadora. Steady. That's it. Good. Stay focused."

Demetrius tried to listen to what Callia was telling Isadora but couldn't catch his own damn breath. Panic tightened his chest and forced every bit of air out of his lungs.

Propped up in a bed in the medical clinic, Isadora squeezed his hand. She blew out a short breath, then managed a weak smile. "It's going to be okay."

There she was. His rock. Reassuring him when *she* was the one in danger.

He looked to Callia, on the other side of the bed. "We need to take her home."

"No," Callia said calmly, encouraging Isadora through another contraction. She glanced at the readout on the heart-rate monitor strapped to Isadora's belly. "It's too late for that. She's having this baby right here."

Demetrius ground his teeth but kept his thoughts to himself. He didn't want Isadora stressing, but he didn't like her being here. Not when daemons and satyrs and, *fuck*, Hades were on the other side of the lake. He should be out there with the other Argonauts and Skyla right now, battling back the beasts, making sure they couldn't get to her, but he couldn't leave her side. The soul mate bond would barely even let him leave the room.

Isadora blew out another breath. "Don't...talk about me...like I'm not here."

"We wouldn't dream of it." Callia chuckled. "There, that one's over. Not so bad, right?"

Isadora swiped at the sweat on her brow. Her shoulders shrank, and now that the contraction had passed, she looked pale and exhausted. And ten times too small for the bed she was lying in. "Whoever said this was a beautiful experience obviously never went through labor."

Callia smiled, but it was forced. Footsteps echoed, and she looked toward the door, but Demetrius was too focused on his mate to care who showed up. Isadora's eyes had fallen closed, her head resting back against the pillow. Between contractions, it was if her entire body relaxed, gathering strength for the next attack. His stomach twisted with fear and sickness. He'd never felt so helpless. There was nothing he could do to ease her pain, nothing he could do to speed things up. And when he remembered all that blood...

He swallowed hard and squeezed her hand tighter in his. He wasn't going to lose her. How could he have ever thought he could walk away from her?

"I heard there was a party happening here."

Isadora's lashes lifted, and when she caught sight of her other sister, Casey, she smiled. "I didn't know if you'd come."

Casey moved into the room. Demetrius tugged his chair down the bed to make room for her but didn't let go of Isadora's hand. Casey stopped near the head of Isadora's bed and brushed a damp lock of hair from Isadora's brow. "Nothing could keep me away."

"Does Theron know you're here?"

She scrunched her nose. "Probably best not to tell him."

"The colonists?"

"All in Argolea. Max and Maelea are helping the castle staff get everyone situated until we know what's happening. That Max... He's got some talent in the delegation department."

Isadora managed a weak smile. "Royal genes."

"Must be. Don't worry, Isa. Everyone's safe."

Isadora blew out a breath of relief. Her eyes slid closed. "Thank gods."

Awe rippled through Demetrius. Even now, she was worrying over others. Her father would never have cared what happened to the half-breeds. Demetrius's mate—his *queen*—was the most compassionate person he'd ever known.

"Zander?" Callia called. "Can you keep Isadora company for a minute? I need Casey and Demetrius to help me gather supplies."

"Sure, *thea*." Zander moved away from the window he'd been staring out and stepped toward the bed. Like Demetrius, the soul mate bond wouldn't allow Zander to leave Callia either.

Isadora's eyes shot open, and worry rippled across her face. "What's wrong?"

Callia smoothed a hand over Isadora's brow. "Nothing. Everything's fine. Rest for a minute. We'll be right back."

Reluctantly, Demetrius let go of Isadora's hand, kissed her brow, and whispered, "I'm right outside if you need me." But he didn't miss the look that shot between Callia and Zander. The one that said she was lying.

In the hall, Callia's features turned serious. "Okay, here's the situation. The placenta is partially lying across her cervix, which is why she's bleeding. She's already too unstable to cross the portal, so we're not going anywhere until that baby's out. Lena's already prepping the operating room."

Lena, the half-breed healer, had stayed to help. But that didn't ease Demetrius's fear. Surgery. Gods, please…

"How long?" Casey asked.

"Fifteen minutes, max. I think the sooner we get this done, the better. Isadora's strong, but the blood loss is weakening her faster than I'd like."

And weakening them. Demetrius looked from one sister to the other. He hadn't noticed until right now, but both sisters were pale too. All three were physically connected. What one experienced, the others felt. "You can't operate on her."

"I won't be," Callia answered. "Lena will take the lead. I'm only assisting. She's done this hundreds of times, Demetrius, so don't worry. I have complete faith everything will go smoothly, but you need to know things will happen quickly." She looked between them. "This is not what Isadora was planning for a delivery, so I need you both to be her moral support."

Moral support. He could do that. For her, he would do anything. *Just don't take her from me…*

"And Zander?" Casey asked.

Callia looked her sister's way, and in her eyes Demetrius saw the first hint of fear. "I told him he needed to join the other Argonauts outside, but he won't go."

Because he was scared too, Demetrius realized. He wasn't about to leave his mate with danger so close. The only reason Theron wasn't here guarding Casey was because he didn't know she'd crossed to the human realm.

Callia gestured for them to head back to the room. Inside, Demetrius immediately moved to the bed. Isadora was panting through another contraction, gripping Zander's hand until it turned white. Zander stared at the screen next to her, beeping and flashing with numbers. "Um...*thea*..."

Demetrius reached for her other hand. She pushed up to sitting and wrapped her fingers around his so tightly, pain shot straight up his arm.

Callia crossed the floor quickly, looked from the machine to Isadora, then nudged her mate out of the way. Holding her hands over Isadora's belly, she closed her eyes, using her healer senses to check on the baby.

Her eyes popped open. She turned toward Zander. "We need to move to the OR *now*. Go get Lena."

Zander rushed out of the room. Isadora's eyes flew wide. "Wh-*what?*"

"Honey," Callia said calmly, unhooking wires from the bed, "the baby's heart-rate is dropping. We need to get him out now."

"Oh, gods...."

"Casey?" Callia called. "A little help here?"

Fear pummeled Demetrius from every side. But he had to stay strong for her. He turned Isadora's face toward his. "Look at me. I'm not leaving. I'm right here with you."

She panted through the contraction, but her gaze never left his. And though he knew she was scared, strength—a strength she'd always had deep inside her—shone in her eyes. A strength he felt all the way to the bottom of his soul.

"I love you," he whispered. "You are the best thing that ever happened to me."

She reached for his hand, placed it on her swollen belly, and covered it with her own. Through labored breaths, she said,

"Promise…if anything goes wrong…you'll love this baby…the same way."

His heart squeezed tight. He closed his eyes and rested his forehead against hers. *Don't take her from me…* "Everything will be okay, *kardia*."

"Promise…me."

Please, Dimiourgos…

"I promise."

Her breathing slowed. The contraction eased. Drawing in a last steadying breath, she looked deep into his eyes and brushed her fingers over his jaw. "I love you, too. Just you. No matter what happens, Demetrius, you are my heart."

His chest felt as if it grew ten times its normal size. But before he could kiss her, before he could tell her the same, Callia announced, "Okay, you two. I hate to break this up, but we have a baby to deliver."

Eyes damp, he eased away from the bed. Reluctantly, he let go of Isadora's hand. With a grunt, Callia pushed the bed forward. Casey helped her guide it toward the door.

Where Nick stood, covered in dirt and blood from the fighting, blocking their path.

CHAPTER SEVENTEEN

Titus stared into the fire he'd built and watched the dancing flames lick across a branch then devour it whole.

His link to the Argonauts screamed he wasn't where he was supposed to be, that they needed him. Doubt teased the edges of his mind, but he pushed it back.

Whatever was happening at the half-breed colony wasn't his concern anymore. He'd made his choice. He and Natasa had spent the entire day hiking around the island and hadn't found any sign of Calypso. He knew Natasa was already discouraged—her mood had darkened with every degree the sun had dropped in the sky— but they still had at least half the island to search. Tomorrow they'd find her. He was sure of it. And the Argonauts...

That screaming grew louder. The Argonauts were highly trained. They didn't need him. Not really. Not like Natasa.

"You seem to be somewhere else."

Her voice drew him back to the fire. To her. The flickering flames lit up her hair, made her skin look warmer, her gemlike eyes brighter. "Just thinking."

"Hm." She clasped her hands, hooked them over one bare knee, and looked into the fire herself. She'd put her dusty white T-shirt back on and was sitting on a nearby log. Close, but not close enough to touch. And though he needed the warmth from the fire to ease the night chill, she'd moved a few feet away from it where he couldn't reach her.

He pushed to his feet, crossed, and sat next to her on the log. She scooted a few inches away. He followed.

Frowning, she looked into his eyes. "You have more than enough room."

"I don't want room. I want you."

Something dark flashed in her eyes, but he couldn't read it. She looked quickly away and rose to her feet. "I'm tired."

"Want me to help you relax?"

"No. I want to sleep. Alone."

A definite brush-off. And a one-hundred-and-eighty degree change from earlier.

He watched as she moved to a mossy area under a giant tree and lay down on her side. Tucking her hands up by her head, she closed her eyes, drew in a breath, and let it back out.

She'd bypassed the soft coat he'd laid out for her. Chosen, instead, to move farther away from him. Something was up with her. She hadn't eaten much either. Granted, the fish he'd caught and cooked hadn't been that tasty, but it was food, and they both needed to keep their strength up. He ran through their earlier conversations, but couldn't figure out what had triggered this change.

He looked back into the crackling fire and watched a swirling flame pop and sizzle.

Volatile...

He hadn't touched her in several hours. Her temperature had been warm during the day—not as hot as it had been at the colony—but hotter than when they'd tangled in bed. Way hotter than it had been at the Amazon city. When he had to wear all that stuffy, formal Argonaut gear and was overheated, he was a bear to deal with. She lived with that feeling daily. No wonder she wasn't in the best of moods.

Quietly, he rose to his feet and crossed to where she lay. Her breaths were already slow and steady. She hadn't been lying about being tired. Easing down next to her, he gently wrapped an arm around her waist and spooned against her back.

Heat rushed from her into him.

She was definitely getting hotter. The element inside her was growing more and more unstable with every passing hour. And, he realized...he hadn't picked up a single thought from her since the colony. Before long, the traces of water left in him wouldn't be enough to cool her.

Duty warred with desire, but he refused to let it change his mind. She was his soul mate. He was the water to her fire. They'd find her father before it was too late.

For her—for the world—they had to.

Natasa gasped, the heat so strong it jerked the breath from her lungs.

She turned right and left. Twisting, curling, angry flames licked toward the sky in every direction, blocking her in. She covered her mouth with her hand, coughing through the smoke filling her lungs, and fought back the panic. Somewhere overhead, an eagle swooped over the flames and screamed. An eagle that should be flying high and far, far away.

Stupid bird. Stupid her for following it. She was trapped. No way out. Growing hotter with every second. Burning from the inside... Igniting into flames...

"I can help you. Come to me and live. You have but to give me one tiny thing..."

A roar echoed. She looked up above the edges of the flames, rising high in the sky. The ground shook. The heavens opened. Water rushed in on a wave, filling her mouth, her lungs, dragging her down. She screamed, but the sound was muffled, the force so strong it knocked her off her feet.

Liquid closed over her head. She struggled against the pull, kicked her legs, and reached for the surface. Watery light lingered above. Grew darker.

"Oh yes. When the fire consumes you, our deal will be complete. And the element will belong to me..."

"Tasa, open your eyes."

Natasa jerked back. Her center of gravity tilted, and she went down. Water filled her lungs again. She panicked. Sputtered. Kicked and clawed out. Strong hands wrapped around her biceps, pulling her up. Sweet, blessed air rushed into her mouth.

"I've got you," Titus said. "Hold on to me."

She gasped and grabbed on to him for support. Drawing in deep, gulping breaths, she realized his hair was wet and slicked back from his face. Cool, clear water surrounded them, moonlight reflecting off its dark surface, illuminating the trees and brush around the small lake.

The lake. Where they'd stopped for the night after scouting Ogygia for most of the day. Where Titus had built a fire to cook the fish he'd caught for dinner. Where she'd fallen asleep thinking about her father and the deal she'd made to stay alive and how she could possibly fix the mess she'd gotten into.

"That's it," he said softly, running his hand up and down her back. "I've got you. Just breathe."

She held on tighter. Poseidon hadn't said anything about taking the element when it consumed her. She'd agreed to give it to him only *if* she found her father. But giving and taking were two very different things, and being a god, he probably assumed the same thing she had. That *if* she found him, Prometheus would know a way to free her from that bargain.

A horrible realization caused the air to catch in her throat.

Epimetheus hadn't betrayed her. Poseidon had. He'd purposely drawn her off course, sent her to Epimetheus in search of Maelea, knowing it would force Natasa to waste valuable time. He'd given her just enough extra "time" for the element to become unstable, guaranteeing she wouldn't reach her father before the element took control. And now he was waiting for it to burn through her so he could swoop in and claim his prize.

"*Skata.*" Titus's arms flexed around her. "You scared the crap out of me. You were screaming in your sleep. That must have been some dream."

Not a dream. The reality of what was waiting for her. When she reached the end of this road. Long before she ever lived up to some meaningless destiny.

An eagle swooped low over the water, then rose high into the sky. An eagle just as in her dream. A shudder ran through her.

"Hey." His voice softened. "You're trembling. Are you cold?"

"I'm just..." She couldn't get close enough. "Don't let go of me yet."

His soothing breath spread across her neck and shoulders. He held her tight, just as she wanted. Long seconds passed. Finally, he whispered, "Wanna talk about it?"

She shook her head again. Couldn't find the words to answer. What the hell was she going to do now? Every day they spent together put his life in jeopardy. There was no telling when she might spontaneously combust and spew fire across the earth. Theron had been right. Titus was blind to her. He wasn't thinking logically. If he were...

Her heart felt like it could shatter with the smallest tap. If he were thinking logically, he wouldn't be here with her now. He'd have let his Argonauts lock her away. He'd be with his order now. Fighting to save the world like he'd been doing since long before she'd ever stumbled into his life.

All the times he'd offered her help, the numerous ways he'd saved her life, the compassion he'd showered on her again and again tumbled through her soul. She wasn't going to be the reason he died. She wasn't going to be the reason millions of innocents died. She wasn't like the gods, selfish and only concerned with herself. As a thousand frantic thoughts raced through her mind, one solution solidified. One that she never would have considered until now.

A renewed sense of purpose washed through her, easing the fear. She drew in a deep breath, let it out, and forced herself to be strong, forced herself not to give anything away. Because she knew in her heart if Titus caught wind of what she planned to do, he'd never let it happen.

"H-how did we get in the water?"

"You were burning. I needed to do something to cool you. As soon as I carried you in, though, you started flailing around. Scared me," he added on a whisper.

That explained the dream. But it didn't change what she knew was coming.

She pressed her face against his neck and drew in the sweet scent of his skin, loving the rasp of his stubbly cheek against her flesh.

"Why do I get the feeling you're holding something back?" he asked softly.

Because he was smart. And because even in the short amount of time they'd been together, he'd learned more about her than anyone else in her entire life. "I believe in signs. I never did before but…I dreamed about you."

"You did?"

She nodded. "I think I have for a while, I just…I didn't know it was you. But now…" She swallowed hard. "I should have waited for you. It's the biggest regret I have. I'm sorry I didn't wait."

He pulled back and stared at her face. She saw the questions in his eyes, saw that he had no idea what she was talking about, but she didn't care. Words were tumbling from her mouth now. Words she needed to get out. "The fire element inside me messes with your gift, or curse, or whatever you want to call it. It's why you can touch me when you can't touch others."

"Maybe," he said slowly. "And maybe I can touch you because you're my soul mate."

No…it was the fire element. And maybe it was the trace of the water element inside him too. She wasn't sure. She only knew that he was trying to ignore the obvious…like she'd been doing since the day they'd met.

She tightened her arms around him. Didn't ever want to let go. Knew she'd have to soon. "This isn't going to end well, you know. Fate has different plans for me."

He eased back again and stared down at her. Moonlight accentuated his strong jawline, the stubble on his cheeks, his rugged and sexy features. But this time the curiosity was gone. Stone-cold resolve filled his eyes. "The Fates are just going to have to change their plans."

She opened her mouth to argue, wanting him to be at least a little prepared for what was coming, but he let go of her waist, brought his hands up to frame her face, stopping the words on her tongue. Water dripped from his fingers, splashed against her shoulders, a refreshing chill that spread over her skin before it warmed again. But it was the look in his eyes, the determined no-one-messes-with-me-and-wins look that consumed her.

"I'm not going to lose you, Natasa. I spent too long thinking I didn't need a soul mate to find her and then have her taken from me. Tomorrow we're going to locate Calypso, and she's going to tell us where your father is. And then he's going to remove that damn element so we can be together. Something more than the Orb brought us together. Something deeper is at work here."

She couldn't take it anymore. She wrapped her arms around his neck again and buried her face in his hair. Silence settled over them, the only sound the gurgle of water from the stream that dumped into the lake. Her heart danced with joy over the things he'd said, and yet it was breaking at the same time. Fate was playing a cruel game, spinning a never-ending web of impossibility. One that she knew now she couldn't escape. No matter how hard she tried.

"I have a house," he said softly. "In the mountains outside Tiyrns. It's not fancy, and I rarely go there, but it sits on a river, and it's the only place that's ever felt like home for me. There's a pool, a lot like this, that's perfect for swimming in the summer months. I've never taken anyone there. I want to take you."

The space beneath her ribs contracted. Of course he'd be drawn to water. She squeezed her eyes tight and pictured the wood-and-glass house on the riverbanks, the rushing water, the towering trees, and the swimming hole. Pictured him sliding into all that refreshing water, dusty and sweaty from a hard day of work, then coming up dripping and so damn mouth-watering, he took her breath away.

"I doubt your Argonaut kin would approve of that," she managed. "They didn't much like me being in your realm."

"They'll just have to get used to it. Some things in life are more important than duty and honor."

Gods, how she wished that were true. "Nothing in life is more important than duty and honor, Titus."

He cradled her face in his hands again. "You are."

That was it. All she could take. A desperate need to be close to him one last time overwhelmed every thought and action. She pressed her mouth to his and kissed him hard. His arms closed around her waist with the strength of a vise, and she gasped, then lost herself in the sweet taste of his tongue stroking urgently across hers.

"I want you," she whispered against his lips. Desperation clawed at her soul.

She pressed her lips to his again, opened, and licked into his mouth. Warmth, wetness, hunger caressed her tongue in an erotic dance. She trailed one hand down his bare chest, over the waistband of his pants, and squeezed his cock through the layers of fabric between them.

He was already semihard. It wouldn't take much. Fire burned between her thighs, made her wet with need. She ran her fingers up his shaft, down again, groaning when his tongue thrust deeply into her mouth the way she ached for the long, rigid shaft in her hand to do to her body.

The muscles in his arms and stomach flexed. "You're playing with fire, *ligos Vesuvius*."

"No, I am fire." She stroked him again. Finding the button on his waistband, she flicked it free. "And I want to erupt. With you."

"*Skata*, Tasa. When you talk like that…" He drew back from her mouth. His lips were swollen, his eyes heavy with desire. But there was worry there. He was holding back. "I don't want you overheating."

She didn't want gentle anymore. She wanted hard and deep and desperate.

Her fingers slid beneath the waistband of his pants, down his lower belly and finally wrapped around the length of his cock. He sucked in a breath. She stroked him, base to tip and back down again. "So fuck me here. In the water. I need you, Titus. I need to feel you inside me."

He shuddered as her fingers closed over his erection. Indecision raced across his features, but she wasn't going to be deterred. She kissed him again, sliding her tongue into his mouth. Then squeezed the glorious hard shaft in her hand and brushed her thumb over the underside of the flared head.

He tore his mouth from hers. "Come here."

His arm closed around her waist, and he moved back, dragging her through the water with an urgency that brought every inch of her body to life.

She wrapped her arms around his shoulders again and slid her legs around his waist. Then groaned long and deep when the bulge of his arousal pressed against her mound.

Water splashed somewhere close, but she didn't care where. Her mouth found his, and she kissed him again. Couldn't get enough. His hand landed on her ass, squeezed, and pulled her into him. "I'm gonna make you scream. In a minute, you won't be thinking about anything but me."

She trembled. She was already only thinking of him. Sliding her fingers into his hair, she licked into his mouth. He jerked away before she'd tasted her fill and whipped her around to face a handful of rocks. Water splashed into her face, and she sputtered, then realized he'd pulled her into a small waterfall. Water cascaded over fist-sized stones, rushed into her shirt and across her breasts, tickling her nipples and dragging another gasp from her lips.

"You can stand here." Titus's hands brushed against her belly and raced under her shirt. She found her footing in the soft sand beneath her just as he dragged the garment up over her head. It landed somewhere on the bank, followed by her bra. His hands moved back to her skin, molding her breasts, his fingers rolling her nipples, sending electric vibrations all through her pelvis. Making her frantic for more.

"You make me so hot, Tasa." He breathed warm against her ear, driving her mad with his hands, with the water against her nipples. "There are so many things I want to do to this body."

She braced her palms on the rocks in front of her and tipped her head to the side. His slick tongue traced the curve of her ear. She closed her eyes and moaned. Oh, she wanted him. Wanted him now... "So do them."

His lips curled against her throat. One hand slid from her breast to the waistband of her shorts, then beneath. "I'd love to, but you're not ready for them."

"Yes, I am."

"No." His fingers grazed her lower belly, brushing the top of her mound. Her entire body quaked. "I'd rather not scare you off just yet."

"I'm not going anywhere." *Liar.* She pushed her hips back against his, rubbed her ass against his cock, wanting his fingers lower, deeper, *inside.* "Tell me."

He nipped at her earlobe, then suckled. "I told you there were certain things I liked."

His fingers slid into her wetness, and she groaned at the first touch. He flicked her clit. She arched her back and pressed against him.

"Yeah, that's it. Ride my hand. Gods, you're so sexy."

His soothing breath, his fingers circling her clit, his husky voice... It all felt so good. So wicked. So right. She tilted her head back, resting it against his shoulder. Rode his fingers like he wanted—like *she* wanted. But it wasn't enough. She wanted more. And his words...*things he liked*...circled in her mind, making her even hotter. "Tell me. Tell me what you want to do to me."

He pressed his cock against her ass and nibbled at the side of her neck. "I want you bound."

"Y-yes." *Gods, yes.*

"Like the others." He searched lower. His talented fingers slid along her slick folds. One thick digit pressed inside. She groaned. Shuddered. Clenched tight around him. "But unlike them, I want you naked. And then I want to touch and kiss and lick every single inch of you."

A dark thrill rushed through her when she imagined it. Imagined being bound, for him, at his mercy, letting him do any and every sinful thing he wanted to her.

She pushed back against him and moaned at the exquisite feel. He drew his finger out and pressed back in with two. Flicked her clit with his thumb. "Come for me, baby. I want to feel you come on my fingers before I fuck you so hard."

Sensations rocked her body—the cool water flowing against her breasts, the hard man rubbing against her back, his fingers driving deep where she wanted his cock, his thumb swirling her clit again and again, and his words. Oh…his erotic, suggestive words…

Heat and electricity gathered in her belly, then shot to her center. Stars fired off behind her eyes. The orgasm condensed and exploded, dragging the air from her lungs and a deep groan from her throat.

Her arms gave out, and she fell forward against the rocks. She turned to rest her head on her hand. Water flowed over her fingers, her cheek. She tried to catch her breath.

Frantic fingers unsnapped her shorts, pushed them down her legs, dragged them over her feet and tossed them through the air. Wet garments slapped against the shore. Titus's hard, very naked body pressed against her back.

Desire rebuilt. Sizzled through her core like a match being struck. She spread her legs, pressed back against him. Braced her hands against the rocks and lifted to look over her shoulder.

Desire flushed his face. His eyes were as intense as she'd ever seen them. He looked down into the water where they touched and bent his legs. The hard, thick, blunt head of his erection slid through her sex, found her opening. She groaned as her body stretched around him. Leaning her head back against her shoulder, she turned her mouth toward his.

This. Yes. Just this…

His lips closed over hers. His tongue licked hot into her mouth. His cock drove hard into her body. Flames ignited every nerve ending when he slid out, when he drove in even deeper. Turned her cells to liquid fire. Turned her mind to only him.

"Titus…"

His hands moved to her hips. Her body fell forward against the rocks. Running water tormented her aching nipples. His fingers dug into her skin, and she knew she'd have bruises in the morning, but she didn't care. He thrust home again and again, stroking that special spot so far inside, her eyes rolled back in her head.

"Yes, baby. Feel me inside. Feel me so deep. No one could ever make you feel the way I do."

One hand dipped between her legs and slid over her clit. She jerked at the thousand-watt sensation. He flicked in time with his thrusts. Her orgasm spiraled and roared toward her with the strength of a firestorm. His other hand skimmed her belly, palming her breast,

He tugged her back tight against his body, closed his mouth over hers, claiming every part of her. She moaned, kissed him back, reached behind her to grasp his hip and pull him closer.

"I'm not letting you go." The hand at her breast closed around her jaw, holding the back of her head tight against his shoulder. His thrusts grew harder. His fingers faster. Water slapped against their bodies, against the rocks in front of her. "Say you're mine."

Her heart raced. Her body felt like it could burst into flames at any moment. She kissed him again and again, arching so he could press deeper, so she could feel him everywhere.

"Say it," he growled.

"I'm yours."

Everything inside her exploded. White light erupted behind her eyes. Vibrations shook her core. Against her, he groaned and trembled through his own release.

Her legs buckled, and she fell back against him. But unlike her, he wasn't limp and boneless. He caught her, turned her gently, cradled her in his arms, then lowered them both in the water until cool, clear liquid brushed her shoulders.

Sweet lips pressed against her ear. Tantalizing breath ran down her neck, sending shivers all along her spine. His heart pounded hard in time with hers, but it was his strong, muscular arms holding her close, cherishing her, that she would remember most about this night.

Gods, what he did to her… The things he made her feel…

He kissed the sensitive spot behind her ear. "You constantly amaze me."

She trembled again then sighed. "That's what I do best. Shock and awe."

"I said amaze. There's a big difference."

Not to her. Not anymore.

She stared at the sleek surface of the water while her pulse slowed. Now that her voracious need had been sated, she didn't want to let reality slink back in to their cozy cocoon, but knew she couldn't keep it at bay for long. "There are things you don't know about me, Titus."

"I'm learning. Slowly." He brushed a curl away from her forehead. "And I like every single thing I see."

She didn't have the strength to warn him away. And she didn't want to. Not tonight. "You might not. When you know more."

"I'm going to have all the time in the world to get to know every one of your quirks, *ligos Vesuvius*. And trust me, I plan to explore each one in depth. Nothing I learn is going to change how I feel about you."

Her heart bumped, even though she knew he was wrong. On both counts. But she wasn't about to say so. For the rest of tonight, for what little time she had left, she wanted to pretend like tomorrow didn't exist.

She framed his face with her hands and brushed her mouth against his, a whisper-soft caress that sent chills all along her spine and desire reforming in her core. His arms closed around her, holding her tight. His lips and tongue moved against hers as if they were made for each other. And when they were both breathless, she eased back, tangled her fingers in his hair, and knew—without a doubt—that what she planned to do tomorrow was the only choice she could make.

"What would you say about doing a little more of that…exploring…right now?" she asked.

His lips curled into a gorgeous smile, one that lit up his entire face and crinkled the skin around his eyes. A full-blown grin she hadn't seen before. One that made him not just sexy as hell, but devastatingly handsome. "I'd say…get me out of this water, and I will explore until you scream."

She could think of no better way to spend her last night. "You're on."

CHAPTER EIGHTEEN

A chill spread down Demetrius's spine, one born not just of the cool air in the room but of fear.

Behind the drape, Callia spoke quietly with the Misos healer, Lena, and a nurse who'd stayed behind to help with the delivery. Metal clanked against metal as they picked up or put down instruments. The scent of antiseptic cleaners filled the operating room.

He looked down at Isadora and brushed a lock of hair back that had slipped free of the cap on her head. "You did great at the ceremony the other day. I didn't get a chance to tell you. You had the Council quaking with your speech."

She tipped her head toward him. A faint smile tugged at her lips, but her eyes were closed. "Thanks. But we both know you exaggerate. The Council has never been intimidated by me."

"Yeah, they are. You're stronger than your father, and they know it. They're afraid of change, and you're bringing it. I'll never forget the looks on their faces when you charged into that hall and stopped my execution."

Her eyes drifted open. Fathomless, chocolate eyes he could look into forever. "I'll never forget that moment either. Seeing you strung up like that... It was the worst moment of my life."

His heart took a long, hard roll. "And seeing you was my very best."

"Oh, Demetrius..."

He wanted to hold her hand, but her arms were strapped down for the surgery, so instead he brushed his fingers against the cap on her head and lowered his forehead to hers. *Please don't take her from me...* "There's more for you to do. Still so many things in Argolea that only you can change."

A weak smile tugged at her mouth. "You worry too much about me."

"I always have. That's nothing new."

"I'm going to be fine, Demetrius. It's our baby I'm worried ab—"

Isadora's body jostled from whatever they were doing behind the curtain, and she sucked in a sudden breath, as if in pain. He tensed, and then, from beyond the drape, a tiny cough echoed, followed by a high-pitched infant scream.

Isadora's eyes grew wide. She lifted her head but couldn't move any other part of her body. "Is it...".?

"It's a girl," Callia announced, a smile in her voice. "Give us a minute to get her cleaned up."

"A girl?" Isadora looked toward Demetrius with wide eyes. "Are you sure? Look again. It has to be a boy. I dreamt about it."

A hundred emotions pummeled Demetrius's chest but he was too afraid the Fates were about to rip his world out from under him to smile. "Your gift of foresight isn't reliable when it comes to you, *kardia*." To Callia, he asked, "Is she okay?"

"She's perfect," Callia answered. "Ten fingers, ten toes. A little small, but so is her mom."

The baby screamed louder, and Callia laughed. "Can you hear that? I'd say she definitely has some Argonaut genes in her."

Dressed in scrubs, Callia emerged from behind the screen, a smile bright on her face. In her arms, she held a tiny bundle wrapped in a pale blue blanket. "Here you go, Daddy."

Demetrius pushed to his feet. The rolling chair he'd been sitting on skidded backwards. Callia handed him the bundle. Nerves pinged through his stomach, and his arms shook as he cradled the small package against his chest.

There were two moments in his life he would never forget. The day Isadora had saved his life, and this. The baby stopped screaming, stared up at him with big, gray eyes. And blinked several times.

All these months he'd been afraid, not just for Isadora's health but for what he'd see in his child's eyes. Would she be evil, like his mother Atlanta? Would she fight an inner darkness, as he and Nick did on a daily basis? Or would the light from Isadora and her link to the Horae be enough to overpower everything else?

But when he looked into his daughter's eyes for the first time, he didn't see darkness. He didn't see hatred or revenge or the million other things his mother had hoped for in an heir. He saw the future. And he saw love.

Tears pricked his eyes. He smiled, blinked several times to clear his vision, and whispered, "Heaven."

"Demetrius?"

He swiped at his eyes with his shoulder, turned, and lowered the baby so Isadora could see her. "Say hi to your *matéras*, sweet baby girl."

Isadora lifted her head. The baby stared at her, then opened her little mouth wide and yawned.

"Oh my gods," Isadora whispered. "She's beautiful."

Demetrius smiled at the tears filling his mate's eyes. "She's not a boy."

"Are you kidding? Boys are useless. She's...perfect."

At Demetrius's side, Callia laughed. She patted Demetrius's shoulder and looked down at her sister. "We're almost done here, Isa. Once we get you stitched up, we'll let you hold your baby."

She moved back behind the curtain, and Demetrius sniffled and pushed the blanket down so Isadora could see their daughter's tiny hands.

"Oh...see?" Isadora blinked back tears. "I told you everything was going to be okay. Didn't I tell you?"

"You did. I'll never doubt you again. Gods, I love you so damn much." He pressed his lips against Isadora's, then laughed when the baby grunted from being squeezed between them.

He eased back and swiped at the tear sliding down Isadora's temple. Love flooded his heart—for his wife, for his baby, for everything he'd never expected and now couldn't live without. "She needs a name, *kardia*."

Isadora tipped her head and studied their daughter. "You said heaven when you first saw her. What about...Elysia?"

From Elysium, the Isles of the Blessed, the afterlife where the heroes were said to dwell. He looked down at his daughter's picture-perfect face and smiled. "Elysia. I like that. It fits. It's how I feel when I'm with you."

Isadora's gaze drifted up, held his and softened. "I love you too. Thank you. Thank you for her."

He lowered his lips to hers again and kissed her gently, sweetly. The baby yawned again, content now between them.

"Um, Callia..." From behind the curtain, Lena's voice rang out. "I need you. Her blood pressure's dropping."

Demetrius drew back from Isadora. Her face paled. Her eyes grew distant. From behind the screen, Callia's tense voice said, "Hold on. Let me just—"

Isadora's eyes drifted closed. A crash echoed, and Lena yelled, "Callia!"

All that relief Demetrius had felt jolted to bone-chilling panic. "*Kardia?*"

Oh gods...

The door to the operating room pushed open. Voices flooded the space. Zander's. Lena's arguing with him to get out. Casey's as she rushed in to help.

But all Demetrius could focus on was his mate. Lying still as death. Growing paler by the second. He handed the baby to Casey and pulled the cap off Isadora's head. "*Kardia*, stay with me. Stay with me!"

"Shit," Lena muttered. Metal clanked against metal. "Come on, Isadora..."

Nick turned for the grand stairs, his heart a knot beneath his ribs. If he'd had any hope that Isadora might need him, that he could help her if something were wrong, he'd realized his stupidity the second he'd seen her and Demetrius together.

He had to let this go. There was nothing he could do for her. He wasn't her mate. That wasn't his baby. She—

A slash of pain raked through his chest. He sucked in a breath and gripped the banister at his side. Darkness rolled through the castle like a black, slinking fog.

He was here. Hades had found a way in. Only he wasn't here to conquer like the daemons and satyrs outside. He was here to take.

Nick turned, raced back up the steps, and tore down the hall.

He burst through the door into the waiting room of the medical clinic. It was empty. His boots echoed through the corridor as he ran for the operating room. He pushed the door open, then froze.

Isadora lay motionless on the table. A machine beeped slowly behind her head, so slowly even he knew it was ticking down the seconds of her life. At her side stood Demetrius, a heart-stricken expression across his face. Next to him, Casey, looking almost as pale as Isadora, held a bundle of blankets. Zander was kneeling on the floor next to Callia, who—also pale—sat leaning against the wall, a hand over her stomach. And Lena, dressed in scrubs and covered in blood, stood motionless near Isadora's feet.

No one noticed him. No one moved. No one spoke. Everyone was too busy staring at the seven-foot-tall god dressed all in black in the center of the room.

Hades's gaze raked the group, then slid over Isadora. "Oh, this *is* a good day. The half-breed colony *and* the little queen. I did not expect she'd be mine so soon, but I am not complaining."

Fury erupted over Demetrius's face. He moved out from behind the bed and launched himself at Hades. "You won't touch her!"

Hades lifted a hand. An arc of electricity erupted from his palm, shooting through Demetrius. His body flew back, crashed against medical equipment, and hit the wall. He slumped to the ground in a mess of machinery.

"None of you can stop this," Hades announced, looking from face to face. "A deal with the King of the Underworld cannot be revoked. In a few seconds, that deal will be fulfilled, and her soul will belong to me."

At Isadora's side, Casey's face paled even more. She held the baby close. Nick's gaze shot from her to Callia, then back to Isadora.

Isadora had made a deal with Hades to save Casey's life. One soul for another. But if Isadora died, it wouldn't just be her life that was forfeit. All three sisters would perish.

The machine near Isadora's head slowed its beeping even more.

"That's it, little queen," Hades encouraged. "Come to me. We're going to have so much fun together."

"*Kardia…*"

Demetrius tried to push up, but Hades blasted him with another jolt of electricity. Nick's gaze shot to his brother, then back to their soul mate. And everything inside him—all the hope and disappointment and heartache—coalesced in the space that should hold his heart.

"If you spare her, I'll tell you where the therillium stores are hidden."

Hades turned, and surprise, followed by confusion, flickered over the god's face. "You...you're the leader of the half-breeds."

He was negotiating with the god of darkness. This could go downhill fast. Nick spread his stance. He wasn't about to back down. "Spare her, and the therillium is yours."

"Nick," Zander breathed in warning.

Nick ignored him. To Hades, he said, "I know you want the invisibility ore. And I know it's more important to you than her."

Hades's gaze narrowed. And in his soulless eyes, Nick could see the god was contemplating.

Yes...take the deal...

"I have such plans for her." Hades looked over Isadora once again. His gaze lingered. Lust and indecision swirled in his eyes. Abruptly, he turned and fully faced Nick. "Though I am always amenable to a trade."

The god was going for the ore. "The therillium is—"

"Not just the ore." Hades's black stare homed in on Nick. "You. I want you. Not when you die, but now. There will be no trading of souls this time. You come to me freely, here and now, and in exchange I will spare the little queen's life and relinquish my claim to her soul. That is the deal. Take it or leave it."

Nick was a pure-blood demigod—the son of Atalanta, a goddess, and a human father he'd never met. As a pure hero, it made sense his soul would be more valuable to Hades than an Argolean, royalty or not, but Nick couldn't figure out why Hades would want him now. Options, scenarios, possibilities raced through his mind.

He looked back at Isadora's pale features. And remembered how happy she'd been at the party in Argolea, how she'd smiled and sparkled under those chandelier lights. How much love had been in her eyes when she'd gazed upon his brother.

The empty space around his heart twisted hard. She'd never be his. Not the way he wanted. But he could do something for her his brother couldn't.

"Fine." His gaze shot back to Hades. "My life for hers. I agree."

"Niko," Demetrius said in a weak voice, trying to push up.

A wide smile broke across Hades's face. Metal shackles connected by a heavy chain appeared from nowhere and snapped over Nick's wrists. And a dark gloom pressed down hard on Nick's chest, sucking the air from his lungs.

A poof of black smoke erupted in the room, and another god appeared. This one Nick knew well.

"We were winning out there," Zagreus snapped. "You force me to fucking fight, then you summon me from the battle for—"

"I summoned you," Hades said, "to greet your newest prisoner."

Zagreus turned to face Nick. Disgust reflected in his eyes. "A demigod? I'm not impressed."

Hades placed a hand on Zagreus's shoulder. "Not just a demigod, son. Forget Prometheus's daughter. Let Zeus and Poseidon fight over her. You're going to repay your betrayal to me by joining my army. We now have everything we need to harness Krónos's powers. My father's bastard son is going to win this war for us."

Titus awoke with a shiver. His living blanket wasn't cuddled up to him like she'd been when they'd drifted to sleep.

He rolled to his back and pushed up on the soft moss under the tree where they'd fallen asleep after making love. "Tasa?"

Water gurgled from the nearby stream. The first rays of dawn spread watery light over the forest. Somewhere close, a bird cawed.

He moved to sitting and looked around the sparse trees. Nothing but stumps and branches and tree trunks as far as he could see. Natasa's clothes were gone.

A whisper of unease rushed through him. He dragged on his shirt, then stood and pulled on his pants. "Tasa?"

Nothing.

Skata. Where the hell had she run off to? He hoped she was just hungry, looking for something to eat. Or maybe she was back at the lake, taking a quick dip to cool down. He headed that direction, searching the area around the lake and stream and the small clearing beyond.

No sign of her.

"Tasa?" he called again.

He stood on the edge of a meadow, tall grasses tickling his hands where they perched on his hips. Turning, he scanned the area. It was warm out here in the sunlight—warmer than he expected. Sweat slid down his back, pooling at the base of his spine beneath his thin shirt. His panic jumped another notch. If he was sweating, Natasa had to be on fire.

"Come on, *ligos Vesuvius*," he muttered. "Where in Hades did you go?"

He moved across the meadow. Halfway to the other side, an eagle swooped down in his path. His feet drew to a stop. He watched the eagle soar through the sky, then dip low and land on the branch of a great oak off to his left.

The eagle was the emblem of Zeus. And Zeus had imprisoned Natasa's father. His heart beat faster.

He turned, some unseen hand drawing him toward the oak instead of the woods on the other side of the meadow he'd plan to search. When he was five feet away, the eagle screeched, its great wings flapped, and it took off into the sky.

Titus wasn't sure what to do. He was losing it, thinking he was seeing signs in a bird. Just when he was about to turn around and head back the way he'd come, he caught sight of what looked like a bare foot, lying still against the ground through the tall grass.

Foreboding slid down his spine. He parted the grass with his hands, then sucked in a shocked and horrified breath.

"Tasa…?" *Oh, shit.*

She lay motionless on the ground, her curly red hair fanned out beneath her, her skin pale and dry. He reached for her arm resting on her stomach and placed the back of his hand against her forehead. Her skin was cool, not hot, and the pulse in her wrist was abnormally slow.

"Tasa? Baby, open your eyes and look at me." She didn't respond. He pried her eyelids open. Her pupils were dilated.

This wasn't the element burning her. This was something else. He looked around, trying to figure out what had happened to her. A clump of long-stalked, yellow-and-white flowers rested in her hand.

Shaking, he reached for the flowers. The roots were missing, the stalks broken and ripped. He looked from the flowers to her face and the trail of drool down the side of her mouth.

No. No, no, no...

He dropped the flowers against the ground and reached for her shoulders. "Tasa, dammit!"

Her leg twitched. Her eyes fluttered open.

"Tasa...baby..." He cradled her face, then pushed the hair back from her eyes. "*Skata*, what did you do?" His voice hitched. "Tell me what you did."

"For you," she rasped. "So he can't...have the element."

"He who?"

Her eyes fell closed again. Her head sagged to the side. Panic, fear and helplessness coalesced inside Titus. He dragged her into his lap. "I don't care about the damn element. Don't you know that? I care about you. Open your eyes, Tasa. Come on, baby..."

Her body fell limp against him.

"Tasa?" He shook her again, but she didn't respond. Tears blurred his vision. Never before had he thought he'd miss her fever, but this cold chill was worse than anything he could imagine. Pain ripped through his chest, his heart, his very soul. The one thing in the world he'd never wanted was now the only thing he couldn't live without.

A scream echoed from the sky. Through watery vision he looked up and saw the eagle again. It dove straight for them, swooping low—so close he could have reached out and touched it. The great bird glided through the meadow and landed in a tree on the far side. Then stared at him, as if to say, *Follow me.*

I believe in signs...

She'd said that to him last night, in the water. When she'd been rambling about the elements and dreaming about him and not waiting. His mind flashed back to the day he'd chased her in Argolea, when he'd climbed the trellis on that castle wall. An eagle had swooped low then too. An eagle he hadn't remembered until just now.

He wasn't sure he believed in signs, but if he hadn't followed that eagle moments ago, he never would have found her. If she hadn't seen it dive-bomb him on that wall walk, it was possible she might not have come back and saved him.

He didn't have time to second-guess. Moving on autopilot, he pushed to his feet, lifted her in his arms, and turned toward the eagle. It lurched off the branch, flapping its wings, then screeched again. But it didn't fly off. It hovered over the ground, as if waiting for him to catch up.

Calypso was somewhere on this island. She was a nymph, immortal, and she had use of magic and spells. If anyone could save Natasa, it would be her. He just hoped like hell this eagle knew where the nymph was hiding and was taking them to her, instead of leading them both to their deaths.

CHAPTER NINETEEN

"**H**ang on, Tasa."

Titus shifted Natasa in his arms. His muscles ached, and sweat slicked his skin. She was cool against him, but he knew he hadn't lost her yet. Her occasional twitch and the soft moan when he shook her encouraged him and kept him going.

He reached the peak of the ridge they'd been climbing. The eagle screamed, fluttered its wings, then dove down into the small valley. There, nestled between two mountains and built beside a lake, sat a small, well-tended cottage.

The soft notes of a gentle song drifted to his ears. Calypso. It had to be. His aching muscles pushed forward all on their own.

Natasa groaned in his arms with every jostling step down the hillside. "Not long now, baby. I'm gonna get you help."

Rock and dust gave way to packed, even ground. His boots sloshed through the small stream flowing out of the lake as he crossed to the house. Just as he rounded the far corner, a female carrying a bucket stepped in front of him, drew up short, and gasped.

Calypso didn't look like an immortal deity. She wasn't tall like Persephone, nor dressed in rich gowns. She wore a common cotton dress. Her curly dark hair was pinned up on the top of her head, and her cheeks were pink and sun-kissed. The only hint he had it was her was the music she'd been singing before he'd startled her. Music that had drawn him toward her like a sailor to a siren.

Her eyes widened, then narrowed. And she uttered one word. "Odysseus."

"No," he said quickly. "Titus. She's hurt." He nodded down at Natasa passed out in his arms. "She needs help."

He didn't wait for the nymph to answer. He stepped into the open door of the cottage, looked around, and finally decided the best place for the nymph to work her magic was on the table.

He laid Natasa on the old scarred surface and moved the few cups sitting close to the sideboard at his back. Calypso stepped into the cottage after him, eyed Natasa warily, then set her bucket on the counter in the adjoining kitchen. "You are not...Odysseus? I sense him in you."

"I'm his descendant. And we've been looking for you."

Her expression was full of speculation, but slowly, it relaxed. "What happened to her?"

"I'm not sure." The nymph was blocking him from reading her mind. That or he was too frazzled to make his gift work. He raked a hand through his hair. She had to help him. She had to...

He took a deep breath to calm the raging panic. "I think she ate something she shouldn't have. She was holding a clump of flowers in her hand when I found her passed out on the ground."

Calypso leaned over Natasa, pried her eyelids apart and looked at her pupils. She ran her fingers over Natasa's throat and felt for a pulse. Easing back, she looked down Natasa's body and back up to her face. "What did the flowers look like?"

"Um..." Titus tried to remember. "Long stalks, yellow-and-white umbrella-shaped flowers."

"The roots. Were they tuberous?"

"There were no roots. They were broken off. Ripped."

Calypso was quiet as she held her hands out, hovering them over Natasa's belly. "She burns hot inside, yet her skin is cold and clammy."

Titus didn't answer. Didn't know what to say. She had to help. She had to do something...

The nymph slowly lowered her hands. "Tell me, does she know she carries the fire element inside her?"

He swallowed hard. There was no sense lying. Not now. "Yeah."

Her gaze flicked to his. Soft, light blue, compassionate eyes his forefather had once gazed into. "She ate hemlock. The fact the roots were missing tells me she knew that was the most poisonous part of the plant."

"Can you heal her?"

The nymph's gaze dropped to Natasa's face. "No. The damage is already done. Her pulse is slow, but paralysis has yet to set in. She has, maybe, twenty-four hours left. Probably less."

Titus's eyes slid shut, and he braced his hands against the table, letting his head drop between his arms. He'd failed. They'd been so close to finding Calypso and locating her father and she'd gone and done something so stupid, so selfish...

"You care for her."

It wasn't a question but a statement. And why it unleashed a rush of fury inside him, he'd never know. He pushed away from the table and threw his arm out. Felt like slamming his fist through a wall. "I don't just care about her. I love her, dammit. And she went and threw it away like it didn't even matter."

Calypso looked back at Natasa, lying still against the table. "Sometimes we have to let go of those we love in order to save them. I did that for Odysseus. He would have died here, trapped forever. He was meant to be free. She did this for you, so that you could live."

For you...so he couldn't have it.

He didn't want to understand, but he did. She'd done this to kill the fire element within her. Too keep Prometheus's wrath against the Olympians from being unleashed. To save him. Again.

Titus closed his eyes and sank against the back of a chair, nearly swept under by a tidal wave of misery so high it was all he could see.

"You came this far, Guardian," Calypso said softly. "Use your gift."

"The only way for the element to be free is at her rebirth."

Calypso's thought penetrated the despair. And in a rush, all the knowledge he'd received from the Orb came flooding back. Calypso was Atlas's daughter, and Prometheus was her uncle. Zeus forbade the gods from uttering words about the Titan, but he didn't prohibit thinking.

Death. Rebirth. The name *Natasa* was Old Greek, and it meant, literally, resurrection.

He pushed away from the chair, a renewed sense of urgency coursing through him. "Can he save her? Prometheus?"

"He can free her," Calypso thought. *"But he has to do it before the poison claims her and destroys the element."*

Titus didn't care about the damn element anymore. All he cared about was the woman lying still against the table.

He reached for the nymph's hand. "Touch me."

Calypso's brow wrinkled, but she lifted her hand and slowly lowered her palm against his.

Electricity flowed from her into him, a million thoughts and memories and emotions. A wave of nausea rushed through Titus's body, and his knees buckled, but he gripped the table with his free hand, ground his teeth against the pain, and fought to stay in control.

When the transfer finished, he let go of her and sagged to his knees.

Calypso reached out to help him up.

He blocked her with his arm. Once was all he needed. "I'm"— he hissed out a breath—"fine."

His strength returned quicker than in the past. A sign he was mastering control? He didn't know, nor did he care. He pushed to his feet and reached out to pick up Natasa. "Thank you."

The nymph closed a hand over Natasa's arm. "Leave her. Where you're going it's not safe for her to travel. Find him, bring him here. I will watch over her. You have my vow."

Titus didn't want to leave Natasa, but the nymph was right. Thanks to the memory transfer, he knew exactly where Prometheus was chained, and he knew there was no way he could keep Natasa safe where he was going.

Swallowing the lump in his throat, he nodded, leaned down toward Natasa, and brushed the hair back from her brow. "I'll be back soon, *ligos Vesuvius*. I promise."

She groaned and tipped her head his way as if she'd heard his words. Tears pricked his eyes, and his heart felt like it cracked open wide in his chest. He pressed his lips gently against her cheek, then whispered in her ear, "I love you, fire-girl. I'm not letting go of you. Don't you dare let go of me."

"Hades's and Zagreus's armies have withdrawn. Phin's with Cerek, Orpheus and Skyla, burning the bodies and cleaning up the mess."

Isadora sat perched against a pile of pillows in a bed in one of the suites of the colony, cuddling Elysia in her arms, listening to updates from Theron. Seated on the bed beside her, Demetrius leaned close and brushed his fingers over their daughter's hand. Elysia yawned, then grabbed on to him, her tiny little hand barely wrapping around his masculine index finger.

Demetrius hadn't left Isadora's side, not since she'd gone into labor, and after everything that had happened in the delivery room, and everything he and Callia and Casey had told her had happened with Hades and Nick, she could see the guilt and fear eating away at him. She knew he was desperate to go after the brother he'd never seen eye to eye with but now felt he owed. But she also knew he was torn. He was already head over heels in love with their daughter—a fact that warmed Isadora from the inside out—and couldn't bear leaving either of them just yet.

She understood. She felt the same. She didn't want him anywhere but at her side. But Nick…

She looked up at Theron, who'd been none too pleased when he found out Casey had crossed to the human realm to help, and how close she'd come to death when Isadora's situation had turned dire. Guilt washed through her, that she'd caused so much trouble for everyone during an already tumultuous time, but this was always the way it was going to be. Anytime any one of the three sisters was in jeopardy, the others would be affected. And Zander too, since Callia was his vulnerability.

Her gaze cut to Callia and Zander standing on the other side of the bed, he behind her rubbing her shoulders, she looking down at Elysia with a wide smile. This time, thankfully, tragedy had been averted.

It wouldn't always be.

Her gaze slid back to Theron. She pushed thoughts of *what could have happened* out of her mind and focused on what they needed to do next. "The Misos can't come back here. Now that Hades knows where they're located, they won't be safe. And with Nick gone…" Her heart pinched, and she cuddled Elysia closer, so very thankful for what Nick had done for her but afraid for him at the same time. "They'll need to stay in Argolea."

"The Council will throw a fit about that," Demetrius said at her side.

Isadora didn't care. She had bigger problems to deal with. Like how they were going to find Nick and save him from a hell he'd sacrificed himself to, all for her. It didn't matter if he was Krónos's son—though her stomach rolled at just the thought. All that mattered was that he'd saved her. Saved *them*. "The Council can kiss my ass."

"When can she go back?" Theron asked Callia. "I don't think it's safe for her to be here where Hades knows he can reach her. Even with Nick as a prize, he's going to be pissed he lost her soul. Especially since we now have Maelea."

Thank the gods Maelea and Gryphon were back in Argolea with Max, getting the colonists settled. Things could have gone from bad to worse had Persephone's daughter been in the room when Hades showed up.

"Tomorrow, probably," Callia answered. "She should be strong enough by then."

"We still have to deal with the issue of the fire element," Casey said from Theron's side. "Even if Zagreus can use Nick to harness Krónos's powers and...crap....I don't know, figure out how to somehow free the Titan, we still need that element. And having Prometheus on our side would be a huge boost."

Theron crossed his arms over his chest and scowled at Zander. Isadora knew from talking to Callia that Zander had let Titus and Natasa go in search of her father. She leaned into Demetrius, totally understanding the reasoning, but every second that passed without word from them amped her worry another degree.

"What of her 'unquenchable fire'?" she asked, looking up at the rest of them.

"Titus isn't going to let that happen," Zander said. When all eyes turned his way, he added, "Trust me. I saw the guy. He's got it bad for her. No way he's letting her out of his sight."

Theron rubbed his forehead. "According to Phin, he had it bad for her before any of this even happened."

"You say that like it's a bad thing." Casey's lips curled in a smile. "I remember a time when you 'had it bad.'"

Theron's arm wrapped around Casey and he pulled her close to his side. "I still have it bad, *meli*. Especially when you pull stunts like that last one. But that doesn't change the fact the object of his obsession is more of a loose cannon than Zagreus ever was."

Footsteps echoed from the hallway. Isadora looked past Theron and the others who were turning to see what the ruckus was about. Surprise registered when Titus appeared in the doorway. Unlike the last time Isadora had seen him, there was a wild look in his hazel eyes. His clothes were wrinkled and covered in dirt, his hair free of the usual leather strap, hanging in messy waves around his face. And there was enough stubble on his jaw to tell her he hadn't thought of shaving in days.

Theron dropped his arm from Casey's waist. "Titus—"

"You." Titus looked past the leader of the Argonauts and zeroed in on Demetrius. "I need you right now."

"What's happened?" Demetrius let go of Isadora and the baby and pushed to his feet.

Titus took one step into the room. "I have to get to Prometheus before it's too late. He's the only one who can stop it. I know where he is…I just don't know how to get there."

"Stop what?" Theron asked.

"Where?" Demetrius said.

"Pandora." Titus didn't even look Theron's way. "He's being held in a cave high in the mountains."

Pandora. Isadora's pulse picked up speed. She looked up at her mate, who was suddenly looking down at her. Prometheus was on the island where she and Demetrius had been trapped together by Atalanta. Where Zeus had dumped all the worst of the monsters and beasts from the ancient days. They'd been within walking distance of the Titan and hadn't even known it. "Oh my gods," she muttered.

She didn't have to ask what Titus was trying to stop. Everyone knew.

"How long?" Demetrius looked back at Titus.

Titus scrubbed a hand through his messy hair. Panic filled his eyes. "I don't know. Eighteen hours, maybe less."

"Holy *skata*," Theron muttered. "And you're just now telling us?" He looked to Zander with a *see what kind of mess you caused?* look. "We have to make sure she's contained before—"

Fury flashed in Titus's eyes, and he hurled himself toward Theron, slamming the leader of the Argonauts back against the wall beside Isadora with a crack. "You're not touching her!"

Isadora gasped and pulled the baby close to her body in a protective move. Casey and Callia scrambled toward the bed to protect her.

"Son of a bitch." Demetrius lurched around the bed. Zander's boots scuffed the floor. Theron's head hit the wall with a crack, but the leader of the Argonauts had the strength of Heracles on his side. Isadora knew he wasn't really hurt, just surprised....as were they all.

"Dammit, Titus." Zander grasped him by one arm. Demetrius got hold of the other. Together they yanked Titus back from the death grip he had on Theron's throat.

"What the *fuck* has gotten into you?" Theron roared.

Titus's face looked pained, but he jerked against the hold Zander and Demetrius had him in. "You're not putting her in a cage. She's not a freakin' animal!"

"Holy Hades." Exasperated, Theron ran a hand down his face as if to calm himself, then pinned Titus with a hard look. "You're losing it, man. Pull your shit together and remember what's at stake here. Do you have any idea what she really is?"

"She's a person. Not an object and not a pawn that you"—he yanked his arms out of the guardians' grips—"can manipulate in your vendetta against the gods."

Theron's eyes darkened. Isadora tensed, realizing how close the leader of the Argonauts was to losing it. He stalked forward, getting right in Titus's space. "I don't give a rip about the gods right now. I'm focused solely on what we—as guardians—took an oath to defend. Start thinking with your brain, Titus, instead of your dick. She's the end of the fucking human world."

"Since when do you care what happens to the human realm?" Contempt filled Titus's eyes. "You never did before Casey came into your life. You forget shit so fast. Once you realized she was your soul mate, you were willing to sacrifice everything for her— everyone in this room and all of Argolea. I'm not asking you to do that. I'm not even asking for your friggin' help. All I need is for Demetrius to tell me where the island is located before Natasa dies."

"Lena said her temperature might continue to rise," Callia said warily. "Is she overheating?"

"No," Titus answered, staring at Theron, distrust and anger swirling in his eyes. "She ate hemlock. Poisoned herself in the middle of the night so it would kill her before the element could ignite inside her. And she did it to *save* the human realm, not destroy it like you all think she's hot to do."

Theron's eyes widened.

"Shit," someone muttered. "Fuck me," someone else whispered. In the shock reverberating through the room, Isadora's gaze found Demetrius's. She nodded.

Demetrius looked at Titus. "I'll take you to Pandora."

Relief rushed over Titus's features. He moved quickly toward the hall. "We don't have a lot of time."

"Titus—" Theron called.

Titus stalked through the door and disappeared around the corner without another word.

Looking as shocked as Isadora felt, Theron turned toward Demetrius. "We'll need charmed weapons if we have any hope of getting past those beasts on Pandora."

"Pretty sure what we'll need we can find in the Hall of heroes," Demetrius answered.

Theron was going with Demetrius and Titus. Though fear shot through Isadora's belly at the thought of Demetrius back on that nightmare of an island, a little of her anxiety eased. She knew Theron had only been performing his duty, protecting the human world as best he could, but Titus had a point. Theron had been willing to give up everything for Casey. And Titus had every right to be pissed at all of them for not giving Natasa the same benefit of the doubt, no matter who she was.

"Should we gather the rest of the guardians?" Zander asked.

"No," Theron answered. "We don't want to do anything to attract unwanted attention from the gods. Cerek and Phin can keep cleaning up. I'll alert Orpheus and Skyla to watch over the Horae until the queen is clear to travel back to Argolea." He turned toward Casey. "Can you contact Gryphon and tell him to keep everything under wraps? The last thing we need is the Council figuring out shit's going down."

Casey nodded, stepped forward, and wrapped her arms around Theron's waist. "I will. Don't worry, everything here will be fine. Just help Titus find Prometheus before it's too late for Natasa."

Theron frowned down at his mate. "My help's the last thing he wants right now. But he was right. I would have given up everything for you, *meli*."

Casey eased up on her toes and kissed him. "That's what makes you human. It's what makes you different from the gods. It's what I love about you."

He frowned. "My stubbornness?"

"Your flaws. And your ability to admit when you're wrong."

Isadora watched the exchange, regret spreading through her. She was as much to blame as Theron. Sometimes she got so wrapped up in doing for the good of the whole, she forgot that it was the individual relationships that made life so precious.

Demetrius leaned close and kissed Elysia on the forehead. When he lifted his dark eyes to Isadora's, she ran her fingers over his rugged jawline, aware that Natasa's life wasn't the only one in peril here. "Be careful. Please don't do anything stupid. We need you."

Demetrius pressed his lips against hers. "Nothing will ever keep me away from you, *kardia*. Take care of our princess."

Her heart rolled as he eased away, as he joined the others and headed for the door. Her sisters—Callia and Casey—sat on opposite sides of the bed, and through her connection to both of them, she could feel their worry and fear for their own mates

"They'll be back," Casey announced, brushing her fingers over Elysia's little head. "They'll find Prometheus in time."

Isadora hoped so. Not only because she knew losing his soul mate might just break Titus, but because, regardless of what any of them had or hadn't said, they couldn't afford for Natasa's fire to burn free.

CHAPTER TWENTY

The Hall of Heroes was nothing more than ruins set high on a hill on the island of Pandora. The Mediterranean Sea crashed against rocks far below the broken outpost, and off in the trees on the hillside behind them, the splitting of trees hitting earth followed by an occasional screech or bellow echoed.

Titus didn't know what the hell was making that noise or what was in those trees, but he had a bad feeling they'd soon find out. Demetrius had told them about his time on Pandora—about the hydra and chimera and ker he'd encountered while he'd been here. A ripple of worry skittered through Titus, but he forced it back. All he wanted to do was find Prometheus and leave.

His heart squeezed tight. He wasn't going to lose her. He couldn't. He kept his mouth shut as he followed Demetrius inside the ruins. Behind him, Theron and Zander spoke in hushed words. He didn't know why the fuck the leader of the Argonauts had joined them, but he wasn't going to be stupid. He knew Theron was most concerned about the element, not that he cared what happened to Natasa. Titus had already made an important decision before coming here: when he got Natasa out of this mess, he was leaving the Argonauts. He'd had it with doing what everyone wanted. When it came right down to it his guardian kin didn't care about his happiness or his needs; they only cared about what he could do for them. About the fact they could use his ability to read minds to gain the upper hand in whatever battle or quest they were engaged in. And he was sick of it all.

Demetrius stopped in front of a stone wall and muttered words in ancient Greek. Air rasped, and then the entire door slid open to reveal a secret passageway and a curved set of dark stairs.

"Sweet," Zander muttered at Titus's back.

Demetrius reached for a torch from a holder on the wall, waved his hand, and used magic to ignite a small flame. Then he ushered them to follow.

Boots clomped against stone. The flame illuminated the dark staircase. Moving off the last step, Demetrius waved his hand over the torch, and the flame grew brighter, illuminating a hall with a vast ceiling and soaring columns, and seven trunks, each marked with a different seal of the great heroes. They formed a U shape with Heracles's trunk the center of attention.

"Holy mother of gods," Zander said, awe and wonder alight in his voice. "I honestly didn't think this place was real. I mean…I know you told us but…"

"I lived it," Demetrius said, setting the torch in a holder on one of the columns. "And most days I don't believe it's real." He waved his hand again and other torches around the room came to life. "Fan out and look for what might be of help."

They spread out. Titus moved toward the trunk marked with the seal of Odysseus. Metal groaned as he flipped the lid open and eased it back. Behind him, the guardians talked in low voices as they went through the other trunks.

A sword, a shield, a wooden statue of Athena—which Titus immediately recognized as the Palladium of Troy that Odysseus had stolen during the Trojan war—a cylindrical-shaped reed closed off on both ends that sloshed as if water were capped inside, and a small branch with a clump of bright orange, perfectly preserved berries still clinging to the vine.

He uncapped one end of the reed and sniffed. Quicklime, saltpeter, resin and a few other components he couldn't decipher. He looked to the vine. At his back, he could hear the other guardians showing off spears and poisoned arrows.

He should be awed by the history in this one room, but he wasn't. He was too frantic to get help for Natasa. Recapping the small tube, he thought logically. Odysseus had been a great warrior and a better thinker. Magical weapons might help, but they weren't going to save Natasa's life. He was.

He stuffed the reed into one pocket, the berries in another, then gathered the sword and shield and closed the lid of the trunk. "Let's go. "We're running out of time."

Trunks closed. Demetrius and Zander headed for the door. Titus turned to follow Z, only to be stopped by Theron's hand against the sleeve of his shirt. "T, hold up."

Thankfully, Theron didn't touch his skin, but Titus could read the Argonaut leader's mind. And he already knew the guardian was fumbling for something to say after their run-in. "Don't. I don't want to hear excuses. I just want to get this done."

He pulled his arm free and turned for the stairs.

"I didn't know she was your soul mate."

Titus harrumphed. "It wouldn't have stopped you from trying to use her. I know that better than anyone."

"There."

Titus swiped the sweat from his brow. They'd battled three harpies—winged, screeching creatures that were a grotesque cross between woman and bird; a hydra—a nine-headed dragonlike beast hell-bent on keeping them from reaching the opposite side of a giant lake; and an orthrus—a two-headed serpent-tailed dog that, luckily, went down with the help of Demetrius's magic and the strength left in Achilles's spear. Hours had passed since he'd left Natasa, and every second that spun by amped Titus's fear. Time was running out. If they didn't free Prometheus and get him to his daughter...

His heart twisted. Zander, Theron, and Demetrius—each equally battle-weary and as sweaty as he—moved up on his side. All four eyed the dark cave dead ahead.

"I don't hear anything," Theron said in low voice.

No, Titus didn't hear anything either. An eerie silence echoed over the rugged mountains. He knew Prometheus was in there. Lies could be told but not felt. Calypso couldn't have fooled him.

Demetrius scanned the rock formation above the cave entrance. "You think that giant eagle's inside with him or lurking somewhere out here?"

Titus's gaze jumped from rock to rock. He tuned in to his gift and tried to locate the eagle's thoughts. Couldn't.

"We could look for another way in," Zander said.

"That could take hours." Demetrius's gaze narrowed on the cave opening. "Natasa doesn't have hours."

Theron drew his blade. "Then let's be quiet and quick and get the hell out of here."

Zander, Theron, and Demetrius moved forward. Titus hesitated, hundreds of thousands of years of war strategy rolling like a wave through his mind. If he were Zeus, he'd lock Prometheus somewhere no one could reach him. In a place with only one entrance that, to the naked eye, might seem harmless but was actually impenetrable.

Rock was impenetrable. But one thing could destroy it.

He turned to Theron. "Gimme the bow and arrow you took from Heracles's trunk."

Theron slid the quiver from his back, handing it and the bow to Titus. "What are you going to do?"

"Use my brain."

He headed for the boulders and rock-face and reached for a handhold to pull himself up.

The others quietly moved for the cave entrance. When Titus reached the top of the cliff minutes later, sweaty and breathing heavily, he realized this part of the mountain didn't peak like the ones around it. A domelike rock structure stretched out in front of him.

He'd bet his life Prometheus was being held inside. A perfectly designed prison. From below, the screech of an eagle similar to the one who'd led him to Natasa echoed, and shouts and hollers of the eternal guardians followed.

Urgency coursed through him. He hiked out to the far side of the dome, reached into his pocket, and drew out the reed. Liquid sloshed inside the cylinder. He set it at his feet, then moved back to the other edge. Stepping behind a boulder, he grabbed Heracles's bow and reached for an arrow from the quiver at his back.

C'mon, Odysseus...don't fail me now. If Prometheus was in there, he hoped like Hades the god wasn't on the far side of the cave.

He closed one eye, lined up his target, and let go.

The arrow whirred through the air and struck the reed standing on end.

Thunder echoed, a plume of black smoke shot into the sky, and a fireball erupted, incinerating the rock and everything around it. The dome collapsed with a roar. Shielding his face from the toxic fumes, Titus rushed to the edge of the destruction and peered inside the hole left behind.

Debris littered the floor of what used to be a giant cave. Frantic, he searched through the smoke and finally found what he was looking for. Chains. Just barely visible, sticking out from beneath a pile of rock.

He pulled rope from his back pocket, tied off one end around a boulder, and rappelled into the cave. The eagle's scream echoed from a tunnel to his left. From the rocks, coughing echoed, followed by a weak voice calling, "Who's there?"

Energy rushed through Titus's veins. He lifted rocks and moved them out of the way. A bloody hand emerged from the stones. His adrenaline surged.

He worked faster, finally clearing enough debris to see a face.

Deep green eyes peered up at him. The face was old and wrinkled, the hair salt-and-pepper, stringy and covered in dust. But power resonated from the frail body chained to the rocks. Power and purpose.

"Who are you?"

A dozen emotions ripped through Titus. Anger for a situation he and the guardians shouldn't be in, frustration that this was taking so freakin' long, hatred for a father who'd condemned his daughter to pure torture…but mostly faith that he was going to be the one to free her from her bonds. "The one who's saving your sorry ass."

He reached for the chain locking Prometheus to the rocks. The eagle blasted a screech that tore through Titus's eardrums and knocked him off his feet.

He pushed up on his hands and stared wide-eyed at the giant beast. This wasn't the same eagle he'd followed before. Not even close to the one who'd swooped over him on the castle wall in Argolea. This thing was as big as a house, with bloodred eyes and a beak sharp as a machete.

At his back, Prometheus whispered, "Don't move."

Fuck that. Natasa was dying.

Titus jerked the berries he'd taken from Odysseus's trunk from his pocket and hurled them toward the eagle.

They peppered the eagle's face. It blinked, recoiled, then opened its mouth again to scream. But instead of attacking like Titus expected, it lowered its beak and pecked the berries across the ground until they were all gone.

Footsteps pounded across the earth. Zander, Demetrius, and Theron rushed into the cave, weapons drawn. All three were bloodied and bruised, as if they'd taken a beating from the eagle in the tunnels. All three sported *holy fuck* looks on their faces.

The eagle swallowed, then opened its beak to screech again. It's giant red eyes rolled back in its head, and it dropped to the ground like a board.

Surprise was swift and useless. Titus lurched to his feet and reached for Prometheus's chains. One tug and he realized he couldn't break them. "D! I need your magic!"

The guardians rushed over.

"What the hell was that?" Zander asked.

"Lotus fruit."

Demetrius traced the chains, held his hands over them and muttered ancient, magic words.

"How in Hades did you cause that explosion?" Theron asked.

C'mon, c'mon...

Titus swiped at his forehead. "Greek fire. Set off by Heracles's poisoned arrows." When they all stared at him, he shook his head. "They weren't really poisoned. The tips were dipped in potassium nitrate, and the tube I found in Odysseus's chest was filled with the ancient mixture. It just needed to be ignited."

Theron looked to Zander. "Remind me not to underestimate him."

"Don't worry." Zander lifted one brow. "On a good day I can barely keep up with him."

Come on, already. We need to go...

"How did you find me?"

Titus turned toward Prometheus, who pushed up to a sitting position on the rocks. Blood flowed from a wound in the Titan's side, and he seemed frail and out of sorts, but he was still immortal. No matter how much he suffered—and Titus hoped he suffered a hell of a lot before the end of days—the god wouldn't die. "Calypso."

"The nymph?"

"Yeah. And she's waiting for us to return. Get up, old man. I saved your ass. Now you're gonna save my soul mate's life."

"But I can't," Prometheus protested, slowly rising to his feet when Zander helped him. "Don't you know...? No god but Hades can cheat death."

* * *

Breathe. Focus. Draw on the strength inside you.

Natasa struggled to open her eyes. Instead of a raging fire she'd prepared her whole life to be incinerated by, she rolled on a crashing sea. Giant waves exploded all around her. Water sprayed into her face. She gasped for breath, tried to open her eyes amidst the storming sea, but couldn't.

Focus...

Her mother's voice rang clear in her ears. Encouraging her. Leading her.

The strength is inside you... Focus, Natasa.

"You thought you could get out from under our deal." Her mother's voice shifted, morphed, grew deeper, darker. "You don't double-cross a god, child. Especially not the God of the Sea. "

"Poseidon, don't—"

A scream rang out.

"Silence, nymph! Do not get between me and my...prey."

Calypso. That was Calypso crying out in pain. The island, the hemlock, Titus bringing her to the deity for help...it all rushed through Natasa's mind.

Fear condensed beneath her ribs. The deal she'd made with Poseidon flashed in front of her, as if set on a movie scene.

"I fulfilled my end of the bargain and you repay me with this?" Poseidon snarled. His voice echoed in her ear, and his breath blew hot against her cheek. He was close. She still couldn't open her eyes, but she pictured him leaning over her, all surfer, sun-tanned God of the Stormy Seas. "There will be repercussions for your treachery. I will hunt down that Argonaut you did this for and see his limbs ripped from his body. Then I'll watch as he drowns in his own blood and vomit and remind him he has you to thank for every second of his misery."

No. *No!* A groan tore from Natasa's throat, but the poison was too strong for the sound to reach her ears. Her limbs wouldn't work. She couldn't move her body. Paralysis settled in. Why had she ever thought this would save Titus? Her pulse slowed until only a flicker of life remained.

The scent of the sea reached her nostrils. Natasa tried to suck in deep breaths.

Poseidon chuckled, a dark, menacing sound. "Give my regards to my brother in hell, *traitor.*"

CHAPTER TWENTY-ONE

"**I** already told you," Prometheus insisted again as they flashed to the riverbank outside Calypso's cottage. "Death is in the hands of the Fates. Not the gods."

Fuck the Fates. Where were the Fates when Titus had needed them? Nowhere. They'd appeared to the other guardians when their lives had been in turmoil, but not to him. Probably because they were the ones who'd screwed him over to begin with.

He tamped down the resentment and focused on the only thing that mattered: Natasa. Grinding his teeth, he nodded toward the small house. "Go."

From somewhere inside, a scream echoed. Prometheus's eyes widened.

Titus bolted for the door.

Natasa lay as he'd left her, still as stone on the kitchen table, her head tipped to the side, her red, silky curls falling over the butcher-block surface. His heart lurched. Slowly he stepped next to her and laid his hand over hers against her stomach.

Cold.

"Come on, baby..." He gripped her hand and felt for her pulse at her throat.

Nothing.

Another scream echoed from somewhere in the house, but Titus was too panicked to wonder where it was coming from.

Come on, come on, come on...

Zander and Demetrius tore off toward a back room. Theron moved up slowly on Titus's side. Titus's fingers shook as he continued to feel for any sign of life. "Come on, *ligos Vesuvius*..."

Footsteps echoed at Titus's back. He felt, rather than saw, Prometheus in the room. At the back of the house, a crack sounded, followed by a female scream and the crash of furniture splintering.

A blip. Right there against her throat. Hope surged. Titus gripped Natasa's shoulders. Shook her. "Wake up, baby…"

"*Fotia,*" Prometheus whispered.

"Zeus will be sorry he wasn't here to see this."

A chill spread down Titus's back, and he froze. Very carefully, he lifted his head and looked toward the sound of the voice. In a doorway on the far side of the room, a blond-haired, blindingly beautiful god stood staring his direction. Only he wasn't looking at Titus; he was staring through him, toward Prometheus.

Blood dripped down Prometheus's side. His hair was a wild gray tangle around his head. He stepped out from behind Titus. At his side, Theron moved toward the door and muttered, "T, get back."

"*Well, well. Look who's free?*"

"*Poseidon. Still as big a pussy as your brothers.*"

Thoughts pinged around the room. Titus looked from one menacing face to the next. Prometheus didn't appear fragile anymore. He stood erect, as if he'd grown two feet, and tension flowed in the air, as thick as blood.

Behind Poseidon, Demetrius carried a ragged Calypso in his arms. Her hair was disheveled, her eyes wide and frightened, her dress ripped at the shoulder and hem.

Poseidon spread his feet and nodded toward the blood trickling down Prometheus's side. "Still nursing old wounds, I see, *uncle.*"

"And you're still forcing yourself on unwilling nymphs," Prometheus tossed back. "Why don't you go back to the sea where you belong before you get hurt?"

Poseidon's eyes narrowed. "She's mine, not yours, *thief.*"

Prometheus's eyes flashed. "I only stole that which already belonged to humans. Nothing more. Your king is more of a thief than I could ever be."

They were talking about fire. The fire Prometheus had stolen from Zeus and which had led to his imprisonment.

"And I'm stealing it back," Poseidon answered. "She made a deal with me, and I'm not letting her go. Alive or dead, she belongs to me."

Titus's gaze shot to Natasa, lying unmoving beneath his hands. A deal. She'd made a deal with Poseidon.

For you. So he can't have the element...

She'd made a deal with the god of the oceans to keep her fever in check. Her rambling admission last night that she'd dreamt of him, that she was sorry she hadn't waited, finally made sense

"Stupid, *ligos Vesuvius*," he whispered, leaning close and running his finger over her soft cheek. "Why didn't you tell me?"

"Your deal backfired." Prometheus stretched his arm toward Natasa. "And fire is stronger than water, Olympian. Remember that."

Heat erupted beneath Titus's fingers. The table burst into flames. He jerked his hands back on reflex, cringing at the burn. Natasa's emerald-green eyes flew wide open. Her lips parted, and a blood-curdling scream pushed out her throat.

"No!" Poseidon yelled.

The house shook, and a deluge of rain poured from the ceiling. But the flames beneath and around Natasa only grew higher. The fire spread down the table legs, along the floor and to the walls, climbing in swirling, angry eddies until the entire house was engulfed in flames.

"Titus!" Theron yelled.

Titus ducked as the fire spread across the ceiling. He held up a hand to block the heat from searing his skin. From across the room, Poseidon's eyes flashed brilliant blue. He shot a scathing look toward Prometheus and growled, then disappeared in a crack of thunder.

Zander and Demetrius rushed out of the house with Calypso. Prometheus looked back at Natasa on the table. A sad expression turned his lips, then he lowered his head hastily and followed the Argonauts.

Natasa continued screaming as her body was burned alive. Horrified, Titus reached for her, but the flames erupted around her, as if protecting her from his touch. He fell back on his ass.

"Titus!" Theron yelled again.

Smoke filled his lungs. Heat singed his hair. A hand grasped his sleeve. Yanked him up. Pulled hard toward the exit.

"No! Let me go!" Titus fought against Theron's grasp. "I can't leave her! I can't—"

An earsplitting crack echoed. Titus looked up just as the beams above gave way.

"Go, *now!*"

Theron threw Titus out of the house and onto the grass before they were caught in the inferno. Rain poured down around them, soaking their clothing, their skin, running in rivulets down Titus's face. The small structure exploded in flames. Each droplet of water seemed to spur the blaze higher instead of dampen the fire.

Titus dropped to his knees in the mud and rested his hands on his thighs. He couldn't breathe. Couldn't think. Wet hair hung in clumps in front of his eyes.

Natasa…

His entire world had ignited in that house. Everything he hadn't known he'd needed. Not just his chance to finally be free of his curse, but his heart. A heart that would always belong to her.

Natasa blinked several times.

The fever was gone. The heat inside her still smoldered, but it was contained somewhere…safe. Power gathered at her center, yet it wasn't the same uncontrollable intensity she'd experienced before. This was strong. Directed. Hers.

She unwound her arm from her knees and held her hand out. Imagined flames. Fire ignited in the palm of her hand. Her eyes grew wide with wonder. She closed her hand into a fist, and the flame went out. No pain. No struggle. Just strength. Opening her palm once more, she saw nothing but perfect skin.

"Holy Hera."

The whispered words brought Natasa around. She looked out over smoking ash and rain-soaked grass toward a group of men and one woman. Three men stared in shock. The woman sat on the ground tugging her dress into place. Another man was smiling— this one familiar—and the last was on his knees, his hands on his thighs, his head hanging forward, dark, stringy, wet hair shielding his face.

"*Fotia*," the smiling man said in a low and proud voice. "My rising phoenix."

No, not a man. A god. A Titan.

Her father, Prometheus.

Slowly, the kneeling man lifted his head. Hazel eyes met hers. And warmth exploded deep in her chest.

Titus.

"Oh my gods," he whispered.

He lurched to his feet and sprinted across the mud and ash toward her.

Natasa pushed to her feet, as anxious to get to him as he was to her. His arms closed around her. But before she could grab on, he yanked back and dropped to his knees again, gasping for breath.

"Titus?" She reached out to help him up, afraid he'd slipped in the mud or fallen or—

He held up a hand to block her from touching him again. Slapped his other hand against his chest and rasped in a breath. "Don't. Just…wait."

Understanding dawned at the pain she saw twisting his features. The fire element was contained. It was no longer consuming her. And he could *feel* her.

No, no, no…

"Rising phoenix? Smart move, old man."

Natasa jerked her attention from Titus toward the dark-haired god who'd appeared out of nowhere, moving toward her from the left, a licentious smile curling his lips.

Zeus. She felt the power radiating from him, knew he was the King of the Gods, knew he was here for her.

"I told you this would pay off, brother."

She whipped to her right, where Poseidon was also advancing fast, a blinding, evil light alive in his blue eyes.

"From the transmutation of fire," Poseidon went on, "we can create the other elements. Hades will never be the wiser."

"You were right," Zeus said, his eyes locked on Natasa. He tsked. "I missed you, flame. That was naughty of you to run away."

The three Argonauts drew their weapons, then put themselves between her and the gods. Titus tried to push to his feet in the mud, but dropped back down when his legs gave out. Her father moved toward her, as if he were going to try to protect her.

Instinct crashed in. A need to guard. One that had nothing to do with self-preservation and everything to do with protecting those she loved.

She lifted her hands over her head, swirling them high. Flames erupted in a circle all around her, the Argonauts, the nymph, and her father, blocking the Olympian gods from reaching them.

Poseidon jumped back and cursed. Zeus thrust his hands forward, throwing lightning toward the flames, trying to break them open. The bolts hit the flames and shot back. Zeus scrambled to the side and only just missed being fried. Irate, Poseidon swept his arms toward the lake and back in a fierce move. Water surged forward, flooded the land and crashed against the flames. The wall of fire grew higher, protecting them.

At Natasa's side, her father chuckled and muttered, "Take that, you scheming Olympians."

Wide-eyed, the Argonauts looked from one god's enraged face to the next, then at each other. But it was Titus, Natasa focused on. Still kneeling in the mud, staring up at her with pained, heartbroken, beautiful eyes.

She dropped to her knees in the muddy ash and rested her hands on her thighs. She'd gotten exactly what she'd wanted, but something in the bottom of her soul said it had come with a price.

"You saved me again," he said quietly.

"We saved each other. That's the way it's supposed to be."

A weak smile tugged at his mouth.

She wanted to reach out to him, to gather him in her arms. To kiss away the pain brewing in his eyes. But she was the cause of it. All the heartache he'd experienced, all the panic…it was all because of her. And now…now even her touch caused him agony.

"I'm sorry," she whispered. "I didn't think there was another way. I didn't want Poseidon to have the element, and I made that deal with him before I ever even knew about you. I…I was trying to protect you from getting hurt."

"It's okay."

Tears filled her eyes. "No, it's not. I should have believed that everything I ever needed would find me if I was patient. I don't know how I can ever make that up to you."

The flicker of flames reflected deeply in his eyes. Her flames. "You just did."

Gods, Titus…I love you.

A sad smile turned his lips. Didn't come close to reaching his beautiful eyes. "I know."

Tears ran down her cheeks to mix with the rain. Vaguely she was aware of someone wrapping a wet shirt around her naked body, but she barely cared. All she could see and feel and focus on was the man—*hero*—who'd brought her back to life. Who'd *given* her life.

"I've spent my whole life thinking I didn't need a soul mate," he whispered. "I was wrong. I love you too, Natasa. More than you will ever know."

They were the words she longed to hear, and yet her heart shattered in the rain between them. For months, all she'd hoped and prayed and pleaded for was that the fever would leave her. Now she only wanted it back.

CHAPTER TWENTY-TWO

Krónos's son... Krónos's son...

No. Fucking. Way.

Nick swallowed the revulsion as he followed Zagreus down a long hallway. The walls were made of rock, the floor dirt and mud beneath his feet. Water dripped from cracks in the ceiling, drizzled down the walls and pooled on the ground. They were in some kind of cave. Underground. The chain cuffed to his wrist rattled with every step.

They'd flashed here from the colony. Zagreus had pulled him into the tunnels. Hades... He didn't know where the hell Hades had gone. Questions swirled in his mind—if Isadora was okay, what was happening back at the colony, where his people had gone, and what would become of them. But circling loudest was the biggest question of all, the words Hades had dropped like a bombshell.

Krónos's son...

No. Not possible. His father had been human. His mother— the same blood he shared with Demetrius—a goddess, albeit twisted. He had the markings on his forearms and wrists, proving he was a demigod. Proving what Hades had said couldn't be real.

The crack of a whip echoed through the corridor, followed by a muffled scream, and then a moan.

Nick's adrenaline surged, followed by a thrill, which he couldn't stop, that shot through his veins.

"You're wondering if my father was lying," Zagreus said, not bothering to face him. "I assure you he wasn't. My father doesn't lie. Deceives, yes. But never lies."

Another scream echoed off the stone walls. The darkness inside Nick surged to the forefront, excited, anticipating what lay on the other side of these rocks.

"They'll die. You know this, right? Your Argonaut friends might have survived this battle, but they won't win this war. They're going to waste all their time finding the remaining elements only to destroy the Orb of Krónos, when now it's probably the only thing that can save them." He shot an amused look over his shoulder. "You didn't think Krónos wouldn't have a backup plan, did you?"

Zagreus stopped and turned fully toward Nick. Nick drew up short and held his breath. The god was tall, close to Hades's seven-foot stature, and just as dark—inside and out—as his father. If there was one thing Nick had learned in his dealings with Zagreus's satyrs over the years, it was that the god was unpredictable. Viciously so.

Zagreus tipped his head. "Didn't you ever wonder how Atalanta got out of the Underworld to fuck your father? She couldn't leave there. That was her deal with Hades. Ultimate power combined with the thrill of immortality but confined to her own living hell. Pretty sweet, if you ask me."

Nick clenched his jaw and didn't respond. He wasn't about to antagonize the god. Not when he was shackled and clearly outmatched. More screams echoed off the rock walls, amping the vibrations in his chest.

"Prepare for the unexpected. That's my motto." Zagreus grinned. "Before we go in there" —he nodded toward a door at the end of the corridor—"and you begin your training, I'll satisfy the curiosity I know you won't admit to. Your mother, Atalanta, sought out Krónos in Tartarus. And there she made a deal with him. To free herself from the Underworld and Hades's contract."

Nick knew this already. The prophecy Hades had created said that two siblings would be perfect halves of a whole—one Argolean, one human—and that when they were united, only then would Atalanta be freed from her prison in the Underworld. His mother had tried to create her own prophesy by getting pregnant with him and Demetrius, but it had backfired on her big-time.

"Krónos agreed," Zagreus went on, "some would say in the hopes that she would escape and come back to free him. But we know differently. He agreed to create you. His backup plan, which was a good idea, since Prometheus fucked him over with the Orb. He made your mother mortal for a few hours, impregnated her, then restored her immortality and sent her to Argolea to find your brother's Argonaut father. She thought she'd won, but Krónos was the real winner. You see, you're not just any demigod. You have Krónos's power and darkness within you. And my father wants me to train you to access that power so he can lord it over his scheming brothers and all of Olympus. But I have other plans for you."

Krónos's son… It was true. Bile rose in Nick's throat while Zagreus's voice faded into the background. He'd thought the darkness inside him came from his mother, but he'd been wrong. He was the son of the most malicious and twisted god ever to walk the heavens.

Zagreus moved to the end of the hallway and punched a code into a keypad on the right. The heavy metal door clicked open, and the sounds of torture, of suffering escaped on a breath of heavy air. That darkness jerked inside, drawing Nick forward like a magnet.

Zagreus ducked under the header and moved inside a vast room. Whips echoed through the air; chains rattled. Screams and moans intermixed until Nick couldn't tell which was which.

His heart beat fast. Sweat slicked his skin. His body vibrated as if a live wire were arcing beneath his flesh.

He moved into the room, then drew to a halt.

Oh, holy…*fuck*.

Six women—no, not women, nymphs, he realized—were chained naked to the far wall, some facing the rocks, some with their backs pressed to the cold stone. In front of each one, a satyr held either a whip, a flogger, or a cane. Bruises covered the females' bodies, and beneath their feet, droplets of blood stained the dirt-strewn ground.

Nausea rolled through Nick's stomach. But every crack of leather against skin sent his blood higher. Every scream increased his heart rate. Every moan made the darkness hungry for more.

"Welcome to my own version of hell," Zagreus announced, a smile in his gloating voice. "Cynna, come and meet our newest trainee."

Footsteps echoed. The sweet smell of jasmine reached Nick's nose. Barely able to drag his attention from the torture, he looked toward the female standing in front of him.

Long hair dyed blonde with streaks of blue that didn't match her caramel skin tone. Heavy, dark makeup that accentuated her large, exotic eyes. Breasts that pushed high and all but spilled from the tight leather corset. Toned legs stretching a mile beneath the short leather skirt, before stopping in four-inch-spike-heeled, knee-high boots. And in her hand…a flogger, the ends of each strip of leather anchored with a tiny barb.

His gaze lifted back to her face. To her chocolate irises. To something familiar in her features. He'd met her before, or someone like her. Or maybe he'd just fantasized about her. His blood hummed with darkness and an arousal he couldn't fight. He waited for her to say something, but her lips remained closed. No spark of recognition flashed in her eyes. They were empty. Soulless. Dead. Just like him.

Zagreus wrapped his arm around her waist and tugged her to his side. Her skin was shades darker than Zagreus's. She hooked her hand over his shoulder in a move that spoke of familiarity, but Nick caught the tensing of her jaw and the flash of irritation in her eyes that screamed she didn't want the god's hands on her.

"What do you think, my sweet Cynna?"

She cocked her head, regarding Nick with distaste. "He's not your usual plaything."

Zagreus leaned in close and nipped at her ear. "No, *agapi*. He's not. He's very special. And as a gift to you, I'm leaving his preparation in your hands."

The vibrations turned to a full-blown roar in Nick's blood.

Surprise lit Cynna's familiar eyes. "Me?"

Zagreus grinned. "It's time you took the next step." His expression turned hard and cold. "Break him, Cynna. Or I will break you once and for all."

The knock at the door drew Natasa's head up.

Casey, the queen's sister, had brought her an entire wardrobe of clothing, which Natasa was currently staring at in the walk-in closet of her room in the Argolean castle. Pants, shirts, dresses— she hadn't worn a dress in over three thousand years, and the last one she remembered certainly hadn't looked like these intricate numbers. When the hell was she ever going to wear all this stuff?

A renewed sense of claustrophobia pressed in. She'd been feeling boxed in all afternoon, and she needed some space, needed to think. She wished Titus were here so she at least had a friendly face to gaze upon. These people were nice but...she was overwhelmed.

Casey smiled and hooked the hanger on the bar. "That should be the last of it."

There was more? What else could a person wear?

Head spinning, Natasa followed Casey out into the suite and froze.

Titus stood in the middle of the room, looking big and gorgeous and every bit the hero she'd just been wishing for.

"Casey." He nodded once. His hazel eyes met Natasa's. "Hey."

"Hey."

Her heart beat wildly. The last twenty-four hours had been a blur of activity. The Argonauts bringing her, Prometheus, and Calypso to Argolea, where the gods couldn't touch them. Meeting the queen. Being welcomed instead of hunted. Talking with her father and realizing...he'd passed the fire element to her mother and then to her, to keep it safe. And he'd known all along that it would eventually burn through her but that she'd rise from the ashes. He'd planned it that way.

She wasn't exactly thrilled with that news—it had hurt like hell. Even now she trembled at just the memory of being burned alive—but he'd intended for it to happen long ago, not four thousand years later. Her being imprisoned by Zeus in the air element had altered everything.

But none of that mattered now. All that mattered was that Titus was standing in her room, staring at her with those mesmerizing eyes. Closer than he'd been in hours.

Casey looked to Natasa. "Well, ah, that's probably enough for now. We can talk more tomorrow. It's a big change being here, trust me, I know, but you'll get used to it. And I think you'll like it."

She glanced between them again. Obviously noticed neither was looking at her. "I should go check on Isadora and the baby. Natasa, if you need anything else, just come find me."

Common courtesy kicked in, and Natasa muttered a thank-you, but she still couldn't tear her eyes from Titus.

The door closed behind Casey. Late afternoon light streamed into the room through the arched windows behind him, showcasing the waves in his tied-back hair, the white shirt and crisp black pants he wore. He'd showered, and though he was as handsome as always, there was something different. She stared at him, tried to figure out what, then realized it was the first time she'd seen him freshly shaved.

"What do you think of the room?" he asked.

It took a second for his question to register, but when it did, she tore her gaze away from his smooth jawline and glanced around the room. Small talk. She could do small talk. So long as he stayed.

"Um…" The suite was big, a large sitting area by a fireplace, a desk and chair near the balcony door, and across the room a giant bed she was sure would gobble her up. Combined with the huge walk-in closet and marble bathroom, it was fancier than anywhere she'd lived before, but it didn't feel like home. "It's…nice."

His lips curled, and like a magnet, that smile pulled her gaze right back to his familiar and gorgeous face. She liked the wisps of hair floating free, but she wanted to tug that leather band from his nape. She liked his hair wild, liked sliding her fingers through the silky locks, liked pulling on it when she drew his mouth to hers.

He sucked in a sharp breath and shifted his feet. Looking toward the windows, he scratched his forehead as if he didn't know what to say.

Her gaze settled on his hands. His strong, talented hands covered by leather gloves.

He'd been wearing similar gloves when they'd met. The sight of them reminded her of the Amazons touching him. Of his tortured reaction. Of him falling to his feet in the mud on Ogygia when he'd tried to embrace her after she'd risen from those flames.

"Um. It's getting late," he said. "Are you hungry? I can call down and have the cooks send something up for us."

There were too many tortured emotions running through her to think about food, but he was working hard for normal and she was determined to give him that. They hadn't had any normal in their relationship yet. "Yeah, okay. That would be…nice."

He moved to the desk and lifted a phone. Speaking into the receiver, he ordered—she didn't know what. Nerves rolled through her stomach as she turned a slow circle in the suite and tried to find control.

He hung up, then stepped toward the balcony door. "Have you seen the view? You've got one of the best in the castle."

The only view she wanted was of him, but she didn't say so. When he pushed the door open and stepped outside, she followed—not because she wanted to but because she didn't know what else to do.

He held the glass-paneled door open for her. As she passed, she caught a whiff of his scent. Spicy. Musky. So familiar it brought a rush of memories and a host of tingles to her belly. His heat slid across the space between them to tickle the fine hairs along her neck, reminding her he wasn't just her refreshing chill. He was more. And she wanted him so desperately she was barely holding it together.

She drew in a lungful of his scent. Held it. Was so afraid that this was all of him she was ever going to get.

He cleared his throat and perched his gloved hands on the railing. Then he pointed off toward the sparkling ocean and dramatic cliffs beyond the castle walls. "That's the Olympic Ocean. That big building down there is the Argolian, which houses the Council chambers. Most of the buildings in Tiyrns are made of white marble, hence the term 'White City.' We've got a pretty big port. The Aegis Mountains border us on the north and east, and farmland runs to the south."

She scanned the majestic city as he pointed out landmarks. He was right. They'd given her a room on one of the upper floors, and it really was a gorgeous view, especially with the sun setting over the ocean in swirls of pinks and purples. But she didn't care about the view. All she cared about was the man standing next to her, what was happening between them, and how they were going to fix it.

She cued back into the conversation, realizing he'd paused. Feeling foolish, she cleared her throat. "Where's your home?"

He pointed toward the north and the purple-blue mountains beyond. "Just outside the city. The Thasian River runs in front of my house and dumps into the ocean about four or five miles downstream."

"Oh." She tried to sound interested, but knew she failed. A small part of her was disappointed he hadn't taken her there, that he'd let the queen give her a place to stay in the castle. She knew why, and it made sense—her father was here, and she couldn't touch him, so how the heck did she expect them to have any kind of future together anyway?—but it still stung.

"Hey." His soft voice pulled at her. She looked over. Then sucked in a breath when she realized he was watching her with soft, captivating eyes. "I still want to take you there. I *will* take you there, but Argolea isn't the Utopia people think it is. There's political strife in our country thanks to the Council, and I'm not risking your safety until I know things have calmed down. But know this…home for me isn't a house. It's wherever you are."

Warmth bloomed in her chest. He still wanted her. Even with what felt like a giant ocean forming between them. She inched her hand closer to his on the railing. Desperately wanted to touch him. Emotions brewed in his eyes—the same ones she felt—and he lifted his gloved hand, closed it over hers, and squeezed.

Warmth. Bliss—

He jerked his hand back and cringed.

Her gaze shot to her hand, then to his confused face. "What?"

"I…I don't know. That's never happened before. The gloves always prevent…"

He reached out and touched her again. Drew back just as sharply. And when his eyes met hers, a pained look crossed his handsome features.

No. Tears burned the backs of her eyes. She pulled her hand away from the railing, cradling it against her stomach. Her heart sank into what felt like a pit of despair.

Now he couldn't even touch her with the barrier of cloth or leather? How cruel could the Fates possibly be?

A knock sounded at the door, and Titus turned. He seemed relieved by the interruption as he stepped back into her suite. "That's dinner."

Alone, she closed her eyes and drew a steadying breath. Told herself to be strong. At least until he left.

Darkness pressed in through the window as the sun sank over the water. Candlelight illuminated the small table near the window where they sat and ate, but it wasn't the romantic atmosphere Natasa had hoped for.

She pushed her food around on her plate, pretending to eat. They made small talk. He told her that Calypso was already making plans to leave Argolea against the queen's request and asked bout her conversation with her father. She gave him the bare bones and asked about the Argonauts. He was reluctant to talk about what had happened on Pandora when they'd rescued Prometheus, but she sensed something had gone down between him and the others. She wanted to know more but didn't have the strength to question. When the conversation lulled and he finally asked if she was done, she nodded, relieved the meal was over.

She rose from her seat. He blew out the candles, cleared the dishes, and rolled the cart out into the hall. When he came back in, she was standing in the middle of the room, lost and unsure what to do next.

He must have sensed her worry—or maybe he'd read her mind. She realized through dinner he'd answered her unasked questions several times. He disappeared in the giant closet and came back with a pair of yellow silk pajamas and held them out to her. "Come on. You look exhausted."

Nerves echoed through her belly. She moved to the end of the bed and fingered the silky fabric, careful not to touch him. She could hold her own with Amazons, satyrs, could even best a couple of Olympians, and yet at the moment she felt like the most helpless person in the world. "Are you leaving?"

"Do you want me to?"

She met his eyes. Felt that pull to him in the bottom of her soul—the one she'd felt before. In the redwoods. At the colony. On Ogygia. But this time it was more basic. More electric. More raw. And it overrode everything else.

"No," she breathed.

"Then I'm not going anywhere."

Relief was swift and oh so sweet. She managed what she knew was a feeble smile, moved into the bathroom and changed. When she came back out, he'd turned down the lights and pulled back the covers on her side of the bed.

Her heart picked up speed. Memories of the night they'd spent tangled together at the half-breed colony spiraled through her. Stomach tight with anticipation, she slid into bed and pulled the covers up. He sat on the opposite side, tugged off his boots and dropped them on the floor, but he didn't take off his clothes. And he didn't climb under the blankets with her. Instead, he lay out on top of the comforter, keeping as many layers of fabric between them as he could.

Silence fell over the room. She stared up at the ceiling in the darkness, blinking back tears of anger and frustration. This was so much harder than she'd expected. How were they ever going to make this work? How long until he got tired of her and went back to his "regular" females—the ones he'd told her about? He was a sexy, virile warrior, and though she believed that he loved her, he'd told her he wasn't built to be celibate. With her—now—that was all he could be.

He rolled toward her, tucked his hands up by his face. "Don't think like that," he said softly. "You are the only one I want. We'll get through this."

Great. He was reading her mind again. That was going to get old fast.

She turned her head on the pillow. Moonlight danced across his cheeks, made his hair seem almost white, his skin luminescent. "How?" she whispered.

"I'll talk to the witches about spells or try drugs or…I don't know. I'll think of something."

"Titus—"

"This is my problem, Natasa, not yours. I don't want you to worry. It's gonna be okay."

"It's *our* problem. You can't even touch me with your gloves. How is that ever going to be okay?"

"Because…I can't think about the alternative."

She closed her eyes against a rush of pain.

"Give it some time, baby. Maybe my reaction to you will lessen as the fire element settles." His voice strained. "This isn't going to be our new normal, okay? I won't let it be."

Her heart felt like it was breaking all over again. The fire element was already settled. That wasn't going to change. He was grasping for a thread of hope that wasn't out there. But weakly— for him—she nodded.

"Sleep," he said gently. "We'll figure it out."

He was determined to keep them together, but Hera's soul mate curse niggled at the back of her mind.

The one person he wanted most in the world, but who was the worst possible match for him.

Yeah, that pretty much summed her up perfectly, now didn't it?

CHAPTER TWENTY-THREE

Titus stood on one of the many roofs of the castle in Argolea and leaned against the railing, looking down at the courtyard below.

June had skipped across the land, the heat of summer bursting flowers on trees and vines, replacing the spring buds and occasional rain. But the warm summer wind blowing across his cheeks and under the collar of his shirt didn't ease the chill inside. It only reminded him he was as cold and alone as he'd ever been.

"She looks like she's adjusting fairly well."

Theron.

Titus didn't turn. Just continued to watch Natasa and Prometheus in the courtyard below. Midday sun glinted off her flame-red hair. She was wearing tight jeans that molded to her curvy hips and a fitted green T-shirt that matched her eyes. Holding her hand out, she summoned a giant fireball. He watched in awe as she manipulated the flames into a stalk, a fountain, then finally a tight ball again, which she blew away from her hand. The rolling knot of fire floated up in the air, growing smaller the higher it rose, until it finally burned out and disappeared in the sky.

Theron was right. Over the last two weeks, she had adjusted to life in Argolea. Very well. Though the Council was still griping about all the Misos who'd been evacuated to their land, they hadn't even protested the fact Natasa and her father were here. Of course, the fact Prometheus was a Titan and could smite them in one breath probably didn't hurt matters.

Prometheus, for his part, was helping the Argonauts look for the last remaining element—water—but so far they'd had no luck. Even he didn't know exactly where it had landed after he'd scattered the elements in the human world. After thousands of years, the shape of the planet had changed, and water was the most variable of all.

In his spare time, Prometheus was educating the queen about the gods and Krónos and teaching Natasa to use her new gifts. Titus still sometimes had trouble realizing she was the real deal— unquenchable fire. But unlike the Armageddon the ancient texts all made her out to be, she was more. She had the strength to release or control it all within herself. And though eventually she'd be able to manipulate fire into the other elements, she couldn't yet. Titus still harbored a shitload of anger toward the god who'd passed the fire element to his daughter, knowing it would cause her intense suffering until it consumed and resurrected her, but even he could see Prometheus cared for her.

An eagle soared through the sky, swept over the castle wall, and screeched as it flew above Natasa and her father. It landed a few feet from Natasa on the green grass, spread its wings, and screeched again as if to say, *Come over here and pay attention to me.* Natasa smiled and held out her hand, then took a step toward the bird. Just before she reached it, the bird fluttered its wings and took off for the sky again. She shielded her eyes against the sun and watched it fly away. But there was a look in her eyes…a sadness…a longing…

Pain.

His heart twisted into a hard knot beneath his ribs. It killed him to see her so unhappy. They'd spent the last two weeks tip-toeing around each other. He was still spending nights with her in her room, but they were both growing increasingly frustrated with the situation. And lying next to her at night when she was asleep was pure agony. To be near her like that and not be able to touch her…

Gods, he hated this. Hated, even more, that Theron was standing behind him now, watching him suffer. He'd decided to stay with the Argonauts—mostly at Natasa's insistence—but he was only half-committed at best. And Theron knew it.

"How did you find me?" Titus finally asked, unable to stand the silence—and prying eyes.

"I followed the sound of ultimate misery."

Fucker. Titus huffed. "You're a comedian now. Great."

Theron grinned. Then his features sobered, and he stuffed his hands in his front pockets. "I've been where you are, T. More times than I want to count. And each time I thought I'd lost Acacia…" Theron's voice grew thick. "I know it's torture

It wasn't just torture. It was a living hell, watching your soul mate suffer and nearly die. Except in Theron's case, he could wrap his arms around Casey and hold her close. Reassure himself. And her. Convince them both that life went on. That everything would be fine. Titus couldn't do that.

Theron pulled his hands from his pockets and leaned his forearms against the railing next to Titus. "It probably won't make you feel any better to know it never gets easier, but I can tell you nothing is better, either. Finding your soul mate… I'd rather cherish one day with Acacia than live a lifetime alone. Not knowing her…that would be the true definition of torture."

Below, Natasa turned to look up his way, and he tried to smile, to reassure her that everything was good, but from the worry he saw in her eyes, he knew he failed.

That knot twisted tighter.

"Anyway," Theron went on, "I want you to know she's one of us now. Not because of what's inside her or what she can do, or even because Prometheus is her father, but because she's your soul mate. We take care of our own."

Brotherhood reverberated through Titus's chest—a feeling he hadn't felt with his kin in…he didn't know how long.

"She always has a place with us," Theron said. "No matter what happens with the Orb. No matter what happens between the two of you."

A lump formed in Titus's throat. He tried to swallow it back. Couldn't. No one knew what was happening with the Orb just yet. Whether or not Natasa would be able to conjure tangible fire in the form of an element to place inside the Orb. Whether or not they'd eventually locate the water element. Whether or not the Orb could even really be destroyed once they did. But most importantly, none of them knew what was happening with Nick. And yet…one thing became crystal clear to Titus in that moment.

He would never be free of his duty. And…deep down, he didn't want to be free. He was an Argonaut, not because of any vow he'd taken or any gift he'd been given, but because doing the right thing and protecting those around him were as much a part of him as was his heart. To shun that side of himself would be shunning what had drawn him to Natasa in the first place.

"Thanks," he managed, not knowing what else to say.

Theron stepped away from the railing. He stared at Titus. But whatever else he was thinking, he blocked from Titus's ability to read. Which was good. Because Titus wasn't sure he could handle any more just now.

"I think you should take some time off from the Argonauts," Theron said. "As much as you need. Things are quiet right now, and with O and Skyla here, we can cover for you for a while. When you're ready to come back, we'll be here."

That lump grew bigger. *Just great.* All the Argonauts knew he was fucked-up right now. This was why he'd never wanted to find his soul mate. Because he knew once he did, he'd never be the same. But even realizing that, he knew he wouldn't go back to the way he'd been before, even if he could.

He forced himself to nod and looked back down at Natasa. She was manipulating fire again with Prometheus, but this time she was smiling and laughing. A glowing, twisting, swirling light in the middle of a world Titus had only known as dark and dreary.

"Okay," Theron said in quiet voice. He moved for the door that led back inside.

"Theron?"

The leader of the Argonauts stopped with one hand on the door handle. "Yeah?"

"You might want to prepare yourself for a little more of that torture."

"Why?"

Titus glanced over his shoulder. "Casey's pregnant. Her thoughts have been banging off the castle walls. I tried to ignore them, but *skata*, the female projects…loudly."

Theron's face paled. "Oh my gods."

Titus smiled. The first real smile he'd felt in weeks. "I'm sure she'll tell you soon. She's been trying to figure out a way. Try to act surprised when she does."

Excitement brightened Theron's features, then lurched to ice-cold fear. "Holy shit."

Titus chuckled. "Torture. Yep." He turned back to the courtyard. "Payback's a bitch, ain't it?"

The door slammed. Theron's footsteps faded into the warm midmorning air.

Alone, Titus crossed his arms on the railing and leaned his chin against his arms. The humor he'd felt before leaked out as he watched Natasa and was replaced with the most intense yearning he'd ever felt.

Theron was right. Spending just one day with her was better than a lifetime of being alone, even if he couldn't touch her. But gods, he missed her. Missed feeling her skin against his, missed holding her, missed falling asleep with her in his arms and waking with her draped over his body, warming him, making him feel something other than empty.

"She's in front of you. Stop moping and go get her."

Startled by the voice, Titus jerked up and turned. The petite, frail creature dressed in diaphanous white sat on the far railing, studying him with a *What the hell are you waiting for?* expression.

Lachesis. The Fate. The one who spun the thread of life. His pulse picked up speed. But instead of awe and surprise, anger and frustration condensed inside him. "What do you want?"

Her wrinkled cheeks creased with a smile. Her hair was long and white, her feet so small he wondered how she stood on them. "I've had unwelcoming greetings, but yours, descendant of Odysseus, probably tops them all."

Titus clenched his jaw. She wanted him to be thankful she was here? Where had she been when he'd been alone all these years? Where had she been when his life had been in the shitter? When Natasa had been suffering because of that damn element?

"I've always been here, Guardian. You just weren't paying attention."

In that moment, he knew instinctively that she wasn't here to change their situation. If she could—if she *wanted* to—she'd have done it already.

He moved for the door.

"I watch you always. Some guardians need me to steer them in the right direction when they blow off course. But not you. You're one who hasn't needed my advice. Until now."

He turned and glared at her, then opened his mouth to tell her just what she could do with her advice.

"The knowledge you hold doesn't just come from the Orb," she said. "Or Odysseus. It comes from inside you. You were given a gift no other guardian could handle. The ability to read minds. That is an incredible power, Titus."

Incredible power. Yeah right. "And I was punished for it."

"You were cursed with feeling others' emotions because you lacked self-control. The Fates never expected you to be perfect. But we're very impressed with the way you've mastered that control over these long years."

"So take the curse away."

"I can't. The curse did not come from the Fates. It came from witchcraft. And that is something neither I, nor my sisters, can change."

Then why the fuck were they having this conversation? Titus took another step for the door.

"Think, Guardian. How does Natasa regulate the fire inside her?"

Titus's feet stilled, and a tingling started in his chest then drifted through every limb. Slowly, he looked over the railing down toward Natasa.

"She made a great sacrifice for you," Lachesis said softly. "Sometimes sacrifice can only be met with sacrifice."

He glanced back at the Fate. But instead of the elderly female he'd been talking with, an eagle sat perched on the far railing.

He stared at the bird, then remembered the eagle that had swooped over him when he'd climbed the castle wall after Natasa. The one who'd led him to Natasa in that field. Who'd taken him to Calypso's cottage. And the one that had sailed over this courtyard only moments before, taunting and screaming, as if…encouraging him.

The eagle spread its wings, screamed an ear-piercing squawk that vibrated through every cell in his body, then lurched from the railing. It flew over his head and dive-bombed the courtyard.

He rushed to the railing, gripped it in both hands and looked down. The eagle pulled up just before it reached Natasa. Her father yelled. She shielded her head. Gently, the eagle tapped the crown of her head with its claws, then screeched again and sailed high.

Surprised, Natasa looked up. The eagle circled the courtyard once, then soared through the sky, heading for the sun.

Natasa twisted, glancing up at the roofline to where Titus stood. Confusion and disbelief swirled in her gemlike eyes.

And in that moment, everything finally made sense. Every touch, every breath, every hour had come to this. She'd sacrificed all that she was for him. He had to be willing to sacrifice the same for her. Even if he failed, she had to know what he was willing to do for her.

For the first time in weeks, something other than misery bloomed inside Titus.

CHAPTER TWENTY-FOUR

"**W**hat are we doing here?"

The service elevator shook, and Natasa waited—impatiently—for Titus to manually open the old wooden doors and tell her what was going on.

He didn't answer her question. Just pried the first set of doors open, then separated the next. Metal hinges groaned. His musky scent slid across the space between them, igniting a burn low in her stomach. Muscles in his arms and shoulders flexed beneath the thin, black, long-sleeved T-shirt he wore, reminding her of what he looked like under that soft cotton. What he felt like pressed up against her.

Need seared her skin, shooting through her stomach and hips. She hated this. Hated being close to him, knowing one small brush of her hand could cause him excruciating pain. Hated that even after two weeks, he was all she could think about. She was supposed to be focusing on training her gifts, on helping the queen and the Argonauts locate the last element and the leader of the Misos Colony. But she was acting at best when she was with those who'd given her sanctuary. The only home she wanted was inches from her, and she couldn't reach him.

"Come on," Titus said, stepping off the lift. "Almost there."

She didn't know where *there* was. When Titus had caught up with her in the castle hallway, looking frazzled and gorgeous and had asked her to come with him tonight, saying that he had something important to discuss with her, she hadn't known what to think. Or expect.

She stepped off the lift and stared down the dark corridor. They were in the basement of some kind of empty warehouse on the outskirts of Tiyrns.

Why did she have this ominous feeling something bad was going to happen tonight? A chill spread down her spine, and she shivered.

"Are you cold?"

"What?" She dragged her gaze from the steel door at the end of the hall and turned his way. Nerves gathered in her belly. "No, I'm fine. Titus, what's going on? What did you bring me all the way out here to talk about? Why couldn't we have talked back at the castle?"

He ran a hand over his wavy hair. It was tied at the nape of his neck again. She missed the way it had hung loose around his face when they'd been searching for her father, missed burying her face in those soft locks when he held her close.

"Don't, *ligos Vesuvius*," he said in a low voice. "Not yet. Thoughts like that are going to push me over the edge. And I'm barely holding on here as it is."

She swallowed, and those nerves turned to a mix of pain and heartache she didn't know how to stop. She kept forgetting that he could read her thoughts now. He was right. She had to find control. At least while they were together. When she was alone...then she could wallow in her misery.

She looked down at the concrete floor and clasped her hands in front of her to keep from reaching for him. "I'm sorry."

"Don't be sorry either." His voice was stronger, louder, and she looked up into his clear hazel eyes. Her heart squeezed even tighter under that intense stare. This wasn't going to work. She wasn't going to be able to stay in this realm. She could barely handle sharing her suite with him at night even though she couldn't bear the thought of leaving him.

His eyes softened. He glanced toward the steel door. "I brought you here because there's something I want to show you." He looked back at her, and a nervous expression crossed his features. "I can't do that at the castle. I... I think you'll understand when you see for yourself."

The ominous feeling she'd experienced the whole way here doubled. He pulled a key from his pocket and slid it into the lock.

Something inside her said she didn't want to know what was on the other side of that door.

"Titus—"

"This building's abandoned. There used to be a club upstairs, but it shut down a few years ago." He pushed the door open and stepped inside. Holding the door open, he waited for her to follow.

Her pulse picked up speed, and her breaths grew fast and shallow. He wouldn't let anything bad happen to her. But if he'd brought her here to tell her he was moving out of her suite or something worse, she didn't want to know.

"Come on, *ligos Vesuvius*. It'll be okay. I promise."

Heart thundering, she stepped into the room. The door closed behind her, the click echoing through the vast, dark space.

His footsteps sounded across the floor, and then he flipped a switch on the wall. One lone light hanging from a long wire illuminated the room.

Natasa sucked in a breath. To her right, a rack held various items—different lengths and colors of rope, leather cuffs, shackles, gags, masks, blindfolds…hooks she didn't know how to describe.

She swallowed hard as she glanced toward the "furniture" in the room. A padded bench, a wooden contraption that looked like an X, a swing of some kind hanging from chains suspended in the ceiling, and a bed. Only this wasn't a normal bed. It was a four-poster covered in black silk sheets, and in each of the four posts were hooks to tie or strap something—or someone—to.

Sickness gathered in her stomach, and she took a giant step back, toward the door and freedom.

Titus crossed the distance between them in two steps and held up his hands. "Don't freak out yet. Just…just listen." Panic filled his voice. "I told you before that there were things I…like. I brought you here because I wanted you to see. And because…" He drew in a shaky breath. "This is me. There have been so many secrets between us, I…I don't want that anymore. I don't want to hide anything from you."

His expression was a mix of uncertainty, hopefulness and fear. Wide-eyed, Natasa tore her gaze from his and looked back at the contraptions in the room. Her stomach rolled again.

"I'm not a sadist," he said quickly. "I know that's what you're thinking. There are no whips or floggers or canes over there. Look."

Her gaze strayed to the rack again, and she realized he was right. There were restraints. Nothing more.

She glanced back to the furniture, specifically the padded bench in the middle of the room, one end higher than the other. The conversation they'd had back at the colony replayed in her mind. He tied females to these things. It was the only way he could have sex.

She stared at the bench. Imagined being strapped down, unable to move. Completely at his mercy. Her cheeks warmed. And deep inside, a slow stirring heated her blood.

"Yes," he whispered. Her gaze jerked back to his. "I would love to tie you to that bench, *ligos Vesuvius*. On your back, with your hands bound above your head so I can watch your eyes when I take you."

Heat shot all through her body, condensed in her belly, and slid lower. She pressed her hands against her burning cheeks, realizing he'd read her mind again. "I hate how you do that."

He smiled, a mesmerizing grin that made him so damn sexy, her blood grew even warmer. "You'll learn to block me soon enough."

"I will?"

He nodded. "The guardians all do, and they're not half as powerful as you."

That didn't ease her anxiety at the moment. She looked back to the contraptions in the room. She knew he was as frustrated with the situation as she was. But he couldn't touch her, even with his gloves. What did he think restraining her was going to solve?

The thought of him tying those other females down and using them for his pleasure brought a fresh wave of nausea to her stomach. And then realization hit.

He hadn't brought her here to tie her up in the same way. He'd brought her here to show her what he needed. To tell her he was going back to that life.

No. *No, no, no...*

Pain ripped through her heart and soul, and she took another step back.

"I told you I don't want anyone but you, Tasa." His harsh voice drew her gaze his way. Determination glowed in his eyes. A determination that kept her rooted in place. "That hasn't changed and won't. Ever."

Her heart raced. Confusion clouded her mind. Confusion and heartbreak. So much it felt as if it were dragging her under.

He pulled his gaze from hers and crossed the floor. His gloved hands closed over a length of red rope. He unhooked it from the rack, then came back to her.

She stared at the rope in his hand. Didn't know what he was doing. Didn't know anything.

"You're right," he said softly. "I don't want to bind you. I want you to restrain me. And then I want you to touch me. Wherever and however you want."

Natasa's gaze jerked up to his face. "What? No."

"Yes."

Thoughts swirled. Over the last few weeks, he'd tried almost everything—magic, spells, herbs, drugs—nothing had worked. But maybe, if he was proposing this…

A tiny sliver of hope cut through her doubt. "Has something changed?"

His lips thinned. His eyes searched hers. He was so silent, her pulse soared. Finally he said, "No. Nothing's changed, but I want this."

What? No. She stepped back until her spine hit the solid, cold door. She wasn't doing it. She'd seen the pain she could cause him with just a casual brush, and that was when his skin was covered with leather. She wouldn't purposely hurt him. Not even if that was the kind of thing he "liked."

"Tasa…" He stepped in front of her, blocking her view of the room. "Look at me."

She squeezed her eyes tight and shook her head. Then she felt his arms cage her in against the door even if he didn't touch her.

"Please, baby. Just look at me."

Fear and sickness rolled through her. But there was such panic in his voice, she slowly pried her eyes open and met his hazel gaze. Helplessness swirled in his gorgeous eyes. "I need you. I'm dying here. Every second I can't touch you is pure torture."

"It's torture for me too. But I can't—"

"Yes, you can. You're the strongest person I know. You gave up everything for me. When I think about what you did on that island…"

His voice hitched, and his eyelids fell closed. Her heart squeezed even tighter when he opened them again, when she saw the tears flooding his beautiful eyes. "I want to give you this. All of me."

"Titus…" Tears blurred her own vision. "What you're asking me to do… I can't intentionally hurt you."

"Please? Please?" he said again, panic cutting through his voice. "I'll tell you if it gets to be too much. I just…gods, I miss you. And I love you so much. Please just let me do this for you."

She stared into his eyes. His warmth and sweet scent made her light-headed, made her weak. Her heart thumped a wild rhythm beneath her breast. "I love you too," she whispered. "I…"

Indecision swept through her. Gods, she wanted—needed—him too. So much. But she was afraid. And she couldn't handle being the source of any more pain for him.

"I'll be okay," he said, reading her mind. "Stay with me, and nothing bad will happen."

"I would never leave you."

"I know you wouldn't." He placed the rope in her hand. The threads were some kind of nylon or fabric, not rough like she'd expected.

Slowly, he stepped back. Her palms grew sweaty as she watched him drag his long-sleeved T-shirt over his head, as she watched him drop it on the floor, rip off his gloves and drop those too, then step toward the padded bench and bend to raise the lower side.

"No." Was that her voice? It was thick. Raspy. It didn't sound like her. She cleared her throat. "N-not there."

He stopped. Muscles in his arms and back flexed. She swallowed hard and scanned the room again. She pointed toward the bed. "There."

A slow smile spread across his face. A gorgeous, heated smile that did wicked things to her blood. He straightened and moved for the bed. "Whatever you want, *ligos Vesuvius*. This is all about you."

No, this wasn't about her, it was about him, and she couldn't believe she'd agreed to this insanity.

She looked down at the rope in her hand. Couldn't even imagine tying it around his wrists. If he pulled or twisted, it would bite into his flesh. That would hurt too.

She eyed the rack and noticed the leather cuffs.

The clicking of her shoes sounded like an ominous warning as she crossed the concrete floor. She hooked the rope back on the rack and reached for the cuffs.

"Ankles too," he said from the bed.

Her hand paused against the restraints. Her eyes slid closed. She tried to stop her spinning stomach. Couldn't.

"I don't want to accidentally kick you," he added.

Oh, gods...

She drew in a ragged breath and slowly let it out. She could do this. She could try. For him.

Resolve firmly in place, she opened her eyes, grasped both sets of cuffs, and moved back to the bed where he was sitting. He'd taken off his boots and socks. Dressed in low-cut denim and nothing else, he sat in the middle of the mattress, waiting for her.

Oh...he was gorgeous. Even his feet. Sculpted muscle and smooth, tanned skin. Her mouth watered as he pulled the tie from his hair and tossed it on the ground. Thick, dark waves fell around his handsome face. "Hook the restraints to my wrists and ankles, then attach them to the bolts in the frame."

Her hands shook as she did what he said, careful to keep her fingers against the wide leather strap so she didn't accidentally brush his skin. When she finished attaching the ankle cuffs to the bolts, he lay back on the mattress and held his arms out so she could restrain them as well.

Her gaze shot from the dark hair fanned out beneath him to his wrists. This was a bad idea. It was so wrong. And she hated that a tiny part of her was excited by it all.

"It's okay, Tasa. Just breathe."

Breathe. Right. Easier said than done.

She finished with the cuffs, then stepped back and looked at him. He was spread eagle, laid out on black silk sheets, looking like her own private offering. Looking like Prometheus must have looked to her mother.

A burst of rolling fear rushed through every inch of her body.

"Take off your shirt, baby, and come here."

She hesitated.

"I want to feel your skin against mine when you touch me."

Her heart beat so fast it felt like it might just fly right out of her chest. Shaking, she kicked off her shoes, then slowly reached for the hem of her shirt and dragged it over her head. It landed on the cold concrete floor next to his.

"Bra too."

Her pulse skyrocketed. But she did as he asked, reached back, unhooked her bra, let it slide into her hands, and dropped it to the floor as well.

"Gods, you are so beautiful."

The awe in his voice, the passion, overrode everything else. Hunger stole through her, a deep, intense craving to be close to only him. She moved to the foot of the bed and carefully pressed her hands against the mattress. Silk brushed her palms. The mattress dipped as she climbed over him.

She made sure her hands and knees weren't close to his skin, sweeping her hair to one side so it didn't hit him in the face. But seeing him bound like that below her…waiting… She licked her lips and fought back the burning arousal…she wanted him. *Needed* any part of him she could get.

"I—I want to kiss you," she managed. "Is that okay? I won't touch you anywhere else yet."

"Yes," he exhaled. "That's more than okay. Just go slow."

Carefully, she lowered her face to his, making sure to keep her weight on her hands and her knees wide. Her hair skimmed his shoulder. His muscles tensed, but he didn't tell her to move back. And his warmth—how could she have ever thought he was cool?—enveloped every part of her.

She paused when she was a breath away. Looked deep into his eyes. And knew no one—in the history of the world—had ever felt the way she did right now. "I love you, Titus."

"Show me."

Her lips lowered to his. A whisper of a kiss. The softest caress of skin against skin. Beneath her, she sensed his whole body contract. But he didn't pull away, so she did it again. Added a tiny bit of pressure. From the corner of her vision, she watched his hands curl into fists.

She pulled back. "That hurts, doesn't it?"

His eyes were tightly closed. He breathed heavily through his nose. "A little, but I can handle it. I want you to do it again. And this time I want you to do it like you mean it."

She couldn't stop the smile playing with the corner of her mouth. Gods, she wanted that too. What he was giving her... It was the biggest sacrifice he could ever make for her.

Slowly, she leaned forward again. Her hair fell against his cheek. She lowered her mouth to his once more. Trailed the tip of her tongue against his bottom lip, then gently kissed the corner of his mouth. He groaned. Her adrenaline surged with fear and doubt. She was hurting him. She had to pull back.

"Titus—"

He lifted his head, captured his name from her lips before she could get more than an inch away, and slid his tongue into her mouth.

Heat spiraled through her body. And the connection she'd felt to him before—the passion and love he'd ignited in her—swirled like a firestorm, overwhelming everything, even her fear.

She moaned, sank into the kiss, tangled her tongue with his, and reveled in the taste of him all over again.

He kissed her back, his lips turning greedy against her own. She wanted more. Needed more. She nipped at his bottom lip and licked into his mouth again. Could go on kissing him like this forever.

"Gods, Tasa," he groaned. "Touch me. Use your hands."

Slowly, she transferred her weight to one hand and brushed the other over his bare shoulder.

He jerked at the first touch. She pulled back from his mouth and yanked her hand away. "I'm sorry. I didn't mean to—"

"*Skata*, don't stop now."

His voice was strained. Every muscle in his body tight. And he was still breathing so fast and shallow. But there was a look in his eyes as he stared up at the ceiling. One she couldn't quite decipher. Yes, there was pain, but there was also something else.

Pleasure.

He was enjoying this.

"You're killing me, baby. Touch me, dammit."

Her heart thundered. She leaned back so she was resting her weight on her thighs. The fabric of her jeans just barely pressed against his ribs. Starting at his shoulders, she slid both hands against his bare skin, then ran her fingers down his naked chest."

His body jerked like he'd been shocked. "Oh *gods...*"

His eyes fell closed. Between her knees, his entire body tensed. When she would have pulled away, he hissed, "Don't stop. Keep going."

Her pulse was a roar in her ears, but she pressed on. And knowing what he was going through for her, her heart cracked open wide for him. If she'd loved him before, it didn't even compare to how much she loved him now.

Lightly, she ran her hands across his pecs, down his six-pack stomach, then up again, circling the tips of his nipples with her thumbs. He groaned, so she did it again. Tiny quakes shook his body, but he seemed to like them. Gaining confidence, she leaned forward. Her bare breasts grazed his stomach. He moaned low in his throat. She breathed hot against his chest then licked his dusky nipple.

"Oh...*fuck*."

His whole body bucked beneath her. Startled, she drew back. His face was beet red and he was straining against the cuffs. Pleasure condensed into panic. "I'm hurting you, aren't I? Titus?"

"Let me go," he rasped. "Unstrap me. Right *now*."

She scrambled off him and unlatched the leg restraints in seconds. Horrified, she rushed around the bed and reached for his right arm, freeing it. He lurched away from her, freed his other arm. He couldn't get away from her fast enough. Tears burned her eyes. She'd known this was a bad idea. Why had she let him talk her into this? Why...?

He whipped back to her. His arm hooked around her bare waist. Her feet left the ground. She yelped as air rushed over her spine.

Her back hit the mattress, and he climbed over her. She gasped, and then his mouth was on hers. Hot. Hungry. Greedy. And she felt him. His bare skin pressing against hers. His hands...everywhere.

Cloth tore. He ripped off the rest of her clothes, stripped himself of his own, never once slowing his assault on her mouth. Her hands streaked up into his hair. Fisted. She tried to pull him closer. Tried to taste him deeper. She lifted her hips. Wrapped her legs around his back. Needed him. So much...

He thrust into her violently, and she screamed in absolute pleasure. He wasn't gentle, and she didn't want him to be. She wanted this. Him, wild for her. Not holding back. As frantic and desperate and crazy for her as she was for him.

He plunged deep again and again. Ravished her mouth, her body. One hand found hers. His fingers entwined with hers. He slammed her hand against the mattress near her head. His grip tightened. She gave herself over to him, tried to hold back but couldn't. Her climax exploded before she saw it coming, sending ripples of energy and white-hot light through each cell, warming every place inside that had gone cold these last weeks without him.

"Tasa…" He shook hard against her. And she felt him spilling inside her. Felt his racing heart, his sweat-slicked skin sliding over hers, his tight muscles quivering with the power of his own release.

It went on, longer than she expected. Longer than she remembered. And then he collapsed against her. No longer taut and rigid but like liquid honey against her flesh.

She pried her hand from his, wrapped her arms around his shoulders, sifted her fingers in his hair, and kissed his temple, his forehead, anything she could reach. Happiness swept over her like a blanket, cocooning them, warming them, protecting them.

He twitched.

Her heart lurched into her throat.

He did it again. And in a moment of panic, she realized…now that his sexual need had been sated, he was feeling pain once more.

"Don't even think about it, *ligos Vesuvius.*"

"But I'm hurting you."

He smiled against her shoulder. "Yeah, you are."

She pushed against him.

He chuckled, an immovable weight, and nipped at her throat. "You're hurting me and, gods, I love it."

She stilled her fight. "That's…twisted."

He pushed up on one hand so he could look down at her, but didn't put any other space between them. "I never claimed not to be."

He wasn't lying. Every time he twitched, his face would tighten in pain for just a split second but he wasn't climbing off her. He wasn't trying to get away from her. And inside her body, he was still hard. Like steel. "Wh-what does it feel like?"

"Like I'm being shocked. Tiny little electrical zaps. But after…the sweetest pleasure."

Confusion drew her brows together. "Sounds like you're describing an orgasm."

His hazel eyes filled with heat. "No, that was…*skata*, out of this world. I felt everything. Everything you felt. It was the most intense climax I've ever had."

She searched his features, could see from the excitement lurking there that he was telling the truth. "Why? Why can you handle touching me now, when before…"

She looked down at the dusting of hair on his chest, hating the memory of how he'd collapsed in the mud when he'd reached for her. How just the tiniest touch from her since had caused him to jerk away.

"Because I was prepared for it this time. And because you love me." She lifted her gaze to his. "That makes your touch bearable above all others. No," he smiled, correcting himself, "not just bearable. It makes it intense. Incredible. Everything I never knew I needed."

Hope sprang forth. Love enveloped her.

He jerked, then sank against her and sighed. "Holy gods, I felt that. Do it again."

She wrapped her arms around him, closed her eyes, held him close, and let love carry them both across the distance that had separated them. Fire and water. Ancient philosophers theorized that the soul was made up of equal parts fire and water. She knew now that was true. He was the missing half of a soul she hadn't known she'd been searching thousands of years for.

"Does this mean we're okay?" she whispered, fighting back tears of joy. "That we can be together?"

He pushed up on his hand. Twitched. Grinned again. "For as long as you can put up with me."

Relief stole through her. "Thank the gods."

"No, *ligos Vesuvius*. Thank the Fates for you. I've spent my life wishing I wasn't cursed. Now I wouldn't trade it for anything, because without it, I wouldn't have this." He twitched. And sighed in pleasure all over again. "Without it I would never have found you."

"Oh, Titus…" She lifted to his kiss, returning it with everything she had. Every emotion in her heart and soul went out to him, and she felt his pleasured response against her skin, *inside* her body. But a thought made her pull back before she could get lost in his kiss all over again. "Wait."

"What?"

She bit her lip. "No offense, but I really hate this room. I don't mind the restraints and you tying me up now and then if you want—"

His eyes glinted. "You don't?"

"No." Her cheeks heated. "Not so long as I get to return the favor."

"Baby." He glanced at the leather cuff hanging from the corner of the bed, and inside her body, his erection twitched. "As you can tell, I am totally in for that."

She smiled. Hesitated.

His eyes narrowed. "*Skata*, you're already doing it."

"Doing what?"

"Blocking my ability to read your thoughts. Damn, but you are quick."

Oh...*wow*... "Does that bother you?"

"No, because no matter how hard you try you won't ever be able to block me from your emotions." He reached for her hand and kissed her knuckles. But his lips stilled against her skin. "What else?"

Oh, this was going to take getting used to. He'd obviously felt her nervousness. One touch and he was always going to know when she was upset or pissed or so desperate for him she couldn't hold still. But she loved that. Loved him.

She drew in a breath. Let it out.

"Tell me, Tasa."

"I..." She worked up the courage to look in his eyes. Knew it was useless not to. "I can't stand to think of you here with anyone else. I know confident women aren't supposed to be jealous but...I am. Blame the turbulent fire inside me if you want, but I don't like even the *thought* of sharing space in your memories. It makes my blood...boil."

His eyes softened. "No one before you was ever memorable. And I want to be the only thing that makes your blood hot." He slid his arms around her and rolled so that she was on top. "As for this place... You're the only one I want to remember here. After tonight, it's history."

"Can I torch it?"

He laughed, lifted his head, and kissed her. "You can do anything you damn well please, just so long as you do it with me."

She stretched out over him so they were touching, toes to lips. Kissed him, softly, gently, loving each and every jolt and twitch of his body against hers and the deep, pleasure-filled sighs that followed. "That's a deal I can definitely live with for as long as *you* can put up with *me*."

"Ah, *ligos Vesuvius*. That will be for always."

Eternal Guardians Lexicon

adelfos. Brother

agapi. Term of endearment; my love.

ándras; pl. *ándres.* Male Argolean

archdaemon. Head of the daemon order; has enhanced powers
   from Atalanta

Argolea. Realm established by Zeus for the blessed heroes and
   their descendants

Argonauts. Eternal guardian warriors who protect Argolea. In
   every generation, one from the original seven bloodlines
   (Heracles, Achilles, Jason, Odysseus, Perseus, Theseus, and
   Bellerophon) is chosen to continue the guardian tradition.

Chosen. One Argolean, one human; two individuals who, when
   united, completed the Argolean Prophecy and broke Atalanta's
   contract with Hades, thereby ejecting her from the Underworld
   and ending her immortality.

Council of Elders. Twelve lords of Argolea who advise the king

daemons. Beasts who were once human, recruited from the Fields
   of Asphodel (purgatory) by Atalanta to join her army.

*Dimiourgo*s. Creator

doulas. Slave

élencho. Mind-control technique Argonauts use on humans

Fates. Three goddesses who control the thread of life for all
   mortals from birth until death

Fields of Asphodel. Purgatory

fotia. Term of endearment. My fire.

gigia. Grandmother

gynaíka; pl. *gynaíkes.* Female Argolean

Horae. Three goddesses of balance controlling life and order

Isles of the Blessed. Heaven

ilithios. Idiot

kardia. Term of endearment; my heart

Kore. Another name for the goddess Persephone. "The maiden"

ligos-Vesuvius. Term of endearment; little volcano

matéras. Mother

meli. Term of endearment; beloved

Misos. Half-human/half-Argolean race that lives hidden among humans

Olympians. Current ruling gods of the Greek pantheon, led by Zeus; meddle in human life

oraios. Beautiful

Orb of Krónos. Four-chambered disk that, when filled with the four classic elements—earth, wind, fire, and water—has the power to release the Titans from Tartarus

patéras. Father

sotiria. Term of endearment; my salvation

Siren Order. Zeus's elite band of personal warriors. Commanded by Athena

skata. Swearword

syzygos. Wife

Tartarus. Realm of the Underworld similar to hell

therillium. Invisibility ore, sought after by all the gods

Titans. The ruling gods before the Olympians

Titanomachy. The war between the Olympians and the Titans, which resulted in Krónos being cast into Tartarus and the Olympians becoming the ruling gods.

thea. Term of endearment; goddess

yios. Son

Read on for a sneak peek at

WAIT FOR ME

The *New York Times* bestselling book about
love, loss, and the power of second chances.

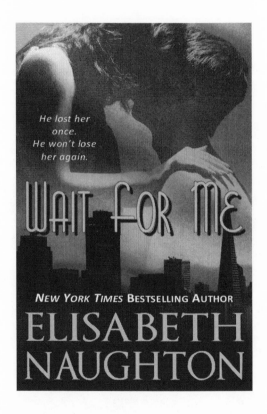

He lost her
once.
He won't lose
her again.

WAIT FOR ME

NEW YORK TIMES BESTSELLING AUTHOR

ELISABETH
NAUGHTON

A woman without a past…
A man desperate for a reason to live…
Two lives about to converge.

CHAPTER ONE

There was torture, and then there was rip-your-fingernails-out-by-the-roots-with-pliers pure agony. Right now, Kate Alexander was in the midst of the latter. Or at least it felt like she was.

She ground her teeth and tried to think of something besides the sweat slicking her skin, the ceiling entirely too close to her face, the fact she could barely breathe in this claustrophobic box. Nothing worked. The only thought revolving in her mind was the fact if she didn't get out of here soon, she was going to go batshit crazy on the tech behind the glass to her left.

"A little longer, Kate."

Great. Fabulous. Just what she wanted to hear. She knew not to move—that would only prolong her misery—but this little test had already taken way longer than it should. What the hell was he doing in there, throwing a party?

Patience had never been her strong suit. Her doctors had told her that lack of patience was probably the reason she hadn't stayed dead in the first place—that she'd given up waiting for the light to get stronger and had decided just to turn around and come back because she'd grown impatient. Kate wasn't convinced of that fact—she didn't remember any light. She didn't remember much of anything. But thanks to the trusty staff at Baylor University Medical Center in Dallas, Texas, her "death" had lasted only a mere ninety seconds. Ninety seconds that had changed her life forever.

She had no memory of the car accident that had left her snazzy Mercedes in a lump of twisted metal. No memory of the driver of the other vehicle who'd walked away while she'd lain on a cold slab fighting for her life. No memory of her life before the accident, period. But she'd learned one very important lesson that day: some things in life were worth fighting for.

Her mind drifted to Jake, their anniversary and the special dinner she had planned. Seven years… It didn't feel like seven years. In many ways, it felt like she barely knew him. The past eighteen months had been a blur of tests and more tests, settling into life in Houston, reacquainting herself with her husband and their friends all over again. A side effect of the accident he'd told her, one they'd get through together. Except…he traveled so much for work, it seemed like she was doing all that reacquainting by herself.

She wanted to sigh but knew not to. Okay, so he was dedicated to his job. He loved his work. She had to admire his passion. So what if their marriage was far from perfect? No one had a perfect marriage. But she'd been given a second chance. She planned to make the most of it.

She quietly rejoiced when the machine buzzed again and the table began retracting from the tunnel. Done. Finally. Twenty minutes of hell. And she hadn't needed to flip the tech off after all. A smile curled her lips at the thought.

The tech emerged from the screening room and unstrapped Kate's head and shoulders from the restraints. "Not so bad. How are you feeling?"

Kate sat up and rubbed the long scar on the side of her scalp. "Like a sardine."

He chuckled. "I hear that a lot. You'll need to hang around for a bit while we review the images and make sure we got everything we need."

She nodded, knowing the routine. She'd been through it before, and this wouldn't be the last.

She dressed then headed out into the waiting area where TVs flickered with a surreal image. Several people gathered around the three screens, staring at what looked like a war scene. Flames and billowing smoke, sirens blaring, lights flashing. Prickly fingers of fear ran over Kate's skin as she watched the horror unfold.

The camera zoomed in on plane wreckage. A ticker across the bottom of the screen flashed "Breaking News."

"The crash happened at roughly ten-forty five, Pacific Time. Flight 524 from San Francisco to Houston crashed just after takeoff. Witnesses say the plane burst into a fireball only yards from the runway. NTSB officials are on scene, and an investigation is already under way. Early reports estimate there are no survivors."

The air caught in Kate's lungs. She scrambled for her purse, one strap sliding down her arm as she frantically searched among receipts and fruit snacks for the note Jake had left her. His flight information and where he'd been staying for the conference in San Francisco.

"Kate? Is everything okay?"

She didn't look up to see who was talking to her. Couldn't focus. The purse slipped off her shoulder, landed at her feet with a clank. She dropped to her knees, frantically pawing through the contents, looking for his note. It wasn't the same flight. It couldn't be. He was probably landing right this minute. He'd laugh when she told him she'd dumped her entire purse on the floor at the clinic.

"Kate? What is it? What do you need?"

Vaguely, she realized Gina, the nurse, was helping her. Tears blurred her eyes. She shook her head. "A note. Jake's note. I have to find it. I have to—"

"We'll find it. Relax. Just breathe. I'm sure everything's okay."

She drew a deep breath, let it out. Gina was right. She was overreacting. Jake was fine. Blinking back tears, she scanned the floor and finally spotted Jake's slanted handwriting on a slip of paper just to the right of her hand. Her fingers shook as she drew it close so she could read the words.

My flight info:
Outgoing: Houston to San Francisco, Flight # 1498
Return: San Francisco to Houston, Flight # 524

The paper slipped out of her fingers. The room spun. Blackness circled in.

The CT scan, the anniversary dinner she'd shopped for earlier, the last eighteen months of her life swirled behind her eyes and mingled with Gina's voice, muffled now, calling to her from what seemed like a great distance. Only one thing made sense. Only one thought remained.

Her life had just shifted direction all over again. And this time, death had won.

* * *

"**Y**ou really need to eat something." Mindy, Kate's next-door neighbor, set the steaming mug of tea on the kitchen table in front of Kate and sat in the chair to her right.

Without looking, Kate knew Mindy's freckled features were drawn and somber. The woman had adored Jake. Everyone had. None of their friends had known about his mood swings. Or the fact he purposely stayed away from home. Or that he and Kate fought about his work. But they didn't need to know those things now. No one did.

"Thanks." With shaky fingers, Kate wrapped her hands around the mug, holding on to the warmth. "I think I might just be ill if I smell one more cup of coffee."

There'd been a steady stream of friends through the house all afternoon and into the early evening. This was the first quiet moment Kate had found. And now…now she wondered why she'd wanted it.

"The tea should help you relax," Mindy said, pushing her red hair over her shoulder. "It's been a long day. How about a little soup?"

Kate shook her head. Food was the last thing on her mind. Her stomach would revolt if she tried to eat. Waving a hand, she blinked back tears that wanted to fall. She wasn't going to give in again. Not now. She'd save the waterfall for when she was alone. In that big bedroom she was too used to sleeping in all by herself.

"I'm not hungry." Silence enveloped the room. She knew Mindy disapproved, but she had a thousand other things on her mind besides food. "God, Mindy. I have so much to do."

Mindy's hand clamped over hers on the table. "There's plenty of time for all that."

"No. If I don't get it all taken care of, I'll go nuts." She leaned back in her chair. "I can't stay here."

"You have to give it time. You can't make rash decisions right now."

"No. This house was his idea. Living here…" Her eyes slid shut. "He made every major decision in our lives."

"He was your husband. And you've been through so much this last year and a half with the accident. Of course he made all the decisions. It's logical given your medical history."

Her medical history. The memory loss. It had been Jake's excuse for everything. Why he ran their finances, why he arranged it so she was never alone, why he'd chosen which publisher she freelanced for.

She should have insisted he include her in decisions. She should have played a bigger role in planning for a day like this. She didn't even know where to look for his life insurance policy.

Her stomach rolled, and she swallowed back the bile. Leaning forward to rest her elbows on the table and her head in her hands, she knew she needed to get as far from this house as possible. She'd felt the pull to leave months ago, but she'd fought it because of Jake. Because her life was here. Now…now she didn't know what to think anymore.

"Jake was the one who loved Houston. Not me." Her head throbbed. She wasn't taking pain medication tonight. Not when her mind was already in a fog.

"It's your home, Kate. You can't just leave. Jake's family's here."

A pathetic laugh erupted from Kate's lips. "He and his father haven't spoken in more than a year. The man barely even acknowledges he has a grandson. That's not the type of family I want for Reed." No family was better than that in her mind.

"Just promise me you won't make any spur-of-the-moment decisions. Please?"

Concerned brown eyes gazed into Kate's face. Mindy wouldn't get it. Not really. She wouldn't understand that this feeling of not belonging had been festering for a long time. That it had been haunting her ever since the accident. And tonight wasn't the night to get into it with her.

Kate squeezed Mindy's hand. "Sure. I'm not really thinking clearly tonight." Rising, she took the untouched mug of tea to the sink. "I need to turn in. Thanks for everything today. I don't know how I would have gotten through it all without you."

Mindy rose from her seat and rested both hands on Kate's shoulders. "Will you be okay tonight? Reed's already asleep upstairs, but I could take him over to my house if you need some time alone."

Kate looked to the kitchen stairs that led up to the second floor where her four-year-old son was sound asleep, then shook her head. She hadn't told him the news yet. She didn't want him hearing it from the neighbors. "No, but thanks. I need to be with him if he wakes. We'll be fine."

"I'm always here for you, Kate. Remember that. If you need anything, I'm just across the street."

"Thanks." Kate forced a smile she didn't feel.

With a quick hug, Mindy made her way to the front of the house. When the heavy mahogany door clicked shut, Kate turned and surveyed the empty house. She was alone. Totally alone. No car would be pulling into the drive in the middle of the night. Jake wouldn't come bounding through the door, apologizing for missing yet another dinner. She wouldn't see his face or feel his arms around her again. It didn't matter if he'd been a lousy husband. He'd been her husband. And now he was gone. From now on, it would just be her and Reed.

Shaky lips blew out a long sigh. She tamped down the grief that wanted to pour over her again. Even though it was close to midnight, she knew there was no way she'd be able to drift into a slumber, peaceful or otherwise.

Making her way into Jake's office, she rubbed the chill from her arms, then sank into the chair behind his desk, letting the butter-soft leather cushion her aching body. With trembling fingers, her hand feathered the dark wood in front of her.

Her gaze washed over the room. A tall bookshelf graced one long wall. Medical books packed the shelves from floor to ceiling. A computer blinked on the short arm of the L-shaped desk. A picture of Reed smiling in the summer sun faced her.

Jake's room, Jake's things. She'd rarely come in here because it was his private space. An odd sense of unease settled over her as she sat in his chair.

She flipped on the Tiffany lamp sitting next to the phone and fanned through the stack of mail on the corner of his desk. The mundane task took her mind off details she had yet to address, calmed her frayed nerves.

Bills, a renewal for a medical journal, a letter claiming they'd won ten-million dollars in a sweepstakes. She tossed junk mail into the garbage can at her knee, sifted Jake's professional mail into one stack, their personal mail into another.

She reached for the letter opener in the pencil holder and found it missing. Pulling open a drawer, she pawed through the contents, then another when she couldn't find it.

In the back of the third drawer, she found it, along with another unopened letter. Kate shook her head, a melancholy sensation deepening her sadness. Reed had probably put these here. He was always getting into stuff he shouldn't. Jake always got so upset when Reed moved his things.

But no one would have to worry about that anymore. With renewed sadness she ripped open the letter and glanced at the bill in her hand. Her brow creased when she saw her name. She reached for the envelope she'd just torn. Jake's medical office was listed as the address on the outside, but it was clearly a bill for her time in the hospital after her car accident. A revolving balance showed an amount of ten thousand dollars still owed.

Jake had told her their insurance had covered everything. Looking closer, she realized it wasn't a hospital bill at all, but an invoice from a nursing home.

Nursing home? That wasn't right. She'd been in the hospital for a little more than a week. Four days in a coma in ICU, another three until they moved her to a regular room, then five on the med/surge floor recovering from her injuries.

She looked at the bill again.

San Francisco.

No, that wasn't right either. The accident had happened outside Dallas. She'd been driving home from a geology conference in Ft. Worth. Her journal had been covering the event. She'd never even been to San Francisco.

The dates of service were wrong as well. They spanned more than two years.

Her hands shook as she set the invoice on the desk. A chill settled over her.

Medical records. Jake was meticulous about his files.

She swiveled toward the file cabinet and flipped through the files, looking for one with her name.

Nothing.

She yanked open the second drawer. Taxes, appraisal information on the house, medical journals he belonged to. The man even had a file with all his grades from college. He was OCD to the max.

But where were her files?

Impatience settled over her, a dismal feeling she didn't want to acknowledge. She yanked open the third drawer, breathing out a sigh of relief when she saw medical folders for Jake, Reed, and herself.

Yes, it would be here. Someone had screwed up, billed the wrong person.

She drew her folder open on the desk, flipped through the stack of forms. A claim for stitches in her toe when she'd stepped on a piece of glass last month. A dental claim when she had to have a tooth repaired last spring. Medical updates from Dr. Reynolds, the neurosurgeon she'd been seeing since the accident. Forms and evaluations spanned the last year and a half of her life, then stopped.

No records on her pregnancy, none on Reed's birth. Nothing from her stay at Baylor University Medical Center where she'd been treated after the accident.

They had to be in different folders. Something separate, marked "delivery" and "accident". She closed the drawer, reached for the bottom one. It wouldn't budge.

She pulled again, only to realize it was locked.

She fumbled through the drawers of his desk, searching for a key. An odd sense of urgency pushed her forward. She tried the few keys she found but none fit the lock. Swallowing the growing lump in her throat, she pawed through his shelves.

Still no key.

The blood rushed to her head, intensifying that dull ache around her scar.

She scrambled up to the bedroom they'd once shared and yanked open his dresser drawers, fumbling through socks and underwear and old T-shirts.

It had to be somewhere. He wouldn't have locked the drawer and thrown away the key. Her fingers skimmed cotton and finally settled on cold metal.

Pressure settled on her chest as she pulled the key ring from the back of the drawer. Two keys glittered in the low light, one bigger than the other. On wobbly legs, she made her way back down to the office, kneeling on the floor in front of the file cabinet.

Don't open it. Forget about the key. Forget about the drawer. Forget about that stupid bill. Nothing good can come from this. You've already been through enough today.

She swallowed the lump in her throat. Before she could change her mind, she turned the key in the lock. The drawer gave with a pop.

Inside, a long metal box rested on the bottom of the drawer. She set it carefully on the desk, then sat in his chair and rubbed damp palms along her slacks. The second key slid into the lockbox with ease.

Drawing in a deep breath, she opened the lid. Medical forms, evaluations, bills filled the box. She extracted each paper, scanned the dates and contents. All referenced the nursing home in San Francisco. All mentioned dates two to five years in the past.

According to the papers, she'd been in a coma for almost three years, not four days. Reed had been born by C-section when she'd been in that coma.

Her eyes slid shut. It couldn't be. She'd had a long labor—over twenty-four hours. Jake had held her hand through the pain. She'd been wheeled into surgery when the labor had stopped progressing. Jake had been with her as her son was cut from her. He'd told her all about it. He'd relayed the story of Reed's birth so many times, she could see it in her mind.

Tears pooled in her eyes. She looked at the papers again as her brain warred with what she'd been told and the facts in front of her.

There were no pictures. No pictures of her pregnancy. None anywhere in the house. Jake had told her it was because she'd hated being pregnant, that she didn't want to remember what she'd looked like.

But there were none of her smiling in a hospital gown, either. None of her nursing her baby. She'd believed him when he'd said he'd forgotten the camera the day Reed was born.

She ran to the family room, yanked picture albums off the shelves, flipped through each page. Jake holding a newborn Reed. Jake giving him a bath. Jake feeding him his first solids. Oh, God. Jake smiling with him on his first birthday. In every picture, it was Jake. Not a single one of her and Reed until after his second birthday.

Panic washed over her. She'd always assumed she'd been the one taking the photos. She'd never even questioned it. Rubbing a hand over the pain in her chest, she tried to rationalize the moment. Couldn't.

He was a doctor. He was her husband. She'd believed him. It had never even occurred to her not to. Why? Why would he lie?

No, no, no. This can't be real.

On legs that threatened to give out, she made her way back into his office. Her eyes focused on an evaluation from a neurosurgeon she didn't recognize.

DAMAGE TO THE LATERAL CORTEX OF THE ANTERIOR TEMPORAL LOBE AS A RESULT OF SEVERE TRAUMA.

PROGNOSIS: MEMORY LOSS, POSSIBLY PERMANENT AND IRREVERSIBLE.

Permanent memory loss. Coma. Three years.

Choking back tears, she continued flipping through the forms. Her stomach pitched when she saw Jake's signature on several of the papers. He'd been an attending physician.

Her attending physician.

No, no, no. Her husband never would have been allowed to oversee her recovery. Never. Not in a million years. She wasn't a doctor, but she knew the rules.

Sweat beaded on her neck, trickled down her back. There had to be an explanation. Something. Anything!

She lifted each paper out of the box in an urgent need to find the truth. Questions continued to swirl in her mind, memories she wasn't sure were real or contrived. When she drew out the last paper, the floor moved under her feet.

Her legs buckled, and she dropped into the chair. In the bottom of the box rested a photo. Her breath clogged in her throat. With shaking fingers, she extracted the picture, just as a stabbing pain cut right through her heart.

It was a photo of a young girl, roughly five years of age. She was sitting on a boat. Water sparkled behind her. Trees glinted off in the distance. A young girl with a disturbingly familiar face, a curly mop of brown hair, and the greenest eyes Kate had ever seen.

Kate's eyes. The same shape, size, color...the same exact eyes Kate stared at everyday in the mirror.

Oh, God. Oh, God.

The air clogged in her lungs. And a place deep inside told her this girl couldn't possibly be anything other than her daughter.

To learn more about WAIT FOR ME
and all of Elisabeth's books,
visit
www.ElisabethNaughton.com

About the Author

Photo by Almquist Studios

Bestselling Author Elisabeth Naughton writes full time from her home in western Oregon where she lives with her husband and three children. Her books have appeared on every major bestsellers list, including the *New York Times*, the *USA Today*, the *Wall Street Journal*, *Digital Book World* and *IndieReader*, and have been translated into audio and a dozen different languages. Her work has also been nominated for numerous awards such as the prestigious RITA® awards by Romance Writers of America, the Australian Romance Reader Awards, The Golden Leaf and the Golden Heart.

When not writing, Elisabeth can be found training for her next half marathon, hanging out at the ballpark with her kids, or dreaming up new and exciting adventures.

Visit her at www.ElisabethNaughton.com to learn more about her books.